Nyifie Brothers Publishing

PRETTY KILLER

JOHNNY B. TRUANT

NOLON KING

PRETTY KILLER

A NOTE ON VERACITY

The drug Nyperal — and its generic, rodostazem — do not actually exist and are our inventions, as the authors of this book. You will not find them at your local pharmacy, in the *Physician's Desk Reference*, or in any of Eminem's songs about his drug abuse.

The food described herein, on the other hand, very deliciously *does* exist.

Bon appétit.

You are Cordially Invited

to an Exclusive, Intimate Dinner

Held at Crave Restaurant

Cielo del Mar, California

May 26th, 2029

At 7 o'Clock PM

Drinks

ONE

"It's not even seven," Ella told her husband.

The elevator moved, and the floor beneath her high-heels purred. Noah, beside her and facing forward, said nothing.

Ella exhaled. She sent her eyes on a circuit of the interior. The display above the elevator doors was faux-antique: a fan-shaped thing that looked like half a clock. The stainless steel arrow appeared too modern on its face. The buttons were inlaid with glass and glowing from within. There were no fingerprints, despite the elevator's daily use. But someone either wiped the thing after every trip, or the metal itself — brushed, almost matte — was immune to smudges.

She looked at her watch again — a gift from Noah's stepfather, Damon — then sighed and dropped her arm. The building had fourteen floors, with Crave occupying the top two. The dial was now sweeping number nine.

"Barely 6:45," Ella said.

"Right on time," Noah replied.

"The invitation said seven."

"Sure did."

The doors dinged open on the 13th floor. Noah didn't move, waiting for her. Ella rolled her eyes and stepped out into the plush lobby. An tropical aquarium ran along one entire wall, blue-lit from behind. A hostess behind her podium was the room's lone human fixture.

"See?" Ella said. "No one here."

"No big deal. We'll just wait."

"I told you."

Noah finally snapped. "Oh, what, Ella? *What* did you tell me?"

This time Ella said nothing.

Noah looked like he might speak. Instead, he approached the hostess. She was dressed better than Ella, though in a sober lady-suit that communicated her servitude. Ella, by contrast, had inspected herself thoroughly before leaving home and declared herself ready for a night on the town. And at least she was pulling off her leg-show of a dress, unlike the hostess.

By the time Noah was back at her side, Ella had a hand on her hip.

"She's going to fetch our host," he explained.

"We have a host?"

"I told you. This is an exclusive affair. We're actually at *Crave.*"

"So what?"

"What do you mean, so what? I couldn't get reservations no matter how hard I tried."

"No," Ella said. *"You* couldn't."

Noah looked at the wall. Then he moved to one of the lobby's oversized sofas and collapsed into the cushions.

"We have to wait?" Ella asked.

"Until she finds our host, yes."

Ella scoffed. Then she muttered to herself: "We have to wait."

Noah's eyes found the tops of their sockets. He took a deep breath. "How about we try to have a good time tonight, Ella?"

"Oh, I'm trying."

"No, you're really not." Then sharper: "I think you're trying to win. What if I just grant you the victory? Do you want to go back outside? Maybe drive around the block a few times? We can come back at 7:30, after everyone is saying, 'Where's Noah Boyer?' Or actually, 'Where is Ella? Where is that schlub's very important wife? Her delay is only making us want her more!'"

"Very funny."

"What's the big deal? So we're on time. Or — God forbid — a few minutes early. Why is that worth ruining our evening?"

"Ruining," Ella repeated, scoffing.

"Look. Maybe you were right. Maybe you shouldn't have come.

Bayshore wants me on the alumni board. That's a pretty big honor in my book, but I guess you don't give a shit. So, whatever. Go ahead, Ella, take the car. I can find my way home."

Ella, still on her feet, met Noah's eyes. She wasn't used to him standing up to her like this. Even his dark brown beard said *quiet pushover,* and she'd gotten used to pushing. She'd stopped hiding her despair just like she'd stopped hiding the pills. If things kept going like they were she'd stop hiding the rest in no time. But right now, looking at Noah, Ella felt like maybe she'd lost the upper hand. He meant his threat and knew her performance was mostly air.

She looked away. As little as Ella had wanted to attend the Bayshore dinner, the graveyard silence of their empty home would have been even worse. The twins were at his mother's and wouldn't be home until morning. Demons called in the dark, when the ache was at its worst and her addiction the sweetest.

Noah must have seen her weakness, because he scooted farther down on the couch, no longer occupying its middle. Then he patted the seat. "Come sit."

"I'm good."

Noah stood, took Ella's hand, and guided her to the couch. She protested less than she probably should have.

"What is it, El? Are you pissed that the board didn't select you, too?"

"Are you kidding? I don't want to be on the stupid Bayshore board."

Noah nodded almost imperceptibly. Ella should have said that she didn't want to be on *a* board. Instead, she'd called out Bayshore's specifically. A slip. Noah knew better than anyone why Bayshore's board was the problem (same for the entire evening, if Ella were honest), but she still didn't like to remind her husband of who she used to be. Who they both used to be.

"Look," he said. "Damon was on Bayshore's board, and you know how he is. He kind of rescued me when Mom and I were still struggling. Not all of my memories of school are good — Bayshore in particular. But this nomination caps it for me. It matters, because of Damon. This makes it all right."

Ella laughed again, but this time it sounded brittle.

"But it's not a big deal for you," Noah continued. "And I know it's a pain in your ass. So I'm serious. I can go alone. Take the car. Or I can order you a FASTr."

Ella thought about the empty house. The darkness and the quiet. The pills, just waiting for her weakness. Every time she swallowed another, she found her mind wandering to other circumstances and other bottles. Alone, the ghosts would haunt her. Especially given the decently buried memories this event had stirred from the floor of her mind, like sediment from a cavernous lake.

She was about to find an excuse for reversing her opinion when a thin man with piercing blue eyes and a dark beard came through double doors behind the hostess stand. He was wearing a perfectly-cut black suit, a dark purple shirt, and a black tie. He extended a hand to greet them as Ella and Noah stood.

The man smiled wide. "Mr. and Mrs. Boyer! It's so nice to finally meet you!"

An awkward moment. Were they supposed to know this man? He looked familiar — even *very* familiar. But Noah seemed even more at a loss than Ella.

The man took Noah's hand. "My name is Donovan. Your host has asked me to greet you and get you anything you would like or need."

"You're not with Bayshore's board?" Ella asked, still searching the corners of her mind for the man's identity. He couldn't have been Class of 2018, or else surely she would have recognized him.

"I'm more like your concierge." He turned to Ella, shook her hand, and repeated, "Donovan," as if maybe she hadn't heard.

"Ella."

"Ella might not be joining me," Noah said, giving Ella an uncertain eye behind Donovan's back. "She's feeling a bit ill."

Big blue eyes turned on her, full of sympathy. "Oh, I'm so sorry to hear it! But you should stay. You're expected!"

Ella forced a smile. "I'm not expected. I'm a 'plus one.'"

Donovan shook his head. "You misunderstand. There are no plus ones. You were invited, same as your husband."

Noah and Ella traded a confused glance. *Noah* was joining the board — there'd been nothing vague about that.

"There are places to lie down upstairs, and I'd be happy to run out if you need anything. Medicine? Pillows, even? I'm at your command." This man meant every word.

Bayshore had more money than it could spend. The school had rented out at least one full room at Cielo del Mar's most in-demand restaurant (well, other than Bella by the Sea, of course). It wouldn't surprise Ella if they'd hired a servant for the evening as well.

Donovan took Ella's hand as if to steady her. "Anything you need. But please, at least stay through reception."

"All right," Ella nodded. "Maybe I just need a drink."

And yes, she decided, she *did* need a drink. Maybe two, or even three. An alumni board event wasn't the same as being back at school, but Ella still felt eighteen in Bayshore's shadow, trying to recover her center in the aftermath of an ugly fateful night.

Noah, seeming to feel none of the old trepidation, put his arm around her shoulder. She thought about brushing it away, but didn't.

Donovan nodded toward the still-open double doors behind the hostess stand, and the stairs leading to a private outdoor patio.

"If you'll follow me, please?"

"Come on," Noah whispered to Ella. "It'll be fun. I promise."

Ella did her best to smile, to believe what he told her.

But eleven years ago felt like now, surrounding her, squeezing, like a hand at her throat.

TWO

Mason drove past Crave, then kept right on driving. He'd looked the place up online after getting his invitation, but the photos were liars that didn't come close. The building was situated on one of Cielo's most prestigious strips, high enough in the hills to command an impressive view of both city and sea. Where parking, like cots in many of the beach houses scattered along the coast, cost more per hour than minimum wage.

But that's not why Mason eventually parked where he did: in an alley a half-mile away, behind a dumpster. Paying to park at Crave wasn't an issue; Predip's email clearly indicated he'd called ahead and prepaid for both valet and tip. The valet itself was the problem. The Voight could only be polished and vacuumed so much. Even after all the spit-shining in the world, the car remained Mason's faithful turd.

He killed the engine, suspecting that he'd return to either an impound or a homeless person sleeping inside it. The door locks were just one of the things that didn't work. *Good.* He *hoped* The Voight would get messed up out here. The longer the shitbox kept running, the longer he'd have to keep it. He needed an excuse to buy something less embarrassing.

Mason opened his door. He closed it again, remembering that last piece of personal business. The side mirror wobbled with the door's motion, so he rolled down the window using the ancient crank and squeezed it back in place. Again.

He pulled out his Doodad and dialed.

A familiar bitchy voice answered, and Mason stepped through the conversational preliminaries. Jessica said she hoped he didn't give his shitty car to the valet like he'd threatened; Mason said The Voight was awesome even though he didn't remotely feel that way; he eventually admitted to parking down the street. It went as well as it could, given her mood.

He rushed through Jessica's questions. Ambivalent emotions made this sort of thing tricky.

"Yes, I'll be there ... that's why I'm calling ... 9:30 am at Mercy Hospital; got it ... I'll just follow the signs to ultrasound ... they have that coffee shop in the lobby ... do you want a mocha or something? ... we already talked about that, baby — I have work at seven, and it's in the opposite direction. I'll just meet you there like I said. And I'll come over right afterward. Promise. Don't ... well, we can talk about that later. It's just the money, but if Predip's news is ... Yeah. Yeah. I hope so too. And Jess?"

Suspicious: "What?"

"I'm grateful to have you. I really am."

Jessica mumbled thanks, but she never responded especially well to his kindness. She could probably tell that he was convincing himself, sort of like a terrified air traveler mumbling "I'm okay, I'm okay" during takeoff.

Mason and Jessica exchanged *goodbyes* and *I-love-yous*, though Jessica's sounded almost despondent. She'd been much more interested in the part about Mason's dinner date with the headhunter, or possibly the part where he'd waffled, yet again, on the issue of their getting a place. But Mason still talked to himself a lot, trying to shove aside his dislike of Jessica as a person in favor of his duty as a soon-to-be father.

Even with the ultrasound time confirmed, Mason stalled before exiting The Voight. Crave was close, but his comfort was miles away. His emotions were all over the place. He had piled a lot of hope on top of tonight. Predip Batra had a history of finding fantastic, high-paying jobs — particularly for his fellow Bayshore Prep School alumni. With the right hook-up, Mason would be able to buy a real car, rent a decent apartment with Jessica, and provide for his unborn child whether things worked out with its mother or not.

But if Predip had bad news? Well, then leaving the car would just be the next step on a long road of failure. Another chance to screw up. Ruin things for the people he cared about.

"It's good news," Mason told the empty car, brushing the sagging ceiling with his head. "He'd let me down at a Denny's. Or, hell, over the phone."

A deep breath and he opened the door. It banged into concrete. He'd parked too close to the wall. Rather than driving out to make more room, Mason slid across the bench seat and got out on the passenger side. Out of habit, he clicked the broken lock. He closed the door softly to keep the side mirror in place. It fell off anyway.

"Fucking Voight," Mason mumbled.

The alley was dark, but this was still Cielo del Mar. He exited unmolested, then turned and nearly crashed into a woman loaded with bags. Was there even shopping up here? She looked like she'd hiked up from the Palms Couture where Mason used to hang — right down to the tight skirt, long legs, silicon, and poison in her face.

"Watch where you're going," she said, then waited for Mason to step aside and let her pass.

"Have a nice night," he said to her silent back.

He hiked to Crave in the early evening air. It had been hot, and with the sun still in the sky, he was warm in his blazer. The usually generous ocean breeze was surprisingly scant. He considered removing the blazer, but by the time he thought about keeping sweat from his shirt, Crave was lighting the remainder of his way. He didn't want to be seen walking up, so he kept his movements small. There was a half-moon driveway where he should have pulled through to valet, and the valets themselves were assembled behind a stand by the door.

They saw him coming, looking on. There was no escape.

"I had a meeting just down the street," Mason explained.

"Yes, sir," said the valet.

"Welcome to Crave," said the doorman.

Mason nodded, wondering if he was supposed to tip.

The lobby was like a 5-star hotel. A spray of expensive-looking furniture: cut-glass lamps and chandeliers. Orchids everywhere. He was confused. Mason couldn't see diners or smell food. *Was* this a hotel? He saw what looked like an empty reception desk. There was a bar in the corner, empty and unlit. The stools along it were vacant, as were the chairs arranged in pits for conversation.

Brow furrowed, Mason reached into his pocket. Predip hadn't given him a number; they'd spoken only by email, and that would have to do. If he was in the wrong place, he needed to know before—

With his feet still moving and his eyes down, Mason nearly collided with another woman.

But this one hadn't noticed. She was smartly dressed with blonde hair brushing her shoulders, standing in front of the elevator.

The woman gave Mason a polite smile. And then, a tickle in his head. Something vaguely familiar. She was older than him — upper thirties, perhaps. Very pretty: smooth skin, a figure that her otherwise conservative pants-and-blouse ensemble managed to make sexy. She had a small, delicate nose. And Mason could've *sworn* he knew her. But from where? His circle was small. Did she work out at his gym? A manager at his supermarket? He wasn't sure, but neither felt right.

"Looking for the restaurant?"

"Yeah," Mason answered.

The woman indicated a sign on a brass stand:

CRAVE LOBBY
THIRTEENTH FLOOR

Mason smiled thanks and came forward. The button was already lit. The elevator was either slow or out of order. He resisted the urge to press it again. He was working on himself, and patience was one of his biggies. That and tolerance: two things he'd need to abide Jessica and be there for his child.

"I think this thing might be broken," she said, pushing the button.

Yes, Mason definitely knew her. She had hazel eyes and a small mouth. High, arching eyebrows. A runner's body. Maybe a swimmer.

And her eyes, now, were ... curious?

"I have cheese dust on my face, don't I? Mom told me not to eat dinner before I came here."

"I'm sorry." The woman laughed, seeming flustered. "You just look really familiar. Do you live in Cielo?"

"No, but I used to."

She shook her head, frustrated. "What's your name, if you don't mind?"

"Mason ... Pace."

"Sounds familiar ..." She shook her head, lips pressed.

The elevator dinged. Slowly, the doors opened.

"Dare we?" Mason asked. "Seems like it might be a half-hour ride."

They stepped inside, Mason turning to the double row of brushed-steel floor buttons. His finger went to 13 but stopped short of pressing it. "Last chance."

"What the hell," she said. "I've had a good life."

Mason pressed the button and the doors closed. They moved for seconds in silence, both watching the half-circle display above the doors, ticking past the numbers at a snail's pace.

She turned to Mason. "It must be nothing, but *man*, do you seem familiar. I guess I'm crazy."

"No, you look familiar to me, too."

"Bindi." She touched her chest with delicate, painted fingernails.

A distinct name, but not one he could—

"Wait. Not 'Bridges'? Your last name isn't 'Bridges,' is it?"

Bindi nodded.

Mason laughed. Right now a brush of familiarity felt like a port in the storm. "You were a guidance counselor. At Bayshore Academy. Right?"

"Did you go to Bayshore?"

"Yes! You were my counselor!"

They laughed.

"No wonder it took so long. Nobody remembers their guidance counselors. I'm shocked you figured it out. We must have met a time or two." She put a finger beside her mouth. "Let me guess: you wanted to go to UCLA, but I told you that any decent Bayshore grad should go to Coastline."

But no, it wasn't that. Mason couldn't place what it was. He, like most of the students he'd known eleven years ago, hadn't made the most of the staff. Yet Bindi — who he'd have known as "Miss Bridges" at the time — was more familiar than that. The association felt more like comfort.

"What year did you graduate?"

"2018."

"That's why I can't remember. You'd have been a senior during my first year, and that whole time was a blur. Figuring out where everything was, getting to know the students and staff. And I think that was the year that ..."

Her smile faded. Mason understood. He remembered senior year all too well. And guidance counselors were the closest thing most kids had to therapy.

An awkward moment lasted too long. The elevator's arm was only on 7. Mason forced his face to brighten. "It's funny that Bayshore would come up. I'm actually meeting a fellow alumnus for dinner. Predip Batra? He was class of 2021."

Bindi shook her head. "I only stayed for three years. He was after my time."

"Did you move to another school?"

"No. I'm in private practice."

"Practice. You mean as a psychiatrist?"

"Psychologist."

"Sounds nice."

"Most of the time."

A beat.

"What brings you to Crave?"

"Oh." She blinked as if Mason had asked about her underwear. "Just meeting someone."

"Hot date?"

"No, just ... nothing special."

Mason looked down. Her left ring finger wore a dual engagement ring and wedding band, soldered together. Her thumb went to its underside as he watched, fidgeting.

Silence descended. He looked forward again, hands clasped in front of his waist. It couldn't have been more than three seconds before the silver arm reached its destination and the elevator dinged to announce their arrival on the 13th floor, but it felt to Mason like a minute of waiting for test results. A shame. Bindi seemed so nice, and it was his fault things had gotten weird.

The doors opened to the restaurant lobby.

A well-dressed man came forward, extending his hand in front of Bindi. "Welcome to Crave. My name is Donovan. Bindi Bridges; am I right?"

Bindi looked at Mason before nodding slowly to Donovan, confused. "Yes."

He shook Mason's hand. "And Mr. Pace?"

"How do you know us?" Mason asked.

"Customer service," Donovan smiled. "Some restaurants pretend to know what that means. Crave lives it. Only Bella by the Sea can do it better — but to be fair, they have a serious advantage." His smile widened, genuine but all teeth. Then he gestured toward a propped-open set of doors behind a polished-wood hostess stand. "Please. Your parties await."

Mason shrugged at Bindi, impressed. The building wasn't nearly as tiny as Bella's — a place Mason used to fantasize about dining at back in school, when he hung out at the Palms and sipped coffee at Buns, watching the hot girls pass — so the fact that the wait staff knew its diners by name and face was quite a feat. With that feeling came another: Predip was probably already here. But with what news? Was Mason about to live life in the fast lane, or spend another year dragging ass in The Voight?

But Bindi looked uncomfortable. "Donovan, is it?"

"Yes, Ms. Bridges."

"Could I ask you a question?" She gave Mason an apologetic look. "In private?"

"It's fine," Donovan said. "Please don't worry. All of tonight's details have already been handled. I promise you'll get everything you're after."

"But—"

"This way, please."

He walked ahead of them, past the hostess, and up a wide set of stairs. Mason followed, intrigued by the pomp and grandeur. This was the kind of high-class pampering he could get used to. Maybe Predip was preparing him now.

They emerged onto what was essentially a rooftop patio, though there was an interior section to the left that covered a fraction of the building's footprint. There was both an indoor and outdoor bar, the shelves of both tastefully lit with concealed blue lights. The view was stunning, the Pacific glittering behind the lights of Cielo as it darkened. The deck was empty, save a man and a woman standing near the far rail. A sign by Mason's hip read *THE LOUNGE.*

"Please," Donovan said. "Ask the bartender for anything you'd like. All drinks are on the house."

"Thanks. But where can I find ..." Mason trailed off, seeing that Donovan was already halfway down the stairs. He turned to Bindi, wondering if they were supposed to go inside to find their parties. "I guess they don't give you a table. People meeting up have to wander until they encounter each other by accident."

Bindi smiled, seemingly more uncomfortable than amused. She was looking toward the smoked glass fronting the inside bar as well, both of them trying to see inside before stepping forward to look. But before either could move, there came a voice from the other direction.

"Mason?" Shuffling feet. *"Mason Pace?"*

He turned. The couple from the railing were walking forward. These people he immediately recognized. Noah Boyer. And Ella ... well, he guessed she was Ella Boyer, now.

"You're being nominated to the board too?" Noah turned to Bindi. "And ... *Miss Bridges?*"

Bindi was looking toward the inside bar again, seeming to consider whether to seek her appointment or stay here for this odd coincidence — the second in the last five minutes.

Her hazel eyes flicked like fireflies: to Mason, to Ella, to Noah.

Bayshore grads all, from the proud and troubled class of 2018.

THREE

S imon was watching the sidewalk, waiting for the end.

"... so the real trick to it is," the driver was saying, "I'm kind of damned if I don't and damned if I do. There's no equity in the house at all anymore. The bottom dropped out of the neighborhood just as my wife was finalizing the construction loan. You see what I'm saying?"

Tedious. Boring.

Simon had his messenger bag open and a plain paper notepad on his lap, with a fresh sheet ready for his notes. He also had a thin but substantial silver pen in his left hand — a pen that had, in more prosperous times, cost him nearly a thousand dollars. His tablet wasn't in the bag. He never traveled with it, even to business dinners. He did his best thinking with dead trees and ink. But the page was blank, thanks to his pinheaded driver.

"You know what I mean?" he said, just in case Simon hadn't heard.

But he had. All about the driver's problems with his home, which he and his wife had over-leveraged, vainly hoping that the market would appreciate enough to turn their "vanity construction project" into "bankable capital." Things never worked out that way. The driver was stupid. He was driving for FASTr. Simon made deals.

"This is it."

The driver had been about to pass the restaurant. He decelerated too fast, banging Simon's head against the front seat. The valets came forward.

"Pull farther up. They think you want them to park it."

"If you just want to hop out."

"I don't want anyone to think I own this piece of shit," Simon explained.

The driver seemed like he might be offended, but then dutifully pulled forward. Simon opened the door, then stopped. "How much is it?"

"I don't know. It's in the app."

"I pay you through my Doodad?"

"Y-yes." The driver seemed confused.

"I've never done this before. I usually drive my Tesla Prime. I didn't drive it tonight because I thought I could get some work done on the way."

"Tesla Prime?" The man sounded impressed.

"I got it by not getting loans on my primary residence that I couldn't pay back, and not driving other people around."

"Excuse me?"

Simon stepped out. He looked at his Doodad's screen, then pocketed the thing and leaned back through the window.

"Listen. What's your name again?"

"Alan."

"Listen, Alan. The solution you're looking for is actually pretty simple. You said you had your mother's inheritance money in a trust."

"Right. But I can't get at that money until—"

Simon waved him silent. "Don't try to take the money out of the trust. Just liquidate the retirement funds and annuities inside it. Then take that money, *still in the trust,* and use it as a down payment to buy yourself a second property. The trust owns the property and pays the mortgage, but you rent the home from the trust. Have the trust charge you whatever rent you want, something you can afford. It's eventually all your money anyway. Then finish the construction on your current house and—"

"It's upside-down. We can't sell it."

"I didn't say to sell it," Simon said patiently. "Rent it out. Put it on Airbnb. If it's really just two blocks from the beach, the value will come back. You're not trying to make a profit, you're trying to ride a dip in the market. Your goal is to pay expenses on your primary residence so you can keep it until the price rebounds. After that happens, you can either re-fi and move back in or sell it. Either way, your problem is solved. Do you understand?"

His brow wrinkled. "I ... think so."

"Good. Then that should take care of the tip."

Simon slammed the door and walked away before the driver could respond. He fished his Doodad back out and indicated no tip, *fare only.*

He looked up. Somewhere at the top of this building, Walter Kagen and Simon would make beautiful things together. Then Simon, too, would ride the dip in his personal market. So what if he was in debt? He could pay for things with his brain.

Ostensibly, they were meeting to see if Walter was interested in promoting Simon's once-expansive, temporarily-struggling internet business. But Simon knew his persuasion skills better than to worry about that part. Kagen was sold. This puppy was in the bag and already barking.

Simon took a few steps toward the restaurant then stopped, suddenly impeded. The valet was helping a brunette out of a car now blocking his way. Her silhouette was impressive. Sleek black dress, silver something-or-other around her neck, sparkly earrings swaying as she shifted. Short heels, but her legs were the kind that would look great in flats. Not a slutty high-society type, though. Simon could tell that by the way she moved. It read *Crave* above the door. But her darting gaze said, *Isn't Crave much higher?*

"Simon?"

His attention was ripped from the woman. Her companion — date, husband, walking wallet, whatever — had exited the car's other side and circled to Simon's.

"It's Teek," said the man, touching his chest. "Teek Sheridan?" He glanced at the woman from across the car's roof and something unsaid passed between them. Then to Simon, Teek added, "Are you joining the board, too?"

Board?

Too?

Simon blinked. His mind reset, finding this strange new frame. He remembered Teek just fine. He'd always been a puppy, eager to chum along at his heels.

His face transformed. A smile bloomed. It wasn't unnatural, but it wasn't quite natural, either. Simon was excellent at being gregarious when it counted.

"Teek!" he trumpeted, taking the man and dragging him into a sideways bro-hug. Only when it was over did he realize that something was amiss. Teek hadn't really returned the hug, and right now he looked like the exchange had caught him by awkward surprise. Almost as if he wasn't eager to lick Simon's sack like he used to.

The woman was coming around the car, holding a tiny purse with both hands, painted fingers over the top like a mouse perched on cheese. He *did* know her. She'd been one of the quiet ones in high school. Immune to his charm.

"Honey," Teek said, taking one of her hands. He paused for a fractional second with uncertain eyes, as if deciding whether or not to continue. "You remember Simon, from Bayshore? And Simon ... you remember my wife Taylor?"

Another glance. Simon couldn't read the unspoken *whatever* passing between them.

Had they just been fighting in the car, and he'd interrupted them?

"*Wife?*" Simon said. "Well, good for you."

Taylor gave him a small, half-smiling nod and said hello. She didn't open up for a hug as Teek had, even though Simon flexed to try. He settled for a handshake, and Taylor seemed put-out even by that.

"Time's been good to you, Taylor," he said.

"Thanks."

There was an odd moment. Teek and Taylor both looked into the lobby as if preferring escape over small talk. Then Teek said, "So ... how about this alumni dinner thing?"

"Alumni dinner?" Simon repeated.

"Excuse me," said a fourth voice. Simon turned to see the valet, who was dangerously close to touching him on the shoulder. "I'm sorry, but would you mind moving inside? You're ..." He gestured toward a pair of cars: Teek's, with a second valet behind the wheel, and a new one behind it with a woman driving.

"Oh!" Taylor jumped a little, seeing the jam. "We're sorry."

She skirted obediently aside, to the threshold, taking Teek with her. For a few seconds, Simon was the lone roadblock. He glanced at

Teek's car — his Tesla was better by at least 50K — and came forward to meet them.

"I had no idea you'd been asked to join the alumni board, too," Teek said as Simon kept walking, past them and into the lobby. "How ... ?" A glance back at Taylor. Then when it became clear they'd need to ride up together: "How have you been?"

Simon pressed the elevator button. "I'm here for a business meeting."

"Oh. Weird."

"It's not weird. This place is fantastic." Simon studied the couple: good clothes, hardly great. Teek's shoes had square toes. Maybe he didn't know. "So is it your anniversary or something?"

"No, it's—"

"Birthday?"

"No."

"What are you celebrating?"

Teek looked confused. "We're here for the alumni dinner."

"Oh. I assumed you meant that was after."

"Dinner after dinner?"

"Never mind. It's great. It's great that the board chose Crave. And hey, they're picking up the tab, right? Sounds like a deal."

"Isn't the restaurant upstairs?" Teek asked.

"Sorry. That's right. I forget you haven't been here before." They hadn't said as much, but come on, it was obvious. "Crave has its own entrance. The lobby has a bar, so people who didn't think ahead to make reservations or don't know someone can wait without having to sit on hard plastic chairs."

"Hard plastic chairs?"

"Like when you have to wait in the lobby at Olive Garden, I assume."

"Taylor loves Olive Garden," Teek said.

Simon smiled at Taylor as if she were retarded.

After a moment of silence, Teek said, "So you're meeting someone about business?"

"Yep."

"What business are you in? I tried to keep up with you on Live-Lyfe after graduation, but your profile is set to private. I sent a request, but never heard back."

"It's just for friends," Simon explained.

"Oh."

"I market and sell educational products online," Simon said. "Courses. And I do promotions for others. I'm also part of this group that ... you've heard of GameStorming, right?"

"You had something to do with GameStorming?" Teek asked, impressed.

"We're building software that plugs into it, through the API."

"Oh," Teek said again.

"It's a big deal. We raised $2 million in VC funding. 'VC' is 'venture capital.' It's complicated."

"You made two million bucks on it?"

"No." Simon forced his voice to stay pleasant, patient. "It's funding. Investors' money, put up in advance to build the software."

"Sorry. I was never good at that kind of thing. Taylor is."

"Mmm?" said Taylor.

Awkwardness.

"Seems like you're doing well," Teek said to fill the silence.

Simon nodded. He should be doing well, yes. And he had been, a few different times. How long had it been since he'd seen this guy? A decade? More? During that time, Simon had personally earned over eight figures. Teek and Taylor were just meeting him at a low spot.

"My meeting tonight is with Walter Kagen."

Nothing. No reaction.

"You don't know *Walter. Fucking. Kagen.*"

Teek wasn't meeting his eyes. Intimidated. He shrugged.

"He's a player," Simon explained. "He's got the biggest lists on the internet."

"Lists of what?"

"Of buyers."

"Oh. That's good."

"Damn right. He already likes what my company is building. All of it, across the board. You don't just *get* a meeting with Walter Kagen. He came to *me*. And tonight? Walter 10X's my shit."

Teek and Taylor waited. They hadn't known what VC was. Probably didn't know "10X" either.

"All it would take is one email from Walter, sent to any one of his lists, and ..." Simon smacked his hands together. *"Boom!* Ten times the business I already have, overnight."

The elevator dinged. The doors opened to Crave's upstairs lobby.

A well-dressed man with a dark, close-trimmed beard was ready to greet them.

Simon took the lead, stepping ahead of Teek and Taylor. He shook the man's hand with a bill in his palm. "Simon Wyatt. I'm meeting Walter Kagen. Do you know if he's here yet?"

"I'm sorry, Mr. Wyatt. Mr. Kagen hasn't arrived."

His lips pressed tight. Simon willed them open. The elevator ride had made him tense. He hadn't liked elevators for years now. Not since that one time, since Elmer.

"I'd rather not wait in the downstairs bar. It seems deserted anyway."

"The lobby bar isn't open tonight. We're at limited seating. But—"

"Why?"

"The restaurant is closed to the public, for a private event."

"What private event?"

But now the greeter had moved on to Teek and Taylor, shaking hands, exchanging names. Taylor smiled wider at him than she had for Simon, probably because the last decade had made her a bitch.

The greeter's name was Donovan. Simon noted it because for now, he seemed to be in charge. And names were any network's bread and butter.

"I was just about to show all of you up to the Lounge," Donovan said. "Drinks are on the house."

"Oh, they're not with me," Simon explained, taking a step to distance himself.

"If you'll all follow me," Donovan said.

Up a short flight of stairs, holding drinks around the rooftop bar, were more people. Simon noted faces he recognized — probably part of the alumni thing. At first, he could only place Noah Boyer and that tall guy who'd gotten all caught up in that thing before the big senior party. What was his name? Martin. Morton? Simon didn't remember. They hadn't been close. But he did know the woman with Noah, now that he really looked. It was Ella. She'd been friends with Taylor, although she'd been much tighter with Casey Davis and—

"Heidi?" Taylor turned toward a short woman with reddish-brown hair who'd just come up the stairs behind them, probably in the other elevator, apparently unescorted. Taylor scuttled toward her, repeating with delight, *"Heidi Friggin' Blanchard?"*

They embraced. Simon was annoyed. He'd already noticed five or more people from his graduating class. Were they all here for the alumni dinner? The board had invited *this* crowd ... but hadn't asked Simon Wyatt?

He walked away, more eager than ever to escape this carnival of mediocrity and get to business. He slipped the Doodad from his pocket. He'd call his office for something to do. Or his assistant at home. Kagen wasn't here? He'd damn well better show up fast. Kagen could 10X his shit with a blink, but Simon kept his preferred way of seeing tonight firmly in mind: *It was Kagen, not Simon, who'd end up lucky to have been here.*

He moved toward the patio's edge, away from the miniature reunion, listening to voices that were high in both pitch and artifice. He didn't have time or patience for such bullshit. Stupid Bayview board, planning their event on the same night and in the same exclusive venue as his deal with Kagen. Crave wasn't supposed to be a place for just anyone. Only people with big futures and big values, like Simon. What was this, an Applebee's?

But his email wouldn't load. And he couldn't reach his office. He had no service. And yet he'd had it outside when he'd paid the driver. How the hell did that make sense: to have a signal on the ground but not 14 stories in the air?

Simon was waving his Doodad in the air, backing up, searching for a signal, when he collided with someone. Turning, he saw Heidi Blanchard, who'd peeled herself away from Taylor to get a drink from the bar.

"Simon Wyatt? Holy shit ... are you here for the alumni dinner too?"

Simon, knowing it was futile to be angry with no recourse (he'd learned that lesson before), found the salesman's smile trying to crawl back onto his face. He lowered his arm, then put the Doodad away. "No, but congratulations to the rest of you."

Heidi looked surprised. She glanced over her shoulder, then back at Simon.

"Me? I'm not here because I'm joining the board." She laughed. "Hell of a coincidence though, right?"

FOUR

"**P**IMPLE TITS!"

Melissa Lynch looked up from her Doodad, which she'd been hurriedly abusing with both thumbs, to see a short Indian woman rushing across the parking lot with tiny little steps. Melissa stopped mid-text, then returned the device to her purse. She'd been shushing the Donovan guy behind her every time he tried to interrupt, but she'd stop for Imogen.

How long had it been since they'd last seen each other? Since that banquet encounter, and the unpleasantness that drove them apart?

Too long, if Melissa was honest with herself.

"Ohmygod ohmygod, *Melissa!*" Imogen gushed, grabbing Melissa by both of her waif-thin, black-draped forearms. "Fuck you you little whore, what the hell are *you* doing here? You know what? Blow it off. Whatever it is, just screw it. I'll blow my shit off, too. Let's go to the bar and get wasted. Class of 2017, fuck yeah!"

"Yeah" ended in a squeal. Imogen raised a hand for Melissa to high-five, then lowered it without breaking her smile when she was, of course, left hanging. The smaller woman giggled, bouncing in a series of rapid-fire calf raises. Melissa wanted to punch and hug her old friend. As it had always been between them.

"Ladies? I wonder if we could head upstairs now," Donovan interrupted, pushing himself toward the space between them,

Imogen's hands still on Melissa's milk-white skin. How long before her old sorority sister called her a vampire? They'd always looked like the before and after in an ad for Coppertone.

Imogen glanced up at Donovan, seeming only now to notice his presence. Then she reeled Melissa farther down the curb. Once away, she resumed speaking to Melissa at her usual manic pace.

"Ohmygod, look at you. You're still such a skank. How long has it been? Did you know I'm into cooking now? Was I into cooking when we saw each other last?"

"Of course. Don't you remember when you—?"

"Oh, that's right. That thing with McFuckface. After college. Ugh, I try not to think about it. But never mind. So anyway, I had this idea for this TV show — called *Fork & Spoon*? It's pretty much just a normal cooking show, but you know those bitches on the Food Channel need some curry with their white bread. *Fork & Spoon*, bitches! It's not a variety show or a travel-cooking show or whatever, it's just me in front of a stove. So what? There are no brownies on the network. They get it. But ... isn't that wow? Can you believe it?"

Melissa felt vertigo. Good thing she didn't give a shit. "Believe what?"

"Ohmygod, that's right. I didn't even say. I can't believe you're here! Look at you with your stupid little no tits. Elder Conway. You have to know Elder Conway?"

"Chef guy. Always shouting."

"Right. Well. He's interested! They did this thing? The network I mean. Like ... a pitch competition. I figured why not, what the hell, wrote up my idea for *Fork & Spoon*, tossed in a lot of my dad's family recipes for extra cred. I don't know. But they liked my pitch. And now *Elder. Fucking. Conway* wants to talk to me about it!" She squealed, then pivoted to a new topic without a hitch. "How are you, though? You still look like a fucking goth reject. What's—?"

Donovan was back between them. "Ladies, we really should—"

Imogen dragged Melissa down the curb again. Just a few feet from Donovan, enough to be insulting. He closed half the distance, not yet between them again but within easy earshot. She hooked a thumb toward Donovan and said to Melissa, "Who the hell is this guy?"

"He's from the restaurant."

"So you're not with him?"

Melissa scoffed and said no. Donovan was kind of hot with those icy blue eyes, but way too formal. A girl like her would break him in half, then leave him crushed and crying. Melissa's dry wit was a weapon. The expression went, "the pen is mightier than the sword." Melissa's tongue was mightier than the pen, and she wielded both like a pro.

An old-fashioned car horn brayed from Imogen's small, chic purse. She was wearing a yellow dress with a purple belt. Her purse matched exactly, as if the belt and bag came as a set. Imogen's hand dove as the horn repeated, then emerged holding her Doodad. She checked the screen, rolled her eyes dramatically, then stuffed it back inside. "Some people," she said. "Anyway, where were we?"

"I have no idea."

But Imogen opened the purse just enough to peek, shoved aside a prescription bottle that struck Melissa as familiar (and only half in a good way), seemed to note the still-lit display, and closed it again. The conversation had for a second seemed like it was drifting toward Melissa, but then it spun back around to Imogen's favorite subject: *herself.*

"My sister. O-M-G, she won't leave me alone. She thinks Elder Conway is hot. Do you think he's hot?"

"Too old."

"Me neither. She keeps texting me. Wants to know if I met him yet. I'm supposed to take a picture for her to post on LiveLyfe. Slut. Anyway, speaking of pictures — say 'Diamond Society'!" Her Doodad was back like a magic trick. Imogen was holding it out, hugging up next to Melissa to snap a selfie. "Wait. Don't say that. There are no good sounds in 'Diamond Society.' Just say cheese."

The camera steadied. Imogen said "CHEESE!" but Melissa said nothing. Imogen flipped the Doodad and showed the photo, but it looked like a hostage situation to Melissa.

"So what are you here for, anyway?" Imogen asked. "A date?"

Melissa scoffed again.

"What then?"

"I might be getting a gig writing on *Fat Vampire*."

"Ohmygod! I love that show. So you're a TV writer now?"

"Hopefully after tonight. I'm meeting one of the showrunners and a network executive or something. Right now I write for Shared."

"What's that?"

"It's an online news syndicate. Kind of like Buzzfeed, if you remember it. I write viral content. I guess you didn't see my masterpiece, '21 Gross Things That All Girls Do In Secret That Will FUCK YOU UP'?"

"Excuse me," Donovan interrupted, yet again.

"Excuse *us*," Imogen snapped. "We're kind of having a conversation here."

"Perhaps you can continue it upstairs? You're both running late."

"Who are you?" Melissa asked. "My dad?"

"Can you believe this guy?" Imogen said as if Donovan weren't present.

"Thinks he's my dad."

Imogen said, "Your dad is hot."

"You're just saying that because he fucks all the high school girls. Like my stepmom when they met."

"Serious?"

"Ladies?" Donovan said.

"*Man?*" Melissa said back.

"I'm kinda warm anyway," Imogen said to Melissa. "Let's go into the air conditioning so at least he'll stop bothering us."

"Good idea."

Donovan said nothing. Clearly, he wasn't invited to this conversation.

The women turned and approached the doors ahead of Donovan. Melissa glanced back a few times. She didn't like having people behind her. She'd been followed before. She'd been stalked. Nothing had come of it, except for the weird paranoia.

Melissa fancied herself like an iceberg: There was what the world saw, but most of her best psychological shit was under the surface. People thought she was distant and dark? *Ha.* They had no idea. That Contract Confessions website? She could blow it open if she spilled her insides. You couldn't be funny and provocative for a living without wanting to kill yourself a little. Melissa had even cut herself a few times — not "just to feel something" like the emo girls did, but so she could understand just how stupid emo girls really were. That little experiment had resulted in an article that had 1.4 million shares on LiveLyfe. Snark was Melissa's currency, but it came at a price.

At the elevator, Donovan came closer. They were nearly a threesome. Melissa looked him over again while Imogen went on and on with her inanity. She decided that yes, Donovan was handsome. Cute. She'd do him. If he could handle it.

The doors opened. They stepped inside and the box began to rise. It was a while before anyone spoke. Then:

"Why is there nobody here?" Imogen asked, probably referring to the empty lobby on the ground floor. "It's Friday night."

"Crave is closed for a private party," Donovan explained.

"What party?"

"Your party."

"We're not here for a party. We didn't even come together," Melissa said, already searching her Doodad, wondering if she'd gotten the day wrong, despite knowing that May 26th was circled twice on her calendar at home.

"I meant *including* your groups," Donovan said.

"Why would the restaurant close just for us?"

Donovan's smile was so pleasant, Melissa almost didn't notice that he neglected the question.

Imogen was studying him. "Where do I know you from?"

The elevator dinged. The doors opened. And finally: *life*. Melissa could see and hear chatter through propped-open doors, up the stairs toward a rooftop deck. So they weren't being led into an abandoned murder warehouse.

Imogen looked around the lobby and said to Melissa, "So is your TV executive here?"

"I don't know. I'm a little early. I don't know if she's been seated already or what."

Donovan said, "Your party has yet to arrive."

"How do you even know who I'm talking about?"

"Nobody is seated. Only the bar is open. For drinks, upstairs on the deck."

Melissa's eyebrows drew together. She traded glances with Imogen. "What are you talking about, *nobody is seated*? Isn't this a restaurant?"

"Please, if you'll just head upstairs. Drinks are on the house. Make yourself at home." Then, as if remembering something, Donovan looked at his watch. "I should be getting back downstairs. There's just one more person I still need to catch."

"You mean *my* person," Melissa said, "who 'hasn't arrived yet.'"

But Imogen already had Melissa by the arm, hooked through like two kids about to skip down the street. Her head was still turned toward Donovan as Imogen led her away, lured by the siren song of free alcohol.

"What are the chances? You and me here at the same time, both about to blow our shit up!"

Melissa didn't answer. She was wondering the same thing.

FIVE

Summer bustled ahead of her husband, in a hurry but guilty for even the small act of leaving him behind. She was trying to shave seconds off her entrance.

She stopped. Looked back. Waited for John to catch her then muttered, "I'm sorry."

"What are you sorry for?"

"I didn't mean to be snippy in the car. I'm just frustrated. This is kind of a big deal, and of course, here we are late again. It's my fault. But still ... *grrr.*"

John slipped an arm around his wife's shoulders, just below the bob of her curly blonde hair. "Who cares? It's only five after. We're fine."

"I hate being late."

"You've been late since I met you. Remember the first time I came to your sorority house to interview you? Being late is part of what makes you adorable."

"Doesn't mean I can't hate it," Summer said.

There was more to this tirade. She'd given it to John more than a few times — and like the Boy Scout he was, John always offered the simple solution of "leave ten minutes earlier than you think you need to" when he thought she genuinely wanted to change. Most times he simply listened, knowing that change was moot.

John was an excellent, *neutral* companion. He wasn't bland, but he had a way of going with any flow Summer threw his way. That mattered, given how busy their lives had become, but it had mattered a lot more when their relationship was new. Summer's edges were rougher in college, even after the event that had made her take many long, hard looks in the mirror. The fact that John forgave her faults was a testament to the benefits of having a solid, dependable man. Was he a thrill a minute? No. Even his haircut was predictable. But moderation made him ideal. It's what made him John.

A bearded man was waiting for them in the lobby. He was wearing a suit, standing at attention, hands clasped on a small notebook at his waist. He must be with the restaurant. He was too young for such an old-guard organization as the board. Summer had been shocked by her invitation to join, and hoped it wasn't a room full of old white men waiting to greet her.

She sighed and offered the man her PTA smile.

"*Hi,*" she said, drawing the word out with a self-effacing bob of her head. "I'm Summer Merritt. I know we're late."

"It's no problem, Mrs. Merritt. Drinks are just now being served."

"The kids wouldn't let me leave. They act like they'll never see me again!" She laughed a little, knowing how much this sounded like small talk. That was another thing she didn't exactly love about herself. Summer didn't care what others thought nearly as much as she once had — but still, she was always on-stage.

"No worries at all." He extended his hand. "I'm Donovan. You're the last to arrive."

"I'm sorry."

"I didn't mean it like that." He closed his notebook: probably a record of the alumni dinner guests, all but one name checked off. "They'll be pleased to get started."

Summer looked around. "This place looks deserted."

"It's closed for your event. If you'll follow me to the elevator?"

"The Bayshore Alumni Board booked the entire restaurant?" John said.

It was as if Donovan had just noticed him. He stopped, turned, and offered the tiniest bow. "It did." He glanced at his small notebook before extending his hand to John. "Donovan."

"John."

Summer looked at the men, curious why John's introduction had been separate from hers. And why Donovan had paused and checked the book before making it.

"Will you be waiting here," Donovan asked, "or would you like me to have the valet bring your car back around? I'm sorry; I would have told them not to park it if I'd known."

"If you'd known what?" Summer asked.

"That you were dropping off."

Summer's instinct was to respond one way, but she answered in another. Keeping her voice noncommittal just in case, she said, "I don't understand. What do you mean?"

"Well ..." Summer read Donovan's face. He was uncomfortable, unsure of how to proceed. "The invitation was exclusively for you, Mrs. Merritt."

"But it's a dinner. It's not just a meeting. John is my plus one."

"Summer ..." John said.

She put a hand on his arm. "No, no, it's fine. You're my plus one."

"I'm so sorry for the misunderstanding," Donovan said. "Guests are not permitted."

"How could guests not be permitted? We've donated to groups for years and been invited to plenty of events. Things like this are *always* plus one."

"Not this time, I'm afraid. There simply isn't space in the private room."

"You said they rented the whole restaurant," Summer pointed out.

"I'm very sorry."

Her dander was rising — part of the strange regression she'd felt since first seeing the Bayshore coat of arms on the invitation. "I'm sure an exception can be made."

"I'm sorry," he repeated.

"If you'd please just check."

Donovan gave his head a polite but definite shake. "My instructions were explicit."

"What did it say on the invitation?" John asked Summer.

"It didn't say anything," Summer snapped, harsher than she'd intended.

"Did you bring it?"

"No, I didn't *bring it.* I knew where the restaurant was, I'm able to remember a time and day, and my purse is the size of a matchbox."

Hearing the hardness in her voice, she found an ill-fitting smile. She raised her tiny purse for inspection, as if to soften the affair with a joke. Truth was, she ordinarily would have packed the invitation, but Summer was glad she hadn't because she remembered the bold red text along the bottom. It had clearly read, *NO GUESTS, PLEASE.*

But the idea of returning to Bayshore's memory without the comfort of her husband? That bothered Summer in a way she could barely articulate — and that John, bless his heart, would never fully understand. At least not if she could help it.

Summer turned to Donovan. "Look. I really don't mean to be pushy. But we live nowhere near here, our kids are with a sitter, and who knows how late this thing will go? I really don't want my husband to have to sit down here in an empty lobby. The board can afford another meal," Summer said.

"It's not a matter of—"

"Don't be ridiculous," John cut in. "I can pay for myself."

"There simply isn't room. I really am sorry."

"Maybe you can call someone and ask." Summer propped her palms on her hips and met Donovan's eye, not wanting to explicitly say what she meant: that if someone was going to tell her *no* tonight, it for damn sure wouldn't be the board's lackey. Let Gloria Dunham herself come down here and deny them. Crusty old Gloria had been on the board since Summer graduated, and rumor said she slept on a pile of gold coins like a dragon atop a hoard.

Donovan took a breath, then nodded and stepped a few paces away. Once alone, Summer turned to John. He seemed amused by his wife's manhandling of the porter.

"Don't tell me you'll just sit down here, John. It's not right. If they want me to volunteer my time for their stupid board, they can buy us *both* dinner. The board isn't that big and they've got more money than they know what to do with."

"Whatever you say, dear."

"I guess I should have let you stay at home. But it really seemed like you wanted to go."

"Either way," John said.

"Am I being ridiculous?" She was suddenly sure she was. "I'm sorry. You *didn't* want to come. I just thought—"

"No. It's fine. I want to be here."

"It's just some stupid alumni thing. You won't have anyone to talk to."

"I'll have you."

"Do you want to go home? It just seems like such a long ride in a FASTr … "

"No. I don't want to go home." He took Summer by the shoulders to halt her downward spiral and smiled. "I'm here."

Summer smiled back, feeling self-conscious, flustered by all of this, and all the sour memories. She'd been so sure he'd never want to attend this fussy alumni thing, so she'd jumped at his flicker of interest. He was always trying to help.

"Hi," Donovan said into a Doodad, a dozen feet away. "It's me."

Summer heard the distorted voice of a woman on the other end, seeming to ask a question.

"Yes. But she has her husband with her. There was some sort of misunderstanding." His eyes flitted to Summer and John. "Right. She brought him along. As a guest … John … Merritt … What? I'm sorry; I didn't hear what you said." Donovan looked uncertain. "Are you sure that's a good idea?" The woman said something else. "I suggested he wait downstairs. Or I could call a FASTr."

The woman became momentarily louder. Summer thought she might have heard a laugh.

"We could offer him a voucher for another restaurant in the area. Maybe a movie?"

"You're not going to send my husband to a movie by himself," Summer said, projecting. "If *that's* how this is going to be, we can—"

Donovan raised a finger, then turned his back to the couple. Summer listened to the woman's still-indecipherable voice, intrigued by its pleasant, accommodating tone.

"Well … all right," Donovan said. "If that's what you want to do …"

He hung up. He looked at Summer, then fully at John. Finally, he nodded and extended a hand toward the elevator. "If you'll please both follow me upstairs to the Lounge?"

SIX

At seven minutes past seven, with the sun now moving in earnest from yellow to tangerine, Heidi Blanchard looked over Teek Sheridan's shoulder and saw someone who seemed very familiar. She'd already recognized a few other people (not just Teek and Taylor, but also Ella, who seemed now to be with Noah Boyer), but this person was particularly unexpected. From a different slice of Heidi's life.

She excused herself and walked toward the bar, noting the tall blonde's narrow nose and concerned — almost worried — expression. She almost slammed into Simon Wyatt, who Heidi hadn't yet recognized and still didn't, even now. The two mumbled apologies, but with Heidi focused on her target and Simon fixed on getting cell reception, neither truly saw the other.

Not until later.

Heidi reached the bar. "Bindi? What are *you* doing here?"

"Heidi?"

The two smiled at each other, both uncomfortable. Heidi was used to baring her soul to her therapist in the comfort of Bindi's office, but it felt somehow dangerous to be with her in the open air, where secrets had no walls to bar them.

"I thought you were done with all things Bayshore," Heidi said.

"I am."

"But you're on the alumni board?"

Bindi shook her head, confused. "No. What makes you ... ?" She trailed off, tried again. "Are you here to meet Mason?"

"Mason?"

"Mason Pace? I think he was in your class."

It hit her in the gut like a sledgehammer. *Mason* is here?"

Bindi wasn't listening, scanning the crowd of familiar faces, searching for whoever was here to tell her about her husband Donald — and the unknown woman who'd tempted him into an affair.

Meanwhile, Simon, at the roof's edge, shook his Doodad with rage, slapping its side as if it were an ancient TV. Still no bars. He should go back outside. But how would it look if Kagen arrived while Simon was standing beside the valet stand, trying desperately to get in touch?

No. He needed to play it cool. He wasn't desperate for help, and *Kagen* was the lucky one.

Going outside was a chump move.

Simon turned his attention to anything that might provide a distraction. He scanned the crowd, found John Merritt and thought the man looked like a middle-manager in some anonymous office cubicle. He held two drinks in elegant glassware: one brown, clinking with ice in an old-fashioned glass, and a cosmo for his wife. Simon put on his usual smile, not intending to stop.

But John nodded and spoke. "Doesn't seem like a big enough party to close the whole restaurant, does it?"

Simon stopped. *Small talk.* Obnoxious.

"John," he said, setting down one of his drinks and extending a hand.

"Simon."

"Are you on the alumni board at Bayshore?" John asked.

"No."

"With someone who is?"

"No. I'm here for a business appointment."

John said, "I thought the restaurant was closed for the alumni dinner."

Simon kept his smile firmly in place, but this was getting stupid. Embarrassing, really. "I hope not, because if so I'm in the wrong place."

But now that he'd said it, Simon was starting to wonder if it were true. He wasn't an idiot. He could read an email and respond to an invitation without ending up in the wrong place and time. But if that was right, why was the Bayshore crew here instead of Kagen?

Simon reached into his pocket, desperate to verify the invitation's details. But then he remembered: no service.

John watched Simon go for his Doodad and retract an empty hand. There was something odd on his face. So to Simon, he said, "What?"

"Do you have cell service up here?"

John reached into his pocket, then consulted his screen with a frown. "No, actually." He looked around, toward the horizon, as if digital waves would be visible things. "Weird. I had it in the car."

Twenty feet away, the women were watching.

"Your husband looks familiar. Should I know him?" Imogen asked Summer Merritt, who she'd greeted as "Summer Nixon." Imogen followed her eyes as John made conversation with ... *Is that Simon Wyatt? He* isn't on the board, is he?

Imogen didn't know Simon much better than the rest of the people here, but she recognized most of them from Bayshore, a year behind Summer.

"Maybe," Summer said. "He went to Coastline."

"Was he in a frat or something?"

"No. He was on the newspaper staff. We met after ..." Summer let the sentence hang. The memory was uncomfortable, for all of them.

Imogen squinted. "I feel like I should know him. You said his name is John?"

"Yes."

"Like Jonathan."

"No, the other kind of John. With an H."

"There are two kinds of Johns?" Imogen asked.

"The kind you shit in," Melissa explained, "and the kind you marry."

Summer ignored Melissa and addressed Imogen, still watching her husband talk to Simon Wyatt, wary. "He was a senior when we were freshmen. But he's not exactly a party guy."

"What's he do for a living?"

"He manages a Greens."

Melissa Lynch, standing beside Imogen, laughed loudly. Things were still uncomfortable between the three of them after what happened freshman year, but it seemed Melissa hadn't lost her edge, same for Imogen and her vacuousness.

"He works in a grocery store?" Melissa asked.

Summer looked away from John and Simon to face Imogen and Melissa. They weren't much, these two, but they were all she had other than John. The stodgy board members were still MIA.

"He *manages* a store," Summer clarified. A waiter passed, so she raised her finger for a drink. *Two* fingers. This might be a long night.

"*That's* where I must have seen him," Imogen said. "That's so funny! Isn't that funny, Melissa?"

Melissa didn't reply. She'd stopped hearing Imogen a while ago. She'd already looked through the entire restaurant on a detour from a trip to the bathroom. She was, as they stood beside Summer Nixon of all people, rehearsing witty lines she intended to try on the network people. There was a balance to strike. On one hand, she very much wanted the gig they were supposedly going to offer — seeing as *Fat Vampire* was, in Melissa's opinion, the only show worth writing for right now. But on the other hand, it was important that she not give a shit.

Still, she kept sneaking peeks at the ornate clock. It was almost quarter past seven. She'd arrived on time, and the executives hadn't. They were TV types, working in LA, embracing the cliché and being inconsiderate assholes from *Go*.

"Why do you keep looking at the time?" Imogen asked Melissa as Summer excused herself.

"I'm curious how fast I can get drunk," Melissa said.

As Teek and Taylor stood at the roof's edge, looking at Noah and Ella, watching Heidi talk to a woman at the bar who struck them both as somehow familiar, Taylor took her husband's hands by the fingers and tried to hold on.

The fight was still raw. If that's what it was. Taylor was unsure what to think of Teek right now, and she imagined that he felt the same. The discomfort wasn't new; only the reasons.

Maybe that was good — lancing a festering wound so they could heal in the open.

But mostly, Taylor watched Simon circling with a scowl, turning friendly each time he passed a cluster of people. Simon Wyatt, of all people. Here. Tonight. So soon after Teek's confession.

"You okay, Tay?" Teek asked, looking over. She was shivering.

"Just cold."

Teek gave Taylor a long look. He was still warm. He took off his jacket and opened for his wife to slip into as—

—Ella studied Taylor's profile across the room, everything eating her insides.

They hadn't chatted long. And the distance she might have imagined in Taylor's words made Ella uneasy. It had been eleven years. Was Taylor still holding a grudge? Certainly not — and yet here they were, Taylor almost turning but not quite, seeing Ella but pretending she didn't, the two women sharing an awkward almost-glance across the long rooftop.

It wasn't the way old friends usually acted. Ella's familiar neuroses were already spiraling, imagining Taylor's possible thoughts and judgments tumbling one after the other. Self-destruction — always so near these days — sniffed at the edges of her mind.

Ella slipped away from Noah, and Taylor's field of view. She couldn't take the wondering. And besides, she needed to call the babysitter and check on the twins, knowing without wanting to admit it that she really planned to stalk Chance Baskin's LiveLyfe profile for the third time this week as soon as she got the chance.

She couldn't help it. Being here made her feel exposed, and she needed the calm.

It was an unhealthy compulsion, but these days checking in on Chance was the least harmless of her damaging habits. Better than sneaking more pills. She'd had enough today already, and tonight she'd be drinking. Oh boy, would she be drinking.

But when she reached the shadows, Ella looked at her Doodad and swore. No service. Watching its blank screen, she felt alone — even more than she did with Noah. Claustrophobic.

In the dark, closed part of the Lounge bar, with the tables still stacked with last night's chairs, it felt like the world was closing in. Her breath was short, and her heart was beating too hard.

Did she even *have* any of her painkillers? She opened her purse. But no, of course not; she'd made a point to leave them at home to exile temptation.

But she needed something to dull this curious edge.

She took out the tiny bottle. Opened it, knowing she'd find only Excedrin and ibuprofen. *"Goddammit!"*

"Headache?"

Ella looked up. It took less than a second to recognize Mason Pace.

His expression dropped like a piping hot plate. He recognized her, too.

Ella held it together. She hadn't known him well. Just enough to put things into motion all those years ago.

"I'm fine."

Now that he'd realized who she was, he looked like he wanted to leave. Not just the room, but the building. Still, Mason stood straight, apparently intending to be an adult. They were almost thirty, after all.

"Are you sure? I might even have—" He reached into his pocket, but Ella cut him off.

"I don't think you can help me. I need something for …"

Lifelessness. Depression. Desperation. The fear of coping with everyday life.

"… menstrual cramps."

"Oh." Then, with effort, he smiled. "Fresh out."

Mason straightened further. He was about to be a father. A husband, if Jessica let him. He was bigger than this. Bigger than his past. Everyone had paid their dues, Ella included.

"Out of *pills,*" Mason clarified. "Definitely not out of cramps."

The joke surprised a laugh out of Ella. An inappropriate bark. Her hand went to her mouth, but the noise was already gone.

Imogen. Imogen Shah always used to carry something stronger than ibuprofen. Maybe she still did. Maybe Ella could chat her up, then ask.

Ella and Mason faced each other in the dark.

"It's Ella, right?"

Ella nodded then verified his name, though of course she already knew. Some of her forgetting was real. Some was feigned. Protection: her mind barring breath from the past.

"I didn't think the board would want so many '18s," Ella said, wanting to fill the silence.

"What do you mean?"

"You're the class of 2018, right? Like me and my husband?"

"Who's your husband?"

"Noah Boyer."

"Oh," Mason said. "Congratulations."

There was no point in congratulations. Not with enough years for love — or codependence — to sour.

"I'm class of '18, yeah," Mason went on.

"Right. That's what I was saying. I'm surprised the alumni board would nominate so many people from the same class. You, Noah, all these others ..."

Mason looked confused.

And Ella said, "You're not here for the alumni dinner, are you?"

Twenty feet away, Donovan Bruce crossed the Lounge, moving from the bar to the stairway. He tried not to look around; he was supposed to stay more or less invisible. Servants were meant to be seen and not heard, *definitely* not recognized in the vague way several of the guests already almost had. He couldn't afford to attract gazes or garner attention. He'd just do his job. And service the gathering's unseen host.

Donovan reached the lower floor with the cocktail chatter now muted consonants above him, then stopped to look around. The lobby was deserted. The hostess had left her station on schedule, moving into the kitchen for her next role. The bartender, after drinks were sufficiently dispensed, would double as a waiter. The light staff was important tonight: just enough hands to cook and serve. Ambiance without excess, as insisted upon by their host.

Donovan walked to the elevators, then used a small key to open a large brass panel. He put both units into service mode, breaking the circuit and de-clutching the motors. He closed the panel as his Doodad began to vibrate. It, unlike the units topside, had plenty of bars. It, unlike the others, was on the jammer's whitelist, its signal clear for the evening's duration.

"Yes," Donovan told the caller. "They're all here. Twelve, if you count Summer's husband." He listened, then nodded. "I asked the kitchen to prepare another plate, and they've made room in the Buvette for one more setting. Six on each side now, with your place at the head. We're still short an envelope, though. I'll leave that to you."

He listened again.

"Maybe a half hour. We're just about to begin serving appetizers. I checked on them a while ago. And good news. I was able to find some decent pancetta to wrap the shrimp." He stopped and listened again. "Of course. It's delicious."

Donovan listened a third time. After a few seconds, his lips turned up into a smile.

"We'll be ready."

He slipped the Doodad into his pocket then went to the fire door. He inserted a key into the recently added lock and turned it.

Before heading into the kitchen to oversee the Starters course, Donovan slipped the key to Crave's only exit into his pocket as well.

Appetizers

Pancetta-Wrapped Shrimp
With Serrano-Infused Lime Juice
And Sambal Oelek Romesco

SEVEN

May 11, 2018

"Oh, *come on*." Ella was lying on her stomach, moving her whole body in a convulsion so she could bounce without getting up from the bed: a lazy girl's way of showing enthusiasm. "We *have* to do it if we want to get in!"

"Then do it," Casey said. "By all means, Ella. You're 18 friggin' years old. You don't need my permission."

"We're not going to do it without you, you know."

Casey looked up from her phone, which she'd been using as an excuse for barely paying attention. She was in the corner of Ella's dorm room, sitting in the secondhand chair that Ella's brother Daniel had hefted up the elevator and into place at the start of the school year. Her stepmother had been sitting in that chair on moving day, holding her baby half-brother, when Daniel had hefted a heavy end table and almost dropped it on them both. That felt like a forever ago. Time expanded, contracted, and sometimes disappeared. It felt to Ella that their little Girl Squad foursome had known each other from birth, and yet it had only been three and a half years since they'd been boarding school freshmen, living away from home for the first time.

Casey gave Ella a condescending eye.

"Don't look at me like that. Don't act like I'm the crazy one." Ella turned. "Heidi, back me up."

"You have to do what they say," Heidi agreed. "Every new class does it."

"But we're not even in college yet," Casey said. "You don't rush sororities until you're actually *in college.*"

"Exactly. That's why they call it *pre*-rush," Ella pointed out.

Casey rolled her eyes. With her high-arching eyebrows and fiery hair, she could make anyone feel patronized without even trying. "There's no such thing as pre-rush."

"No such ...!" Heidi gave an exasperated sigh and picked up the piece of paper she'd been brandishing during the past 48 hours of on-and-off debate. She shook it, making a noise like miniature Chinese firecrackers, then slapped a finger to a bold headline at the paper's top. *"Pre-rush!"*

"It's dumb," Casey said. "I'm not going to do anything that stupid. Especially for a sorority. And ... Heidi, come on! Especially for *Diamond Society!*"

"They're the best sorority!"

"Says you! How much time have you spent on campus?"

"And *you* know all about what's best?" Heidi countered. "Diamond Society is the one you shoot for. The other sororities take their sloppy seconds. Everyone knows that."

"No, they don't. Diamond might actually be the laughing stock of Coastline. They put out good PR. In reality, everyone might make fun of them."

Ella made a disgruntled noise. Half a groan. She looked at Taylor, in the corner, but of course, Taylor wasn't any help.

In the quiet moment that followed, Casey picked up one of Ella's stuffed animals. She wouldn't make fun of Ella for owning it like Heidi did because of course she had stuffed animals of her own. She named them, sometimes talked to them when she was trying to figure things out. Had a bunch more at home, too. With home not far away and her sister Kimmy still there to watch the animals, it was easy to feel young whenever she wanted.

There was no need to grow up quite as quickly as the world sometimes wanted, and definitely no need to debase oneself for those Diamond Society bitches.

"Fine. Forget about which sorority is best. I'm saying that rushing, in general, is ridiculous. I mean ... let's talk about hazing."

"They've cracked down on all of that, Casey," Ella said. "They *can't* haze."

"Of course they can. What do you call making pledges do all the chores? That's hazing."

"That's hardly hazing. It's a far cry from—"

"It's a slippery slope," Casey cut her off. "And nobody's policing it. If nobody rats them out, they can do whatever they want. This girl I know? Sky? She pledged at UCLA and they had all the pledges stand in front of a wall. They couldn't move for a full hour. Anyone who so much as flinched, one of the 'sisters' would slam her head into the wall."

"Oh, come on."

"And another time, they made her sit on top of a running washing machine in her underwear and circled anything that jiggled with a marker. Why would you want to be part of anything like that?"

"That's UCLA!" Heidi threw her hands in the air. "They still eat people there when times get tough."

Casey shook her head, still petting the stuffed animal. A little dog, with a red collar. She'd heard Ella call it Ralphie when she wasn't so busy trying to fit in and be awesome.

Ella got off her stomach, then sat on the edge. Composing herself to appear more earnest, she said, "Look. Okay. So there are some bad stories out there. But this is Coastline, and Diamond Society. You know they've got their fingers in everything. Macy Laze. You know how she got her job?"

"Who's Macy Laze?"

"Sounds like a porn star," said Taylor.

"She's the executive vice president of Garment. I assume you've heard of *them?*"

Casey rolled her eyes again.

"My friend Annabelle knows Macy," Ella went on. "Says she's a total airhead. Can't tie her shoes. Macy only got that cush job because the owner of Garment is a Diamond Society alumnus. Same as Leigh Masterson's job at Outward Unlimited. If you want to be someone, you need to rush Diamond because that's how doors open up for you. And that's not even considering their connections in—"

"Did they send you a brochure or something?" Casey interrupted.

Ella gave a heavier sigh, then moved over to sit on the arm of Casey's chair. Softer, she said, "Come on, Casey. I really want to join."

"Go ahead. No one's stopping you."

But that wasn't what Ella wanted to hear, and Casey knew it. The Squad stayed together. *Period.* That's how they'd sworn it'd always be.

"I want you to join with me. With *us.*"

Casey must have heard something in Ella's voice, because she softened, too. "I'll think about it."

"Don't think too long. It's coming up fast."

"What is?"

"Pre-rush," Taylor said from her spot in the corner. Sometimes, it was easy to forget she was there. They each had their roles. Ella was the dominant one, Heidi was the enthusiastic and popular one, Casey was the smart and sensible one, and Taylor was the quiet, thoughtful one. Taylor could also be surprisingly funny, but mainly because nobody saw her jokes coming.

"I promise to think about Diamond Society," Casey clarified, "but I'm not falling for 'pre-rush'."

"What's to fall for?" Ella asked, exasperated. "This is how they do things. If you wait to rush until college, you'll never have a chance!"

Casey scoffed.

"Come on. Pre-rush with us. Please?"

"No way, Ella," Casey said.

"Well ... what are we supposed to tell Summer?" Heidi asked.

Casey froze. She looked at Taylor, in the corner, and Ella, still on the chair. Finally, she returned her attention to Heidi. She spoke again, her voice now cold. "Summer *Nixon?*"

"You remember her," Heidi said, oblivious. "She graduated last year. She's at Coastline now, in Diamond Society."

"Of course I remember her." Casey turned to Ella, her green eyes stern. With Ella perched above her, she had to look up to do it. "Is that what this is all about, you guys? *Summer Fucking Nixon?*"

Ella looked away, annoyed. Heidi and her big mouth. Of course, mentioning Summer would trigger Casey. Heidi should have known that. Summer had basically run Bayshore until she'd graduated. Heidi had always admired her popularity. Casey hated that whole clique's pretense ... and Summer in particular.

Heidi stood. "She invited me personally, Casey! She was at Bayshore talking to 'promising senior girls' about joining Diamond next year and she *sought me out,* Casey! Me specifically!"

Ella watched her friends with the fascination of a train wreck. Heidi thought that earning Summer's attention was an achievement, but it seemed pathetic to Casey. In this moment they were oil and water. Anything could happen next.

But instead of mocking Heidi, Casey paused. They all knew how insecure Heidi was under her bubbly exterior, and how scared she was of trading prep school for college. The thought of the Girl Squad living different places on the same campus was less-than-ideal for Casey — but for Heidi, it felt tragic.

Casey sighed with a small shake of her head. So the answer was pity. *Pity* would happen next.

She snatched Heidi's flier. "I'll consider it, but I can't make this meeting. I already have plans on Friday."

"We don't have plans, do we?" Taylor asked.

Ella, looking at them, wasn't sure whether Taylor's "we" referred to all four or only Taylor and Casey. Officially they were a foursome, but two pairs were dominant between them: Heidi and Ella, and Taylor and Casey.

"No," Casey said. "I meant just me."

"You and who? Jackie? 'Jackie' is more important than us?"

Casey gave Taylor a look. None of them knew Jackie enough to be jealous or otherwise, but Taylor, with her dry wit, was busting ovaries.

"Or," Ella said, "is it with your secret boyfriend?"

"I keep telling you guys, I don't have a secret boyfriend!"

But Ella thought that was a lie. Casey did things on her own a lot and always came back rosy.

"Just reschedule him," Taylor said, "whoever he is."

"There's no 'him,' Taylor." Casey handed the flier back to Heidi. "But I really can't make this. Sorry."

Heidi sat back down, looking crushed.

"Look," Casey said. "You all go if you want to, and—"

"*I* don't really want to," Taylor interrupted. Ella wished Taylor hadn't said that, but she'd been on the ledge from the start and would probably lean the same as Casey.

"Just you two, then," Casey said to Ella and Heidi. "Make our excuses. If they can't consider me and Taylor because we don't want to jump at the last minute, screw 'em. I guess you can ask. But no promises. In fact, I'm kinda sure I won't do this stupid crap no matter what, but I'll hear you out. Okay?"

Heidi nodded. "Just give it a chance. Don't do that thing where you pre-decide and then act too good for it."

But the fight was over, so Casey smiled. "Like I'm the one who acts too good for things?"

Ella shoved her.

A pillow hit Casey in the face. It seemed to have come from Heidi, while her head was turned, but then Ella noticed Taylor whistling and looking away, in the corner, near a pile of linens and ammunition. It must have fooled Casey because she returned fire at a protesting Heidi.

Then, the room fell apart.

Feeling far too old for pillow fights, Ella pulled a cushion from the mini couch and joined the fray. With college on the horizon and Ella's nerves wary, being immature felt good.

"I'll show *you* hazing!" Casey bellowed, as Ella's lamp shattered on the floor.

They all laughed. And then the battle continued.

EIGHT

"Ohmygod, Melissa," said the girl whose name Noah had already forgotten, her mouth full, the hand not holding her appetizer plate standing guard by her lips lest food try to escape. "This is totally the shit. Tell her it's the shit, Noah."

"It's the shit," Noah repeated, though he felt like a poseur before Crave's delicate portions. He'd taken one bite of shrimp after rubbing it through the crescent-shaped squirt of light orange sauce and found it to be a pleasing mix of tang and spice — lemon and hot pepper or something. Half of the large shrimp was still on his plate, and, watching the girl chew, Noah suspected he'd eaten his wrong. She'd taken her entire appetizer down in a pop, sparing only the tail.

"Ohmygod. Ohmygod." Fingers straight, shielding her lips as if obeying a hush. "You. Hey." Arm darting out to grab a server by the sleeve. He reacted mildly, turning his head, managing to not drop his tray. She pointed at the sauce with a shaped red fingernail. "What is this? Oelek romesco?"

"Sambal oelek romesco. Yes, Miss."

"With ham," Melissa added.

"Prosciutto," Noah corrected.

"*Pancetta,*" said the chewing girl. "You idiots."

"Yes, Miss," said the server.

"You have to take me back to the kitchen so I can watch them make it. There's lime in this. And some other chili."

"Serrano," said the server.

"Is the chef a guy? Tell me it's a guy. Because I'm going to get down on my knees and blow him to see how this is made."

"Miss?"

"Let the poor guy go, Imogen," said Melissa. "Let him earn his minimum wage."

The server, torn between gratefulness at being freed and annoyance at the insult, turned to leave. And Noah thought, *Imogen. That's right.* He used to be more cosmopolitan, but these days Ella kept him in a white upper-middle-class isolation chamber.

It was a pretty name, and Noah didn't want to forget it again.

Imogen turned to Noah. She was like a billion-watt bulb. In a few minutes of idle conversation, she'd paid him more attention than Ella had over a dicy half-decade.

"I'm serious. I'd blow the chef for this recipe. You hear things about Crave's cuisine, but the reviews don't tell you that it tastes like sex. Right now, shrimp is fucking pancetta in my mouth, using lime juice and sambal as lube. Right?"

"Sure," Noah said.

"Keep a secret?"

Noah leaned in.

"I wonder if Elder Conway had something to do with this."

"Who's Elder Conway?"

"Fuck you, 'Who's Elder Conway!'" Imogen blurted, slapping Noah on the arm.

"What? Am I supposed to know?"

"No," said Melissa.

"He's only one of the most famous chefs in the world." Then lower: "I'm meeting him here tonight."

Noah still didn't know Elder Conway, but he was obviously supposed to be impressed. And was, if only for the novelty.

"That's what she thinks, anyway," said Melissa.

Noah looked back. If Imogen was a billion-watt bulb, Melissa was a set of blackout curtains. She was understatedly pretty, but dressed almost entirely in black, with too much black eyeliner, black fingernail polish, subtle black lipstick, and a manner only slightly more cordial than a scorpion's. She looked like an advertisement for apathy.

"He was supposed to be here at seven," Melissa continued. "I think she got stood up."

Noah glanced at his watch: 7:35. The sun was mostly down and the sky was dim enough to see the glow of Cielo. Strings of white lights above would soon provide most of the illumination.

"He didn't stand me up. Melissa is just being a bitch because *she* got stood up."

"You're here on a date?" It felt like playful banter, but also slightly flirty. Noah wasn't sure how he'd ended up talking with these two. He liked them both and, truth be told, was attracted to them each in different ways.

"I'm meeting some network people about a TV writing gig."

"Really?"

Melissa responded by looking at her fingernails.

"You're not here for the alumni board dinner?"

"What?" Imogen asked.

"The Bayshore board." Noah was suddenly confused. "I just assumed."

Melissa gave a derisive scoff.

"Is that what you're here for?" Imogen asked. "There's some dumb Bayshore thing while I'm supposed to be interviewing with Elder Friggin' Conway?"

"If he ever shows up," Melissa said.

"Where are *your* people, tramp?"

"Fashionably late."

Noah's eyes searched the room. If this wasn't a Bayshore gathering, what was it? He recognized pretty much everyone, including Ella's old clique — minus Casey Davis, of course. Their little "Girl Squad" used to be tight, especially Ella and Heidi Blanchard. But tonight, even those conversations were strained. Ella had vanished, but she wasn't talking to Heidi or Taylor; Noah could see them both. Time really did let relationships drift. Or it pried them apart with bars and hammers.

"But I saw you guys talking to Summer Nixon." Noah wanted to add, *That's why I thought I knew you.*

But *did* he even know them if they weren't here for the alumni dinner? They seemed so familiar. And up until now, they'd been having so much casual fun. Imogen and Melissa's mix of hot and cold somehow worked, like lime and peppers. Better than Ella's usual dial tone.

"We know Summer from Coastline College. We didn't go to *Bayshore*." Melissa said it like a disease rather than one of the country's most prestigious prep schools.

Noah's brow furrowed when a cold hit his left arm. He turned to his wife as she entered the circle and offered the remaining half of his shrimp. "Try this. It's like shrimp and ham having sex in your mouth."

Ella was looking at a smiling Melissa.

"Ella, this is Melissa and Imogen." He turned to the others. "This is my wife, Ella."

Imogen shook hands with Ella, expression curious, as if she might know her.

Melissa shook her hand and said, "We've met."

"Oh, that's right," said Imogen. "What was your name again?"

"Ellen," said Melissa.

Ella took Noah's arm, ignoring the shrimp. "Can I talk to you for a minute?"

"No, no," Melissa said. "It's *Helen*."

"You three *know each other?*"

"Vaguely," said Melissa, still smiling. But as far as Noah could tell, only Melissa and Ella had made the connection. Imogen still looked curious. But then her attention was pulled to a fresh tray of appetizers en route atop a passing waiter's hand.

"Noah," Ella said, now tugging.

"How do you know each other?" Watching the interaction had only deepened Noah's itch. Something was weird. It was supposed to be an alumni dinner, but there were no senior board members, no oversight, just a bunch of people from his class. These were the only two outliers, here for a meeting with a chef and TV executives respectively, and yet Ella clearly recognized even them.

"From school," Ella said.

"They didn't go to Bayshore."

"College, Noah."

"She pledged our sorority," Melissa said. "Good times — huh, Bella?"

With this, Imogen gave Ella a look that said, *So that's who you are!*

"Noah. Come on. I'm not feeling well."

"Cramps," Melissa decided.

"I think I have something," Imogen said brightly. Then she looked around. "Where did I leave my purse?"

Ella's eyes lingered too long on Imogen as she scoured the visible deck with her eye. It seemed hard for her to pull away, to pull Noah away.

"Noah. Come on. There's someone I want to talk to."

"You should go talk, then." Melissa looked at Noah, her eyebrows rising, amused.

But you should stay here. Maybe we really like you. Maybe we'd even have sex with you. Maybe ...

"Noah ..."

Ella, walking away.

Noah, knowing he should follow.

He gave Melissa a nod. Imogen's eyes were still searching, her attention totally gone.

"So nice to see you again, Stella," Melissa said, raising her drink.

NINE

Ella was fighting with herself. Again.

She hauled her husband away from Melissa Lynch and Imogen Shah, both of whose full names she easily remembered, neither of whom had any business being here. So why were they here, along with all these other familiar faces?

You didn't even talk to her, said one voice in Ella's head. *You didn't even ask.*

Why did I need to? There's nothing she'd have that I need.

Ella had noticed Imogen earlier; that's how she'd known to seek her out. Melissa was a nasty surprise, same as always.

"Where are we going?"

She'd been dragging Noah along like a naughty toddler, barely aware of his weight. "I just need some fresh air."

"We're outside, Ella."

And fairly comfortable. As the sky darkened, mute employees had circulated and turned on several tall outdoor heaters. They weren't the cheap mushroom-top chrome things, either. These were six-foot, narrow triangles with what looked like a plasma torch burning through their centers, encased in a clear glass tube.

"I need a moment, Noah."

"You've got all the moments you need. I was talking to them. That was pretty rude, the way you dragged me off like that."

"I didn't drag you."

Noah looked at his wrist, where Ella's thin fingers had anchored him for dragging.

"I mean, I didn't drag you away from them," she corrected.

"Just once we were away. That's when you started dragging."

"Do you have something you'd like to say, Noah?"

"Do *you* have something *you'd* like to say, Ella?"

She stopped. Hands on hips. Looked at the horizon. Was she on the verge of crying?

"Look ..." Noah said.

"I don't really want to talk about it."

Another moment of silence. Then, "So are you actually feeling sick?"

"I'm fine."

"That Donovan guy said he could get you some pills."

"What's that supposed to mean?" Ella spat.

Noah raised his hands, palms out. "I meant Excedrin or something. Jesus. Not everything is an accusation."

Just most things.

But she bit her tongue.

"You said there was someone you wanted to talk to. Do you want to ..."

The sentence had no end, probably because Noah wasn't sure whether her request to talk to someone else was another means of escape. His voice was on eggshells. Ella wasn't sure whether she preferred to accept his surrender or feel insulted by it.

"Where is the board meeting, Noah?"

"It's here. All around us. What's gotten into you?"

"This isn't the Bayshore board. You get their emails. It's all old rich women with nothing better to do. Do you know who I ran into a minute ago? Mason Pace."

Searching his mind: "Mason Pace ..."

"He's right over there. With that blonde woman and Heidi."

"Looks familiar. I can't place him."

"The video, Noah. With Casey?"

Noah must have remembered, because he blinked, then looked over at Ella again.

"Weird. I think I remember him being an okay guy, though." Noah was discrete enough not to add, *The problem was you.*

But why? Why was Mason here?

No board, no school authorities, no hosts to this rather small party at the hottest restaurant in town, where big stars like Stitch Freeman and Harper Knox were rumored to dine. Acres of buried memories. When dark descended and the need came calling, Ella got paranoid. That feeling was on her now, like creeping fingers on a wary shoulder.

"I changed my mind," she said. "I want to go home."

"All right. I can call you a car."

"I want you to go, too."

"Why?"

But she wouldn't say why, because that would flatter him. She wanted Noah's comfort. She wanted to grasp his arm as the fear hit, and withdrawal waged its war. She shouldn't have gone without tonight. Ella thought she was strong enough — but as usual, she was not.

"You just need some food. The appetizers are great. I want like ten more. And you know I'm not supposed to eat shellfish. Because of Hell or something. Come on," he said, trying to make her laugh. "Don't you want to see me go to Hell?"

A smile touched her lips as he took her arm. A moment of weakness. Of giving in.

"Look," Noah said, pointing down the patio's edge at a well-dressed man who seemed to be waving his hands wildly around. "It's Simon Wyatt. Remember him? You know that bastard needs someone to talk to about himself. I'll bet half of Contract Confessions is just him confessing to how amazing he is. Wannago catch up?"

"No."

And she meant it. Simon had been many a class favorite, swagger and wealth with the power to match. Ella had always found him grating. A little too much Simon almost all of the time.

"Do you think he's trying to signal his home planet?"

They watched Simon, too caught up in whatever he was doing to notice their observation. At first, it did look like he was fishing in the sky, swinging an invisible lasso, or possibly rolling with a one-man dance mob. But within seconds Ella understood: he was holding his Doodad up and working for a signal. Pacing, wagging it in the air as if shaking would bring better reception. His face was angry. Ella gave even odds that he'd eventually hurl it over the edge to shatter fourteen floors below.

"Let's say hi," Noah said.

"No."

But Noah, despite his faults, had his ways of getting pleasantly under her skin. There were times he could still arouse her, despite the numbness. She didn't want to snicker. Clinging to her sorrow was self-defense.

"*Simon!*"

"Noah. Seriously. Stop."

Laughing now. "*Simon Wyatt!*"

Simon turned. It took a full second for his face to reset, and then he was all teeth. His arm was still up, still gripping the Doodad like a human antenna. Then it lowered. Simon turned, slightly embarrassed.

"You look good," Noah said before Simon could fully compose himself.

"I'm expecting a call," he explained.

"I didn't know they'd asked you to be on the board. The wonders never cease."

It wasn't an insult, but for a moment Ella thought Simon might take it as one. Instead, his face birthed a wide, toothy, panty-melting sort of smile. He shoved Noah playfully and said, "Oh, fuck you."

"You remember us?"

All PR now, all smiles, no frustration. "Of course I remember you. Noah. Ella. Lots of you here tonight."

"Lots of *us?*"

"Alumni. That's not what I'm here for. Somehow my business dinner ended up on the same night. Crazy coincidence, right?"

But Ella thought: *Melissa and Imogen aren't here for the alumni dinner, either.* They weren't even alumni.

And yet they all knew each other — old friends under a silver moon.

The men shook hands. Simon dragged Noah into a hug that he clearly wasn't expecting. Ella, seeing the inevitable writing on the wall, leaned into her hug when it came. They hadn't been best friends, any of them, but they'd shared halls and rooms and awkward times. The acquaintances were de facto: the *why not* that came after years passed, when grudges, reticence, and teen angst all stepped aside to make room for the present.

"How are you doing, man?" Simon asked.

"Good," Noah said, then looked at Ella. "Work's good. We're married."

"Kids?"

They looked at each other as if the answer was unknown. Noah's face was strange. Then Ella said, "Two. Twins."

"You?" Noah asked.

Simon shook his head, then straightened his jacket collar as he looked toward the ocean. "Nah. No time. Too much else going on."

"Like what?"

Ella zoned out while Simon explained. To her, his business sounded vaguely like a scam. Sketchy at least. Simon had much to say, and it was all worthy of praise, which he heaped upon himself. Neither Noah nor Ella said anything for a long time. In her mind, She was sorting social media icons — a boring job she had coming up at work, and wasn't looking forward to at all.

"Well, that's great," Noah said, though he clearly didn't understand most of what Simon had said.

"This guy Kagen, that I'm meeting? Serious game-changer. For me and for him. You just wait."

"I'll do that," said Noah. "Good luck."

"If he ever shows up." Simon laughed, but it had a recognizable edge — a fake laugh she'd used many times herself.

Simon eyed the horizon, then turned back to the couple and concluded their conversation. "Actually, I think he must have his information wrong about tonight. Got held up or something. I should call someone in my office about it. I need to ..." He indicated the air, his pocket — vague gestures meaning ... *to leave you and make a call.*

"Oh, sure," Noah said.

Simon turned halfway, then back as if he'd just remembered something. "Do you have cell service, by the way?"

Noah and Ella both went for their Doodads. After a quick glance, they shook their heads, confused. Nope, neither had any. In all this clear air, near a major metropolitan center.

Simon said nothing more as he walked away, down the patio's dark edge, phone held aloft. But his mention of coordinating schedules had jarred something loose in Ella's head.

"It's the 26th, right?" she asked Noah.

Noah thought, then agreed.

"Is it something special? This date?"

"You mean like Arbor Day? Flag Day? The day we first bought bedsheets, or tried dragonfruit?"

"I'd swear it's something," Ella said.

Noah shrugged. He put his unwanted arm around her and led them toward the bar.

Ella frowned but came up empty. The date meant nothing. It was just another day.

So why did she feel such a terrible chill?

TEN

"Hello, Mr. Wyatt." The butler or whoever was now standing beside the doors leading down to the lower lobby, heels together, arms behind his back. "Are you enjoying the Starters?"

"You told me when I got here that Walter Kagen hadn't arrived yet."

"That's correct, sir."

"So you know who Kagen is."

"Yes, Mr. Wyatt. Although the most important thing I know about Mr. Kagen right now is that he is a customer of this restaurant."

Simon felt his eyes wanting to roll. He stayed them, reminding himself that it wasn't Donovan's fault that Kagen was making him wait. "Has he shown up yet?"

"No, sir. Unfortunately not."

"We had reservations at seven."

"I believe so, yes."

"Can you double-check?"

Donovan had a small notebook in the inside pocket of his black jacket. He opened it and flipped through. What was Donovan to Crave, anyway? The maître d'? Did the maître d' really keep a minia-ture version of the reservations docket on him at all times?

Simon tried to get a glance, but it was gone too fast.

"Yes, sir. Your reservation with Mr. Kagen was for seven."

"It's after 7:30."

"Perhaps he was held up."

"Will we still get our table?"

Donovan nodded. "Yes, of course. We're happy to hold it until he arrives."

But it had been an absurd thing for Simon to ask and a ridiculous answer for Donovan to give. Simon had been waiting long enough to see that even on the rooftop, there were enough bunkered tables to seat an army of Kagens. On the level below, there must be many more. Simon had seen only seen Donovan, the hostess, and the dozen or so people from the Bayshore alumni thing. It didn't feel right. Not for Crave.

His fists wanted to clench. Someone had screwed up. Bayshore had four-walled the most exclusive restaurant in town and neither Simon nor Kagen were supposed to be present. Crave had probably notified Kagen that his reservation was canceled, so he'd stayed at home to reschedule or find a new venue. Nobody had bothered to tell Simon or even this Donovan guy. Kagen was probably trying to reach him right now. Simon could practically feel his opportunity getting away. His patience slipped a notch.

He stepped past Donovan, toward the stairwell. Ten seconds later he was stabbing the elevator call button with the frenzy of a Vegas slots player, but the thing refused to light up.

His skin crawled. The walls seemed to close in. What was wrong with these stupid slide boxes? With no light or sound behind the doors, they must be broken. Simon hated elevators. The idea of getting into one that might be malfunctioning made his heart thrum like a tympani.

He stabbed the button again. And again. And again and again and again and again. Behind him, there was a distant clink — probably flatware in the kitchen. Maybe it was his imagination, but it seemed like someone had heard Simon punishing the button and stopped what they were doing, curious to hear what might happen next. Watching him unseen. Spying.

Simon took a breath.

Relax. Nobody's watching you. This will all work out. Kagen might have gotten delayed or confused or redirected, but he'll meet with you eventually. Or maybe the guy is right; he is still coming. Either way, impatience helps no one. You're in charge here.

Another breath. The elevators still weren't humming, the button still unlit. He pressed it again, imagining himself stepping into whichever temperamental car decided to wake up first.

Fuck it.

Simon told himself that he wasn't afraid of elevators. His time was simply too valuable to waste. He'd walk down to the lobby. Step outside, get reception, check his messages, and make some calls. In another five minutes, he'd be out of the dark. He'd know the plan. Five minutes, and everything would be better.

Simon went to the stairs. On the door's metal face was a set of instructions explaining what to do in a fire, or a tornado. Reinforced concrete blocks made stairwells strong. The only catch was you had to stay in that tiny dark place while the wind raged, knowing the storm might warp the doors and turn them into your coffin's lid. No big deal.

Fuck this, Simon thought with his hand on the door's handlebar, willing himself to open it.

Fuck this place; fuck those elevators; fuck this stairwell; fuck Donovan and Kagen and the Bayshore board and everyone's general inability to follow instructions.

Simon had been here on time, well-dressed and ready to impress. Why couldn't anyone else do their part?

Big inhale. He depressed the latch and pulled the handle.

The door didn't budge.

He pulled harder, now even more annoyed. This time, his tug elicited a clang: a steel deadbolt ringing against the door's insides. But it was locked.

A motherfucking *fire door* was *locked.*

Simon looked around the lobby and saw no other doors, save the one going upstairs and another that likely led to more dining and the kitchen.

He stormed through the latter, past several well-appointed rooms and many tables with chairs up, their legs pointing at a decorative ceiling. A troupe of waiters looked over as he passed. The walls were decorated with elaborately framed movie posters (*The God Particle, Death Nail,* others), actress Harper Knox's face dominating most of them.

One of the waiters raised a hand and seemed ready to call out, but Simon kept moving.

Across a large, dimly lit room, he finally found another fire door. The building couldn't have just one exit. You had to have at least two stairwells, on opposite ends. That was the law.

But the second stairway door was also locked.

"Goddammit!"

The waiters were out of sight, but Simon heard utensils stop clinking.

Across the room again. Past the waiters. Through the door, and up to the patio.

Simon stopped in front of Donovan, who wore an infuriating smirk. "Maybe you can explain something to me?"

"Are you looking for the restrooms?" Donovan began to point.

"Maybe you can explain why the elevators aren't working. Or why the fire doors have locks on them."

"I'm sorry, but you must be mistaken. Fire doors can't be locked."

"Do you want me to show you?"

"Perhaps you'd like a cocktail," Donovan said, unperturbed. "What's your pleasure?"

"Don't fuck with me. Why are—?"

"There's no need for profanity, Mr. Wyatt," Donovan said, still in his host's voice. "I took the liberty of calling Mr. Kagen since you seemed concerned as to his whereabouts. He asked me to apologize and tell you that traffic coming from LA was particularly terrible and that he'll be here soon."

"Bullshit. You didn't call anyone. There's no service up here."

Donovan frowned, then took a Doodad from his pocket. He looked at the screen, and showed it to Simon. Full bars and lit like a Christmas tree.

"I need to borrow your Doodad," Simon said.

"I'm sorry. It's one of Crave's, and contains contact information for many customers who are very particular about privacy."

"I'm not going to run through the address book. I need to call my assistant. You can watch me dial if you don't trust me."

"I'm afraid that's impossible, sir."

Simon's jaw scissored side to side. "How the hell do *you* have Walter Kagen's phone number?"

"He left it when he made the reservation."

"I need to go outside so I can get service."

"I'm afraid that's impossible as well, Mr. Wyatt."

Simon glared. "I'm sorry?"

"No, sir. I'm the one who's sorry."

"You're actually telling me *I can't leave?* You need to go downstairs and open the door."

"I can't do that, Mr. Wyatt. But please. Settle in. Mr. Kagen will be arriving shortly and the first course is to die for. Cold smoked asparagus soup with Dungeness crab and a truffle butter crouton."

"*I don't give a shit about any crouton!*"

It was like a record scratching in a redneck bar. The chatter died as heads turned toward Simon's shout.

"Please, sir, if you'd just rejoin your friends and be patient a little while longer."

Quieter, embarrassed, Simon said, "I'm not with them."

"Ms. Blanchard said that she knew you?" Donovan nodded past Simon's right shoulder.

Simon looked and saw Heidi Blanchard talking to Ella Richards, or *Boyer*, or whatever the fuck her last name was. "Who cares? What business is it of yours?"

"Just trying to make sure everyone has a good time. It's part of my job."

"I'll have a good time if you open the doors." Simon was struggling to keep his nerves. The patio had felt open and airy until the moment he couldn't leave. Now it felt like a box, triggering all the old memories.

Instead of replying, Donovan's eyebrows rose. "Look. Here comes Ms. Blanchard now."

"Go down and unlock the door. Now."

"Ms. Blanchard!" Donovan gushed, ignoring him. "Are you enjoying the starters?"

"They're great," Heidi said.

"I understand you and Mr. Wyatt know each other?"

Heidi extended a hand, pausing but not retracting it when she noticed what must have been a sour look on Simon's face. They'd seen each other, hadn't yet made contact. Simon had been preoccupied and was right now.

"Yes. Hi, Simon. It's been so long. I had no idea the alumni board had—"

But Simon was gone, desperate for air.

He headed for the roof's edge, aware of the drop, working his hands into and out of fists.

Donovan had said Kagen was on the way. Maybe he was, and this was even Kagen's doing. The man was richer than rich, a philanthropist, a hopeless entrepreneur who couldn't keep his hands out of new projects. He was smart but reputedly difficult to work with — not because he was an ass, but because he had such an odd sense of humor. He'd loosed a truckload of ducks on one of his own ribbon-cutting ceremonies because he thought it would be funny. It was good news if that was happening now. Kagen only laughed with people he liked.

Yes. That's what this was. Walter Kagen pranking him.

Simon looked down at his watch.

Fifteen more minutes.

He'd give this idiocy another quarter hour, then throw punches if he had to.

He looked back toward Donovan, the sentry. Heidi was still with him, and both were looking his way. Simon forced himself to nod. To smile. Then to walk back over and make small talk, if only to make the time go faster.

He shook her hand. The best thing he could do right now was to accept any distractions and give his dust time to settle.

Fifteen minutes, to be precise.

He made himself smile. To pull it off, he pretended Heidi was an important business connection or a girl he was trying to have sex with. Either would do, though Heidi had always struck him as more pretty than smart. His smile widened, a bit more natural. Panic retreated a step. He took her arm and led her away from Donovan.

"I had no idea the alumni dinner would be here," Simon said, answering the question he'd stormed away from a moment before. "I didn't expect to see so many familiar faces."

Heidi's eyes ticked toward a blonde at the bar who Simon had seen her talking to earlier. He'd been watching the blonde for a while. She was older than the others but still seemed somehow familiar. Simon had seen her pestering Donovan. Maybe she was also waiting for someone. Her name seemed to be "Bindi."

A strange name striking a stranger chord.

"I didn't really expect it either." Heidi shrugged. "The guy who called about the job didn't mention it."

"Job?"

"They invited me to teach English at Bayshore." Heidi saw something new on Simon's face and said, "You're not here for the alumni dinner either?"

He pressed his lips together, feeling his smile go rotten. He throttled the feeling. He didn't want to think about Kagen now. Not for another thirteen minutes.

He reinforced his publicity grin, like patchwork behind a cracking dam.

"Never mind that," Simon said. "What have *you* been doing since high school?"

ELEVEN

May 23, 2029

Bindi sat upright in her plush chair and forced herself to pay attention.

"... I mean it's not like I think my friends don't believe in Tommy. There's no reason to doubt. What are they going to do, follow me home and see if they can spot him?" Heidi half-laughed — one of her patient's telltale defense mechanisms. Bindi made a note, fighting boredom, knowing she needed to say almost nothing. More and more in her sessions, Bindi needed only to stay awake. Once Heidi got to rolling, a quarter hour could pass before it was her turn to speak.

"But I wonder, you know? Like ..." Heidi seemed to focus, to try and articulate. "It's like I'm a fraud. I don't like lying. I don't even know why I started. And really, it's not like Tommy *isn't* real. He's just not *entirely* real. As described, I mean. He's a composite, right? And that means he needs to be a composite *of* something. Mostly Dylan, but it's not like I'm going to tell my friends I'm dating *Dylan*."

"Of course not." Bindi crossed one leg over the other. "But as we discussed, it's also not good to keep secrets."

"But who is it hurting?"

"Dylan's wife, for one. But *you* mostly, Heidi."

"Anyway," Heidi said, flapping a hand. With the gesture, Bindi lost the volley. Heidi had been a too-perfect patient at first, tiptoeing and asking permission, guarding all of her answers as if afraid of being impolite. Back then, Heidi had shown Bindi the same social mask she showed her friends. Back then, she'd told Bindi lies like the one about her fake boyfriend Tommy Caruthers. Now, two years of hard work later, Heidi was her honest self — at least with Bindi. In therapeutic terms, it was an improvement. But it also meant that all of Heidi's issues were now in play, and there were many. It was most efficient to fight only the biggest battles.

"I guess the question," Bindi said, "is why you feel the *need* to lie."

"About Tommy? Just because it's easier than—"

"About anything," Bindi interrupted.

Heidi shrugged.

Bindi shifted position and made another note on her pad. Sensing futility, she said, "I'd like to do a little exercise."

"Great," Heidi said. "I'll do it with you. I'm starting to put on some weight."

Bindi waited for Heidi's smile to fade. She had no weight to lose. Obsession with her physical appearance was just one of the ways that Heidi had chosen to process her past, and defensive jokes helped no one.

Heidi looked at the carpet. "Sorry."

"I'd like you to list all of the things you've said you want to work on while we've been having our sessions. Just run them down."

"Okay. Well, I guess I lie for the hell of it. I'd like to knock that off. I also invented a fake boyfriend. And some other stuff, like last week with that Amazon credit."

Bindi scribbled the items on her pad. "Okay."

"And of course, I'm cheating."

"Are you cheating on Dylan? You're not seeing anyone else."

Heidi nodded, accepting Bindi's clarification. "Okay, then I'm encouraging *him* to cheat, I guess. I mean, if I wasn't with him, I sort of get the feeling Dylan's the kind of guy who'd still be screwing around on his wife. But that doesn't excuse my part in it, right?"

"What do you think?"

"I'm clearly giving him something he needs that he isn't getting from his wife."

"So you think it's okay." She kept her voice neutral, withholding judgment.

"I guess not," Heidi admitted.

Bindi made another note. "What about all of your shopping? You said before that you wanted to work on that."

"It's a little compulsive, I guess. If you say so."

"It's not important what I say, Heidi. Does it feel compulsive to *you?*"

She thought. "Not really. People shop."

"As much as you do?"

"Well, no. But I'm extraordinary." She really did have a pretty smile. Bindi waited for it to go away again.

"Sorry."

"Don't apologize," Bindi said. "Just answer the question."

"Okay. Then ... no. I guess most people don't shop as much as me."

"Does Dylan shop for you?"

"Of course. He's always buying me things."

"Things for him, or things for you?"

"Why would he buy me things for him?"

"Lingerie," Bindi said. "Maybe sex toys. Things he'd benefit from if you used them."

"Some of that. But no, a lot is just stuff for me."

"Like what?"

"Clothes. Music downloads. A few purses. A lamp."

"He bought you a *lamp?*" Bindi made note of that, too. She'd never heard of a man buying his mistress a lamp.

Heidi nodded.

"Why did he buy you a lamp?"

"I told him I liked it."

Bindi had to stuff down a laugh. She'd forgotten this quirk of Heidi's insecurity. Not long before she'd started coming to therapy, Heidi discovered that she could get men to buy her things for no reason, with no chance for reciprocity. She'd made a game of it. Even started keeping score.

"I have to ask you this," Bindi said. "Was there ever a time in which you'd have considered yourself a sex addict?"

Heidi tried to laugh, but it was clear that had stung her.

"You said you used to be promiscuous."

"I told you about that," Heidi replied, an edge in her voice. Defensive.

Bindi nodded. "You said it stopped. That you became a one-man girl."

"That's right."

But Bindi remembered the times her promiscuity had come up before, and the numbers Heidi had tossed to her prying: two or three men a week at the max, plus so much masturbation that she'd reported going raw. Maybe Bindi shouldn't have pushed as hard as she did to uncover those tidbits, but she'd been curious about Heidi Blanchard and the others ever since graduation. What had become of them? It was half personal curiosity and half professional obligation. She'd helped nobody back in 2018, but maybe she could help Heidi today.

"Did it stop around the time you started playing your game: getting men to shop for you?"

"I don't know. Maybe." Arms crossed.

"I'm just trying to help you, Heidi."

"I know."

"When did it start — the promiscuity?"

"I don't know. Eighteen or nineteen."

"And you lost your virginity when?"

"Eighteen. I was a late bloomer."

Bindi scribbled on her pad.

"I don't think you've ever mentioned taking drugs."

"That's right. Never. Not even weed."

"But you smoked."

"I stopped that, too."

"Did you ever steal for kicks?"

"A time or two. I told you about that."

Bindi tapped her pad.

Heidi leaned forward. "I thought you said this was an exercise,"

"It is." Bindi shifted. "So, consider that list. What do you think all of those 'issues' have in common?"

"I don't know. I'm a mess?" Her smile was back. She no longer seemed defensive. That's how complete her wall was — even Heidi wasn't allowed to see when Heidi was hurting. A clump of hair fell beside her cheek. She pushed it behind her ear — something she did four or five times every minute. Bindi had counted once, determined an average.

"Think about it."

"I ... I don't know."

Bindi considered giving the obvious answer: that Heidi was clearly trying to fill a hole inside her, and had been doing so nonstop since age 18. Compulsive shopping and sex, manipulation of men, addictive smoking, and the gamification and scorekeeping built into her life all pointed to a need for artificial stimulation. She was a person who needed constant activity and material reinforcement to distract herself from her thoughts — to build a wall of things and fake successes to protect herself. Even her affair was downright Freudian. What filled a hole better than stolen cock?

"What's the answer?" Heidi asked.

But Bindi knew better than to barf it out. If Heidi wasn't seeing it yet, she wasn't ready.

"Is this about my job?"

"Why do you think it might be about your job?"

"Because last week we talked so much about my job."

"That's what you wanted to talk about, Heidi. No, this has nothing to do with your job."

"Because if it's about my job, I figure there's something you should know."

Bindi looked up from her pad. "What?"

"I decided to take it."

"Take what?"

"The new job at Bayshore. Teaching English."

"I thought that was just a possibility. They formally offered?"

Heidi nodded. Seeing it, Bindi felt her agenda shift. Yes, Heidi needed to explore the pattern in all of her addictive behaviors, but the seed planted, her mind would probably turn it over between now and next week's appointment. This new thread was welcome. Bindi could see genuine pride on her patient's face, and that didn't come easily to Heidi Blanchard.

Heidi knew she was broken; she knew she was wrong to lie about her fake boyfriend and to carry on with her secret real one; she knew it wasn't right to steal and chain smoke and rub her clit to a callus. Beneath her false cheer, Heidi carried guilt and a hideous self-image.

If this Bayshore job struck Heidi as positive, Bindi wanted her to feel the victory.

"Well, that's great, Heidi. How do you feel about it?"

"Pretty good." Then a pause. "Is that okay?"

"Why wouldn't it be okay?"

"Well, I hate to be ungrateful for my court reporter job. The pay and benefits are really good, and my boss—"

"Your boss isn't part of this. This is about you."

"Sure, but when I leave, they'll have to find another—"

"And they will. It's okay, Heidi. I want you to enjoy this. So think. How does it feel, when you imagine being an English teacher?"

A new smile arrived. A blessed, *genuine* smile.

"It'd be nice to have a job where my degree actually matters. I mean, court reporter pays well and is really interesting most of the time, but I could have done it if I'd dropped out and not even gone to college."

"And the people from Bayshore must respect you, Heidi. If I remember from last week, you didn't even apply for the job."

"Nope." Heidi shook her head. "They called me."

"You were unsure last week. What made you decide to accept?"

"I thought about what you told me. And I just went for it."

"That's great. But I didn't do anything. You did." Now a real smile touched Bindi's lips. "When do you start?"

"I'm not sure. I'm meeting with them this weekend. But it's not an interview. The job's in the bag."

Heidi smiled a few seconds longer. Bindi had almost asked her about this last week when Heidi mentioned the gig. She didn't want to risk soiling Heidi's moment of glory and thus considered letting it go. But there was something here that her patient might not be seeing.

Soberly: "How do you feel about returning to Bayshore?"

"What do you mean?"

"I think you know what I mean, Heidi."

A moment of quiet. Then finally, "It'll be good to be there again."

"Will it?"

"Why wouldn't it?"

"Come on, Heidi. We've talked about this. You, and Ella, and Taylor, and—"

"That's ancient history."

"Is it?"

"*Is it? Will it?* Why don't you just tell me if you're so sure of something instead of trying to get me to guess?"

"I didn't mean anything by it. I just want to make sure you—"

"I told you I didn't want to talk about high school," Heidi snapped, her manner suddenly turned. "I want to deal with what I've got going on now. The past is the past. Who cares how I got to where I am? Maybe my daddy didn't love me enough. Maybe mommy was cold and distant. Who gives a shit? I'm twenty-nine fucking years old and I can't hold a normal relationship to save my life. Two years of therapy and I'm just now starting to believe there's another side to this. So can we please just stick with what's working?"

But that's exactly the problem, Heidi. If you won't open up, I can only guess what's working and what isn't. Without knowing your causes, I'm a mechanic working with the hood shut.

Only twice had she been able to ask about what happened back in 2018, and even then Heidi had only offered what Bindi already knew — what the entire community already knew. She knew the names *Ella* and *Taylor* and *Casey* from her time as a Bayshore counselor but had always been dead curious what truly happened among them.

Eventually, if she wanted to heal, Heidi would need to come forth and deal with it. Then maybe Bindi could deal with it a little, too.

Bindi, like many therapists, had her own help. Dr. Slater had asked her: *Are you pushing your client's comfort zone to alleviate her pain ... or to satisfy your own morbid curiosity?*

Bindi, facing Heidi's eyes, sighed. "Okay. Fine. I'm sorry."

Heidi immediately forgave. It took seconds, and then all of her old walls were back up. She prattled on about her job now, and her job in the future. Bindi let it all go, kept her mouth shut, and scribbled. They only had a few minutes left anyway.

If what lurked deep in Heidi had lurked deep in Bindi, returning to Bayshore would be the last thing that she'd want.

Her mind wandered, despite her best efforts.

Taylor McKay.

Ella Richards.
Casey Davis.

Bindi turned her mind inward, trying to remember what she'd been told, what she'd been allowed to see.

There'd been that thing. With the big guy with the square jaw.

What had his name been?

TWELVE

"Mason," he repeated. "Mason Pace."

Bindi rolled her pretty green eyes, embarrassed. She put a palm to her forehead: a slow-motion slap for forgetfulness.

"That's right. I'm sorry. I suck with names. You'd think I'd remember, seeing as we did the whole introduction dance earlier. I knew it was an M name, but I was thinking Michael or Milton."

"Who's named Milton these days?" Mason wasn't remotely bothered by the way Bindi had forgotten, but was enjoying the flirtation that came with poking fun. If he wasn't with Jessica, he might be very interested in Ms. Bridges. She wasn't that much older than him, and he'd never noticed how adorable and engaging she was back in high school.

"I have a patient named Milton. He's big and muscular. Probably kick your ass for making fun of his name."

"Hey, I'm not making fun. I'm big and muscular, too."

"Besides, didn't you see *Life, Liberty,* and *The Pursuit of Happiness?*" Bindi asked.

"I saw *Life* and *Liberty*."

"You didn't finish the trilogy?"

He shook his head. "Too artsy for me."

"It swept the Oscars, you know."

"It's almost as if I don't care about the Oscars," Mason said. "Why?"

"There was a character named Milton in the last one."

"Oh. Fascinating."

They both bobbed heads, small-talk going nowhere.

Mason took a sip of his Old Fashioned. "So do you like it? Being a psychiatrist?"

"I'm actually a psychologist."

"What's the difference?"

"Drugs."

Mason pretended to consider, then bobbed his head, extended a hand, and said, "Sure. Why not?"

Bindi laughed. "I can't prescribe drugs. Psychiatrists can."

"Not even Valium?"

"Not even Valium."

"Not even Thorazine?"

"Do you need some?" She said it with a smile.

When he'd approached her at the bar, she'd seemed troubled. He always had a way of thawing even the thickest ice. He set his drink on a coaster, settling onto the barstool beside Bindi.

"Maybe. I'm about to become a father."

"Congratulations!"

Mason tipped his head, looking into his drink: a miniature shrug. "Maybe. I'm not sure I'm ready."

"Oh, nobody thinks they're ready."

"Do you have kids?"

Bindi shook her head. She looked bothered.

"I'm sorry. That's a pretty familiar thing to ask."

"Not at all." She gave a tiny, dismissive wave. "No, I don't have kids. But I have a lot of clients who talk to me about theirs, including new parents." *Sip.* "Trust me: nobody ever feels ready. It's like jumping into a cold pool. If you're going into parenthood, you just have to leap."

"Is this your official advice? Because if I have a shrink in front of me, I'm damn well taking advantage."

He wished he hadn't said it. His smile wilted at the corners. It was supposed to be a joke about his current state: impending fatherhood, distant girlfriend, trying to be a better person. All were ripe for digging into with a bit of free therapy. But only now was he thinking of the issue he truly needed help with for over a decade now. Only now was he remembering that he'd *gone* to Bindi once in high school, to tackle that very topic, but had punked out at the last minute. Would she remember that botched appointment? Did she recall the way he'd sat in her office for an entire half-hour one day in May, telling her nothing was wrong despite all signs to the contrary?

"I don't know," Bindi deflected. "How's your insurance?"

Before Mason could laugh, an exclamation of *"Bullshit!"* from the stairs caught his attention. They both turned to look.

"Do you know that guy?" Bindi asked.

Mason nodded, now watching. "That's Simon Wyatt."

"Sounds familiar."

"He was in my class. He'd have been at Bayshore when you were." Mason sipped, then swallowed through his first syllable. "He's kind of an ass, but in a good way. Everyone hates Simon until they love him, and *that's* when he becomes the guy you love to hate."

They watched Simon and Donovan for a while. Heidi Blanchard wasn't far off, also watching. Mason saw the three as a diorama, trying to decide what was occurring between them, studying their still-life like a critic.

"He sounds kind of like an ass right now," Bindi said.

Mason squinted, nodding. "I know, right? I heard him yelling at the same guy a while ago. Apparently, they weren't finished. I think he's waiting for someone who hasn't shown up yet."

"And he's taking it out on the maître d'?"

A shrug. "Gotta take it out on someone."

Bindi looked around the patio. Black-jacketed waiters were still circulating with shrimp, and taking drink orders. The sky was quiet, washed of stars by the coastal lights just down the low rolling hill. The street, fourteen stories below, was quiet. Chatter and clinking glasses. Shuffling feet. Mostly there was dim light, aromas from the kitchen, and curiosity in the air.

"You said you're here to meet a headhunter?" Bindi asked.

"Predip Batra." But then he looked at his Doodad, realizing just how much time had passed. It was already quarter to eight.

"He's late?"

"Yeah." Mason tapped at his Doodad, no service. "He was supposed to be here at seven."

"The person I'm meeting was supposed to be here at seven, too."

"Who are you meeting?"

"I don't know." She sipped the rest of her drink, and when she set the glass down, Mason realized he had yet to see her more than a few feet from the bar. Her glassy eyes and casual air were new. His old guidance counselor wasn't drunk, but she was definitely buzzing.

"You don't know?"

"It's a surprise."

"What — a blind date or something?"

"Or something," she repeated.

Simon kept getting louder. Again they turned to look.

"*He's* here for a business meeting," Bindi said. "You're here to meet a headhunter and I'm here for ... something else. I've sort of kept up with Heidi over the years—" Here, Bindi's eyes ticked away, and Mason gathered that there was more to the women's relationship than *keeping up*. "—and Heidi told me she's here for a job at Bayshore. I knew she was meeting them this weekend but was surprised that it just so happened to be *here, now,* at the same place I was going. A lot of people are here for a reunion, or an alumni thing, or whatever."

The bartender had delivered a new drink; Bindi must have told him to keep them coming. She sipped it and said, "Doesn't it seem weird that everyone here knows each other?"

Mason indicated the Indian woman standing next to the waifish girl with jet black hair. "I don't know them."

"No, but the man talking to them is *that* woman's husband." Bindi pointed.

"That's Summer Nixon."

Bindi took another sip and gave Mason a look as if to say, *Well, there you go.*

"What ... do you think something weird is going on?"

Across the patio, Simon had his hand on Donovan's chest. Heidi had moved between them as if playing referee.

"I don't know," Bindi said, not moving her eyes from the trio at the door, "but maybe we're about to find out."

Mason was so focused on Bindi's words that the slap on his back nearly made him shit his pants. He jumped and his head spun, finding Teek Sheridan behind him with a giant grin.

"*Mason fucking Pace!*"

"Oh, hey, Teek."

"Good to see you, man! It's been absolutely forever. I saw you earlier but didn't realize it was you. But ... wow!"

Mason nodded, unsure what to say. He'd seen Teek just fine, but his hug seemed to indicate a closer bond than the one they shared. They'd barely known each other. But Teek always had been eager for other people's approval. Or maybe he was naturally good with others, unlike Mason.

He settled on: "So what's new with you?"

"Lots, lots." Teek's head bobbed. "Do you remember Taylor McKay?"

"Of course." Mason had thought about Taylor plenty. Those thoughts weren't sexual or obsessive; she was pretty, but too brainy for him. He admired her, because she was different from Heidi and Ella, had done the right thing when it counted.

In school and after, Mason and Taylor had barely spoken.

But in a way, they'd both been victims.

"We're married now. Me and Taylor."

"That's cool."

"She didn't take my name."

"Oh."

Teek tipped his head toward Bindi with a smile. "Are you going to introduce me?"

"Teek." He made a dumb little gesture; Teek should know her as well as Mason. "This is Bindi Bridges."

Teek looked at them both and shook his head. "She was one of our guidance counselors. At Bayshore."

Bindi extended a hand. "Good to see you again. *Teek*, is it?"

His smile evaporated. He shook Bindi's hand, but only barely. Looking at Mason he said, "Guidance counselor?"

"I don't think you ever came in to see me. It's okay. Not many people remember their high school counselors." Bindi smiled, all charm.

Teek's eyes were darting from one to the other. "No. That's right. I never came in." He looked confused, seeming to search his memory.

Mason saved him. "Bindi is a psychologist now."

"*I can see into your soul!*" Bindi joked with theatrical hands.

"What do *you* do, Teek?" Mason asked.

"I'm a sound designer," he said after a few second's pause.

"What does a sound designer do?"

Teek looked over at Bindi, almost as if he'd forgotten she was there. "I arrange music. Also some scoring."

"Scoring," Bindi said. "Like having sex with women?"

"I'm married!"

Mason clapped Teek on the back. "Have a drink, Teek. Hard day?"

"No."

"You seem stressed."

"I'm not stressed."

"What made you choose that job?" Bindi asked. "It sounds really interesting."

"Had to do something." It looked like Teek was *trying* to smile. "It was the only creative thing I could find that paid well."

"Well ..." Bindi nodded and raised her drink. "If you'd come to me in high school, I'd have approved that logic."

"Thanks."

Teek took Mason by the arm. "Did you talk to Taylor yet?"

"No."

"She wants to say hi."

"Okay." Mason could see Taylor from here. She wasn't looking over.

"Come on." Teek pulled.

Mason shrugged at Bindi. "I'll catch up with you later, okay? Need some of that free therapy!"

Bindi nodded toward Simon, Donovan, and Heidi still standing at the exit.

It looked like that trio might soon come to blows.

"You're not the only one," she said to herself.

THIRTEEN

Summer found herself reaching out to grab a large man by the arm. He was passing by with the squirrelly little guy who, she remembered from her time on student council, had acted like Simon's lap dog. She'd had a few drinks; seeing Melissa and Imogen had dredged up some muck. Maybe the alcohol was making her friendly, reverting her to an earlier form — a Summer who'd stopped existing late in college, before Mother Summer took over.

"Hey," she said to the guy. "I swear I know you. What's your name?"

"Mason."

"Oh, that's right." She laughed but didn't like it. "I know who you are. Everyone knew who *you* were, right?"

Summer looked around for applause, but nobody was there to hear her one-liner. John had gone to the bar forever ago, but she'd watched him stop to talk to Simon Wyatt, then to Melissa and Imogen. She should have joined them a while ago, but the proper order of things demanded that those two come back to *her* rather than the other way around.

"What do you mean?"

Summer met Mason's eyes. He'd been a year behind her like Heidi and Ella, but from what she recalled, he'd struck her as a big, soft moose. A genuinely nice guy, who she'd felt bad for plenty in the years since high school. It hadn't been his fault. So why was she baiting him now? Fucking high school. It was twisting her all over again, just like Frodo with the One Ring.

Pretend you meant something else, the adult part of Summer's brain told her juvenile twin.

"You played football, right?"

"Yeah ..."

"Well, there was that one game ..." Summer stalled, unsure of her finish. Not only had she never cared about football, but Mason would have had his glory year after Summer was already at Coastline.

"Do you mean the comeback against Orchard? When I scored three touchdowns?"

Summer had to work for a genuine smile, facing him as Summer Merritt, the 30-year-old mother of two instead of 18-year-old Summer Nixon, *she-who'd-run-things.* Forcing the switch was harder than it should have been.

"Yeah," Summer said. "I *knew* I remembered you."

Mason glanced to his right, at the squirrelly guy. He was a few paces away, looking back at Mason as if expecting him to follow.

But Mason squared himself instead and said, "You're Summer, right? Summer Nixon?"

"Summer Merritt now. That's my husband over there."

"Are you here for the alumni dinner?"

"Yeah. You?"

"I'm actually here to meet someone about a job."

"So is Imogen! Are you a chef, too?"

His brow furrowed. "A chef? No."

"Imogen is."

"Imogen is what?" Imogen asked, arriving behind Summer.

"A bitch," Summer answered like a reflex. Alcohol seemed to be helping her forget the baggage between her and the other Diamond alums, sending her back to a time before all the trouble.

"Oh, shut up, you slut!" Imogen blurted.

They giggled like teenagers. Mason waited patiently, but it went on long enough that he wondered if he should leave — maybe join the guy who was still between him and Taylor McKay. The guy who Summer also recognized, now. *Teek.*

Apparently one time after gym class, Teek had forgotten his deodorant. One day; that's all it had taken. In Summer's group, he'd been known as *Reek* forevermore.

"Do you know Mason?" Summer asked Imogen.

"You're hot," Imogen said.

"Mason," he said, ignoring the compliment, extending a hand.

"This is Imogen," Summer said for Imogen when she was oblivious — too caught up in shaking Mason's hand and letting alcohol encourage her to gaze into his big blue eyes. "She's always like this, so don't be offended that she's staring at you."

"Oh, *shut up!* Like *you* don't want to fuck him!"

"I'm married," she said.

But it was still funny — especially seeing how Mason was clearly embarrassed — and Summer laughed just a little.

"Like 'married' means your pussy falls out!" Imogen turned to Mason. "She's still got a pussy, you know. Although it's probably all hairy now, stretched out by two kids like an old sock. Back in college, she used to parade that thing around like a little hairless clam."

"Oh my God, Imogen!" Summer looked away, pushed the other woman, and erupted into something that could only be described as snorts of glee.

"Are you married, Mason?" Imogen asked.

"Um ..."

"It's okay if you are. Nobody thinks it made your dick fall off like Summer's pussy."

A new voice. "Hey, did you want to go see Taylor?" It was Teek, or Reek, arriving right on time to rescue Mason.

"How is Taylor's pussy?" Imogen asked Teek. "Intact, or hanging by a thread?"

"Imogen!"

Teek looked confused. It seemed that he wanted to ask Imogen, *Do I know you?* The mature part of Summer felt bad for him, trapped this way. But it was too funny, so she looked at Imogen and practically guffawed.

"I'm sorry she's like this," Summer said after catching her breath.

John was suddenly at her arm, tucked neatly between Summer and Teek like the steady companion he always was. "Looks like I missed something."

Imogen reached across the little circle to grab John's arm. She turned him toward Mason.

"Ohmygod, Mason. Do you know this guy? This guy is a *grocer.* Like, he works in a *grocery store.* Isn't that kickass?"

"I still don't see why that's so amazing," John said.

Summer looked at her husband, then at Imogen. This seemed to be part of a pre-existing conversation — probably what had been going on between the two of them and Melissa at the other table. John was smiling, probably not realizing that at least some of the joke was on him.

"John," he said, extending a hand toward Mason.

"Mason."

They shook, but John was eyeing Mason, seeming to wonder. They couldn't know each other, could they? Surely not. John had one of those faces: an everyman in everyman's clothes.

"Do you know these two?" John oscillated a finger between Summer and Imogen. "Because I don't."

Summer shoved John playfully. Imogen let go of his wrist.

"I know Summer," Mason said. "Sort of."

For a blink, Summer felt awful. She and Mason did know each other in a third-degree sort of way, but did Mason even know? Their biggest connection had been her fault. But then it was gone, and Simon was back to raising his voice over by the stairs.

"Ohmygod, Summer," Imogen said, pulling her attention to the group. Summer blinked up and got a face full of Imogen's giggly brown eyes. "Do you remember the time we got those guys to do a beer run for us? They were that loser frat but Holly and Leslie came up with their tits half out and were like, *'You'll do it for us, right? Please?'* and then they came back with total hard-ons and you just shut the door on them?"

"You just shut the door on them?" John repeated.

"College," Summer muttered. "You know how it is."

John did know. He'd gone to Coastline, too. That's where they'd met, though Summer had gone to great lengths to ensure that he never knew what she'd been like back then ... or her role in the events that brought them together.

"Who are you?" Imogen asked, turning to Reek.

"Teek."

"You know everyone, too?"

"I know Summer."

"How?" Summer asked although she knew just fine.

"I went to Bayshore."

"I don't remember you," Summer lied. "Did I see you at a party or something?"

Imogen laughed.

And a voice inside her head said, *Why are you pretending you don't know him?*

John was watching her, curious. He'd never seen this side of his wife, rolling with all the easy laughs.

"I was a year behind you in school," Teek said. "I was—"

"That's right. *Teek.*" Summer flapped a dismissive hand, feeling the alcohol. "Now I remember. You had that shitty car, right?" She touched his arm so it didn't sound like an insult. It was, though. Teek attended Bayshore on scholarship. He'd always been self-conscious.

Teek's eyebrows were bunched. His eyes kept darting to John. Summer felt a devil on one shoulder and an angel on the other, floating outside her body, watching herself like an exhibit, wondering which voice she planned to obey.

The devil's was stronger, and in that moment Summer felt sure that her husband knew it.

Relax. You left this part of yourself behind a long time ago. What good did it do you? What grief did it give you? Of course you know Teek. Move away from Imogen. Stop laughing like a hyena. You're a mother now, for Christ's sake.

Looking around, Imogen muttered, "Where's my purse? Dammit, not again!"

"Did you lose something?" Mason asked.

Imogen was already wandering back toward Melissa and her misplaced purse.

Teek tried again. "I was on student council your senior year."

"I know," Summer said. "I—"

But he was bulldozing. From what she remembered of this guy, he needed to be liked.

"You knew Heidi, right? She was on council, too. She talked about you all the time. Simon was on it, too." He looked up at an angle, thinking. "Oh, and Casey Davis."

Summer's hand tightened. John looked over. He gripped her hand in return. Subtly, he drew her closer. He was looking at Mason as though something about the man had just dawned on him. But that wasn't possible because John didn't know anyone here.

John's not doing anything. John's not reacting. John doesn't know Mason or anyone else. It's you, Summer.

Another bark from Simon at the door. This time, Summer heard Heidi say, "Maybe we should just get some air."

She felt a squeeze and looked up to see John's eyes on her. A little distance had formed between them and Mason and Teek, so in a low voice he said, "You doing okay?"

"I'm fine."

"You don't seem fine."

"I'm *fine*, John."

"You aren't acting like yourself."

No shit. I'm acting like I did at 19 years old. "It's nothing."

"Even with him mentioning—?"

"Weren't you going to get me a drink?"

John looked around, then back at the bar. He seemed confused. "I *did* get you a drink. I must have set it down somewhere. I stopped to talk to some people."

"Shocking."

"Hey. I'm a natural networker."

Summer squeezed John's hand, trying to feel herself, back inside her own skin. She kissed him. "Only John Merritt could find so many friends at a place where everyone is a stranger."

They kissed again. She was feeling better, more like herself. Then they both looked toward the door, toward the argument.

"What do you think's going on there?" John asked.

"I don't know."

"I was talking to that guy earlier. He seemed nice enough. Simon?"

"Yeah."

"Think I should go over?"

"I'm sure it's nothing."

"I keep getting the feeling they're going to fight."

"I can probably talk to Simon. We—"

John grabbed both of her wrists. "Don't."

The reaction was so immediate and so strange, Summer wasn't sure what to say.

Don't?

"If anyone needs to talk to them, I'll do it."

And that's when Summer realized: she hadn't been imagining

John's earlier reaction. Not entirely. He'd been social during the almost-hour they'd been killing waiting for this soiree to start, but through it all he'd always had one eye on Summer. His gaze hadn't ever settled. It seemed like he was waiting for something to happen. Staying close. Like a guardian, even at a distance.

Ella Boyer had arrived at Summer's shoulder. She had her husband in tow, looking dragged. Ella said something Summer didn't catch, and when she looked back at John, he was gazing into the distance.

"Stay here. I'll get you that drink."

Mason had vanished. Only Teek was standing in their wake, looking around, probably for Taylor. John slapped him on the shoulder and said companionably enough, "Want to help me find something. It's Teek, right?"

After they'd walked off but before Ella could say more, Summer held up a finger and managed a smile.

Something was itching under her skin. Something wasn't right.

"I just want to call to check on my kids," Summer said. Feeling very much, all of a sudden, that she needed to.

But, curious: She didn't have any bars on her Doodad at all.

FOURTEEN

"Look," Imogen was saying. "I—"

Melissa had to cut her off. Immediately. The mood was about to shift, and that couldn't be allowed. Imogen *never* spoke in monosyllables. Her mouth didn't know how it was done. She was an uncorked vomiting-forth of nonsense rhythms and run-on sentences: a travesty of language that was half English, half emojis and texting acronyms. Imogen said things like "OMFGLOL." If she was going to start a sentence with a thoughtful "Look," that meant she intended to get serious. And Melissa didn't need that bullshit right now.

"I'm looking. And you're right. Breastfeeding didn't do Summer any favors."

"It's been a long time since we talked," Imogen said, ignoring the joke.

"If that's what you think, you should record yourself sometime. The talking never stops."

"You know what I mean."

"Yes. I do. It's been a really long time since I've seen you. And it's been awesome, not having your airhead diarrhea in my ears every second. Let's see if we can prolong it a bit more."

"Melissa ..."

"See? Now you went and fucked it up."

Imogen gave her a look. She was on edge. Imogen trying to be serious was walking a tightrope. Melissa just needed to give her a push.

"You suck," Imogen said.

"Then why did you come back to talk to me?"

"I left my purse."

"Now that you've got it, fuck off, pixie."

Imogen rolled her eyes. "You wish."

After a beat, Melissa said, "Hey, look. It's Elder Conway."

Imogen looked around. They'd both been waiting nearly an hour, and it seemed they'd both been stood up. That was another reason Melissa didn't want the conversation to sober. *Officially*, she didn't care at all if she lost the *Fat Vampire* gig. But deep down, being stood up by the executives would cut her — just more proof that she was worthless.

Once she and Imogen stopped laughing, they'd have to admit defeat and go home. That was where the nothingness lived.

"Where's Elder?" Imogen asked, looking around.

"Back home, up his own ass."

Imogen slouched. "You're a bitch."

"We already knew that."

"Besides, where are *your* TV people?"

"Who cares?"

"How can you not care that they didn't even show up?"

"Like this." Melissa slumped on the barstool with her legs sloppily apart, nonexistent gut pooched out, miming smoking a cigarette to go with her tumbler of vodka. Grey Goose, the good shit.

"Have you talked to that guy?" Imogen asked, pointing at the man fighting with the maître d'.

"No."

"Summer kinda knows him. I think I might have seen him at that party once, too. Simon? I heard him saying something about the elevators, like, they're out of order or something. Maybe nobody can come up. Maybe Elder and your people are just outside."

"Wow. Is that what you say to yourself when men don't call you back? 'They really want to hang out with me, but they're trapped outside'?"

"I'm serious! I think something's messed up and we're locked in."

"If that had happened, someone would have sent in a SWAT team to save me from you by now."

They sat in silence for three seconds — the longest Imogen could go without speaking. Melissa started to get worried. If they were out of snarky exchanges, Imogen might make another attempt to bridge the unspoken thing between them.

Melissa hoped not. The incident at the banquet had happened; feelings were hurt; despite certain people's asshat mistakes, nobody died. It had all come out in the wash. Their friendship had been the only casualty — and yet here they were, frenemies all over again.

But just as Imogen looked like she might take another crack at sincerity, that dude walked by again. John — the grocery guy who blushed like a fucking cherub, and still struck Melissa as familiar.

"Hey, Johnny Boy," she called out.

John was walking with another guy — a rocker type with an ironic beard that Melissa felt was trying too hard. John nodded without slowing. He'd already done his time with these two women. Imogen had even given him a second round when she'd wandered into the other group without her purse.

But John couldn't be allowed to escape. With Imogen growing immune to their private dialogue, Melissa needed someone external to fuck with.

"Hey, wait," she called again. "We need you to settle a bet."

John stopped. The guy with the beard stopped too. Beardo wasn't unattractive. He had big blue eyes full of private pain and looked just a little like he might want to slit his wrists. Hot.

They came closer, waiting for the bet.

She didn't have a bet prepared and would have to think fast. She pointed at herself and Imogen. "White or dark meat?"

"I'm sorry?" John asked.

"We were just arguing about what guys want. You know racism is alive and well in America, but I don't know how far it extends in dating."

"We're both married," the other guy said.

"Who asked you, Beard?" Melissa replied.

"When you get married, your dick falls off," Imogen told Melissa.

Melissa shifted on her stool. It was a high stool, but both men still towered over her. Over Imogen, too. But whereas Imogen had some meat on her bones, Melissa was thin enough that she vanished when she turned sideways. The guys she'd dated said they liked it because they could pick her up and fuck her like a Fleshlight, like she wasn't human. To Melissa, that was sexy talk.

"I'm a writer. I told you that, right, John?"

"Yeah."

"It's not as exciting as working in a grocery store, but it's a living."

"I'm actually a—"

"Anyway, I'm writing an article called, '11 Shocking Things Men Think When They Look at You Naked.' It's going to go viral as fuck. And so I want to know what you think when you see a dark-skinned girl like this thing here, versus someone like me."

The men looked at each other.

"I'm not inviting you to a menage-a-four. I have higher standards than that." It wasn't true.

"Um ..."

"Just first impressions," Melissa said.

They'd both climbed off their stools so they could pose. The exchange hadn't started sexual and remained nonsexual, but now that Melissa had established animosity among them all, she was wondering what it would be like to fuck Summer's husband and Hipster Bigfoot at the same time. They'd probably just shove her into a corner, get off, beat her up, then leave her for dead. It'd be awesome.

"Should we all adjourn to a bathroom for a better look?"

John blushed like a stoplight. Bingo. Imogen saw it happen, pointed, and squealed.

"Look at him! Look how embarrassed he is!"

"I'm not embarrassed."

Imogen kept pointing, her shaped fingernail just inches from his face. "Yes, you are! The idea of us being all naked totally weirded you out!"

"I'll bet he's got a raging boner," Melissa said.

Imogen looked down, but John ducked halfway behind his companion. "Have you met Teek?"

"We know each other as of five minutes ago," Teek said.

"And this is ... Melissa?"

"Ogle a girl and forget her name," Melissa said. "Nice."

"Is it not Melissa?"

Melissa was ignoring him. Something about this moment with

John was strengthening the sense that she knew him. It had been growing stronger ever since Summer's introduction. She and Imogen had spent a while trying to figure out why, because John struck her as familiar, too.

"You went to Coastline College, right?" Melissa asked John.

"No, I went to UCLA," Teek said.

"Why are you still here?" Melissa demanded.

"Sorry." Teek started to leave, but Melissa grabbed his wrist.

"Which one is your wife?"

Teek indicated a tall brunette who looked poured into a cocktail dress.

"Okay. She's pretty hot."

"Thanks?" Teek said.

"But how are things in the bedroom?"

"Excuse me?"

Melissa thrived on discomfort. Teek's in this moment made her feel like a vampire who was days past her last feeding. She took his second wrist and stared right into his eyes. "I know this look."

"What look?"

"You're into freaky shit. I know because I'm into freaky shit. Does the missus let you do all the stuff you want?"

"Um ..."

Melissa was still staring.

"I get it. There's a lot of self-hate here. What do you want — for her to slap you around? Wait. No. You want to tie her up. Sexualized misogyny is so boring and predictable."

Teek freed one wrist. He looked far more uncomfortable than John.

"Not that I'm opposed if that kind of thing gets you off. You just let me know if you get tired of the princess's insistence on missionary with the lights off."

Teek nodded toward the door. "I should see what Simon's all pissed off about. It sounds like there might be a fight."

"That'd be hot," Melissa said.

Teek escaped.

Melissa returned her attention to John. "Better. He's hot, but a total drag."

John was watching Teek, wondering what just happened.

"So, Coastline?" Melissa said.

"What?"

"You went to Coastline," she repeated.

"Yeah."

"What dorm? 2017-2018."

"I was a senior that year. I lived off-campus."

She shook her head, frustrated. "So we just know you from dating Summer? But she said she met you her second year."

"I guess so. You saw me around with Summer."

Melissa and Imogen traded a glance.

"Well," Imogen said, "we weren't really around Summer much after freshman year."

"What do you mean?"

"She dropped out of Diamond Society."

"I know," John said. "She did it a few months after I met her. She said she wanted to—"

"And she kind of stopped talking to us."

John paused before responding. Melissa should have filled the pause with a witty retort, but that breakup had been awkward for everyone.

"But you were still in school, right?" John asked.

"Yeah," Melissa said.

"We probably saw each other at the commons. Or walking across campus."

"I know. You took Summer to the Freshman Mixer." Imogen looked at Melissa. "Remember the mixer? That's when—"

"I went to the mixer every year because I was on the planning committee, but I didn't take Summer her freshman year. I didn't know her yet."

The whole thing was starting to dig at Melissa. There was something here — a reason she was *sure* she'd seen John several times before tonight — and she couldn't let it go. She kept seeing him with Summer on his arm, and yet Summer had met him after they'd all stopped talking. It was like trying to place an actor you'd seen but couldn't remember where.

"Did you used to hang out on the quad? Just like, sit down under the same tree or something?"

"Sometimes."

"Maybe that's it. With Summer? Maybe you sat where I used to walk by on my way to work or something."

"Yeah, Summer and I hung out there a lot."

"Under the big tree with the hammock in it."

John shook his head. "I used to like that spot, but not with Summer. They cut that tree down before I met her."

Imogen said to Melissa, "You're thinking of another guy. I remember the guy you're talking about, but it was someone else. He was with a brunette."

"That's not who I'm thinking of."

"How do you know who *I'm* thinking of, skank?" Imogen asked.

"I should really get back to Summer," John said, seeking an exit from this odd conversation. He looked to Teek for help, but Teek was trying to calm that Simon guy.

Melissa shook her head. "I know exactly who you're thinking of, slut. The guy with the big 6 on a jersey he wore all the time. We called him 'Sexy Six.' And Sexy Six's girlfriend had brown hair."

"It wasn't brown; it was red!"

"Brown."

"Red!"

"Who cares?" Melissa said. "It wasn't blonde."

"I used to wear a jersey with a six on it," John said.

"There you go. Sexy Six." Melissa pointed, triumphant.

Imogen was looking at Summer and her bright blonde hair. A frown formed. She turned back to John. "When did you hook up with Summer?"

"Just after her freshman year ended, I think?"

"He's not who I'm thinking of," Imogen told Melissa. "Unless they broke up for a while and he dated someone else, like sophomore year or whatever."

"Except ..." Melissa paused for drama. She'd figured this out, and it now felt critical that she win the discussion.

"What?"

"Summer dyed her hair. Remember? Just the once. It looked ridiculous when it was growing out: brown hair with yellow roots. We would have made so much fun of her if we hadn't stopped talking."

"Except that she dyed it brown," Imogen said.

"Which is the color it was when you saw them together."

"That was red."

"Brown."

"Ladies?" John said.

"Like a reddish brown," Melissa said.

"Brown with strawberry highlights."

"That's ridiculous."

"*Blonde* with strawberry highlights," Imogen tried.

"It was brown!"

"Um ... ladies?"

Melissa's head snapped toward John. She blurted, "What color was Summer's hair that time she—?"

The room was suddenly frozen. Everyone was watching Simon, shouting at Donovan, shoving him, doing everything he could to antagonize the other.

Teek was nearby but only barely interfering.

Then Simon stopped his tirade, noticing the stares. His chest was heaving, his eyes wild and angry.

"He says we can't leave," Simon said, projecting his voice to the watchers. "The elevators and doors are locked, and this son of a bitch won't open them up!"

Someone — Melissa wasn't sure who — uttered a tiny, uncomfortable laugh. That couldn't be true. Simon's salesman's smile had struck Melissa as unstable from the second she saw him.

"It's all a lie," Simon said. "Every bit of it."

The silence was deafening until a clock chimed the time and a line of white-gloved waiters marched up the stairs behind Simon and Donovan.

"Well then," Donovan said, smiling as the servers passed him, literally saved by the bell. "Looks like it's time for dinner."

FIFTEEN

The waiters threaded through the group as Heidi, feeling nerves but unsure about their source, counted them. There were five. Or six, if she included Donovan as a waiter.

So she tallied the guests, a reality just now dawning on her: For the past hour, she'd been wrapped in uncomfortable nostalgia, choosing on some level to ignore that Crave's complement for the evening was lighter than one might expect. The rooms around the Lounge patio were dark, with chairs upside-down atop the tables, anticipating no one. Nobody in the room seemed entirely unfamiliar, and yet she didn't see a single Bayshore authority around to offer her that teaching job.

Twelve guests.

Six servers.

And a host she'd heard whispers about, as new silence bore weight.

Beside Heidi was Taylor McKay, and beside Taylor was Teek Sheridan, and inside Teek's head was the secret he'd so recently disclosed. His eyes darted to Taylor, to Simon by the door, to Bayshore's old guidance counselor, Ms. Bridges. In the tense quiet, Taylor's hand found his. Teek felt momentarily better; the gesture meant she wasn't mad. Or was she? Maybe something else was amiss, and Teek was her port in the storm?

"Who exactly invited you to join the Bayshore board, did you say?" Taylor asked her husband.

"I didn't say."

"Well, who was it?"

"Why the hell does it matter?"

Then he turned his head, wondering why he was snapping at Taylor, who'd done nothing, who'd suffered plenty then and now, who'd always held her center no matter what.

Teek hated himself. At least Taylor could hate him now, too. The thing between them couldn't have come at a worse time. Or a better one.

Not far from Teek and Taylor, a waiter approached Summer and John extending a hand and making an almost imperceptible bow. Summer's hand stayed by her side, near but not holding her husband's. The waiter said, "If you'll follow me to the Buvette?"

Summer watched the group ahead and saw that they were winding toward a hallway that had recently been opened and lit. She thought, decided, hoped, whatever, that the board had set their dinner and arrived late. She'd find the Bayshore board waiting in this "Buvette" room, just down the hallway. Never mind that Imogen and Melissa hadn't attended Bayshore, and yet were headed to the same place.

Summer smiled uneasily at John. He smiled back. The patio behind them had emptied. All twelve guests were filing down the hall, leaving it still. The small white lights were a canopy above: a mask on the not-quite-dark sky beyond. On the coast, Cielo del Mar was a multicolored blur. Los Angeles wasn't far.

But LA had a ghost in the group. At Crave, weeks after it opened, there'd been a celebrity party. The party had been unknown to most, private invite only, with expensive liquor flowing like a river. Donovan had been there. But not as a server.

"I really need to check on the kids," Summer told her husband.

"Okay."

She looked at her Doodad. Which of course had no reception.

"I think I'll need to go outside to do it."

"I'll go with you."

Because John, too, felt something off. Something odd. For John, unlike Summer, the sensation was not unexpected. He looked at the tall, broad man not far ahead: the one he'd first known as 06-24-

2029-23:16/F, who'd given a peculiar sort of confession. The one whose name, it turned out, was Mason. He went to Bayshore, a year behind Summer. Mason, who, unlike John Merritt, had been invited to this party.

As the Merritts broke away to find the exit, questions scurried through John's insides like insects. He had no one to ask for answers. Everyone here had similar doubts, now more than ever as they filed to the new room for dinner.

They headed for the staircase, away from the group. One of the waiters followed, catching them as they arrived at the elevators, as John pressed its button.

Summer apologized, feeling the alcohol, wondering if she was acting as pleasant as her face kept trying to be. She told the waiter that they needed to head downstairs. To step outside, just for a moment. They had to check on their children. The man assured Summer there would be plenty of time for that — but not now. If they'd kindly head back upstairs and rejoin the group, he would personally take them down after everyone was settled, to make sure Summer made her call.

Of course, he had no such plans.

And that's something Simon Wyatt would have told Summer if he'd been downstairs with her. But he wasn't with Summer. A new server held him by the arm. He was the size of a linebacker. Polite, with a clipped British accent. But Simon knew better than to continue his protests. Something dangerous lit the waiter's eyes.

The walls seemed to close in.

Air seemed to escape the room.

And all over again, Simon imagined he was in that tiny little metal box at the airport with the buffoon and seven other people. The buffoon he'd named Elmer. These days Simon avoided elevators in buildings less than seven stories tall. These days, Simon preferred wide open spaces. Hated crowds. Loathed this strongman's hand around his arm, leading him like a toddler.

Simon wanted to ask the man about Walter Kagen. But who was he kidding? Kagen wasn't coming. This was another box. A snare to hold the wily.

Taylor, arriving at a door labeled THE BUVETTE just behind Simon with Teek still at her side, kept her eyes on Simon. Waiting. Knowing him well — better today, she imagined, than ever before.

What would he do? What fuse had Donovan lit? And *were* Simon's paranoid protests correct? *Were* they trapped?

Certainly not. If Taylor had known their host's identity, she would have thought: *double*-certainly not. Teek had been invited to join the board. So had the others. Her mind scrubbed away everything that contradicted that scenario. She ignored the unsettling pall that Simon's words had tossed atop them. He was unstable. Probably always had been.

Bindi marched unescorted, wondering if Donald was here. In the room ahead, waiting for her arrival to spill his guts. Wondering, hope against hope, whether she would get her answers tonight.

Ella was just behind Bindi, entering the large, beautiful, many-windowed room. Beyond the French doors lay a small patio decorated with plants and a pair of gargoyles. At the celebrity party, a leading man and a casting director with a secret exhibitionism fetish had made sweet lust on that patio, her bra left dangling from one of the gargoyles' horns.

Ella looked at that specific stone creature now, and missed the extravagantly plush rug under the long table filling the small room. Her heel caught in its long gray fibers and she almost fell until Noah caught her by the wrist.

Curiously, in the same moment he saved her from cracking her head on the emerald tile surrounding the rug, Ella was thinking about Noah's weak will. She knew what he wanted before they'd started dating all those years ago, before he'd settled for Ella and her addiction, her cheating and private pain. But he'd never acted on it. Spineless like always.

"Thanks," she told him.

But Noah knew something new that Ella didn't want him to know, too. And if he told her — *when* he told her — she'd be hurting plenty.

The pills that Ella had been hoping were in Imogen's purse were indeed there. Had she known, Ella would've pushed ahead to where she and Melissa were already finding their seats and asked for one, or two, or more. Imogen would have surely offered a handful.

Right now, Imogen was thinking about Elder Conway. Assuming this was it: they'd all been held in the Lounge while their parties assembled. Once seated, Elder and Melissa's TV contacts would appear. Had she expected a celebrity chef like

Elder Fucking Conway to hang around for small talk? Of course not.

The evening was on course. Never mind that there were only a dozen seats around the long table.

Imogen drifted. She let herself be transported by the stunning nighttime view through the French doors as she thought of the small people on the streets far below. By the smell of cooking shellfish arriving through the vents. And ... truffles?

But Melissa, pulling out the chair beside her, wasn't transported at all. Imogen was stupid; Melissa felt sure that was the problem. She was a gullible idiot. She'd once let someone talk her into making one of her customers very sick. What kind of chef did that? Not one who would end up on TV. Of that, Melissa felt certain.

As for her own botched rendezvous, Melissa had decided the executives weren't coming. Because she was a hack. That's why she'd ended up writing clickbait articles instead of anything worthwhile.

It so fucking didn't matter. Melissa picked up her fork and decided to jab it hard into the white flesh of her forearm. It'd never draw blood, but that was okay. Cutting yourself was for angsty teens. She didn't need pain to know that she was already dead in every way that mattered.

Within minutes, everyone was settled. Seated, with folded white name cards tented atop plates (straddling a decorative rosemary garnish) before them. The settings were elaborate; three kinds of forks and a large white plate. On the other side, spoons and knives. Delicate stemware, and crystal glasses filled with water.

Heidi next to Taylor next to Teek, on the side nearest the double French doors. Then Melissa, then Imogen, then Bindi.

Bindi glanced down the table's side to Heidi, all the way at the other end, almost apologetically. But would it have been appropriate for them to sit side-by-side?

Summer was across from Bindi. Simon was next, then Noah and Ella. Mason was on the end, opposite Heidi.

John was just about to ask where he was supposed to sit (and how he was supposed to eat) when Donovan took one of the other servers by the sleeve and mumbled something. Word passed discretely from waiter to waiter, then there was a flurry of activity as the place settings on the far side were moved down, clearing a spot between Summer and Simon.

Someone brought a chair to fill it, and clinks foretold of plates and silverware to come.

"My apologies," Donovan told John. "I sent word that you would be joining tonight's party, but my request seems to have been lost somewhere along the chain."

The waiters worked fast. Chairs scooched. There was already a plate at the new spot. Atop it was an immaculate tented name card just like the others, reading JOHN. Beneath it was a sprig of rosemary, aromatic and fresh.

Forks. Round-bladed knives. Spoons. Glasses for water and wine.

Donovan pulled out the chair, and held it for John to sit. "It will be just a while longer. For your parcel."

John looked, as did all the others. The waiters had placed themselves between the seated diners and were setting an elaborate red envelope in front of each one.

John looked up at Donovan, wondering.

"Printing the envelopes is what takes time, Mr. Merritt," Donovan explained. Then he smiled. "It's obvious which of your secrets should go inside."

First Course

Cold Smoked Asparagus Soup
With Dungeness Crab
And Truffle Butter Crouton

SIXTEEN

May 12, 2018

Ella, as she stood in the lobby of the Diamond Society house, decided she liked that girl, Imogen. She was a bundle of energy. Ella had plenty herself. She was too enthusiastic, her father always said. Even her friends tired of it — except Heidi, who had the same affliction — and regularly rolled their eyes.

But Imogen was fun. And cool. It wasn't just that she was in college (though the infinite freedom didn't exactly tarnish her in Ella's eyes); it was that she seemed up for anything. Even Heidi, who was up for plenty, could be a buzz kill. It was her weird moral streak. Heidi was still a virgin, for fuck's sake. At eighteen.

"I really like your necklace," Imogen said. "It's like my personal philosophy."

Ella looked down, cradling the thing toward the ends of her fingers. It was a small yin-yang in black and white glass. She was about to say, *Necklaces are your personal philosophy?* when Imogen ran-on without stopping.

"I was with this guy once? And he had this big giant brown beard, like food would get stuck in it and stuff and that was just *totally* gross, but he had a big dick, so what, was I going to care? You know what I'm talking about."

Imogen smiled secretively and touched Ella's arm. Ella smiled along, even though she'd only had two sexual relationships thus far, and only one had rounded the bases. He hadn't been bearded, or particularly well-endowed.

"Anyway, after we had sex, he used to talk about how it was, like, the planets aligning or something. Like, orgasms transported us to alien planets or into the Milky Way."

Ella didn't point out that they were in the Milky Way now. If you wanted to be cool with college girls, you couldn't fact-check their monologues. Ella nodded along with her big, stupid smile, and glanced over at Heidi. She didn't look back. Her attention, of course, was on Summer Nixon.

Summer turned and saw Ella from across the room, her expression already annoyed. "Am I boring you?"

"No, not at all," Ella said.

"Then what are you doing over there?"

Imogen touched Ella's arm again and said, "Anyway, Peace."

Ella supposed this was her way of linking the story about the hippie and his cosmic orgasms with her original comment, about the yin-yang. Which didn't mean "peace" at all.

"Sorry," Ella said, rising from her nest with Imogen.

Heidi was glaring at Ella, aghast that she'd left Summer for one of her lackeys mid-lecture.

Ella sat in one of the hard, red-plastic common room chairs arranged around Summer like a fan. Why were they talking over here anyway? The couches were much more comfortable.

A chair squeaked as Imogen sat.

"What time is it?" Summer asked.

The black-haired girl (Melissa? Ella had been so overwhelmed by the Diamond Society house that she wasn't sure she'd caught it right) slipped her cell phone from her pocket and said, "Four-oh-six."

Summer looked annoyed.

"I have stuff to do," Melissa said, seeming bored.

Summer turned to Ella. "Do you know if they're coming?"

"Who?"

"Casey. And that other girl you hang out with."

"Taylor," Heidi said.

"They can't make it." Ella didn't start the sentence with "I told you that ..." because it'd probably come off as snotty, and they hadn't come to Coastline for a private help session with three Diamond girls to be rude. Ella planned to keep her hands folded on her lap with her legs demurely crossed. She planned to say please and thank you. Heidi wasn't the only one who wanted to make it into Diamond Society, but she was the one caught up in the four of them making it together.

"But this is pre-rush," Summer said.

Ella blunted her instinct to look around at Summer's statement. If this was pre-rush, it badly needed a party planner. There was no food, music, or decorations. No other people. Summer had met Heidi and Ella at the door, then grabbed Imogen and Melissa to sit in so it wouldn't just be the three of them. They'd gone through a plush living room to something that was half-kitchen, half-dining room in the grand style of college furniture. If it was just five people, Ella had no idea why they hadn't settled somewhere more leisurely.

But Summer must have realized her flub, because she added, "Well. We're here to *talk about* pre-rush. Do Casey and whathername not want to rush Diamond Society?"

"Oh, of course they do," said Heidi.

"They had conflicts," Ella explained.

"I thought you four were a package."

"We are," Heidi said.

"Then why couldn't they be bothered to be here? Don't Casey and ..."

"Taylor," Ella said. Why couldn't Summer remember? She knew Casey's name just fine.

"Don't they realize what an opportunity this is?" Summer finished.

"Sure," Ella nodded. "They just couldn't make it."

"Too far? Couldn't figure out campus parking?"

Ella shot her a look. Only Casey had claimed other plans. Taylor hadn't wanted to come, if Casey was out. They'd probably ended up hanging out, letting Heidi and Ella do all the work of making nice with Diamond Society. Typical. Those two were borderline antisocial, and yet they'd reap the rewards when Heidi and Ella led them into the inner sanctum.

Ella shrugged. It must not have been convincing because Summer's head tilted like a curious dog.

"What?" Summer looked at Heidi, to make sure both knew their private joke wasn't going unnoticed. Were they laughing *at Summer?* "Should I regret reaching out to you?"

"No, of course not!" Heidi exclaimed.

"I told you this was a bad idea," Melissa said.

Summer was shaking her head, irritated.

Ella saw Heidi's crestfallen look and leaned in. Damn Casey, causing problems. If she had come, Taylor would have too. Then none of this would be an issue. They didn't appreciate how rare an opportunity like this was. It wasn't a dog and pony show. So what if you had to lick a little boot and show up when the girls told you to? Everyone had to start somewhere.

"Look," Ella said. "Honestly, they may not want to pre-rush. They—"

Heidi was practically blushing, discombobulated by Summer's change in mood and Ella's heresy. "Oh, no, they will. They just couldn't make this little get-together to—"

"Maybe," Ella said. "*Maybe* they'll pre-rush. Maybe they won't. But Heidi and me, we're really into it. We know how big of an opportunity this is, and we appreciate it. Heidi wants all four of us to rush, pre-rush, whatever it takes. I do too. But Casey is ... well, *Casey*. She's weird. She doesn't really like sororities at all, so—"

"What the hell is wrong with sororities?" Imogen said. "If that girl thinks she's going to be big-tits on campus without support, she's crazy. And if she thinks we're going to vote for her to join when she ..."

Imogen trailed off. Summer's hard look said, *Stop.*

"Oh, like you don't agree, Summer? This was all your idea."

Sounding bored, Melissa said, "Sit down, Imogen."

Imogen sat. Something unknown passed between the college girls.

Summer resumed speaking, her voice almost sweet. "They're thinking of not rushing?"

"*Pre*-rushing," Melissa clarified.

"Maybe," Ella said. "I don't know."

"They're thinking about it," Heidi added. "We're working on them."

Summer's lip turned up for a half second. That had been a dumb thing to say. Joining the Society was an enormous privilege, and maybe their wayward friends could be persuaded to see the error of their ways before Diamond closed the door in their faces.

"I guess I should have said they were undecided," Ella said. "They know it's a big deal to be invited."

Imogen crossed her arms. "A *super* big deal."

"What's her objection?" Summer asked.

"Whose?"

"Casey's."

"What about Taylor?"

"Oh, hers, too."

Ella and Heidi exchanged a glance.

"Casey's just not really a ... a joiner. She's weird. And Taylor usually does what Casey does."

"So Taylor wants to join, but Casey doesn't want her to? Doesn't your friend have a spine?"

"Well ..."

"She's ungrateful," Imogen said. "Maybe they're all ungrateful. Maybe this was a bad idea. Maybe we don't want any of them."

Heidi's eyes widened to all white.

Summer seemed about to say something, but then she flapped a hand in dismissal. "Whatever. It is what it is."

"*This* isn't pre-rush, right?" Heidi asked. "They can still do it if they want to, can't they?"

Melissa looked at them, her eyes indifferent. "If they don't want to join Diamond Society, why should we beg?"

"I mean, if they want to join and you *let* them join; if they—"

"Forget it," Summer said. *"You're* here. *You're* dedicated. I don't care about the others. Maybe they wise up and maybe they don't. It seems silly to me, because college is a big, confusing place and Diamond Society is a home. You could all stay together, you're obviously tight."

Heidi looked from Summer to Ella, then back to Summer, not quite nodding.

"But that doesn't matter right now. Let's talk about you."

"Okay," Ella said.

Summer leaned in, elbows to knees, her eyes bright. "You, at least, have made the right choice. I can tell you're in this. You get it. Right?"

"Absolutely," said Heidi.

Summer waited.

"Yeah," Ella finally said.

"How dedicated are you?"

"What do you mean?" Heidi asked, her voice low.

"What if you have to choose? If your friends don't rush and you do, and if you get in and they don't, we'll be your family. You'll spend more time with us than them. Is that something you'd be okay with?"

"They're going to Coastline for sure," Ella said. "It's not like we'd *have* to choose."

"Well, I don't know about that. They wouldn't be in the house and the house becomes your family. There's a reason we call each other sisters. I need to be sure you're right for pre-rush. You know?"

"Why?" Ella asked.

"It's like sponsorship. I have to know what kind of people I'd be recommending to the others."

"You'd do that for us?" Heidi said.

Summer's eyes went to Heidi, but she waited for Ella to answer.

"I'm sure it'd be fine," Ella said.

"And what about rush?"

"Pre-rush," Melissa interjected.

"What about it?"

"Well, it's hard. You'll have to do some uncomfortable things."

"Like what?"

"Nothing bad. It's more about making sure you're loyal. You'll have chores. Special requests."

"Before we even get to college?" Ella was clearly irritated.

"This is an exclusive early offer," Summer said, a bit harsh. "Everyone gets to sponsor someone, and that means I'd be putting my neck on the line for you. And either Melissa or Imogen — or both and a fourth person if your friends decide to try. It also means that when it comes to actual rush next year, you'll go to the front of the line. Do you know how many people pledge Diamond, versus how many we accept?"

"I didn't mean anything by it," Ella said.

Summer took a moment, then slid her palms across the top of her jeans as if smoothing wrinkles.

"Yes. *Before you get to college.* Pre-rush is like talent scouting. But because you'd be the special ones, we have to know we can count on you. So you need to do what we say. You need to not ask too many questions — especially 'Why?' The answer is, 'Because we said so.' That's how we'll know you're with us. That's how we'll know if you're fit to join this sisterhood and get all the benefits that come with it."

"What kinds of stuff do we have to do?" Ella asked.

"Agreement first," Melissa said. "Assignments later."

"Yeah," Imogen added. "Are you in? Or are you out? Because we could really, super-easily find some other high school girls who are dying to—"

Summer held up a hand. Imogen stopped talking.

"Of course," Heidi said. "Of course we're in."

All eyes turned to Ella. What was the harm?

"We're in," she said.

SEVENTEEN

J ohn said, "My *secrets?*"

But Donovan had already moved aside. With John's place set and a chair in place, he was free to sit. One of the other waiters had pulled the chair out and was gesturing for Mr. Merritt to take his place, as the lone guest still standing.

John glanced at the elaborate red envelopes set in front of each guest. Smooth finish, thick folded stock with padding laid over the top, a gold clasp that looked like a coat of arms, robust gold thread looped around a button to close it. Nobody touched their envelopes. From seat to seat, each guest was regarding the beautiful object atop their plate with something like fear, as if the envelopes had teeth.

John looked up at the waiter. His creeping feeling from several days earlier had returned. He was back in his office, blinds pulled and lights low, listening to Mason tell his story. He hadn't wanted either of them to come tonight. But irrational fears were rarely worth heeding. John's wariness that day had been strong. But his curiosity — and that damnable unsolved question that dogged him for years — had been so much stronger.

"What the hell is happening here?"

"Sir?"

"Is this the Bayshore alumni dinner?" John looked around the table, now projecting his voice to the other guests. "Are you all here for the Bayshore dinner?"

Murmurs.

Summer tugged on his sleeve. "John."

He ignored her and looked back at the waiter. The man was a caricature: smooth white face, slicked-back hair, a little Errol Flynn mustache. He didn't have a towel draped over his forearm, but that was the only thing missing.

"We were invited to an alumni dinner. I think we might be in the wrong place."

"I assure you, Mr. Merritt, you are in the appropriate place."

"Where is the board? Where's the old woman my wife won't stop complaining about? The one whose wealth can't buy her a decent facelift? Is that who this last chair is for?"

"John!"

John stared. Now others were whispering and a pall of oddity descended in the small, elegant room. He'd known something wasn't right since the day he'd met Mason Pace — or in truth, depending on the framing, a lot longer than that.

The hairs on his arm were standing. He wanted to lash out, but it wasn't anger or frustration that drove him. It was fear, and the knowledge that he should have known better.

"We'll be serving momentarily, sir." And then the waiter was gone, leaving a dozen diners around the table alone.

John clamped his mouth shut. He felt his chest rising and falling in oversized waves. His heart hammered against his ribcage, desperate for escape. He looked around the table, seeing only eyes and those big red envelopes. Everyone was staring at him.

Calm down.

But what had Donovan said? *What* were the envelopes for?

Summer took his hand. Patronizing more than supportive. She wasn't nervous. This was business as usual to everyone else. John was the crazy one.

The doors are locked.

"Are you okay?"

It was Imogen, the tiny woman who'd taken such delight in his fake career.

Relax. You don't even know what this is yet.

Summer squeezed his hand. He looked over, then reminded himself to settle. He had to be here for her, and that meant being *here*, not in his head. He was tumbling down that old rabbit hole, but what had set him off? Donovan talking about secrets. Because once exposed, secrets became confessions. It was hard to remember that most people didn't see life through the skewed lens that John had ground for himself.

"I'm fine," he said.

"You seem anxious. Are you anxious?"

"He said he's fine." Simon had pushed up his sleeves. John could see the cables in his forearms because the man couldn't stop making fists.

"I have something that might help to calm you down," Imogen said to John, glancing sideways at Simon.

"You're kidding," said Melissa. "Still with the pills?"

Imogen gave her a look, and in it John saw a hidden thing. He was now excellent at spotting them.

Imogen reached for her purse and removed a small, orange-tinted bottle with a white label around it.

"What is it?" said the woman three places to John's right. *Ella,* maybe? But she shut back down, because the man with the beard seated beside her — Ella's husband, John thought — was glaring at her. Another look, another secret.

"It's okay. They're for anxiety." Imogen handed the bottle to John.

John looked at the bottle. Inside were twenty or thirty small pills. The label read: *Shah, Imogen. Nyperal, 2mg.*

"Let me break one up for you, though, unless you want to sleep through dinner."

"This is rodostazem," John said. "Do you have epilepsy or something?"

But she'd already told him. And the answer was there on the bottle: *Take as needed for social anxiety.* Imogen, with a social anxiety disorder? She could hide it well, or have a thick defensive wall. Maybe she lied to her doctor.

He met her gaze, eyebrows drawn.

Imogen snatched the bottle back, stung. The pills rattled. Down the table, Ella leaned forward, involuntary.

"Have you been hanging out in your grocery store's pharmacy or something?" Imogen asked.

The bottle was gone. *Name the drug, look like a narc.* If John had wanted a quarter-pill to dull the edge on his nerves, the offer had been rescinded.

Summer, sensing the shift in mood, put on her brightest smile. She was great at this. It's where she got her name, John liked to joke. But this was a tough crowd.

"Well, it sure is nice to see you all again."

Melissa sniggered. Imogen rolled her eyes. The blonde across from Summer didn't seem to be paying a lick of attention. Teek, who John had saved from Imogen twice now, smiled, but his wife and the woman at the end (Heidi?) looked pointedly away.

Silence followed.

"Maybe we should play charades or something," Melissa said. "You know, as an icebreaker?"

The man beside Simon pushed back to stand, then stopped when he realized she was being sarcastic. All eyes were on him for a few seconds, so he cleared his throat and said, "Do ... does everyone here know each other?"

"I know you," Melissa said. "You're the guy who was about to stand up and act out 21 *Jump Street*."

"I don't know everyone." Heads turned, and suddenly Mason looked caught. He went on anyway, looking around the table as he counted off. "I know ..." At Heidi, he paused. For the third time, John sensed something buried. "... Heidi, and Taylor, and Teek. Ella and Noah. Summer, kind of. And Miss Bridges."

Everyone looked over at Mason's mention of a title. The woman said, "It's Bindi." Despite her ring, she didn't bother to correct him to "Mrs."

"We pretty much just know each other and Summer," Imogen said.

Melissa laughed.

Then Imogen followed Melissa's eyes and pointed at Ella and Heidi. "Oh, and those two, sort of."

"You don't know anyone else?" Teek asked.

"Not really. Maybe a little. Just sort of, like from that party at Bayshore."

Nobody asked Imogen which. It might as well have been the only one.

"You didn't go to Bayshore?" Bindi asked.

Imogen turned to her left. It was as if she hadn't realized Bindi was there. "No. Did you?"

"I was a counselor. For one year."

"Our *graduation* year," Mason said.

"So?" Imogen said. "You say that like it means something."

"Doesn't it?"

"It wasn't *my* graduation year."

There was stirring behind the closed door — the one John had wondered about. Was it locked, like the elevators and fire doors? Why was nobody focusing on that? Why had everyone taken Simon's protests in stride?

But John knew the answer. The envelopes were keeping them in line, quiet and well-behaved. The nuclear threat of secrets.

"Why are you here?" Mason asked Melissa.

"Why are *you* here?" she countered, apparently taking it as a suggestion that the outliers should leave.

"I'm meeting a headhunter about a job. Predip Batra, also from Bayshore. Know him?"

Mason wasn't looking at Imogen; it was a question for everyone. But she answered first, and with an edge to her voice.

"No. Why would I know him? Because I'm Indian? That's racist. I know all sorts of people. I don't just hang out with people named Misha and Sanjay and all the Patels, like we're all a big—"

Melissa put a hand on Imogen's shoulder. She stopped as if hitting a wall.

Again, the room was silent. Until the door opened and the waiters returned, carrying trays topped with broad, shallow bowls. The guests ceased conversation, waiting for the service to end.

"What the shit is this?" Melissa asked when they were gone. She poked a finger into the green liquid in front of her. There were clumps of something in it and dark green spears rising from the center like a shipwreck in shallow water. She made a face. "It's *cold*."

"Asparagus soup," said Heidi.

"Are you a chef?" asked John.

"No, but this is asparagus," Heidi said, using her spoon to raise one from the depths.

"I'm a chef." Imogen's cheery demeanor was already back. When people looked over she said, "I'm here to meet Elder Conway about getting my own show."

"Really?" said Bindi. "That's amazing."

"Sure is," Melissa agreed, "seeing as he didn't show up."

"Like the suits you were supposed to meet?" Imogen countered.

"Suits?" said Noah.

"She's meeting network executives," Imogen explained. "I'm sure they'll all be here in just a minute."

"They might. And if they don't, who cares? I've got cold green shit." Melissa lifted her spoon, letting it drip back to the bowl and spatter the pristine white tablecloth.

"Maybe," Bindi said, tasting her soup. "There's still a seat left." She indicated the vacant spot between her and Summer.

"I know who's sitting there," said Simon. He'd been such a hole in the room that everyone had forgotten him.

"Who?"

"Walter Kagen."

"Who's that?" Heidi asked.

Simon didn't look up. He just gave a superior little chuckle and began eating his soup.

"So you're not here for a Bayshore thing either?" Bindi asked.

"Of course not. I'm here for Kagen. Or rather, he's here for me. I don't have a clue why he'd want the rest of you."

Bindi and Summer traded a puzzled glance across the table.

Simon saw it and sat up straight. His earlier swagger from before his fight with Donovan was back. "Why are you here ... *Miss Bridges?*"

"I'm meeting someone."

"Who?"

"Does it matter?"

Simon smirked. "Probably not." He turned to Teek. "I guess you're here to hang out with Miss Bridges, too? Or maybe not, seeing how you ran away from her earlier."

"How do you know?" Taylor asked. "Weren't you busy yelling at the butler?"

"I notice things. That's why Kagen wants to meet me. It's why I drive a Tesla Prime."

"What do you think people notice about *you*, Simon?" Taylor retorted.

He turned into the sting, his face puzzled. "What the fuck are you talking about?"

Mason, down from Simon, said, "Hey, there's no need for that."

Now he was fully awake. Simon turned to Mason and said, "No need for what? Does my profanity offend you? Well, fuck fuck fuck fuck fuck. *Fuckity fuckity fuck!*"

"Hey, take it easy," John said.

Simon turned to John. "It's cool. You're new to this group, so I don't blame you for not knowing, but Mason is cool with 'fuck.' He'll fuck all day long in front of a motherfucking window. *Fuck!*" His face split into a maniac's smile. "Hell, you don't believe me? Ask Heidi. Ask Ella. Ask Taylor. Everyone knows—"

"Leave Taylor out of this," said Teek.

"Or what? You gonna 'come at me, bro'?"

Teek looked hurt and defensive. "She wasn't even involved!"

"Involved in what?" Bindi asked.

Simon cackled.

The doors opened. Donovan entered, flanked by waiters with bottles. He made a single lap, then deposited a red envelope in front of John's plate. It was identical to the rest, with his name in cursive across the front.

"If the rest of you would please remove your envelopes from against your wine glasses so we're able to pour?" Donovan said.

Slowly, mutely, the room complied.

"The first course pairing is a nice dry Riesling: Schloss Johannisberger, 2024. If you're interested, please—"

"What are we here for?" John interrupted. "You left before answering when I asked last time."

Donovan shifted, holding his smile. "I assure you, your questions will be answered shortly."

Melissa shrugged. "How about now?"

The waiters circulated, filling glasses.

Teek was fondling his envelope, toying with the gold string. He slowly began to unwind it.

"Please don't open your envelope just yet, Mr. Sheridan. It would please your host if you'd wait."

Melissa picked up her envelope. "Interesting. It'd please *me* to open it now just to fuck with you."

"Who's the host?" Mason asked.

"Relax, Chappy," Melissa answered. "It's not Imogen's friend Dipthong, here to offer you a job."

"I told you who it is," Simon said. But his arms were still full of tendons, his fists still clenched.

"What makes you think it'll be your guy?" Imogen asked.

"What, you think it's going to be Elder Conway?" Taylor said.

"This is a restaurant! It makes more sense than Kagen or whatever."

"Most of us are here for the Bayshore dinner," Summer said. "Why wouldn't it be someone from the board?"

"*One* person?" Ella looked around, annoyed by something. "You know the board is a big old collective dumb-telligence. Why do any of you care?"

Noah turned to his wife. "You're determined to ruin this for me, aren't you?"

"Ruin this weird-ass dinner? I wouldn't dare." She laughed as she went for her soup spoon, but it was dry and humorless.

"I'm through here if that's not Kagen's chair," Simon said, glaring up at Donovan.

"It's not Kagen's chair." Summer was working to hold her composure.

"How do you know *shit* about Kagen?"

"How do you know shit about *shit*, Simon?"

"Oh, look who's in charge all over again," Simon said.

An ugly look crossed Summer's lips. "Hey, does everyone remember Simon's freshman year, when he pissed his pants in class?"

Melissa barked laughter.

Simon's head was down, head shaking. Quietly he said, "None of you are paying attention."

"God forbid we don't pay attention to you, Wet Pants."

John glanced at his wife. She wouldn't meet his eye. Heidi and Taylor were watching her with rapt attention, as if unsure of what might come next. Teek had his mouth half-open and his hand up, trying to get in a word.

"*We are locked in,*" Simon said in a low voice.

"What's that?" Summer demanded. "I can't hear you over all the urine."

"We. Are. *LOCKED! IN!*"

Noah: "Simon, you don't know that we're actually—"

"Are you all stupid? Is nobody listening? *They locked us in!* They won't let us leave! I tried the elevators, and both are off. The fire exits ALL have deadbolts. They—!"

"You can't put locks on a fire exit," John said. "It's against code."

"You really are a fountain of knowledge, aren't you?" Melissa said.

"—just talk in circles whenever one of us asks to go outside! None of us have cell reception up here. We don't even know who put this together. None of the people we expected to show up are here, and I *know* mine came from Kagen because I'm on his list and I know his email address, so that means someone somehow hacked his account and—"

"Simon," Teek said in a patronizing tone. "Relax. It's cool."

Simon stood, his chair thrust backward. It fell to the ground with a clatter.

"And all of you are ignoring the fact that *we all know each other somehow, some way,* and that's one *fucker* of a coincidence considering we're not even here for the same reason. But you're all just sitting there eating and drinking wine while goddammit if there aren't some *SERIOUS FUCKING PROBLEMS* with all of this, and—!"

The room was interrupted by a series of sharp metallic dings.

Simon stopped shouting.

Everyone stopped everything.

Because they'd seen who was at the door, striking her glass with a knife for attention, and no one could believe it.

EIGHTEEN

Bindi wouldn't be the first to say it, despite how obvious it was. Celebrities were spotted all the time in SoCal — especially in areas like Cielo del Mar. But despite running across bit actors and directors, Bindi had never seen a whale. Someone who gave the silver screen a reason for still existing. If she was wrong out loud ... well, that would just make her look stupid.

But no. That was *Harper Fucking Knox* in the doorway.

She was still holding a half-filled wine glass in her left hand and a butter knife in her right. Once she had the room's attention, she returned both items to the empty setting at the head of the table. But instead of sitting, she stood with all eyes on her, as if she'd entered the room on a red carpet. It wasn't put-on or pretentious; on the famous Ms. Knox, the subtle shift of hips and delicate placement of fingers — ready for the paparazzi's lens with her chewing-gum smile — was like breathing.

"Hello, everyone," she practically purred. "Welcome to my party."

No one spoke. Bindi could only hope her mouth wasn't open. Simon had just been ranting about how something was wrong, but something new was *even more wrong*, and in a decidedly different way.

If Harper Knox threw dinner parties like a normal human, none of the present guests should be invited. And no one was reacting.

Nobody was raising a hand to say, *Um, excuse me ... but don't you realize you're famous and we aren't?*

That's what struck Bindi most, other than Harper's height (Bindi was no shortie herself at five-nine, and Harper still seemed impossibly tall — and wore her inches better, of course): if one of the most famous people on the planet was going to show up in a room full of everyday Joes and Janes, someone should at least be clamoring to point it out.

If Harper was uncomfortable with all the staring, she didn't show it. Her smile became less flashy, more pedestrian, falling several notches into a bow of closed, pink-painted lips. Her silver dress brushed the floor — something Bindi could never have pulled off even at Harper's age. What was she — 25? Even younger? It seemed unfair to have taken the world by storm so young, and yet with so much left to look forward to.

Famous, brilliant blue eyes made contact around the table. Bindi wanted to blush when they found her. Some personalities were magnetic, but Harper was the magnet itself.

She bowed slightly. To Bindi, she said, "I don't mean to presume, so I hope you'll excuse me. But it's Bindi Bridges, yes?"

Bindi nodded. Harper extended a long-fingered hand on a milky white arm. Bindi didn't know what to do. Eventually, she shook it.

"I'm Harper."

The bubble popped when Imogen, to Bindi's right, said, "Shit, we know who *you* are!"

She extended a hand to Imogen anyway, leaning across Bindi, her long blonde ringlets — styled for a thousand dollars, probably — swinging before her. "Harper."

"*Ohmygod ohmygod.* Can I Instagram this? At least let me take a picture." Imogen's Doodad was already out, held sideways and aimed. Her eyebrows drew together and she squinted, repeatedly pressing the screen.

Meanwhile, Harper had moved down to an unimpressed Melissa, then Teek, Taylor, and Heidi, all who were.

"Hang on. Hang on." Imogen was muttering to herself. "Heidi, take a picture for us! My Doodad's being an asshole."

Heidi seemed locked into Harper, who was continuing her introductions as if she were an everyday person that nobody knew. Seeing her gave Bindi a strange stir. She wanted a photo same as Imogen, but she felt guilty about it. Harper was beyond beautiful, beyond glamorous, beyond dazzling to the room — but she wasn't acting it. Her manner was gracious and, it seemed to Bindi, genuine.

Did Harper Knox really think she might need an introduction?

Still, Bindi's impulse got the better of her. She had her Doodad out, planning to snap a shot or two from table level when no one was looking. But the dark screen was unresponsive.

"Harper."

"Nice to meet you. Mason." He gave a charming smile. No panty-sniffing. Was he immune to celebrity, or was his casual response the politest of them all?

She moved to Ella. "I'm Harper."

"I loved you in *The God Particle!*"

"You're very kind."

Ella giggled self-consciously. It was funny to see, given her gloom. Bindi hadn't known Ella much at Bayshore and had barely spoken to her tonight, but she'd seen enough to guess that Ella was depressive, overwhelmed, and fighting a lot of hard feelings. It made sense; she'd have all the same problems as Heidi but without her defenses. They shared history. Maybe Bindi could talk to her — offer a discount on therapy. As much as Heidi suffered, Ella was probably suffering more.

"And your name is Ella?"

More giggles.

"Noah," Noah said.

"Harper."

"What are you doing here?" Noah asked.

But then, to Simon: "Hello. I'm Harper."

"Simon Wyatt. I built Swipe4Info and worked with Desmond Valence to launch aRRow. Netted $32 million on the day of the IPO."

"Thank you for coming, Mr. Wyatt."

"Where is Walter Kagen?"

She greeted Summer. Across the table, having given up on her dead phone, Bindi watched. Harper's coifed mane, perfect makeup, and whispery, warm voice was cinema given breath.

"And you must be John," Harper said, with her widest smile so far.

"I am."

"Harper Knox."

"I know. What a coincidence. We just saw you in *Death Nail*."

A tiny laugh. "I'm sorry."

"It was good."

"It wasn't. But that's okay."

Now John was smiling, despite himself.

"I have a confession, John," Harper said.

He head tilted. His smile became something else.

"I hadn't meant to invite you. Only now, after having made some calls, am I realizing that was an oversight." Her eyes ticked toward John's red envelope. "Clearly you should have been here all along. Not because of what's in there, but because of the role you've played."

"What role? In what?"

"He manages a grocery store." Then without reason, Imogen burst into a laughing fit that was the duration and volume of a sneeze.

Harper straightened. She stood behind her chair and plucked her wine glass back from the table. "It was so very kind of you all to come tonight. I know you all have very busy lives. And I appreciate that much of this is taking you by surprise, or has been difficult thus far. Everyone tends most to what is in front and within them. Where you've been is who you are, same as me or anyone."

"What does that mean?" Melissa asked.

Harper raised her glass. "To the past. And the secrets we keep."

Half the people around the table picked up their glasses, including Bindi. Harper ignored the bewildered half, said "Cheers," then sipped her expensive Riesling.

She sat. Donovan scooted her in. Harper regarded the soup with what looked like delight, then picked up a spoon.

"Um ... Miss Knox?"

Harper looked up at Teek. Bindi tried not to focus on Harper, or stare. Five minutes ago, she'd been thinking about Donald: angry, sad, feeling worthless, and more eager than ever considering that her mysterious informant hadn't appeared. Now she was having dinner, her arm nine inches from a movie star. It was vertigo.

"Yes, Teek."

"I ..." He looked around for help. Bindi could sympathize. Why was he having to ask this? It was unfair to drop something so strange onto people and expect them to accept it as normal. "What's going on here?"

"A lovely cold crab and asparagus soup. It's to die for."

"I mean ... why are you here?"

"This is my restaurant. I'm half-owner of Crave."

Teek blinked in the face of Harper's simple answers. She was smiling patiently, waiting for the part where something required explanation.

"I ... I mean ... why are *we* here?"

"You were invited."

"Jesus Fucking Christ," said Melissa.

"I think he means ..." But words didn't come much easier to John. He looked at Summer, then for some reason at Mason. Returning to Harper, he said, "Well ... I mean ..." Again he turned to Summer. "We were supposed to be attending an alumni dinner for Bayshore Academy."

Harper nodded. Donovan moved to stand by the door, hands behind his back. Watching the exit, same as before.

"Yes. The alumni dinner," Harper said. "I believe several of you were inducted."

A volley of nods around the table.

"Who is here for Bayshore's dinner?"

Hands slowly raised: John and Summer of course, but also Ella, Noah, Taylor, and Teek.

Harper said, "How do you know I'm not the board representative?"

Bindi looked at Imogen, who was no help, then Summer. Both appeared clueless.

Harper said. "I've donated to Bayshore. It's a fine establishment. Despite the normal problems with any high school — and they're much more careful about those things now."

"What things?" Mason asked.

"Mason. Why did you come to Crave tonight?"

"I'm meeting someone about a job."

"Of course. With your baby on the way."

Mason's face bunched.

"Heidi?"

"Bayshore. But a teaching job specifically."

"What about you two?" Harper asked, gesturing at Melissa and Imogen.

"I wanted to sip cold green shit from a spoon," Melissa said.

"Ohmygod," Imogen said. "I have a big question about *Life, Liberty,* and *The Pursuit of Happiness.* The whole series. When the gardener—"

"TV jobs, am I right?" Harper said.

"Melissa," Imogen said, bubbling, "if anyone can get you a writing gig, it's this bitch right here!" Pointing at Harper. Apparently this wasn't an insult.

Harper turned to Bindi. "And you?"

"I ..." Bindi scanned the table. "I'd rather not say."

"No. I'm sorry. Of course you wouldn't."

"Do you ... ?" Bindi began. Then quieter: *"What?"*

Harper smiled. "There's an answer for you, Bindi." Her eyes flicked to the right. "And Simon. Mr. Simon Wyatt. What brings *you* to—?"

"Kagen. Walter Kagen." His hands were on the table. "We've been exchanging emails for months."

"I know about Walter Kagen. He's quite the player. I'll bet if the two of you talked, he could totally 10x your shit." The swear left Harper's lips like a kiss.

"He—!" But Simon realized a word too late that Harper had beat him to the punchline. The rage left his face. Evenly he said, "That's right."

Harper nodded toward Donovan. "Donovan told me you've been asking about him. About his 'late arrival.'"

Simon's neck retracted. He didn't seem to appreciate the verbal air quotes Harper had put around "late arrival."

"Where is he?"

"At home, I believe. In Colorado."

"He's supposed to meet me here. We have a deal."

"You don't. I'm very sorry for the deception."

"We've talked about this forever."

"Maybe. But I invited you to dinner tonight. Not Mr. Kagen."

"You?"

Now Harper had everyone's full attention.

"Please. Eat. The crab is exquisite, but best when it's fresh."

There was a long pause, but slowly people began picking up silverware.

Bindi's eyes went to her red envelope. What was happening here? Harper looked at her, so she took her spoon and tried the dish. She realized how hungry she was once the bite was in her mouth, and woozy from drinking.

"Money buys a certain amount of control," Harper said. "It has a way of opening doors and making connections. Things that shouldn't be possible suddenly are. Like re-routing emails and texts between you and Walter Kagen."

"But we've spoken on the phone."

Harper nodded. "I know you have. But it was months ago. You discussed getting together in person, but didn't start making plans until 'Mr. Kagen' mentioned he'd be in Cielo del Mar, and referred you to his assistant via email."

Simon looked more incredulous than angry. "You ... you *hacked my email?*"

"I'm very sorry. I promise I have an excellent reason for bringing you here." She looked around the table. "All of you. There was a fair amount of subterfuge. I don't like to lie, but the deception was necessary. I needed to make sure all of you could attend."

Taylor said, "So ... there's no alumni dinner?"

"No. Nor is Predip Batra coming to speak with you about a job, Mason — nor Elder Conway for you, Imogen, or anyone any of you expected to meet."

"But I talked to The Food Network!" Imogen blurted.

"And maybe they'll offer you a show at some point. Maybe you'll even meet Elder Conway. But not tonight. I have no shows or celebrity chefs to offer."

Mumbling. Raw disbelief. Everyone felt upended, including Bindi. Did this mean she wasn't going to find the answer to her question about Donald? Or maybe she would; Harper had told her that answers were coming. For Bindi specifically.

Simon said, "The doors are locked. We're prisoners."

"You're my *guests.*"

"We can't leave. That makes us prisoners." Simon was speaking reasonably, but his tone was no-bullshit. "I want to leave. Fuck you and fuck all of whatever this is. I came here to make a deal, and if I can't do that I'm out. You want to keep me here? You'll have to tie me down." Then he looked around at the other diners and pointed at Donovan. "If we *all* go, he can't stop us."

Harper paused, dabbed at the corners of her mouth with white linen, and stood.

She walked toward Simon, and for one comically horrible moment, Bindi was sure they'd start throwing punches. Instead, Harper reached out and took one of Simon's hands in hers. He flinched but allowed it. They made a curious tableau, like a couple about to exchange vows.

Simon met her eyes, looking slightly up. In heels, Harper was taller.

"If you wish to go ... then as I said, you're free to leave."

He snatched his hand back and swiveled to Donovan. "Good. Then get the fuck out of my way."

Donovan did him one better. He stepped aside and held the door.

Simon glanced back at the others — probably to convey his disgust at being the only one outraged — and took several purposeful steps. He stopped short when Harper spoke again.

"Of course if you leave, there is the matter of your envelope."

Simon looked back. His eyes fell on the envelope, SIMON written in gold script across the front. His posture said he didn't care, yet still he paused. Bindi could sympathize. She'd been feeling the same oddity since they'd entered the Buvette. The same sense that something was amiss, and she'd better not rock the boat until she knew what it was if she didn't want to drown.

"What about it?"

Harper sighed. She looked down at her lightly clasped hands, then continued with an air of what sounded almost like regret.

"I hope you'll all understand. But once upon a time, something went very, very wrong — in many ways, for *all* of us. It's not something I can abide. It's not just something I can brush aside and let go."

Nobody asked what *it* was. Bindi had no reason or proof, but still she might know. And if so, she understood why nobody asked. Or wanted to raise it.

"I brought you here tonight to find the truth. I've lied to you. I've deceived you. And I've had, in all cases, to seek the help of professionals capable of violating your privacy. I can only assure you that

I've been assaulted just as much, and that what I've done in preparation for tonight was necessary. It's what's *right*."

Still nobody spoke. Harper pointed to Simon's envelope.

"Inside each of your envelopes is a secret you've fought desperately to hide from the world. Something that haunts you. Something that has shaped and formed you. Something that would crush you were it to become known."

Teek cleared his throat. He looked around — *guiltily*, Bindi thought. Heidi was looking away. The room was silent between Harper's words, save the purring from the vents.

"If you choose to leave, you must do so knowing that your secret will be revealed — first to the person it will harm the most, and then to the world."

There was a very, very long pause.

Then Simon wordlessly returned to his chair and Donovan closed the door.

The meal resumed without a sound, all eyes down, the clinking of silver on porcelain the room's only sound.

NINETEEN

May 14, 2018

"Casey," Noah said.

But Casey hadn't heard him. She was still closing things up with Ella and Heidi, both of whom were due to leave as Student Council convened. Miss Bridges arrived, shooing them toward spectator seats or away.

"Okay," Heidi said. "We've gotta go. Text you later."

"See you, Casey," Ella said.

Noah waited, nearby but unseen. Their femininity was intoxicating.

"Later, then," Casey said, hugging her friends. "I love you."

Heidi made a face. "Ugh. Can't you just say 'goodbye' like a normal person?"

"Love you, Heidi!" Casey said too loudly, laughing.

As the girls walked away, Noah tried again: "Casey."

She turned toward him, her enormous smile on full display. It wasn't for Noah; she'd been laughing with Heidi and Ella about things unknown — some delightful girlish secret whose potential filled Noah with a giddy, shameful energy. Their whispered discussion had them blushing with giggles, running fingers through styled hair, opening their mouths in shock or delight, bouncing about in private glee. Noah had watched from the corner of his eye, like a peeping tom peering in on a pillow fight.

The smile stayed on Casey's face, her pale skin still flushed; chest and sweater-clad breasts rising and falling as she waited for Noah to continue.

"Do you have a minute?" he asked.

"Sure. What's up?"

Noah paused. What *was* up? This sort of thing wasn't simple. It couldn't be easily asked or explained. It wasn't like he wanted to copy her homework. "I ..."

Simon slapped him on the back, wearing a smile wider than Casey's. "Noah!"

"Oh. Hey, Simon."

"You ready to turn this mother out?"

"Yes," Noah said, deadpan. "Woo-hoo."

"There's no need for sarcasm," Simon said, still playing. "I know leadership and finance don't always see eye to eye, but my regime is a benevolent one. When I convince the school board to turn my title from 'Student Council President' to 'El Capitan,' I promise to spare you in the ensuing bloodbath so long as you keep doing the books in my favor."

Noah was halfway to crafting a witty response when Casey beat him to it. She turned that big smile on Simon and (MOTHER-FUCKER) touched his arm:

"Your second in command never agreed to give you powers of mutiny."

"Maybe I should overthrow my second in command," Simon retorted.

"Good luck." She took a few strands of red hair between her fingers and said, "See this? Don't you know what they say about redheads?"

"That they're good at being stepchildren?"

"Slander," Casey said. "We're 1%, dammit! We deserve more respect."

"That they shouldn't get in El Capitan's way?"

"That—" Noah began.

"That you should always check to make sure the carpet matches the drapes?"

Casey's face became mock-offended. "You're gross," she said, shoving him.

"What if you dye that shit?" Simon said. Still smiling, charming, and way better looking than Noah. Still an asshole even though Casey was battling laughter.

"Get out of here," she said.

Simon shrugged, moving away. "Okay. But one of these days you'll say yes."

"He's such a dick," Noah said after Simon was gone.

Noah watched him, heading into place at the head of the room, seeing the way Teek Sheridan cozied up to him like a puppy at his master's heels. Student Council was such a farce. It had no power. Noah would never have volunteered as treasurer without the chance of getting closer to Casey.

"He's Simon."

"He gets on my nerves sometimes." He should rein it in; badmouthing him could cost Noah friends. But his pulse had doubled, and half his agitation was focused on Simon's interruption. And the way Casey kept touching his arm. "He's so *loud.*"

"I like him," Casey said.

"You like him? Like ...?"

"Well, not in *that* way." She laughed, also watching Simon and Teek. "Though not for lack of effort on his part."

A weight left his chest.

"It's just that ... you know how phony most people can be?"

"I'm not phony."

She gave him a little smile. Then, blessedly but only for a second, she touched *his* arm, too.

"No. Of course, *you're* not. But most people are, even if they don't mean to be. Everyone wants other people to think they're better than they are. We have all these little lies we tell. Secrets we keep to protect ourselves."

"What secrets?" Asking had a giddy thrill. What was Casey keeping close that she didn't want others to know? Was she hiding crushes? Secret, shameful thrills? Did she touch herself more than necessary when she took a bath, or sleep naked?

She shrugged. "You know, half the pharmacy industry would probably have to close tomorrow if people would just stop keeping so much inside. If we could all learn to be who we really are."

Noah tried on a smile. He didn't know where this was going, but it was already a long conversation with Casey Davis, considering, and he wanted it to last forever.

"What does it have to do with Simon?"

She looked at Simon again and said, "I get that he's an asshole. But at least you know who he is for real. What you see is what you get."

Noah's gut didn't like that much at all. Especially considering Simon's sharp, manly jawline. "You *talk* to Simon?"

"I talked to him just now."

"I meant *talk* talk."

Casey made a *why-not* face: a half-frown on her pretty lips. "No. But—"

A rapping noise came from the front: Simon, using a carved wooden bookend in the shape of a monkey as his president's gavel. Someone closed the doors from the outside, then the dozen or so students inside all shuffled to their seats.

Noah followed Casey toward Simon and Teek (checking out the rear view when he thought he could get away with it) and took his place. The four of them faced the assembly: kids trapped between the end of the school day and the start of their sport of choice with nothing better to do. At the front corner, Miss Bridges sat in one of the little desks with her hands folded as faculty representative. She might've been hot if she wasn't a teacher.

Noah kept replaying his five minutes with Casey before the meeting. Had he been interesting? Maybe. Had he scored any points? Probably not, though he couldn't stop thinking about her touch on his arm and the way she'd said he wasn't a phony. But she'd touched Simon's arm as well, and he apparently wasn't a phony either. Maybe she really would take her troubles to Simon. Maybe they were friends. Maybe Noah, by calling Simon an asshole in front of her, had lost some of her respect.

A little voice inside Noah spoke up: *Hey, pussy! Do you know what loses respect from girls? Obsessing over how you might lose it! You think you've got a shot? HA! You're lord and ruler of the Friend Zone, doomed to stay there forever. So you know what, dipshit? Maybe you should stop closing your eyes and picturing her lips, and just fucking kiss them instead!*

That fantasy went back to 6th grade. Noah couldn't help it; he was doomed to be a nice guy forever, even though the alpha types like Simon didn't give two shits and still got the girls. Was he supposed to change his personality? He'd said nothing all year, even after joining Council. Now here they were, in the last meeting before the end-of-year bash, and he'd said dick — despite his opportunity.

Hey, pussy! Do you know what really turns girls on? Soul-searching and indecision! You want to melt some panties, keep right on wondering when you'll get your perfect chance!

"Now," Simon said from Noah's left, "let's talk about the senior party."

"*KEGGER!*" someone shouted. Others laughed.

"Hang on," said Miss Bridges, drawing the room's attention. "I know that things are going to happen somewhere and at some time, but as long as the official senior party is on the agenda at a Student Council meeting, I can't know anything about alcohol or I'll have to shut it down."

Simon stepped in with his peacemaking smile. "Please, Miss Bridges, ignore Ashton. He's got problems. He still wets the bed. When he sleeps, his brain slides through the goo in his skull and lays on its side. The poor thing is getting a callus."

Chortling from the back. Ashton muttered something about Simon's mother and a guess as to her illicit profession.

"He said 'kegger' because that's a word he thinks means 'party.' Like 'bash' or 'gala' or 'shindig.' We're not actually planning to have a keg."

More chortles. Some boos. Simon shot the group an eye. If they didn't stop playing games, Miss Bridges really would have to shut it down.

"No alcohol, Simon. You want to drink at parties, that's on you. But as long as the student discretionary fund is paying for the band and the school system is being used to invite all of the seniors, you can't do it at this one."

"Of course not. He was only joking."

"Not one beer. I'm serious. I put my neck on the line for you guys about this, and if *anything* happens with *any* kind of—"

Simon raised a hand, palm out: a scout's salute.

"Not one beer. I promise. My parents aren't going out. I made sure of that. You can call them if you want. You should. They're acting as chaperones. And there will be others. You know what?" Simon took out his cell phone and tapped at the screen. He looked back up. "I just sent my mom a text. Said we should go through the house the day of the party and empty the liquor cabinet for the night. Take that and my dad's beer and wine out of the house. If you give me your number, I'll send you her name and information so you can—"

"That's really not necessary," Miss Bridges said, her face friendly all over again. "I'll be at the party on behalf of the school. I'll keep an eye out."

The meeting concluded, again with Noah barely paying attention except for his three minutes delivering the treasurer's report. None of it mattered. They discussed the party and there wasn't another worthy topic. They were all seniors in their final days, phoning in the minimum required to cross the finish line. They might as well have tossed the agenda, popped some corn, and kicked back with a movie instead.

The students filed out. The Council broke up and began stuffing papers into backpacks. Simon left. Teek went with him, still sucking up. Suddenly Noah and Casey were alone again.

Now. Now is the time to be bold.

But who was he kidding?

Casey was three feet away, looking into her backpack, arranging what was inside. Noah took in her profile, the delicate swing of her hair. He could reach out and touch her. Be a man and say what he was thinking — if *that* was what proper men did.

But his hands twitched. His lips strained, trying but unable to speak.

She looked up and smiled at him. "See you, Noah," she said, zipping up and tossing her pack over one shoulder.

"See you."

She walked toward the door.

Now. Asshole, do it now!

"Casey."

She turned.

"What are you up to? You headed anywhere?"

Maybe we could get a burger at the In-N-Out down the block. Or hit Starbucks. Anything. Everything.

Casey's body was present, but her eyes were far away. She was listening to Noah, but he could tell her mind was on somewhere else, on the same something that had preoccupied her throughout the meeting. A gaze that hadn't escaped her face since those whispers with Ella and Heidi.

"Actually, I think I'm supposed to meet someone."

"You *think* you're supposed to?" Noah's forced smile was already fading.

"Yeah. I need to find out."

"Who?"

"Mason Pace," Noah felt something break. The way she looked right now was the way he usually felt. A dreamy look, full of quiet hope.

"Mason?"

"I think so," Casey repeated. "I don't suppose you know where I can find him?"

TWENTY

May 14, 2018

Mason was sitting at one of the tables outside Buns, in the Palms Couture shopping center, taking in the view under a warm May sun.

He sipped his coffee. Mason liked Buns for its ambiance and people-watching, but sitting inside the shop itself was a big mistake. Even if doing so wouldn't obstruct his view of the courtyard (it would) or make him inaccessible for casual conversation with the girls who found him cute (it did), the bakery made his mouth water.

Mason didn't like to be a girl about it, but he did watch his diet. Even 18-year-old football players didn't get six-packs without effort, and the cinnamon rolls at Buns had to be two thousand calories a pop. He'd rather be tempted by the flesh outdoors than the pastries inside.

"Mason? Oh my God."

He turned. Two girls were approaching: Ella Reynolds and Heidi Blanchard.

Ella had spoken, and Mason could tell without clarifying that although she aimed the first word at him, the "Oh my God" was for Heidi. She was greeting Mason, then sharing delight with her friend. *Why?*

Mason sipped his coffee and cast a covert glance at a woman in a miniskirt near the fountain.

The girls giggled and traded a glance. He was used to this. Mason didn't think of himself as conceited (nor did anyone else; he'd earned an annoying reputation as a white knight), but he'd had his share of female attention.

"Hey. What are you two doing here?"

Without asking, the girls pulled out two of the three remaining chairs and sat. Again, they giggled.

"*What?*" Mason said.

"You aren't seeing anyone right now, are you?"

Mason frowned. They weren't asking him out, were they?

"Uh ... no."

"I heard you were going out with Jen Summerall," Heidi said.

"Just once. It's not a thing." That had been a poor fit. Jen was cute but hadn't even wanted to talk. On their first and only date, she'd wanted to go down on him. His dick had been interested more than his brain. Despite what some people thought, Mason wanted a relationship with substance. He wasn't above screwing on the first date (in fact, that was ideal), but it had to be with someone who had a good head on her shoulders and a future in front of her. And most importantly? She had to understand that Mason had a brain in *his* head, too.

"Told you," Ella said. Heidi rolled her eyes.

"Why?" Mason asked.

"Because we know someone who likes you."

"Did she give you a note to pass me after nap time?"

Heidi looked confused.

"You know. Because that's a kindergarten thing to do." He exhaled. "Never mind. Why isn't she here for herself?"

Ella seemed to think this was hilarious. Heidi shrugged.

"Are you messing with me or something?"

"No," Ella said.

"So why isn't she here?"

"Because you're Mason Pace."

"That's what my license says."

Again, the girls stared.

"Who is it?" Mason asked.

"Casey Davis."

Mason blinked and drew back in surprise. He'd written Casey off, after his odd crush the prior year. He wasn't usually intimidated by girls, but she seemed somehow older than her years. He *had* liked Casey. Enough that his natural powers had been useless. He remembered thinking, *This is how some guys feel about* all *girls they like*, but then he shed the discomfort for lower hanging fruit.

"Casey Davis?"

"Do you know her?"

Mason stopped himself from saying, *How the hell could I* not *know her?* "Yeah. You all hang out. With ... Taylor McKay?"

Ella looked at Heidi. There was something in that glance. "Yeah. Taylor," Ella said.

"So she sent you two to do her dirty work?"

"It's not that. It's—"

"But not Taylor. Not today." Mason realized two things as he spoke. First, he didn't know what he was saying. Words were just coming out. And second, he felt a shadow of his usual smile: a dumb, sideways thing that might be at home on a brainless yokel.

You're nervous. You're freaking out a little right now, and that's why you're blubbering and mugging like an idiot.

Which was crazy. Mason didn't get nervous about stuff like this.

Ella and Heidi traded another glance.

Sweetly, Heidi said, "Um ... so what do you think?"

"I don't know." They all looked at each other. It was an impasse. If Mason didn't know what he thought, nobody did. "I mean, she's cute."

Sure, Mason had noticed Casey's sophistication, but that hadn't stopped him from also seeing her ass. Or sneaking peaks at her boobs. They were small and perky. Probably milky white, with little pink hats that would ...

Stop thinking about nipples.

But Mason was eighteen. He thought about nipples often. And Casey's, like the rest of her, were probably adorable. Or downright *hot.*

And now he was kind of getting hard — undignified, somehow, because he'd crushed on Casey before his lust. This was all so out of the blue. He'd given up, and now Heidi and Ella were springing her on him. *And* her nipples.

"You should totally ask her out," Heidi said.

"Isn't that kind of my decision?"

"I'm just saying, you should."

Mason kept looking at the tiles around the courtyard, noticing patterns in their layout, lost in thought. When he finally returned to Heidi and Ella, Ella was looking away, too. Heidi nudged her with an elbow, but Ella said nothing.

"Well, maybe I will."

"She's been into you all year. Hasn't she, Ella?"

"What? Oh, yeah."

"And ..." Heidi leaned toward Ella and whispered. Ella mumbled something back that sounded like, *No way.*

"And what?" Mason asked.

"She totally wants to get with you," Heidi said.

"'Get with'?"

"Heidi!" Ella slapped her friend on the arm.

"Define 'get with.'"

Ella turned to Mason. "You know, go out with."

Heidi said, "That's not what *I* meant."

Ella gave her a darting look: *Shut the fuck up.*

Heidi said, "What the hell else am I *supposed* to say?"

Mason's erection barely noticed their exchange. It was rising like a charmed serpent. It was uncool to think of asking a girl out and immediately start wondering how she moved in bed. Casey deserved better than that. But it's not like Mason (or his dick) could be blamed. Heidi and Ella were painting a picture for him. Of Casey. Her chest heaving, wanting to "get with him."

"So?" Heidi pressed.

"I wouldn't've pegged her as the kind of girl who'd send friends after a guy she liked."

"Why?"

"Redheads are supposed to be bold and fiery."

Mason caught himself wondering if she was red all over. She'd have to be, right? Unless—

"Yeah. But *guys* are supposed to ask *girls* out."

"It's 2018."

"So?" Heidi said.

"She didn't *send* us." Ella reluctantly came alive. "We came because she's a wimp."

"But she's definitely into you," Heidi said.

"Definitely," Ella agreed.

"Talks about it all the time."

Mason looked from one girl to the other, then back.

"And we sort of already told her that you—" Heidi began.

"*Shh!*"

Ella stopped shushing and looked at Mason.

"That I what?"

"*Fine,*" Ella said. "We already told her that you were into her, too."

"What? Why?"

"Are you? You said she was cute."

"Yes, but—"

"We told her you were going to call her," Heidi said.

"What the hell?"

"Why not?" Heidi said. "You're into Casey, right?"

"Sure, I guess, but—"

"She needs to give her vibrator a break," Ella said.

Heidi looked over at her friend, shocked. Ella's face was frozen, seeming not to believe what had just left her mouth. Mason tried to smile along because it was obviously a joke, but now Casey was buzzing in his head in a different way.

"Ella!"

"Well, it's true!"

Mason heard: *It's true.* A trivial, private fact that meant nothing, applied to nothing at the moment. But Casey Davis was hot *and* fun, smart *and* sexy. He felt a little drunk, trying to chase the swirling thoughts.

"Just call her. Give me your cell." Heidi didn't wait. She snatched Mason's phone from the table and entered Casey's information.

"She's been into you forever. We told her at the student council meeting that you'd been asking about her."

"I haven't been asking about her!"

"Oh, come on. Jason Charvat's sister is on the cheer squad. She told me that Jason said you've got a thing for Casey. So—"

"I—"

"—so what you need to do is to man up and call her. You're both hot for each other's bodies and just need to get over yourselves."

"I'm not *hot for*—"

"Look," Ella said. "This could be a good thing."

"Okay. Fine. I'll think about it."

"Just do it, Romeo." Heidi rolled her eyes and pushed Mason's phone into his hand.

"You want me to call her *now?*"

"Yes!"

"No. Wait. I've got an idea." Ella cast a stare in Heidi's direction, seeming to inform her that this was a mandate, and that there'd be no objections. Then to Mason she said, "Get her flowers."

"Yes," Heidi agreed. "That's good."

Ella stood then scampered to the end of the courtyard where a furniture store called nouveau house (all lower case, so everyone would know it was fancy) had a taupe-colored furniture set on display in the sun. The mock room had a vase on an end table, filled with red roses. Ella plucked one and ran back. She handed it to Mason.

"You want me to give her a stolen rose?"

"There's a shop here called La Fleur de Blanc." Ella pointed. "They only sell white flowers. Buy a bouquet and stick this—" She indicated the rose. "—in the middle. Then tell her how unique she is."

Mason laughed. "I'm not doing that."

"Why not?"

"Because it's corny as shit!"

Heidi said, "Casey is corny. That'll make her cream her panties."

Dammit. Now Mason's boner was downright painful.

"She love it," Ella added. "Trust us."

Mason was doubtful. What the girls were talking about was the kind of shit that people did in movies, not real life. But both were now smiling and nodding, practically shoving him out of his chair with their eyes.

"You really think I should do it that way?"

They nodded vigorously.

"Why?"

"Because it's totally romantic!"

"No," Mason said, "I mean, why are you doing *any* of this?"

Because as hard as his heart was pounding and as sweaty as his hands had gotten and as delightful as his thoughts had become and as tight as his jeans felt right now, Mason couldn't help but notice how well-thought-out all of this was. They'd spoken to Casey and knew where to find him; they'd had discussions beforehand. Even Ella's inspiration about the flowers seemed less than spontaneous, and her beeline to the red roses seemed more like performance than inspiration.

"Just because," Heidi said. Then, belatedly: "Because Casey's a good friend."

Ella was looking off toward the ocean.

"Go on," Heidi said, standing to give Mason a shove toward La Fleur. "No time like the present."

With a nervous smile, Mason ticked his gaze between the flower shop and the girls. They were still in place by the Buns table, staying put even as he took a step forward.

"What? Are you going to wait to make sure I do it?"

"If we have to," Ella said.

TWENTY-ONE

"Fuck it."

John looked up to see who'd spoken, but before his ears could get their bearings, a blur of activity came from across the table: Teek, practically ripping his envelope to shreds in a frenzied attempt to open it. The things had simple string-and-button clasps, but he was tugging and clawing as if trying to free the secret inside before its poison could seep out and do him in.

All heads turned. Everyone waited. A few people, including John, looked to Harper to see if she'd object. But she just sat there eating her soup.

Teek's hands shook as he fished a stiff card from the torn envelope's innards. He shielded the thing with his body, scooting back just far enough that neither Taylor and Melissa, flanking him, couldn't see. With the card cupped in his nervous hand, he read. Seconds passed; a clock ticked.

"Teek?" Taylor said.

He was staring at the card. Eyes wide. Stock still. Taking it in.

"Teek?"

When Taylor's outstretched hand tentatively brushed his upper arm, Teek jumped as if shot. His eyes were saucers, whites showing all the way around. He pushed back even more, front leg of the chair snagging on the thick rug, and almost toppled. He turned those giant eyes on Taylor as if he didn't recognize her.

"Teek? Are you—?"

Pulling forward. Chair legs catching again, almost falling but this time forward. Head down, focused, hand with the card half-crumpled, palm down for the table's surface to look up and read. He snatched at the discarded envelope, missed, grasped again. Shaking fingers found the edges and opened the parcel. Teek shoved the card deep inside. To the bottom, surely half-folded or in a wad, as if he wanted to push through the envelope's floor to another world where there was no shame, where his pulse wasn't a swollen bulge in his neck.

"You okay, man?" Noah asked.

Teek blinked. Noah was across from him.

"Yeah."

"You sure?"

"Yeah."

Teek lifted his plate and slipped the envelope beneath so only the four corners showed.

The clock ticked.

Ten seconds passed.

Noah cleared his throat. He took a sip of water. Everyone was watching, as if he and Teek were the only players in a two-man show. Teek had picked up his spoon again, resumed eating. Far off in the kitchen, someone dropped something metal, big but light like an empty pie tin.

Teek looked up. Noah met his eyes.

Mason, down the table from Noah said, "Is it ...?" Teek was sipping wine, imbibing in gulps. He set it down and Mason tried again. "Is it ... *true?*"

Teek's jaw worked.

"The thing in your envelope," Mason said. "Is it true?"

Taylor's hand on Teek's arm, welcome now, slow and moving. "It's okay," she told her husband. "I told you ... it's okay."

"You already know what it is?" Imogen asked.

Taylor leaned in. Whispered something to Teek. He shook his head without meeting her eyes.

John looked down at his envelope. It hadn't been here when they'd entered the Buvette. He'd been right to worry. To wonder and doubt, to feel from the start — from *before* the start, since that day in the office — that nothing was right about this supposed alumni dinner. Practice had given John a PhD in bullshit detection, and seeing when something might be hidden underneath. He'd been right this time, but had let Summer come.

But this was the only way.

Because: *Bayshore. What Mason had said, days ago.* Because of what John had always held inside. What he had failed, despite all his secrets, to unearth.

He was trapped in straight jacket. A man fed a paralyzing drug, eyes open, forced to watch something awful. Even Summer didn't know the real reason they'd met.

What was in *his* envelope?

"Is what's in your envelope true, Teek?" John asked.

He didn't reply, but John could read him just fine. Everyone could.

Simon shook his head and turned to Harper. "This is such fucking bullshit."

Taylor, across the table. "Is it, Simon?"

His head turned toward her as if on a slow hinge.

"Is it bullshit?" Taylor repeated.

"What's your problem?"

"I don't know, Simon. I haven't opened my envelope yet."

John watched them both, seeing something that reeked of their history.

"Maybe you should," he said.

"There's nothing in mine that can hurt me."

"So open it," Simon said. "Open it and read it for all of us."

"Why are you like this? Why have you always been like this?"

Teek had snapped out of his torpor. His hands were on Taylor, trying to quiet her. But she was glaring at Simon in wordless fury.

"Like what?"

"You know what I mean."

"Do I?" Simon gave a single, derisive chuckle. To Teek he said, "And I thought that bitch was the smart one."

"Knock it off, Simon," Teek said.

Now Simon's attention turned to Teek.

"What are you going to do if I don't?" Simon said, rising halfway from his seat.

John's shoulders rolled forward. "Take it easy."

Simon continued: "What are you going to do, Teek? I'm really curious what you'll do to me if I don't stop calling your wife out for being a nosy cunt."

"Hey," John said, standing as well, squaring to Simon beside him. He was younger, but John was bigger and had been in enough scraps to hold his own.

"What's in your envelope, Simon?" Taylor said.

"None of your fucking business."

"Afraid?"

"I don't know. Are *you* afraid?"

Taylor's face set. She pulled her envelope from the table and unwound the thread from the button, never moving her eyes from Simon's. She withdrew the card and peeked. Her jaw set slightly askew and she gave an angry, self-satisfied little smile. A small laugh escaped. Then she turned the card toward Teek, so that he could read it.

"Not too bad?" Ella said. "I mean ... if you showed Teek." To John, it sounded like Ella was talking to herself — trying to believe that Teek's reaction was atypical, and that what lurked yet-unseen wasn't that terrible after all.

"He already knows," Taylor said.

"Care to share with everyone else?" Simon said.

"Of course not."

Simon snickered. "So it's something you did together. What, do you like it up the ass?"

Melissa spooned soup to her mouth. She craned past Teek to look at Taylor in her pretty but conservative dress. *"Her?* I seriously doubt it."

Imogen: "Right. And it's not like *that's* a big, scary secret. You like it up the ass — right, Melissa?"

"I *prefer* it up the ass."

"Don't you have a dildo that's like a fist?"

"A fist on the end of a jackhammer," Melissa said, nodding. "It takes a crew of three men to work it. Not that there's anything wrong with three men."

Bindi said, "Knock it off, you two."

"It's my bedroom. I can have as many dildo crews as I want."

"You know what I mean."

Melissa's lips firmed into something like thinking. "Hmm. I really don't."

"This isn't funny."

"Yes it is. Show of hands. Who thinks a fist-shaped dildo is funny?"

No hands went up.

Bindi turned to Harper. "You can't do this."

Harper said, "I already have."

"It's blackmail."

Harper took another bite of crab and nodded without looking up. "It is."

"Now you," Taylor said, still in an ocular wrestling match with Simon. "I opened mine; now you open yours."

"Forget it."

"So you *are* afraid. You're a little man with a big personality." Taylor shook her head and picked a piece of crouton from her plate, crunching it in an eye-lock with Simon. "I told Teek that about you in school, and I'm telling you right now."

"Teek never had a problem with me. Ask him."

"He respected you! He'd have done anything you asked!"

Simon laughed. Teek protested, but Taylor shoved him away.

After a quiet moment, Taylor sat back in her chair with a smug little shake of her head. "All talk with nothing behind it. You're all hot air. Just a tiny-dick coward. I wonder if the fact that you're dead fucking broke is what's in your envelope? I hope not, because ..." She turned to Harper, who continued to chew, less interested than amused. "Because *really*." Back to Simon. "I looked you up last night. Doesn't take much searching to find out what people in your industry think of you. To find out that you're better at flushing money away than the government, and just scratching for one big score."

Simon flinched forward. His hand struck a drink; his water glass spilled. Then he composed his face, washing that flash of fury away. He ran a hand through styled brown hair and laughed, his winning grin looking like like a threat .

"You don't know what you're talking about," he said.

"I know you won't open your envelope."

Simon took a moment, inhaled, exhaled, then gave an *If you insist* sort of frown. He turned to Harper, and on his face John could see only polite frustration. The anger and denial were all gone, covered by this mask of civility.

"May I open my envelope?"

"Of course."

"You're sure?" He indicated Teek and Taylor. "Some people didn't bother to make sure."

"Go ahead, Simon," Harper said.

John leaned forward to watch as Simon slowly opened his envelope. So did everyone else. He moved back enough to conceal its contents, and almost kept his face straight. *Almost.* But John could see the way his fingertips whitened from pressure on the envelope, the rising of tendons in his neck, the tempo of his breath.

Before he returned the card to its envelope and gave another of his little laughs, his teeth clamped shut. Then he nodded acknowledgement to Harper, but the truth was on his face: If Simon was sure he could get away with it, he'd have jumped at their host already.

"What does it say?" Imogen asked.

"Nothing."

"Nothing," Taylor parroted.

Simon looked like he might engage, but what he'd read on that little white card had clearly punched him in the gut. John could see it all: the concealed rage, the protected soft center, the way Simon was ignoring everyone again while remaining aware of whether or not others around the table were looking.

He probably felt trapped in a glass box, certain that everyone could see his secret like a scarlet letter. Walking a tightrope of fury and shame, working to embrace whatever was on the card: It was his pride; he'd do it all over again, if he had the chance.

But John also knew that Simon would be quiet for a while. Docile, almost — or, possibly, building pressure like a powder keg.

Summer, beside John, slapped her napkin onto the table. A fork jingled. All eyes turned, waiting the half-second it took for Summer to speak.

"Simon was right about one thing. This *is* bullshit."

John started to say something but Summer beat him to it. He stopped, knowing protest was futile from her silencing hand.

She looked around the table. Eyes were mostly on Summer, but John could see fear mixed with the attention in all of them. For now, they were listening. But their eyes made them look like animals backed into corners. Summer was about to say something dangerous. And if it fell apart, they'd protect themselves first — at any cost.

"Do you really think you can just ... get away with this?"

"I'm very sorry," Harper said.

"Yes. *You're sorry.*" Summer looked to the table's opposite end, to Heidi. Then to Taylor, Teek, Melissa, Imogen, and Bindi, right on down the line. And to them she said, "We aren't just going to sit here and let her do this to us. She's one person." A red-nailed finger stabbed the air at Donovan, still by the door. *"He's* one person. What are they going to do if we all just walk out and go to the police?"

Eyes averted. Someone cleared their throat.

"Are you serious?" Summer went on, seeing the others' inaction, her finger still on Donovan like the scope on a rifle. "What's she going to do? Who's she really going to tell, and how? What, is she going to send out a press release? Who cares about us? Who's going to give a shit if she spills our whole life's histories onto the internet?"

Her arm lowered. She set both hands on the table, her body tense like a grasshopper about to spring, and fixed on Harper as she spoke to the others.

"But her? Harper Knox? There's a person the world cares about. What's going to happen if *everyone here* says what they have to say about tonight ... and our 'everything' has one of the world's biggest movie stars creeping around in bushes or whatever it took to get what she needed on us? Do you think *People* would be interested in talking to us after tonight?"

Summer paused, scanning the table, waiting for shouts of approval and uprising. None came.

Imogen said, "Shut up, Summer."

Summer's head swiveled. Blonde ringlets whipped in an arc. "What?"

"Shut up and sit down."

Summer looked around at the others for support. Imogen was being unreasonable. But the others seemed to have noticed what John already had, and it kept their tongues in check: At some point during Summer's rant, Imogen had opened her envelope, its pieces now in her trembling hands. The card had made up her mind. Who cared about Imogen's secret? Clearly, Imogen did.

Summer sat from her half-risen position. She cast a venomous glance around the table, then seemed to fold into herself with a mutter.

John leaned toward her. Summer flinched as if she'd hit him.

"Whatever you want," John said. "Whatever you want to do."

He thought she might insist on leaving, but with her balloon popped, her courage went missing. Now there was only anger, and tremor.

"Eat something," John said. "It'll help."

Summer began to pick at her plate. She hadn't eaten anything. Not off her plate, nor the circulating appetizers. But she'd had plenty to drink.

It's the secret. Whatever Harper knew was eating her alive.

John tried to take her hand under the table. She pushed him away. He leaned closer and whispered, "Open it. Open your envelope."

"No."

Still too quiet for others to hear: "You're making yourself sick. Not knowing is the worst part."

"Don't get Catholic on me again, John."

"Then I'll open mine."

His hand went for the envelope, but Summer grabbed his wrist. "No. We're not playing her game."

"It's okay." He pulled away and this time got the envelope before Summer could stop him.

"I mean it, John. Put it down."

"I want to know."

"I don't."

"Then I won't tell you what's in it." He pulled away again, harsher than he meant to. Summer's hand was a cup and saucer under a yanked-away tablecloth. It dropped, limp, and struck the table's edge.

John reached for her, but now it was Summer who flinched away, holding her banged wrist.

"Summer—"

"Then do it," she snapped, her eyes on his envelope. "If it turns out your daddy sucked dicks to get you into college, don't cry to me."

Her words were a slap. He met her eyes for a long, long moment, feeling the weight of judgment. Everyone had seen and heard that.

"John, I ..." She stopped.

His jaw clenched and he snapped his hand from hers. With thirteen witnesses, he opened his envelope, taking his turn on this unusual stage. His heart beat harder and his hands shook, but the words on the card — in fancy script, like an invite to a debutante ball

— didn't surprise him. He already knew what he dreaded Summer discovering. He'd learned, through harsh experience, what turned his mental keys. It didn't make them any less deadly, or John more eager to reveal.

He reassembled the envelope, piece by luxurious piece.

"So," Melissa said from across the table. "Daddy *did* suck dicks?"

John turned to Harper. "What's this about?" he asked, keeping his voice as steady as he could.

But John had come to Crave with a head start. He might know the answer already.

And Harper said, "This is about Casey Davis."

Murmurs percolated. The air thickened. People gestured and grumbled and stood.

All but John.

A bomb detonated inside him. Alarms were screaming.

Casey Davis.

All the warning feelings John had ignored. All the premonitions. All the certainties and doubts and grips of foreboding that had crawled across his flesh when Summer received her invitation to the Bayshore dinner, as he'd recalled that evening in the dark, screen-lit office, as something had grabbed him by the back of the neck and insisted that none of this was right.

Of course he'd had to go.

Of course he'd needed to accompany Summer.

And of course there'd never been a choice.

Harper's words repeated in his mind like a file with a glitch.

This is about Casey Davis.

Casey Davis.

Casey—

TWENTY-TWO

May 24, 2029

—D avis."

John had been scribbling a reminder (*"check abt S's birthday"*) onto a small yellow Post-It note when he felt the man's words like an ice pick through his neck.

For several curious seconds, his muscles tensed and he couldn't move. Then the feeling passed, and he reached for the screen of the rightmost monitor and tapped to pause it.

To the darkness, John spoke aloud: *"What?"*

He looked back up. The stalled video showed the broad-jawed man with his head halfway bowed, almost reverent through his first sentence. So many of them started this way. The subject would blurt out the worst part in one Heimlich belch ("I'm gay" was common, but John had also heard such gems as "I beat my kids" and "I stole from church"), then sigh to catch their breath. It was a five-second orgasm curve: peak then recovery.

John hit the ten-second rewind icon and played what he thought he'd heard again.

The confessor repeated, "I guess this starts and ends with Casey Davis."

And again, *Pause.*

John sat in the darkness, his mind afire. The blinds were drawn, as if someone might peek in and immediately know what he was up to. As if Summer knew this office existed, and might appear unannounced: *Hey Honey; I need you to watch the kids for a while.*

It was absurd; as far as Summer knew, John left every day to manage the Greens store he'd quit months ago. Still, working in the dark made him feel safer.

Casey Davis.

It couldn't be the same one. How could it be? John went to Forage and typed the words "Casey Davis," in quotes to get exact matches. There were over a half-million results, and scanning through, most of those were recent. Lots of Casey Davises out there. It didn't have to be the one Summer knew all about — the one that, if John had to guess, still haunted her dreams.

Summer's voice, more than once in her sleep, quiet and penitent: *Casey. Casey, I'm sorry.*

His wife hadn't always been such a wonderful woman.

John looked at the screen. The square-jawed man was paused with his head up, athlete/model's face on display, eyes open, baby blues wide and apologetic. The face of someone trying to be a better man, just as Summer broke her back these days to become a better woman.

To atone, John knew — even if Summer had no idea that he did.

The guy in the video wasn't talking about the same Casey.

The world was too big.

But no; his reaction to the name was spot on. After giving his own name (*Mason,* John thought but would want to double-check), the confessor had mumbled some history: a job that went nowhere, regrets that meant nothing, and the prep school he'd gone to: Bayshore Academy. He was about Summer's age, too. So, yes. This was the same story, about to be told from a brand new angle.

This starts and ends with Casey Davis.

Starts.

And ends.

Casey, I'm sorry.

Casey was a ghost that had haunted Summer since before he'd met her — and although John knew more than he let on, he'd never forced his wife to talk it through. So Casey became his ghost, too.

One more burden for the pile. Another reason to kill this business, no matter how much it was banking for his family. He drank poison in this dark little room. A contagion he couldn't shake or shield himself from. Pain he couldn't unsee, unhear, or unfeel.

John stopped moving. He'd heard something. Someone just outside the door. Coming up the stairs. Summer with her fist raised, about to strike the door of this secret, anonymous office.

But that steady drum wasn't coming from the hallway — nor from the office above or below, inexplicably busting out phat beats in the middle of the day to blaze up and bliss out.

It wasn't coming from the other rooms of this office; if only that were possible, if only John had found the guts to hire a staff. But no. It was coming from inside the room. From his own chest, telegraphed through his bones to the fluid in his cochlea.

Heartbeat, fast and loud. Thick enough to hurt.

John stood. He'd been working late by the light of the corner lamp, having told Summer that Perry needed him to run end-of-month inventory and send it up to Greens corporate. Now he turned on the overheads, not as bothered in the moment as he usually was by their fluorescent flicker and buzz. The Greens warehouse had the same lights. If he had stuck around at his old job instead of starting this lucrative sideline, he'd be under the same sick blue glow. Doing whatever Perry told him to do.

Well, John thought with all the precision in his educated mind, *Perry can suck a fattie.*

Although ... sometimes John felt he should reach out to his old boss and let him know what he'd inspired. Perry Wallace had, by most accounts, been an ideal supervisor. Saccharine sweet. The kind that was hard to believe. John had been sure there was something wicked beneath: secrets that Perry didn't want the world to see.

So he'd started his website, Contract Confessions. A place where he could peer into the secrets of others. He never discovered what Perry hid beneath his Sunday morning demeanor, but he'd been right about the world at large: everyone (John included, perhaps especially) had something inside that was dying to get out.

John walked into the next room and turned on the lights. Then he went into the next. It wasn't a small space, just the smallest he'd been able to find. He'd only wanted a room but had ended up with a suite. What the hell. The website could afford it. And eventually, he'd been telling himself, he could always hire staff. Would *need* to, if he wanted to keep his sanity.

But who had John been kidding? He couldn't let anyone else see this.

By the time he returned to the computer room, Mason's face had become a screen saver. Just as well. John didn't need to process the submission soon, considering that Mason had given himself a three-month contract. His confession was fresh, and there were so many more urgent ones — those with contracts of weeks or days — that needed to be queued, and their fuses tentatively lit.

John turned to the second computer, beside the one now displaying Mason. He pulled up the incoming bucket, noted the dates, then looked at his watch. There were only five confessions in the queue. He could review, pass or reject them, then set them up for auto-delivery in about an hour. Maybe less. He could handle Mason's and the other new confessions tomorrow, after he'd lied to his wife again.

Or maybe he could handle Mason's never.

John touched the first confession with his finger. A video came up, of a woman in her thirties.

"Um ..." she told the camera, "I'm Maureen, I guess, and this is my Contract Confession."

John waited for Maureen to find her nerve. In the pause, his eyes flicked to the other monitor.

"I ... I cheated on my husband."

The long pause to refract and gain energy. John knew it well.

"He's a good man. I love him. I ... I'm such a ... *fuck!*"

Maureen took a breath, wiped at her eyes, and looked off to the right. She wasn't crying yet. About three quarters of the time, that changed.

She frowned — an ugly, pinched, bitter-mouthed expression — and shook her head. Her eyes found the camera. Not the screen like most people. John hated when they did this. It was like they were staring into his soul.

"Assuming I clicked the right boxes before starting to record, I've given myself a one-week contract. If I haven't told Sam that I've been screwing around by then, I guess you'll let this video go live." She blinked, looked up. "And ... *shit*. I just realized my aunt Liz is in my contacts, so I guess you've got her address and phone number, too, huh?" Now the tears were coming. She faced the camera again and said, "Too late to back out?"

Uncomfortable laughter. A fist gripped his heart. He didn't know this woman at all. ContractConfessions.com worked on the honor system, and that meant it wasn't too late to back out. Maureen could log in tomorrow and tell the system that she'd fessed up to her husband and it would all go away. John didn't keep copies of the videos or contact lists; holding them felt like cradling a stillborn baby for sentiment.

If people wanted to bury their baggage, then God bless them. But the fist in John's gut stuck around because even if Maureen could cheat the system (and, if she chose, go right on cheating her husband), this was the part that mattered. Confessing was a salve, even if it meant nothing, even if nobody heard it. People paid to confess, paid for the system to rat them out to friends and family if they failed to make good. Advertisers paid a mint for his traffic. It was a service the modern world needed, but still John couldn't help but feel he was selling bullets and knives. Shilling torture and pain, even if such things were allegedly good for the soul.

As with most of the Contract Confessions, Maureen seemed to hold nothing back. A viewer (including Aunt Liz, if she didn't fulfill her promise in time) would learn the sordid details of her two-week affair with Dave Benson, a realtor who promised to put *YOU* in a new home *TODAY* but instead spent most of his time sticking his dick in Maureen.

Locations. Times of day. Excuses to her husband. Positions. Brands of lubricant and varieties of toys, orifices visited.

John clicked the confession to double-speed, unable to take it. He needed to make sure nobody confessed to something the law might want to know. That rarely happened. He could have hired an employee to take over this job weeks ago, given how much money the site was dumping into his life. But Contract Confessions was *John's* secret, and one that could cost him his family — especially after all the site's recent press. Even Summer (an expert at repression) had ranted about it just five nights ago, then again in the morning.

It's a disgrace. People should keep their stuff to themselves, but these parasites are just making it worse!

The video ended and John looked through the contracts entered into the site's backend to make sure everything jibed. The database had been buggy last week but seemed okay now. Sure enough,

Maureen Carter's confession contract was logged: a week from submission (five days from now), everyone in her life would learn her secret if she didn't log back in to tick the box claiming that she'd made everything right.

John scrolled. More confessions had come in while he'd been watching. That was happening faster and faster these days. Not for the first time, now clicking through page after page of freshly logged contracts, John wondered how many people cheated the system. How many people told the site to abort its life-changing broadcasts without fixing their lies? He guessed not many. People *wanted* to get caught. Deep down, they *wanted* punishment for their sins.

And that, right there, was the reason John was inches from making his own confession: promising to come clean to Summer or be exposed by his own creation. He couldn't take it anymore — not the site, not the pain of others, not the stress, not the lies. People thought he was a happy-go-lucky guy, and so far, John had managed to maintain the facade.

But it was getting harder and harder to keep his chin up. He found himself looking around in public, wondering what sordid secrets the people around him were were stuffing inside. The kindly-looking woman pushing the stroller might secretly shake her baby. The restaurant manager might beat off in a beautiful woman's food. Once, John had seen the confession of someone he knew: a favorite teacher, who confessed to molesting students. Fate was cruel, crashing John into that teacher not two weeks later. There'd been nothing to say, no way to make it right. John had shaken his hand with a smile, then spent a sleepless night wrestling the acid inside him.

John eyed the screen-saver.

No, not yet.

He scanned confessions, screening for crimes he'd be legally bound to report. That line had blurred. In the beginning he had sent many videos to the police, including the confession of murder. He'd heard nothing back. No atta-boys from the cops, no reports of crimes solved, no angry confessors wondering how they'd been ratted out days after spilling their guts to a website. He'd more or less given up. There was no right course. He'd either be abetting criminals by keeping their secrets, or betraying those who'd come here seeking discrete absolution. He was a bastard no matter what. So many crimes were committed in the grayest of areas. Robbing a bank was a big deal ... but was stealing the boss's wallet just because he breathed through his mouth in meetings?

The last batch had:

A woman taking hospice care of her aging mother who'd been increasing the dosage of pain meds to accelerate the process of dying.

A teen boy who'd had sex with a very drunk girl at a party, and wasn't sure if what he'd done was consensual.

A man in his nineties, with a German accent, who confessed to having led a post-war Nazi movement.

And a round-faced young woman in a green blouse who confessed to hating all of her children, resenting them for stealing the carefree, globe-trotting life she'd dreamed of having.

Again, John looked at the screen saver. There was no reason to review this new confession.

He tapped the screen to wake it, then resumed Mason's video.

"See, I just found out I'm going to be a dad. Yay!" Mason raised both hands in mock celebration, then tried to laugh at what clearly wasn't funny. "And ... I guess I'm excited. No, I *am* excited. But it changes things. I wasn't expecting to settle down quite yet. Not that I'm a wild man or anything. Just ... Well, this girl. The mother, I mean. Jessica. We had fun, but we're not soulmates. Not that I believe in that sort of thing. But it was kind of about to end. We aren't a good fit. And then she told me she was pregnant. I want to do the right thing, but I'm not sure what that is. Y'know?"

Another uncomfortable laugh.

"I guess you *don't* know. If I get some balls, hopefully *nobody* will know. Or see this, I mean."

John felt a twinge. The site's FAQ clearly stated that no human would ever watch the submissions, and that everything was automated.

Your privacy is guaranteed.

But it wasn't. John started Contract Confessions on a lark after imaging Perry's secret burial ground. A manual process was his best at the time. What was he supposed to do now — hire a web developer? It was ridiculous and embarrassing. Besides, John wasn't sure that the site's promise was legal. Yet another reason he should confess to Summer, then shut the whole thing down.

Who am I kidding? John thought as he sat in the dark. *I've been saying that for weeks.*

"The problem is that I'm lazy," Mason continued. "*Emotionally* lazy. I'm never lazy at work." Deep sigh. "You know, I went to a really good prep school. Five stars, super expensive; I was off to a great start. I graduated in the top fifth of my class, and got a partial ride to college. But then I kind of imploded. Stopped showing up for class, lost my scholarship, and eventually got kicked out of college. I woke up one day and realized that I didn't even care. So I got a shitty job as a glorified copy boy with a company that makes electronic scales, then got myself fired from that. I got on this jag with just not wanting to show up. Like, I felt really, really bad for a while, and couldn't face anyone. It went away, but I still couldn't put anything together for ... for *years*. I guess I just got stuck in a bad spot. Did I mention that earlier?"

John caught himself nodding as if Mason could hear him. Yes, he'd mentioned that and other things during his intro, before the confession's first real salvo with that Casey Davis bomb. And what had happened there? He'd mentioned the source of Summer's shame and nightmares before going into this thing about being a father. John resisted the urge to click ahead.

"Anyway, I'm trying to get a new job. Even got a really good lead. There's this guy, Predip, who was a few years behind me in school. He's a headhunter now. And I guess he must be serious about having something for me, because he wants to meet me on Saturday. What do you think ... does this look like a good sign?"

Mason held something up. Bright blue, about as big as one of those oversized index cards. It came and went too fast for John to see details, but its familiarity punched him in the heart.

"And the place he wants to meet — Crave? I looked it up. *Fancy!* So no matter what you think, *I'm* taking it as a good sign."

Again Mason waved the blue thing. This time John saw it fine, though he paused the video for a few seconds before letting Mason continue. It was an envelope, but inside there would be an invitation card of cream-colored stock. John couldn't read what was on it, but that was okay. Summer's was the same.

Not the sort of thing you got from a headhunter, but definitely the kind of invitation you might expect for an alumni dinner.

Mason set the card down, then inhaled and exhaled. He leaned forward. "The truth? I'm not sure I'm ready to have a kid. I don't have my shit together. And it's not just my empty bank account. I'm still acting like a kid myself. I phone it in with Jessica, and maybe that's why we don't fit. I could do better. Do shit like bring her flowers. I could ask about her day and care about the answers. I could be there more, be out with my friends less. It's time to grow up. For my son or daughter."

John waited. There was still a loose end the size of a fist hanging over this confession.

"I shut down, I think. After something that happened in high school. I've been sort of pondering the past, figuring things out on my own. I'm no shrink, but it feels like that's what happened — the shutting-down, I mean. And hey, I guess I *should* go talk to someone, right?"

There was a snapping sound offscreen then the scratch of a pen as Mason scribbled a note. He took his time before looking up again. His head went down and to the right, then down and to the left. It shook slowly. He looked back up with moisture in his eyes.

"I used to be quite the player. Jock type, you know. I was big, and strong, and I guess the girls liked me. I tried to be respectful, but what the hell; I was a teenager; my dick made the rules. But I tried to be as good as a kid like that can be. The girls I hooked up with had to be cool or we broke up. I had standards. But high school girls? They're mostly the same. Same for the boys. I thought I had it all figured out back then, but ..."

Pause. Indecipherable expression as Mason looked away.

"One day, I was just hanging out and these two girls came up to me. They told me that their friend was into me. And that was cool because I was into Casey, too. She seemed ... *different* ... than the girls I usually went out with. Like she was just more dignified or something. More grown up. Kind of 'above' the drama and bullshit I usually had to deal with from other girls. Super pretty, super nice." Mason smiled. "Bright red hair. Proud of it, too. So I ... ha, shit ... I actually *got her flowers*. I won't get them for Jessica, but I bought a bouquet for Casey; what does that tell you? One red flower in the middle of a bunch of white ones." He laughed. "Who does crap like that?"

John knew how this story ended and his heart was already aching.

"Me and Casey went out twice. Totally hit it off. The second time was at a party being held by those same two girls — Heidi and Ella — who came up to me that first day. We were at one of their houses. I forget which. I just know their parents weren't home. We all hung out for a while, and then the others kind of paired off and vanished to go make out or something, and then it was just me and Casey and the other girls. Heidi and Ella seemed nervous, and at the time I didn't know why. Then they decided all of a sudden to turn on music, really loud, and it was this shitty music, too. I didn't get that at first either, but looking back it was obvious they were trying to get me and Casey to leave the living room — you know, give us a reason to go somewhere private together. We ended up in a bedroom and shut the door to keep the noise down. We started kissing and I asked Casey if I should lock the door. She said yes, and I did. We didn't have sex or anything; Casey drew that line. But we did make out. Kind of hardcore. It snowballed. We both ended up with our shirts off, her bra too. And I started ... you know. With my hand in her pants. And Casey was ..."

Mason made a jacking-off gesture — just a few pumps. He stayed silent, his jaw firming, eyes averted but hard, frustrated, maybe an angry kind of sad. Then he continued with a grudge in his voice.

"The other girls must have been listening. Or watching. The lock didn't mean shit because it was their house. The door exploded open to a gaggle of girls, holding cell phones and laughing. I saw what they recorded later, shot through a gap in the drapes I guess. There we are, grabbing on each other. The photos were just as bad — Casey with her hand on the gearshift before we jumped for our clothes. I guess they thought it was funny. Found out later it was all a big prank. The girls knew Casey liked me, so they tricked me into asking her out. They knew just what to have me say and do to get her all ... you know, *interested*. And dude, the pictures and videos they took? That's the worst part. Right there and then, with Casey totally pissed and trying to cover herself and fucking *crying* in the corner, a bunch of them stopped to upload that shit to the web. Emailed it out to the school directory or something, too, because *everyone* knew about it by Monday. I tried to console Casey. Make her feel better. I told her it was only a joke, that those girls were assholes, shit like that blows over in seconds. But Casey just stared out the window, and wouldn't say a word, even when I was dropping her off."

Mason wiped one eye, then the other. His voice cracked.

"Cruel bitches playing a prank. That's how they saw it, I guess. Figured Casey would get over it, maybe laugh with them later. But the thing is, after ... well, after what happened ... I kept thinking back to how obvious it all was that Heidi and Ella were up to something when they came to me and then in the days after, like they were trying to push us together. Then that stupid, awkward party, and the way they turned on the music. One of them said, 'If you don't like it, there's a room down the hall you can hang out in.' I should have seen it coming, or something like it. Hell, I *did* see *something* coming. I could have grabbed their cameras instead of ..."

Mason trailed off, sighed, and wiped his eyes again.

"I'm sure a shrink would say I'm not to blame. Not for what happened that night ... certainly not for ..."

A shaking head. A long moment.

"Look," Mason said, measuring his words, fitting them into short, controlled bursts. "She didn't deserve that. I should have controlled myself. I didn't have to try and fuck her. We only went that far because I pushed. We kissed but I wanted to feel her tits. That night fucked me up worse than I used to think. I didn't try hard enough to help her. I didn't fight to get those videos and pictures taken down. When Casey brushed me off, I didn't push for her to let me help her. I could have done more, but I didn't. And now? *Fuck!*"

Mason put his head down. One hand wiped both eyes. He sniffed, fighting for control, then looked back up with haunted red eyes.

"I know how this is supposed to work. I'm supposed to confess, then make a 'contract' with myself, promising to do something by a certain date or you'll release this video. My promise is, 'To be a better man. To be the man my unborn kid deserves. To be a good husband to Jessica, if she'll have me.' But I'm not going to come back in here and tell you that I did it. You can't be a better man or a better father *once*. It's something you have to do for the rest of your life, every single day. So I guess you'll just have to release the video. I guess the world gets to see my confession."

John's attention piqued. Listening to Mason, he felt like someone had stepped on his heart. Tied his spine in a knot. When he reached up to wipe his eyes there were tears.

"Fuck me for letting it happen. Fuck me for being involved in that shitty prank, for not being smart enough to see it coming. And fuck me for not taking her by the wrists afterward, and forcing her to talk. I could have stopped what happened after that, and *fuck me* for not."

John swallowed. A new tear wicked from Mason's eye.

"Casey was a nice girl," he said, "and she didn't deserve to die."

TWENTY-THREE

The mood changed at the mention of Casey.

Okay, so there was some old, ugly shit here. Did that change Simon's readiness, now that he'd seen what this famous bitch had somehow dug up? Not for a second. He had to keep his eyes open. For now, Harper had them all in a vise. But as Simon had learned, several times now, there was always an escape.

"Casey?" Heidi was sheet white.

Simon craned forward and looked left. Wary as he was, he still wasn't going to miss the dynamic at the end of the table. Heidi, Taylor, and Ella had been Casey's best friends until the betrayal. Mason, surrounded by the trio, had been a different sort of friendly.

"So you know her." Harper sounded like she was reading a script.

"Of course we know her," Taylor said.

Bindi was a second behind everyone else. She slapped a palm to her open mouth. On Simon's right, John shifted subtly closer to Summer. A protective movement, drawing her near.

"It's interesting, this country," said Harper, sipping her wine. "And all the first world. So much is needed: food for the hungry, clothing for the cold, shelter for the homeless, books and computers for the underprivileged, wisdom for the ignorant ... the list goes on and on. I give wherever I can, and I still have too much. But money can never buy equality. Do you know why?"

"Because of politicians?" Melissa said.

"Because people don't *want* equality. They crave disparity. I've spent my life learning and seeking, and that's what I've discovered again and again. The universe wants entropy — for everything to be the same. Human beings are anti-entropy. If we redistribute wealth, it clumps up again. I can only conclude that we're happy where we are. Some like to rule, and others prefer to be governed."

"That's a great speech," Melissa said. "Have you considered giving it for the ACLU?"

Harper turned toward Melissa and smiled.

"Melissa Diane Lynch. 409 5th Street, number 617. You're too smart to keep a spare apartment key under your doormat, but the person who lived there before you wasn't quite as intelligent. He left one in the sconce — the one by 406, the one that flickers. Are you feeling better, dear? You never picked up your prescription at the Rexall down on 7th."

Melissa was obviously shocked, but she hid it quickly behind a disinterested mask. She said, "Stalker," smiled wryly, then looked to Imogen for a laugh. Imogen seemed not to hear her.

"I could recite your date of birth and social security number, your credit card numbers and bank accounts. Plenty to steal your identity if I wanted. But something tells me it's not an identity worth having. Would you care, if I made it impossible to be *you?* Or would you be relieved, even if it meant starting life again from the gutter?"

Melissa's face went ashen, her mouth formed a straight line. "Is that a threat?"

"Poor people ask such silly questions." Harper stood then slowly circled the table. "I know about you all." She nodded toward John. "Naturally, you're part of this. The curator of so many fascinating secrets, and not just your own ..." She winked.

Summer turned to John. "What's that mean?"

"I don't know," he said.

But Simon knew a lie when he heard one.

"People don't trust the rich because those without wealth tend to believe it goes hand-in-hand with dishonesty," Harper continued. "That's true in many cases, though nowhere near all of them. The real reason is a flip-flop of cause and effect. It's not that the rich *became rich through dishonest means,* which is what many people like to believe. It's more that once someone is wealthy, she suddenly *acquires the means to be dishonest.* A rich man doesn't become rich because he stole your wallet. But once he's rich enough, he can steal your wallet right in front of your face. Wealth doesn't always make people immoral. But if they choose to *become* immoral? Well. Having money makes it so much easier."

"What the hell are you talking about?" Noah asked.

"I am talking about the man with shoulder-length blond hair and permanent stubble, sitting in the doctor's waiting room with you on Tuesday, Noah."

Noah blinked. Simon could tell he was trying to play casual, but Harper had hit a bullseye. Ella turned to her husband. "You had a doctor's appointment this week?"

"I'm talking about the same man who seems to live next door to *you*, Mason, but who actually doesn't. Have you seen him? Instead of saying 'Hi,' he says 'Howdy.' You don't seem to like the way he winks at Jessica when she comes over, but you've probably decided he means nothing by it. Just a friendly neighbor with southern charm, however handsome though he may be. But he doesn't live in that house. His lease is there so he can come and go. So that he can observe."

Mason tried to respond but came up empty.

"Or maybe *you* know who I'm talking about, Imogen. The man who washed dishes in your restaurant for a few days before disappearing. Did you even know his name? He made fast friends with your sous chef, Alex. And he's been with you a long time, hasn't he?" Harper's smile ticked up, an eyebrow flinching. "Since you and Melissa parted ways, at least."

Melissa and Imogen looked at each other. Melissa said, "You've been spying on us?"

"No, of course not. I've been making movies. Don't you read the gossip rags? I'm always in there: heading back from the gym, stopping at Starbucks for a latte, walking my dogs, sitting out on my patio, more vulnerable than I like to believe. You'd think I never went to the set, given the paparazzi's eagerness to catch me being human. Strange the things they've found out about me, and the things I've managed to keep hidden."

She plucked her wine glass from the table and sipped again, tipping it toward Melissa as she concluded her answer.

"But my friend Gavin? He doesn't stay in LA like I do. He takes odd jobs to meet interesting people like you. He worked I.T. three cubicles down from you. He spends time at the salon where Ella probably mistook him for a gossipy woman's husband two months ago when she was getting her nails done at Sensation. Or maybe you thought he was gay?" She shrugged in Ella's direction, then took the opposite tack: "No, I think someone as bold as Ella Boyer knows a straight man on the prowl when she sees one. You're still a woman, after all."

Ella's face froze. Then she laughed while avoiding her husband's eye.

Harper paused in front of the French doors, just behind Teek and Melissa. Simon, now able to watch her without turning his head, studied Harper in the light of this curious turn of events.

She was stunning. Mesmerizing, really. If there was such a thing as "star quality," Harper had it: radiant without appearing to have tried. She would have been at home on the red carpet in her long dress and low neckline, small breasts held high in temptation. Dusty pink lipstick, fingernails painted to match. A sexy look on her — surprising, given that red would have been more predictable. The color was feminine and bold. Focal without screaming for attention.

Simon wondered, quite suddenly and unexpectedly, what it would be like to fuck her. She was Hollywood royalty these days, but even famous girls had to fuck *someone*, right? She put her panties on one leg at a time like the rest of them — and, Simon thought, peeled them off the same way.

Harper finished her half-circle, coming to the table's other end opposite her chair. With her wine glass still in her long white fingers, she looked like the hostess in a mystery, ready to toast. Which, Simon supposed, she damn near was.

"I've been bad, I know," Harper said with every eye on her. "My friend Gavin Cash, though excellent at digging up dirt, has not been my only accomplice over the last dozen years. There is an inequality in our society, and I have taken advantage. You believed in your privacy. You went through your life thinking that if nothing else, what you chose to keep inside was *safe* where you left it. But you were wrong. Secrets create guilt, and guilt leaves traces. I am a careful student of the tracts guilt leaves on us all — on all of *you*. With the right levers, anything can be unearthed. With enough money, anyone can be bought. Deny as you wish, but I know what

I've uncovered about each of you is true. I *earned* those secrets. And paid for them with my blood."

"You mean with dirty money," Summer mumbled.

Harper gave her a tiny little smile.

"I've uncovered so much more than I could fit into one little envelope for each of you, but the effort has been so very worth it. This meal, my friends, is exquisite. I have spared no expense on food or accommodations. The pan-seared Kona kampachi, for instance, is from the big island of Hawaii and had to be flown in on dry ice so it could be served sashimi rare. And this room? The Buvette costs four thousand dollars to reserve, just for the evening. But even that pales to the cost of Crave, which I had to build around it."

Simon searched his memory. He remembered reading about the opening party — Harper and her Hollywood peers. And yes, she had been referred to as an "owner."

"Wealth has bought me many things. Like my way into your private lives. And the loyalty of our serving staff. I encourage you not to waste your time trying to slip them a note. I bought a privacy jammer that ensures we won't be bothered by Doodads or other attempts at outside communication, and should you decide after tonight to tattle on me, I assure you that I have bought the benefit of the doubt with those who would pretend to hear you. Think about it for a second. Who would believe the famous Harper Knox would do such a thing as this? And if you insisted she did, who would believe *you?*"

"What if we *all* insisted?" Summer asked.

Nobody murmured assent; they were too focused on their terrible red envelopes.

"Then you will find that I've bought all the evidence in every direction."

She set her glass down. The table was stewing but silent.

"I have looked and looked for the answers I seek, and in that search I found so many things that people would otherwise choose to keep under their skin. With needles and razors, I have cut that skin back to take what is hidden. But it's never been enough. If I had found what I needed then you wouldn't be here tonight. I would have done what was necessary, not unlike taking the unpleasant steps to treat an infection. But unfortunately, one thing has eluded me. One big question without an answer."

She looked around the table, and this time her expression, though pleasant on the surface, struck Simon as menacing.

"At least one of you has that answer," Harper said. It was a prompt for guesses, but nobody spoke. *"What happened to Casey Davis?"*

Rumbling disquiet. No one spoke, exactly, but the room had its grammar. Bodies shifted. Fabric rustled as limbs sought solace. Heads wobbled, neighbor to neighbor. Simon's eyes, after the briefest of glances inside himself, turned outward. Harper didn't matter. The tells that would frame the balance in all that would follow weren't on her face. They were etched on the others, and Simon was watching them all.

Noah turned to Ella.

Melissa looked at Imogen and Imogen at Melissa.

Summer, across the table, was eyeing them both.

Heidi was watching Taylor. So was Ella. Taylor and Teek were both staring at Simon.

Bindi, across and to the right from Simon, looked at her thumbs while Heidi, at the table's far end, was obviously trying not to look at Bindi.

Most curious, Summer's husband was leaning forward, peering past Simon, Noah, and Ella. Staring at Mason — not overtly, but obviously enough. And it wasn't a curious or knowing stare like the others. No. It was watchful, antennae raised. As if he were bracing for what he thought might be coming.

"Casey killed herself," Taylor finally said. "She committed suicide. That's all there is to it."

"But why? *Why* would she have killed herself?"

"Because of a prank. You know the prank."

"Of course I know the prank," Harper said, still-pleasant, casting glances at Ella and Heidi with a glitter of accusation. "It seems an obvious answer, but I'm sure that it isn't the right one — or at least not *complete*. 'Because someone pranked and humiliated her,' I'm afraid, does not feel like reason enough for Casey to have ended her life. So what's missing? What is the link between the prank and her suicide? What, exactly, went wrong all those years ago?"

"Why do you care?" Noah asked. "Who is Casey to you?"

"That," Harper said, "is *my* secret."

Someone sipped soup. The noise was small and subtle, but

Simon turned toward it. Imogen, lips poised and eyes unmoved, as if nothing strange had occurred.

Harper paced. Her high-heeled shoes — pink, to match her fingernails and lipstick — counted time on the exotic tile floor.

"I knew Casey well," Harper said. "She was bold. Beautiful. Strong, both inside and out. It would take a lot to defeat her. I know the official story of her death, same as all of you. I've dug deepest there, sometimes reaching limits that even money couldn't buy my way past. I've hit one dead end after another ... but I can't shake the feeling that I've been a rat in a maze, with new avenues just inches away, hidden out of sight. It's a puzzle I can only see from one side. A picture that's visible only from above. *You* hold those missing pieces. *That's* why I've brought you here tonight, my friends: to usher what you've kept from the world into the light."

She met each person's gaze. Then:

"Someone here is responsible for Casey's death. I'm as sure of it as I live and breathe. But even with my considerable resources, I've never been able to figure out who it was, or which parts of the story are still hidden. Too much has gone into this evening for me to leave empty-handed. I don't like what I've been forced to do, but I've done what I have and will do what I must. Casey deserves it. *Her memory* deserves it."

A pause. Then stirring from the far side of the table, jarring the room's collective nerves.

"We're leaving," said Ella.

But nobody moved, including her. Teek coughed.

Beside Simon, John was still peering down the table at Mason.

"This proposition, I'm afraid, is all or nothing. If I don't learn the truth, then every secret in these envelopes will see the light of day. It doesn't matter if you stay or leave. It doesn't matter who you try to contact, or tell. I've thought of every contingency. You will find the staff here unhelpful and the authorities uninterested. Argue if you like, but it's only wasting time. Look at your secrets. Simon? Teek? Imogen? John? Are these things you're comfortable sharing? And for the rest of you, is the unknown a risk you're comfortable taking?"

Mumbling. Disquiet.

"Each of you," Harper said, her eyes growing still, "is guilty in your way. Deny it if you want. Shout at me, if you choose. But you are who you are because of the barbs that have grown under your skin. The sooner you believe that, the better."

Harper's face went from deadly to welcome. Turning toward the door leading from the Buvette she said, "But please. Take your time. I understand that such things can't be rushed and that revelations have a way of coming slowly. There is no hurry. This dinner should be savored."

Harper circled back to her seat at the head of the table. She sat, then resumed sipping soup with a napkin primly on her lap. A clock ticked. Clinking came from the kitchen below, trickling through the door where Donovan stood sentinel.

Come and go as you wish. But mind the first step. It's a doozy.

Three full minutes passed. Simon took in the seconds.

Heidi cleared her throat. Heads rose to greet her.

Harper looked politely expectant — ready, as hostess, only to serve.

"So ..." Her voice caught. Sound stopped. She swallowed and tried again. "So if one of us tells you who's responsible ... then we can go, and what's in these envelopes stays secret?"

"Of course," Harper said.

A half-second pause. Then she pointed. "Mason. It's *Mason's* fault that Casey killed herself."

Mason shot to his feet. The backward force of his legs knocked the chair flat, striking the tiles like a gunshot. His napkin fluttered like confetti, his face red, his hands coming up, striking the table's edge, making the silverware rattle.

Ella, beside him, jumped, hand rising toward her throat, protective.

Taylor's eyes went wide as Mason's — blue, Simon saw — seemed to flash crimson.

"*BULLSHIT!*" Mason shouted.

Heidi wasn't backing down, but she was backing *off;* she'd gotten to her feet and was clacking backward with an outstretched arm, looking to Harper and sighting on Mason's chest.

"I'm telling the truth! He was the last one with her!"

"Bull*shit!* I wasn't *close* to the last one with her! She wouldn't even talk to me after—!"

"After you had sex with her then tossed her aside like trash?"

Mason's head was rolling in a big, disbelieving circle. He looked to the ceiling as if sanity might be smiling down from above. "Oh, you motherfucking *bitch!*"

"You want to know what happened?" Heidi ranted. "*Mason* happened. He got with Casey and then just kind of—"

"First off, I didn't *have sex* with her. Second of all, you're conveniently forgetting that you and Ella—"

Heidi waved it away, trying to win by force of volume. "Who cares? She really liked you! Then after—"

"After *what*, Heidi? After you came rushing in, taking all those pictures and posting them to BayNet and she just fell into the corner crying and ..." His mouth twisted: the expression of someone who's finally seen too much stupidity and can no longer manage. He was too irritated to finish his old sentence, so he started a new one. "*You* set me up with her!"

"*Because she liked you!* That didn't mean you had to grope her and leave her!"

Mason turned to Harper.

"Do you know what she did? Set us up. I liked Casey and Casey liked me. *These two knew it—*" He pointed at Heidi and Ella. "—and told me exactly how to ask her out, then they kept bugging us about how things were going ..."

Noah turned toward Ella, confused.

"Oh, like we were bugging," Ella said.

"... and then at this party, they basically drove us out of the front room and into a bedroom, where they must have been watching through the window the whole time with fucking *cameras* like peeping toms ..."

"Ella?" Noah said.

Ella turned to Harper, her line of sight passing Simon like a bullet.

"It wasn't like that. We—"

"It was *exactly* like that!"

"I suppose *we* stuck your hand down her pants and took off her top?"

"Oh for ..." Mason sighed, then turned to Harper: "Just look for the videos. You'll see what they recorded and shared that night. *Nothing* dies on the internet. God knows I haven't been able to get away from them."

Harper, her face set: "I've seen the videos."

"Then you know. If they didn't set us up, why were they filming since before we even went into the room?"

"We saw you go into the room and *then* thought it'd be funny to record you!" Heidi snapped.

"And post it online?"

"We were kids! Teenagers do stupid things!"

Taylor was shaking her head, looking at her soup, her lips firm.

Heidi looked down at her, but said nothing.

Taylor said, "One of your best friends."

"Excuse me? What did you say?"

"You heard me, Ella. She was a friend. She trusted you! I told you not to get involved!"

Noah looked at Ella, then Taylor and finally Heidi. "What are you talking about?"

Taylor said, "Why don't you ask Summer?"

All heads swiveled to Summer, whose mouth peeked open, hands coming off her lap. For a pregnant second nobody spoke.

But Mason wasn't finished with Heidi. "You ..." *Sneer.* "You're just ... a *horrible* person."

Bindi, near Harper, said, "Now, wait just a minute."

Still talking to Heidi, Mason went on. *"Eleven. Fucking. Years."* He shook his head. "So maybe you were a selfish bitch in high school. I get it. I was a stupid jock. Was I hot for Casey? Sure. Did I know we should have gone slower, and that I was maybe pushing more than she wanted? Yeah. But you know what? At least in the last *eleven goddamn years* I figured that out. *You,* on the other hand—"

"Let's all just calm down," Bindi said.

"—didn't learn anything! You still think it was a harmless prank, don't you? How self-absorbed are you? You know what you need? *You* need a goddamn psychiatrist!"

For a moment, Heidi looked beaten. Then she said something that even Simon, who hadn't been within fifteen miles of the prank, saw clearly as a lie:

"You knew what we were doing, Mason."

Mason's whole head retracted: a tortoise pulling its neck into its shell. He blinked, unable to believe what he'd heard. "I *what?"*

Heidi was appealing directly to Harper. "He was in on it. Right, Summer?"

Simon turned his attention to Summer, then kept it there as

Heidi continued. He knew part but not all of this story. The thing inside Simon's envelope would end his career, embarrass him personally, and maybe even send him to prison, but right now he wanted nothing more than to know Summer's secret. Did her husband know what was on that card? She'd pulled it toward her, craning above it like a mother animal over cubs.

No, Simon thought, he didn't. And Summer looked like she would die to keep it that way.

"I ..." Summer stalled.

"How was I *in on it?*" Mason demanded.

"You said you wanted a sex tape." To the table: "He said he wanted us to film them so that he could—"

Mason lashed an arm across the table and snatched Heidi's envelope. She saw him too late; she'd backed up against the doors, standing with her finger *j'accuse*. Heidi dove to try and take the thing back before Mason could grab it, but one high heel caught in the dense rug while the other pushed forward, slipping, losing traction on its tiny footprint.

Heidi fell forward into the space between her vacated chair and Taylor's, hands up to break her fall, but finding nothing. Instead of arresting her descent, Heidi's fingers raked the table, the left one detouring on the recoil to upend her empty bowl.

There was a clatter of fine china immediately followed by a *thunk!* The meaty sound of Heidi's chin striking the table. She hit the floor with a swish of hair as Taylor bent to meet her.

Mason waited with an expression of concern just long enough for Heidi to stir. Once she sat up, with blood in her mouth but clearly alive, his vindictive expression returned.

He unwound the envelope's string, opened the flap, and plucked the creamy white card from its innards. His eyes ticked down, reading.

Then he said, smiling with his eyes on Heidi:

"Listen up, everyone. You're not going to *believe* this."

TWENTY-FOUR

February 8, 2029

Heidi lay flat on her back, covered in sweat, with only the kiss of hotel air conditioning between herself and the world.

Her breathing hadn't slowed; her legs were still spread; her nipples were still standing tall. This was the part where she was probably supposed to feel shame, but today Heidi only wanted a second round. Or a fifth, if she counted from this morning.

"Damn, Dylan."

It took the always-suave, always-composed Dylan Michaels a second to turn his head. He was standing in front of the desk, his backside as bare as hers. Dylan wasn't an astonishing physical specimen (he was almost forty, after all), but he'd done well as far as Heidi was concerned. Avoided the dad body, though maybe that's because he wasn't a father. It didn't matter. Most guys used that as an excuse, same for most women. Not Heidi, though.

She looked down her body. Stomach still flat, legs toned. Of course, she was lying down. Heidi hated the small pooch she got when sitting up. She'd dieted and exercised to distraction, even passed out once. Maybe you really did just get fatter and saggier by the year. Heidi didn't want to buy that answer, but still: the pooch. She'd done her best to never let Dylan see it.

"What?" he asked.

"I came like four times."

Dylan laughed. He had a deep voice with just the right amount of grit. "You come easy."

"Maybe you should get back over here if it's so easy." She rolled toward his turned back, then caught a glimpse of herself in the mirror beside the dresser. Her boobs looked perkier if she sat a bit more upright.

"Do you think I'm 21 or something?" He turned and his penis swung like a pendulum. "How many bullets do you think I have in the chamber?"

Heidi made a pouty face. It vanished when she saw what he'd gone to the table to do. She flopped onto her back, feeling like she'd taken a punch to her big fat gut.

"I hate when you do that," she said.

"What?"

"You know what."

Dylan pulled on his pants. They were suit pants, because officially speaking, he was here on a business trip. But the only business he ever transacted on his "trips" was the kind that put his marriage at risk.

He climbed onto the bed beside Heidi, spooning up beside her. She turned away.

"Don't be like that."

"I told you how much I hate it."

"Look, Heidi," he said in his maddeningly sexy voice. "I'm not playing dumb. I honestly don't know what you're talking about."

Heidi considered freezing him out. But there was no point. One of the things she loved (well, *lusted*) about Dylan was how few shits he gave. He was a rogue, a lone wolf. He made his own rules and didn't play sensitive. There was something delicious about that.

She rolled back. "Your ring. After we have sex, you always go for your wedding ring."

Dylan held up his left hand with his fingers splayed, considering the gold band. Heidi felt another small punch. It was like he was trying to rub it in her face.

"I don't want to lose it. She thinks I never take it off."

"Then *don't* take it off."

He laughed again. "Baby, I'm left-handed. You know where that ring would go if I *didn't* take it off. Maybe Laura and I have lost the spark, and maybe she's turned into an ice queen. Hell, maybe I don't even love her anymore. But that's crossing the line, don't you think?"

Heidi shrugged. Her arms had crossed over her chest.

"Besides, it's loose." He bent over her, tugging the ring with his right hand to demonstrate how easily it moved. "You want me to lose it in there?"

"You're gross."

"Then you'd find it a week later. You'd be like a gumball machine, dropping prizes."

Heidi shoved him, but she was already starting to laugh against her will. Fucking Dylan. He had an infuriating way of defusing anger with humor. But Heidi always laughed. She was trying to hide it now, but too late; Dylan smelled blood in the water. He was on her now. The scent of his skin, the one-day stubble against the hollow of her neck as he egged her on.

He stopped and propped himself up on one elbow. Heidi sighed and shook her head, taking him in. So handsome: strong jaw, piercing eyes, an excellent mane, and a smile that never failed to melt her.

She said, "I can't help feeling like I'm a bad person."

"You're not a bad person."

"I'm *having an affair with a married man.*"

"... whose marriage was over long ago," he said, running fingers along her arm, soft like whispers. "We've been through all of this."

"It still feels wrong."

"Then end it."

Heidi looked up at Dylan. He'd said it as an offer, not a threat, but they'd been through this plenty. She *couldn't* end it. That's something Dylan seemed to understand that her psychiatrist didn't. In Bindi's office, they'd batted the issue back and forth: Heidi was compulsive; she tended to latch onto an addiction as a surrogate for facing her real issues. She shopped; sometimes she stole; in the past, she'd smoked.

Now she had this affair. All were secondary problems that Bindi said Heidi had manufactured to draw her attention away from the self-work that needed doing, like a magician's flourish to distract the eye.

Of course she'd been seeing Bindi before her affair with Dylan began, and Bindi had seen it coming. She said the man sounded like a predator: that Dylan wasn't a smooth-talker so much as an eagle-eye for easy pussy. Men like him could *smell* women who made bad choices.

He knows you're damaged, Heidi. That's why he's with you.

But what did Bindi know?

She exhaled, her eyes leaving Dylan's.

"Look," Dylan said. "I've told you everything, but I'll tell you again. Laura and I met young. She was a different person, and so was I. We used to do all sorts of things together, but now she just sits around the house and complains. Nothing is good enough for her. She doesn't work. The trips I take?" He smiled, realizing the irony. "The trips I *actually* take, I mean. I take them because I get extra pay — 'conference pay,' my company calls it. I don't even like to travel, but I have to. Laura refuses to bring a cent into the household, and we live near the coast, so not exactly cheap. Know what I mean?"

"She sounds horrible." This wasn't new, but Heidi wanted to say the words anyway. Probably to convince herself.

"Exactly. You're not a horrible person. *She* is." Dylan kissed her neck, twice. "And we never have sex."

"You poor man."

His hand found her breast.

"I have to beat off all the time."

"Too much information," Heidi said.

"I'm getting rug burn. From hairy palms."

"You're so immature."

Dylan's hands continued to move. They felt good. Perfect. He was hitting her spots and saying all the right things. They had never, to her recollection, had an argument. If there was an owner's manual out there for Heidi Blanchard, Dylan had read it twice. More often than not, she felt like the man was inside her head. If he *was* a predator, he was a damn good one. Even when Heidi knew she should end this thing, his words and non-arguments made it impossible. It was like hypnosis. Like giving in to all that old pain, and welcoming the insanity.

Heidi sat up, suddenly distracted. "What time is it?"

"Why?"

"There's a flash sale at *Tres Chic* at one."

"You're going to *Tres Chic? Now?*"

But Heidi had already risen from the bed and was pawing through her weekender bag for her Doodad while Dylan reclined on one elbow, amused. He looked toward the nightstand clock, which Heidi had somehow missed. It read 12:51. "You're a little under-dressed."

"It's online."

"Well, by all means, don't you dare miss it."

Now that her breathing and heartbeat had returned to post-orgasmic normal, Heidi felt the chill. She reached for a hotel robe that Dylan had draped over the dresser's edge, but he'd set his bag atop it. She tugged the robe and sent his bag to the floor. Dylan laughed. He claimed he adored her clumsiness, but it was just another thing about herself that Heidi hated.

"Dammit." She stooped to scoop up the bag. But it was open on the wrong end and its contents spilled across the carpet. Dylan laughed harder.

"Don't laugh at me."

"You make it so easy."

She tried again, righted Dylan's bag, and shoved items in without regard for shape or order. The sale was happening promptly at one.

You're deflecting, Bindi would have said.

But what did Bindi know? There'd been a suicide on her watch at Bayshore. And she was always late for their sessions. Bindi had, in a rare breach of personal lines, told Heidi that she wanted kids. Yet, she didn't *have* any. Who was the screwup now? Maybe Bindi's husband had gotten a secret vasectomy. Dylan had. He'd shown Heidi the scar. They'd laughed about Stupid, Unaware Linda together.

Hands arrived to help her. "You have such great dexterity."

"Shut up," Heidi said.

"I've got it."

"No," she insisted, "I'll clean my own mess."

"It's fine."

"I know it's fine. I—"

Something flew from a pile of clothes. Dylan's wallet landed on the floor with a thump, its innards jarring out like paper tongues.

Except that Dylan's wallet was on the dresser. She could see it from her spot on the floor.

"You have two wallets?" she asked, looking between them.

"Uh. Yeah."

Heidi reached for the wallet but Dylan took it as more paper fell out. Strange place for a wallet, buried in his clothes.

"Why?"

"One is a decoy." He put on a smile, smaller than his usual. "In case I'm robbed."

"Who carries a decoy wallet?"

"Smart people."

Heidi reached for the papers still on the carpet. A few were receipts. The stiff one was a business card. Dylan plucked it all from her fingers before Heidi saw its entirety, but she did see VOICE TALENT below the name: *Donald* somebody.

She looked back at Dylan as he stuffed the papers back into his wallet. Decoy or actual? Heidi was curious how that system worked.

"Are you looking to hire a voice actor?" she asked him.

"Maybe," he said, uncharacteristically flustered.

"Why?"

"Something at work," he said. "For a promo video."

"Wouldn't a video be a *regular* actor?"

"There's a radio promotion, too."

Heidi shrugged. She went for her Doodad. Four minutes left. She squinted at Dylan. "Did you get that idea from me? For the voice actor?"

"Yeah."

She tapped around on her Doodad, bringing up *Tres Chic's* webpage. "Whenever you talk to the guy, ask him."

"Ask him what?"

"About voice work."

"That's what we're hiring him for."

"You know what I mean."

Of course he did. Dylan had a voice like silk. Whipped chocolate on devil's cake. He'd make an excellent voice actor, and the occasional gig would be a lot easier than taking extra business trips if the Michaels family needed money. She'd mentioned the idea to Dylan the second she'd heard "voice actor" was a legitimate career, but he'd never bitten. And for some reason, he got weird whenever she mentioned it.

"It's supposed to be good money."

"I know," he said. "You keep bringing it up."

"You could fit voice gigs into your spare time."

"No thanks."

"It wouldn't hurt to ask."

He cleared his throat, then pointed at the clock. "Time to shop."

One last look at Dylan, before the spending began. "My therapist's husband is a voice actor."

And Dylan replied, "So you've told me."

TWENTY-FIVE

The table was silent. Melissa barked laughter. Mason was still at the front of the room, feeling his smug smile melting like wax in the sun.

"You're kidding." Imogen was smiling, trying not to laugh with Melissa. "Ohmygod, that's just too amazing. Is that what it really says?"

Donovan took a step forward. Mason saw the movement from the corner of his eye, his hand moving to something either on his belt or behind his back. He couldn't turn to look. His eyes kept returning to the cream-colored card — the one he'd snatched from Heidi's envelope. On its embossed face was beautiful script that looked like it'd been written by a master calligrapher:

You are having an affair with Bindi Bridges's husband.

And Imogen, rustling for a while before realizing her purse was behind her, pulled out her Doodad and said, "I am so Instagramming this."

"Who still uses Instagram?" Melissa asked. "Do you have the pizza rat video on there, too?"

"Pizza rat?" repeated Teek. "What's—?"

Bindi rose from her chair and came at Heidi like an Olympic sprinter.

She caught the younger woman in a tackle; there was no other word. Mason, who'd spent many formative years on the gridiron and had seen many bone-crushing hits, didn't envy Heidi. Bindi probably only weighed about one-thirty, but she knocked Heidi back with a linebacker's thrust. Heidi, who had to be lighter still, was momentarily airborne.

Hands clawed at Heidi's throat. Mason, still in his idiot mannequin stance, couldn't move. He'd caused this, but was too paralyzed to stop it.

Taylor and Teek were on Bindi, trying to pull her away. But Heidi was fighting back: kicking, trying to swipe at her eyes and grab Bindi's shoulder-length hair.

It took both Teek and Taylor to tear them apart, with Noah, Simon, and John rushing past Mason once the worst was over.

Imogen had her Doodad out, but the thing didn't seem to be working — another techno-trick by their elegant host.

"You bitch! You fucking bitch!" Bindi yelled.

She writhed as Teek held her, Taylor standing between the women like a blockade.

Bindi was an animal. Seeing it, pieces fell into place for Mason. She wasn't reacting in the moment; Bindi was reacting after hours of simmering. He remembered so many of her answers. Everyone's reasons for being at Crave were public knowledge now, except for Bindi's. She was waiting for someone. Bindi had known that her husband was cheating. She'd come here to find out who it was.

"Calm down!" Noah shouted.

"You fucked my husband?"

Heidi, getting to her feet and keeping her distance, looked shocked. Apparently the card had been a surprise to Heidi as well. How was that possible, if it was her secret?

"Please," Harper said, so perfectly calm. "Let's be civilized."

When nothing happened and Bindi continued to shout, she gestured for Donovan. He approached holding the thing he must have been pulling from his belt: a zip-tie like police used.

Bindi saw it coming and kicked, catching Donovan in the groin.

He crumpled.

"I ..." Heidi cried out. *"Bindi!* It's not true!"

Bindi's lips were tight, her face hateful. "Sure. Sure it's not."

Heidi wiped at her mouth. It was still bleeding from when she'd struck the table, and thanks to Bindi's assault she might soon have an egg on her head.

"I've told you all about the guy I'm with! His name is—"

"Dylan Michaels," Harper interrupted.

The women stopped.

Then Harper said, "Or ... Donald Dawson."

She touched a screen on the wall that before now, Mason hadn't noticed. The thing was so carefully integrated into the panels that it vanished when off, and only now came to life. Onscreen, the room saw a passport-style shot of a handsome man in a suit and tie.

"Dylan. Donald. One and the same, it seems. My friend Gavin even learned he carries a second driver's license. But on the positive side, Bindi, it seems your fears are unfounded. Donald isn't impotent. He's just disinterested." A small laugh. "Or *spent*, as it were."

Donovan was inches from Bindi, still holding the zip tie though he hadn't moved to use it. *You be cool and I'll be cool,* his body language seemed to say. Bindi stared at Heidi. At the screen. At Heidi. Her chest was rising and falling in long, steady rhythms.

"Bindi ... she's lying."

Harper tapped the wood beside the screen. "Who is this, Bindi?"

"My husband. Donald."

"And Heidi? Who is this?"

She ignored Harper and spoke directly to Bindi.

"I didn't know. How could I know? He lied to me. He lied about his name, about his wife's name ..."

Bindi bit her lip. "So this is just a coincidence? You're telling me you're totally innocent?"

"I told you I was with someone. And that he was married! But I swear, I had *no idea* he was your husband!"

Imogen was oscillating a finger between the two women. "Are you two ...?"

Bindi said, "I don't believe you."

"You don't—!"

"You lie," Bindi spat, lips peeling back to her teeth. "You do it for fun. You prey on men to get them to buy you things."

"You said *he* was the predator!"

"Indeed." Harper tapped the screen again.

A clumsy shot of a hotel room. Heidi was on all fours with

Donald/Dylan behind her, working the bones. The facial expressions and soundtrack could win an Oscar. Maybe a Grammy.

Heidi went red, then rushed to block the screen. Sounds continued from behind her. She glared at Harper. "You *filmed* us?"

"No. But Donald did." Harper leaned closer to Heidi and whispered, low enough that Mason was just able to hear. *"He broke into his wife's computer and read your file. That's how you met. Isn't it romantic?"*

Bindi had slumped back against the table, hands covering her face. The fury was gone, replaced by what had been beneath it all along: Sorrow. Hurt. Worthlessness. And betrayal.

Heidi touched the screen. The video paused, and the sounds ended.

"Bindi. I'm sorry. If I'd had *any* idea ..."

A deep, rattling breath. Bindi kept her face covered. "Fuck you."

"I didn't know!"

Sobs beat Bindi to pieces. She refused to look up, or move.

"Bindi ..." Heidi looked around the room for help but found none. Nobody felt sympathy for the cheater. And it seemed that she was Bindi's client, so her betrayal had layers. "I never would have—"

Bindi came alive all at once. With tears painting her face, she ripped Taylor's half-empty water glass from the table and threw it at Heidi's head. Her aim was deadly; Heidi barely dodged and the thing detonated against the screen. Donald and Heidi's doggy adventures vanished as the still shattered into a dull gray.

Donovan grabbed Bindi by the arm when she went for Heidi again, this time dragging her to the table's end. He eased her down in a seat beside Harper. Three waiters came through the door, holding nothing, looking like well-dressed escorts. As Bindi fought Donovan, half-shouting and half-crying, the waiters took positions around the room. One ushered a shocked-looking Heidi back to her seat, discreetly excusing himself for picking loose shards of glass from her hair. Another circled behind Mason and righted his chair. He then held it out and tapped Mason on the shoulder. "Sir? If you'd prefer to sit?"

The zip of plastic, the quickly ceased rattle of chair legs against the tile floor as Bindi, now fastened to her seat, seemed to surrender. She wept quietly. Before leaving, Donovan bent over and gently freed her right hand. So she could eat, of course.

The waiters circled as everyone took their seats. One swept up the broken glass and mopped the water while another made swift work of a tablecloth swap at the table's far end. The third brought Heidi a fresh setting to replace the one that had hit the floor.

The room again fell into silence. With no clue what came next and Harper resuming her meal, unsure eyes scanned uncertain faces. Eventually, what remained of the soup was sipped. Wine was drunk. Dinner was enjoyed by all.

Imogen looked to Harper. "So ... you own this place?"

Harper nodded. Imogen took another spoonful of soup.

"The food is delicious," she said.

TWENTY-SIX

Noah finally gave in and finished eating his soup. It was a long five minutes — proof that although time flew when you were having fun, the inverse was also true. Noah spent his eternity waiting for something more to happen: for Bindi, now restrained and one-armed, to come at Heidi using her bound chair as a weapon. Or for Heidi to seek revenge, deciding she'd been beaten up enough for an affair that was somehow accidental while also fully disclosed. Perhaps Harper would insist the rest of them start opening their envelopes, or announce more private tidbits that her pal Gavin had uncovered about her guests.

Or (and Noah's money was on this one) Simon might snap.

On some level, Simon seemed to be clinging to a belief that not only would he leave tonight without incurring Harper's wrath, but that he'd do so with his Kagen deal intact. Teek might have spent high school with his nose faithfully up Simon's crack, but Simon had always struck Noah as an alpha dickhead.

It didn't matter what Casey used to say about Simon. She'd seen him as a friend, but Noah had never stopped seeing Simon as the kind of guy who got girls like Casey, and himself as the kind who got stuck in the Friend Zone.

He kept his head down, eyes glancing up. Everyone around the table seemed to be doing the same thing: feigning civility because soon it would end. What happened between Bindi and Heidi had, by unspoken mutual consent, been forgotten by all. Same for their captivity. They were thirteen people eating dinner. No big deal.

"Ella." Noah said it quietly. The room seemed to demand it.

Taylor and Teek glanced up, then down again. Noah suppressed a flicker of envy. Something large and awkward had seemed to pass between Taylor and Teek not long before coming to Crave, but they were happy as a couple. Still together. They'd been holding hands, even if it seemed to be serving a needed illusion. He remembered when he and Ella had been like that, when times were better. Or *did* he?

He looked Ella's hand. She saw the glance — having looked up after hearing her name — and looked likewise at Noah's. Neither flinched.

"What?" Ella said.

"I didn't know you were in on that Casey thing."

"I wasn't."

"Mason said you were."

Voices too high. Mason seemed to hear his name, then pretended he didn't.

"It's nothing," Ella said, eyes on her empty bowl.

Noah wasn't going to drop it. "What happened with that prank?"

"You know what happened."

"I mean ... with you."

"What do you mean, 'with me'?"

Ella was feigning obliviousness. Her usual defense mechanism (well, one that didn't come with a bottle). She treated life like a toddler. If she covered her eyes, maybe Trouble would go away.

"Did you trick Casey into going out with Mason?"

"No."

Noah waited, not speaking.

"She *wanted* to go out with him," Ella whispered low enough that Mason wouldn't hear.

Then she turned away, drawing her usual wall. Noah knew it well. He had a stronger marriage to it than he did to Ella. He exchanged hellos with the wall every morning. In the evenings, he sat beside the wall while they watched her shows. He slept next to the wall in a California king.

Sometimes, Noah thought about finding ways to break through

the wall. But he rarely bothered. She'd stopped hiding her pill-popping from him, going so far lately as to more or less rub it in his face: it was *his* fault she was fucked-up, *Noah's* fault she was sad. He was sure she was cheating, too, and that might be a problem if they had more than the occasional angry fuck during which Noah's role was to be a punching bag for her purged aggression. It's not like he was going to stop the sex; Ella still turned him on even when they hated each other. *Especially* when they hated each other. But how long would it be before she started rubbing the cheating in his face, too? There'd been two clear signs, though it'd taken him long enough to see them for what they were.

More silence. Another long five minutes.

Harper broke the quiet, surprising her guests enough that Bindi and Summer jumped in their seats. "Mason. Perhaps you'd like to tell us *your* side of the story?"

Mason seemed surprised, but he replied plainly enough. "What story?"

"Heidi says you were the last one with Casey before her suicide."

Mason laughed with the self-assurance of someone who knows his truth is beyond obvious. "Yeah. Right."

"You weren't?"

"Of course not. Ask anyone." He looked around the table. "Simon. The senior party was at your house. Was I even there?"

"I have no idea," Simon said.

"Well, I wasn't. And that was the day after the prank. She didn't kill herself until ... what? Like a week later."

Harper nodded. "She died the following Saturday. May 26th."

"Right. And as to the party, Casey ..."

Mason stopped. *Today* was May 26th.

Acid realization rained on the table. Noah had no umbrella.

Mason shook it off. "Casey went to the party. I didn't. So which one of us was stronger about the whole thing?"

"What the hell does that prove?" Heidi asked.

Harper looked to Heidi. "We've heard your side already. Along with the ... *consequences.*"

Heidi touched her swelling lip.

"Mason?" Harper said.

"I'm sure she talked to a bunch of people at that party. But not me. I stayed home. I was embarrassed, yeah, but mostly I heard Casey *was* going to the party and figured she wanted some space. She wouldn't return my calls. *That's* why I stayed home. I never saw her after. Not for the entire week before she died."

"She wouldn't talk to you at all?" Harper asked.

"Just a few words here and there. She was acting weird. And ..." He paused, and his expression grew curious.

"And what?"

"She sounded ... *apologetic?*" Mason seemed confused by his words. "I know how that sounds, but that's what I kept thinking after everything was over. It was like she was sorry for being ... you know ... non-communicative. Like she'd messed with me instead of me ... well, I didn't *mess* with her, but you know what I mean."

Ella laughed. "Right. That's convenient. Is that the story you've been telling yourself? That you *didn't* drive her to do it?"

His eyes sharpened. Sitting just past Ella, Noah got a secondary blast of the hate that Mason stared her way.

"Did you really just say that?" Mason demanded. "*You?*"

Bodies perked up, waiting for what he would say next.

"Fuck you, Mason."

"Ah. Yes. Fuck me. It was *my* fault. Because I liked her. Is that the bullshit that's been spinning around in *your* head for the last decade? Maybe we moved too fast. But she didn't fucking *kill herself* because we got heavy, Ella. She did it because *you* recorded it and shared it with the whole school!"

A dagger. Noah had seen the video of Mason and Casey together, of course, plus the photos. He'd pretended he hadn't — that he'd heard the rumors and gotten the notifications but erased it right away. But secretly, Noah had watched that video. He'd also saved a copy. Same for every guy at Bayshore, and half the girls. They'd been teenagers. Walking hormones. And as much as Noah believed he'd loved Casey Davis, and as guilty as he'd felt with every view of that video, he'd still done it. Love and lust, at age 17, were awful hard to pry apart.

Noah turned to his wife. "You filmed it?"

Ella mumbled, "You knew that."

But no, he hadn't. Until fifteen minutes ago, he hadn't even known that Ella was involved. He'd known about the prank, and that given the way slut-shaming worked, Mason had "made an excellent score." That had hurt his conflicted heart to the breaking point at the time: watching Casey suffer alone, refusing consolation from everyone. He'd finally had enough, called and called and barged his way over to her house after her fifth day out of school. He'd seen her the morning before she did it and left feeling that she was bruised but strong. After she took her life, his conflicted heart had been shredded, pulped, and made into some cruel asshole's juice. But this? Finding out that he'd given Casey's memory a final fuck-you by marrying one of the people responsible? It was too much.

"Ella ..." Noah said, trying to touch her, to believe the impossible.

She snapped her hand away and hissed low: *"It's none of your goddamn business."*

"Tell us your side, Mason," Harper repeated.

But Mason shook his head. "No disrespect, Miss Knox, but fuck *you*, too."

The table waited. Then:

"I'll tell you his side," Bindi said.

Harper looked to her right. She seemed pleasantly surprised. Mason saw what was coming and started to protest, but then let it drop, resigned.

"I was at Bayshore for one year, and I faced one suicide. Great record, right?" Bindi tried to smile, but with her mascara still smeared from her dustup with Heidi and the subsequent breakdown, the effect was tragic.

Her smile faltered. "It's haunted me. Because if I'd paid more attention, maybe I could have helped her before she did it." She looked at Mason. "I'm sorry. What you shared with me was confidential, but ..." She let the thought hang.

Then, without approval or rejection, Bindi told the story of Mason's visit to her office. The old tale was a fresh wound. But Mason's story, told through Bindi, held nasty surprises as well.

Ella and Heidi, coming to Mason. The suggestion of a bouquet of white flowers, with a single red bloom in the center.

The hookup. The pressure. The way they'd nudged Casey and Mason alone.

Then all those girls, rushing in laughing while the lovers had been half-clothed, taking photos and video from the moment they'd entered the room. Sharing it online, right in front of Casey's crying face.

Noah made fists. He watched Bindi but felt Ella on his other side, behind his back. He refused to look at her. To glance back even when Heidi piped up to defend herself.

If he turned, he'd see Ella. And then he'd snap.

"Just over a week after the prank, Casey committed suicide. Mason kept calling, trying to make an appointment. It was the end of my first school year and I could barely keep my head above water. I put him off, but he was persistent. Said he was worried. Of course I'd seen the prank. And yeah, it was embarrassing. Sick, that girls—" Bindi looked past Noah to Ella and Heidi, but again Noah wouldn't let himself turn. "—would do something like that to a friend, just for some sorority bullshit."

"Sorority bullshit?" John asked.

Bindi laughed. "Yeah. It was a rush prank. Sorry: 'pre-rush.' Ask your wife."

John turned to Summer, his mouth a straight line. Summer, clasping her hands in her lap and staring straight ahead, shivered and pretended not to notice. John seemed about to speak, but Bindi continued.

"I knew Mason was worried about Casey, and his part in all of it. But I figured, 'Whatever; it's just a prank; it'll blow over.' I'd met Casey before. She seemed like a strong girl. I didn't want to sweep it under the rug, but I just didn't have any time. So I kept telling Mason: 'Monday. I can see you next Monday.' But her parents and the police announced that night — *after* Mason and I spoke, and I'd given him what I thought was solid advice — that Casey was dead, and had been since Saturday night."

Bindi sniffed. She seemed about to cry. Noah admired her. He felt like crying himself. Crying and punching and shouting. Fingernails cut his palms. He let them bleed.

"Thank you," Harper said to Bindi. "And thank you, Mason, for trying so hard to get that appointment."

Mason said nothing. Slowly, all heads turned toward him, and Noah finally had to rotate to see what they were looking at.

"I didn't call you," Mason told Bindi.

"What?"

"I didn't call you to make an appointment. I just came in that

Monday." He shrugged, looking to several people around the table, including Noah. "Why would I call when I was right there in the school and could have just dropped by?"

Confused silence. Then Bindi said, "You called the guidance office. Like five times."

"I'm sorry. I didn't. I should have, but I didn't have the guts."

Eleven years had passed. Memories got muddled. But she'd immortalized those calls, same for Mason's too-late visit and her guilt. She'd patched all three things together, but Noah could see the truth on their faces. Mason was right, but so was Bindi.

"Then who kept calling me, worried about Casey?" Bindi asked.

Noah looked around the table and ended on Ella, the face he'd been avoiding. He tried to see remorse. To see the woman he married. The mother of his children. But he could only see the girl with the camera.

Ella faced her husband, saw the accusation in his eyes, and deflected like always.

"Let me guess," she said to Noah. "Was it *you*, loverboy?"

Poison water boiled. Noah could only see rage.

That and the big red envelope in front of Ella.

Did it say inside what he thought it surely must?

He reached. Ella saw it coming and beat him. She clasped the envelope to her chest, pressing it between her breasts as if trying to show it the time of its life.

Noah came at her again.

Ella stood; Noah stood; Mason and Simon stood with hands raised, waiting to intervene.

At the door (a blur to Noah), Donovan flinched a step but came no further.

"Why are you so fucking surprised, Noah? *I've* always gone after what *I* wanted."

She had, Noah knew.

Of course she had.

TWENTY-SEVEN

April 23, 2029

She's terrible. And mean, said one voice inside Noah's head.

But not always, insisted a second voice. *She's still capable of sweetness. Deep down, she's still the same Ella. It's fear and insecurity that's twisted her. She doesn't want to be mean. You only see her worst parts when you're angry. Get past that. Take the high road. Understand rather than condemn her. Then you'll know that you still love her.*

You've stayed with her long enough. She'll never change. She only gets worse. The voice now had less spite and more logic — a tone Noah could respect. *It's not about you. If it were about you, then maybe you could change, and Ella could change, and you could change together. But it's not about you, so there's not a damn thing you can do. Ella's shit is Ella's shit. Unless you want to get in there with a Freudian jackhammer, nothing is going to improve. It's over. Make a clean break. And move on.*

And it was true. These were the thoughts that kept him up at night, usually between 3 am and when he finally collapsed again at 4:30ish. He'd been on the brink of suggesting a divorce for nearly a year, but fear of her reaction kept him paralyzed.

Their beautiful twin boys, James and Diego, needed their family.

In other words, said the hectoring voice, *you're a coward.*

Noah looked down at his hands, clasped lightly in his lap. There were four other men in the waiting room, all middle-aged. One was reading a print book, two were checking their Doodads, and one — the guy across from Noah, slightly to the left — seemed to be sitting with his thoughts. No one made eye contact. Every man in here knew what the other dudes had probably just done in that little back room, and why they were waiting now.

A door opened. The nurse called one of the older man back.

The door closed and Noah wanted to run.

He pulled out his Doodad, then went to Ella's LiveLyfe profile. He always felt trepidation, as if he'd learn something new. It was ludicrous, but the feeling was there. He browsed her pictures with a wary heart, as if he'd run across vacation shots of her with another man. He rolled through her interactions half-expecting to see her in a public dialogue with a pharmacist or a drug dealer. He scrolled through her timeline, wondering if the person on LiveLyfe was more honest than the one who came home.

My husband is such a douchebag, He expected to read. Or: *Thinking about offing myself. Any tips?*

But instead of finding vitriol and wrongdoing, Noah saw something that made him sit forward, elbows on his knees, holding the Doodad with both hands as he focused on the small screen. A shared memory: a photo first posted back in 2021, an open expanse of water behind her and Noah. A thick, white-painted railing at their waists. The cruise they'd taken with her family to celebrate her parents' 30th wedding anniversary.

He zoomed in. How old had they been in this photo? 22, 23 ... something like that? His face was different than he remembered. Seeing himself in the mirror every day had tricked him into believing that he hadn't changed. But they both had. He was smiling. Ella, too. He pinched out. They were even holding hands, and not yet married.

Noah had thought the trip sounded like a terrible idea. Cruises were for the elderly. He'd met his future in-laws, but a week-long dose would be murder. She'd talked him into it anyway, persuading him through conversation and sex. Her glee finally tipped him. The Casey wound had still been fresh. Real happiness had been as rare then as it was now, but at least it existed.

Noah distinctly remembered thinking: *I should do this for her.*

He was surprised to learn that she'd been doing it for *him*. Ella had never gotten along with her parents, but she and Noah were kids; they couldn't afford a vacation. The cruise was her loophole: a way to spend time with her fiancé without breaking the bank. So they'd made a game of it. How long could they go without seeing her parents on the ship? They'd lounged on the less-popular sun deck, swum in the less-popular pool, and chosen on-ship restaurants instead of hitting the dining hall. The trip had been sunshine and sex. Their past had stayed on-shore.

That had been their peak. Without the stress of life, before kids, with the ghost of Casey lifted from Ella's shoulders, at least for a while. Sitting in the waiting room and clinging to his Doodad, Noah desperately longed for those gone days that he could never have again.

He scrolled to Ella's new caption: *So long ago.*

He sighed and stowed the Doodad. Then, inspired, he tapped a text to Ella. Maybe he could try to be the bigger man. Life made her how she was. She hadn't asked for this any more than he had.

Coming home soon. Then after considering, he added, *Hope you had a good day.*

Ella's reply: *Buy stamps.*

The door opened again.

"Noah Boyer?"

Noah followed. The nurse led him into an office and instructed him to sit in one of two wooden chairs opposite a large desk with a blotter on top. Noah made himself comfortable as the nurse stepped out with a promise that Doctor McGuire would be in shortly.

McGuire entered a few minutes later, a big smile on his bearded face. They exchanged pleasantries. The doctor took the chair behind the desk, opened an envelope, examined a single sheet inside it, then set the paper aside.

"How are you, Noah?"

"Fine. You?"

McGuire leaned back. "Did you ever think how weird it is that this is the way we talk to people? I'm your doctor, so it makes sense that I'd ask how you're doing. But you asking me back? I appreciate it, but nobody really cares, do they?"

"I care."

"Well, thank you, Noah. To answer your question, I'm well. My wife's azaleas finally started blooming." McGuire laced his hands behind his head. "Most people don't care. But still, everyone always asks how the other is doing after being asked themselves."

"My wife doesn't."

"Ah. Yes." The doctor shuffled papers. "How is Ella?"

"She's okay."

"Did she share the results of her tests with you?"

"She said everything was normal."

"Yes. Ella's file says it's okay to discuss this with you, so I can confirm that there's nothing in her tests or exam to suggest that she will have any trouble at all getting pregnant again."

"That's good," Noah said.

But was it? He and Ella staying together felt 50/50 at best. On the question of *Should we have more children?* Noah came closer to 25/75 in favor of *No.*

Ella had the occasional mania to accompany her depression. There'd been a rare manic day months ago when she had decided that another child could save them. When sullen, it didn't even seem that Ella liked him, and yet she wanted another kid? Noah hadn't understood. Still, she'd already been off birth control for six months by the time she told him, and by now it was a grudge. Every time they had angry sex, Ella seemed to resent it if she didn't pee a plus sign.

"Yes. Good." McGuire seemed about to say something else, but then stopped, clicked his pen, and began tapping it button-side-down on the desk. "How are things at home, Noah? If that's not too intrusive."

"They're good."

"Stressful at all?"

"Well, you met Ella. She has her moods. Why? Does stress impact fertility?"

"It can. Ironically, certain kinds of stress can make men *more* fertile. Some deep biological mechanism insists they procreate to spread their genes, because a threat to their line is on the horizon." The doctor was still smiling, only less so. He looked at the folder. "And how are your kids? Twin boys, right? What were their names?"

"James and Diego."

"And they're how old now?"

"Six."

"Fun age. Remind me, how long have you and Ella been married?"

"Seven years."

"Exactly six and exactly seven?"

Noah laughed. "Fine; you caught us. Ella was pregnant when we got married. But it wasn't a shotgun wedding. We didn't know she was pregnant until after she asked me."

"She proposed to you?"

"Does the fact that I didn't do the proposing lower my sperm count?" An uncomfortable laugh, first Noah then McGuire. "Why are you asking all of this?"

"How long have you been *together* with Ella? Not just dating. I mean 'seriously.'"

"Since we were ... nineteen?"

"And you were exclusive?"

"Yes."

"And Ella proposed to you."

"Yes." His heart was suddenly pounding. "What's this about?"

What the hell had the doctor discovered? Did he have testicular cancer or something, and it had shown up in the load he'd left in that little plastic cup?

McGuire sat forward, elbows on the desk. "Noah, your sperm count is ... unusual."

"Unusually high?" He wiped wet palms on his pants.

"Unusually *low*."

"I guess it's lucky I had kids before I ran out of shots, then."

"Not just low. You have no sperm in your semen. None. Your count is zero."

"Is that unusual?"

"Not for a man with a vasectomy."

"I didn't have a vasectomy."

McGuire tapped the papers. "Yes, you did. Nature gave you one."

Noah tried to think. Had he been in a crotch-smashing accident in the past six years?

The doctor sighed again. He pulled a printed image from the folder and turned it around to show Noah.

"You have a congenital defect in your vas deferens. You can't have children, Noah. Without going to heroic measures, it's literally impossible."

Noah picked up the image. "When did this happen?"

"Birth."

"You mean when the kids were born?"

McGuire sighed again, but now there was a sad frustration on his face. There was something Noah was supposed to have already understood, and it injured the doctor to nudge him toward it.

"No, Noah. When *you* were born."

Noah held the image with both hands, staring. It was on glossy stock, giving him a ghost of his reflection. The image shook. The paper, for some reason, had begun to tremble.

"Do you understand?"

Noah didn't. Except that he did.

"You can't have children, Noah. You've *never* been able to." McGuire sighed again — his biggest yet. "I'm very sorry to have to be the one to tell you this."

"It's okay," someone said. Noah realized it was himself. "I didn't want to have more kids with Ella anyway."

"I want to make sure you understand—"

"It's okay." Noah stood. He couldn't feel his hands, his feet, his skin. Someone else was controlling this body. "Thank you, Dr. McGuire."

"Noah—"

But McGuire was behind him. Then the closed door. The lobby, the office door, the parking lot. He opened his car and sat. He must have started it, because the engine was running and the radio was on.

A nurse came through the front door, spotted Noah, and rushed forward. He must have pulled out of his parking spot before she reached him, because he was on the highway, passing cars full of people with boringly normal lives.

Leave her, said one voice inside his head.

The other voice said, *Stay. For the kids.*

At a stoplight two blocks from home, Noah pulled out his Doodad and flipped through his photos. He stopped on his favorite shot of the boys. A strange choice. It didn't even show their faces. They were squatting by the shore of a pond — the kind of deep, ass-to-heels squat that only little kids can manage. They were both wearing ball caps, on backward, staring at something in the water.

Stay for the kids. Stay with her ... for the sake of your children.

The garage. The door off the kitchen. Ella wasn't home; the housekeeper was washing the windows. She greeted him and got nothing in return. He was looking for the boys.

The boys.

And then here they were, rushing forward, *Daddy Daddy you're home,* arms wrapping his legs, one each, becoming weights, shackles, hugging him tight. All smiles. Noah felt himself smile. An odd thing, almost an anomaly.

He looked down at James and Diego.

The loves of his life, but the fruit of someone else's loins.

TWENTY-EIGHT

Summer watched Noah extend a hand toward his wife.

"Give me that envelope."

"No."

"Give it to me, Ella."

He grabbed her by one arm, attempting to lever it away.

Ella shouted and thrashed, raking a long fingernail across his cheek.

That stopped him, and they separated. But Ella looked shocked. If Summer were guessing, her expression was a display of regret. And oh boy did she know about that. She'd seen it on Ella and Heidi's faces in the past, and on her own for a decade. Summer tried to forgive and worked to forget. But every day, she saw that same wicked face.

Noah's hand went to his cheek.

"I ... I'm sorry," Ella said.

The whole room was staring at her, the same way it had in the past. With judgment. And condemnation.

"What did you do to Casey?" Noah asked.

"Casey?"

"*Yes, fucking Casey!*" He raised one arm, wiped the spit from his lip. "Isn't that what everyone is here to find out?"

"Take it easy, Noah," Teek said from across the table.

"Sit down, Teek. This is between me and my non-blushing bride."

Ella's eyes were wide. Summer knew the look. She'd been unlucky enough in her Queen Bee days to wear it, a couple of times. Noah probably never stood up to her, but now was his time.

And the room could feel it.

"Tell us all what you did," Noah repeated.

"It wasn't my fault," she finally said.

"*What* wasn't your fault?"

The room was waiting.

"It was a prank. Just kids being kids."

"Be specific, Ella." Noah's voice was frosted past recognition. "Tell us all about it."

Darting eyes. Ella no longer seemed fierce with that envelope against her chest. She looked like something caught in a snare. "Miss Bridges already told you."

"You mean the Miss Bridges whose husband Heidi has been having an affair with."

Heads turned to Bindi, still with one hand zip-tied to the chair, then at Heidi as she looked away.

"What about you, Ella? Have you been screwing Miss Bridges's husband, too?"

"Fuck you, Noah."

"If only. I'm not the one getting fucked these days."

"We had sex last week!"

Uncomfortable laughter. Ella probably hadn't meant to say that.

Noah, near her, was laughing as if at a joke known only to him. "What's it say in your envelope, Ella?"

Paper wrinkled as she hugged the envelope closer.

"It's okay. I probably know."

Teek cleared his throat. "So ... it's true, what Miss Bridges said? About Ella and Heidi and ..."

Teek withered underneath all the eyes.

So Taylor answered. "Yes. It's all true."

Heidi snapped her head toward Taylor. "Oh, you weren't even there!"

"I know it's true."

"How? How exactly do you know it's true when you were sitting at home and—?"

"It's true. Just how Bindi explained it." Mason rehashed it: Ella and Heidi approaching him, the promises, the break-in, the photos and videos, the laughter, and the online slut-shaming that followed.

Noah laughed again.

Taylor said, "She never told you?"

"Not that she was behind it."

"I wasn't behind it!" Ella yelled.

"Not that she betrayed her best friend and caused her to kill herself."

"That's not why she killed herself!"

"Is *that* true, Ella?" Taylor said. "Or just what you keep telling yourself so you can get through the day?"

"Oh, shut up, Taylor."

"Fuck you, Ella!" Pause. "You too, Heidi!"

Summer saw movement on her right and turned to see Harper watching the exchange with wide-eyed fascination.

Noah sat, leaving Ella standing alone. He sipped his wine, rubbing in his nonchalance by swirling and sniffing. To no one, he said, "She tells herself a *lot* to get through the day. If she's the reason Casey committed suicide, I'm not surprised."

Ella looked slapped. Her mouth hung open.

Imogen leaned forward. "Like, what else does she do?"

Ella: "Fuck off, Imogen."

Noah: "She takes pills. A lot of pills."

"She was asking *me* for pills earlier!"

Mason: "You just always carry pills around?"

John, shockingly just eating his soup to Summer's left, said, "Apparently."

"I have anxiety," Imogen snapped.

"Every day, right?" John said. "About a milligram a day's worth of chronic anxiety?"

Defensive: "Usually a half."

Without looking up, John scoffed.

Thirty seconds passed.

"And she cheats," Noah said out of the blue. "Fucks all sorts of other guys."

Melissa laughed out loud.

"I ... I ..."

"What, you think I don't know?" *Sip.* "Hell, you leave evidence all over the place."

Melissa laughed again.

"Where?" Ella demanded.

Summer noted: *That's not a denial.*

"Shit. *All over* the boys' room. In the back seat of our car. Even at the elementary school."

"That's absolutely—!"

Noah pointed at Ella but spoke to Harper. "I'm tired of covering for her. Do you want to know why Casey Davis killed herself? It's because of this bitch." Then he pointed at Heidi. "Oh, and I guess that bitch, too."

Heidi stood like a bullet. Donovan jerked forward but held his ground.

"It was a prank," Heidi said. "A *joke*, okay? We were just kids. If you hadn't been so *in love* with her ..."

"Wait," said Imogen. "Who's in love with who?"

"Whom," Simon corrected.

"Noah loved Casey," Heidi said. "Everyone knew it."

"Is that something to be ashamed of?" Noah demanded.

"Only if you never let it go," Ella said, finally taking her seat — but only its leftmost edge, closer to Mason than Noah. "Only if you marry another person but never stop pining for someone else."

Noah's eyebrows went up. He faced Ella, and she flinched. "Oh. You're one to talk."

"I'm not having an affair! I don't know where you're getting this bullshit about—!"

"Who's Chance Baskin?"

"Who's ... *What?"*

Noah returned to his wine. "You sure seem to visit his LiveLyfe page a lot."

"What, are you *spying* on me?"

"I had probable cause."

"What the hell are you talking about?"

"I don't know, Ella. You and Heidi are the ones who killed Casey Davis."

"WE DIDN'T FUCKING KILL—"

Noah cut her off again, hooking a sideways thumb at his wife while talking around the table. "You guys tell me if she's guilty. I'll leave it to you. I told you about the pills. *Always* with the pills. And I told you about the fucking around—"

"I am *not* fucking around!"

"She lies for fun. And she steals sometimes. She—"

"That's what Heidi does," Bindi said. "All you're describing? We've been talking about it for years in therapy."

Simon said, "That's some great doctor-patient confidentiality."

"She's fucking my husband!"

"See?" Noah said, still sipping wine. "The pair of them, broken. They didn't used to be this way. Doesn't that sound like two people trying hard to swallow their guilt? Along with pills that make you forget." To Bindi, he said, "Does Heidi pop pills like Tic-Tacs?"

"Shut up, Noah," Heidi said.

"Not that she's admitted," Bindi replied. "But she used to smoke like a broken stove."

"Makes sense. Smoking is like sucking a tiny little dick." Melissa turned to Bindi. "You should ask your husband if she has an oral fixation."

Bindi stared hard at Melissa. The table went quiet.

"So," Harper finally said. "Noah, you feel Casey's suicide was Heidi and Ella's fault?"

"Oh yes. Absolutely. Hundred percent."

Ella's face went limp. Noah hadn't just stood up to her; he'd stood on top of her.

"I guess the rest of us can go, then." Melissa started to stand.

Heidi was having none of it; she jabbed an arm so hard toward Melissa that she could have broken Taylor's nose. Her face was wild. *Terrified.* It dawned on Summer that no matter how civil Harper seemed to be, she'd trapped them, severed their ties to the world.

What might come next for the guilty?

"It wasn't our fault!" Heidi shouted. "We were just doing what *they* told us to do!"

"Who?" Simon asked.

Heidi's arm swung over to Summer. John followed it to his wife.

"Summer! Summer ordered the whole goddamn thing! Summer and her little bitch cronies!"

"*Summer?*" said John.

Her mouth opened. "I—"

"You want to blame someone, blame them!" Heidi cast her eyes from Summer to Melissa to Imogen. "Casey didn't even want to be in Diamond Society, but for some reason, Summer had it in for her!"

A flashback: Casey on campus, jaunting around Coastline with that man of hers. She'd seen them that once, from a distance. Casey's red hair like fire on her head. What bothered Summer now, remembering it all, wasn't the unwelcome memory. It was the way her gut responded, same as it had back then:

Who does that bitch think she is, telling her friends not to rush Diamond then strutting around campus with a college man?

The snap was instant, like a reflex. Summer had been so sure she didn't think like that anymore, that her years of self-work had paid off, that she'd become someone better than the girl she used to be.

"They're the reason Casey killed herself, Ms. Knox!" Heidi went on. "They're the ones who brought that stupid pre-rush to Bayshore in the first place!"

Deadly silence. Until Simon laughed.

"There's no such thing as pre-rush," he said.

Then the doors opened, and the waiters returned with the second course.

TWENTY-NINE

John waited for something, anything, that Summer might be willing to offer. He'd known she attended Coastline (of course) and Diamond Society (naturally), and he had much more knowledge about Summer's relationship to Casey Davis than she realized. Because secrets were his business. But he hadn't known this.

"Summer?" he said. "What happened that spring?"

"I told you what happened years ago."

"That's not what I mean."

"Watch out." Summer nodded in the direction of John's place setting. "He wants to take your bowl away."

John leaned back. The waiter took his bowl. Summer avoided his eyes and dove into her thoughts.

In a way, Casey's death brought them together. Even then, Summer had erected a stoic facade. But her front had never fooled John. The day she first spoke to him was the day when the guilt was finally too black to see through. Over the years, they'd talked a bit about Casey, but she'd let him believe that they'd only been friends. Harper's party would change that. John would leave tonight knowing the truth: that without Summer's bitchy college grudge, Casey would probably still be alive. What would her perfect man think about the undiluted truth?

As the waiters worked, John looked away. A refrain played in her mind:

You killed Casey Davis. It's your fault she's dead.

And horribly, her envelope held something else.

Beside John, Simon was calculating balances in his many accounts. That once mighty number was now small. If pressed, he could sell his car at a fire-sale price. Apparently, this thing with Kagen wasn't going to happen. The lack of a Plan B could make a guy edgy. Or desperate.

In Simon's envelope: *You borrowed over one million dollars on fraudulent real estate deals, then defaulted on the loans.*

He had worse secrets by far, but this one could land him in prison. He tried to stay calm, and consider his aces. He couldn't go to jail. He hadn't made his billion.

Imogen, whose envelope contained the message *You poisoned someone,* had taken out her Doodad and was playing Dime Swap. Her friends all played it. *Imogen, girl, you've gotta try it; you'll go broke paying for tokens.* So far Imogen didn't see the big deal. You slid coins back and forth. They were supposed to add up to something before disappearing. Big whoop.

She played anyway.

The second course was a delicate little salad with pink lady apples and what smelled like a blood orange reduction vinaigrette. Paprika in there somewhere, too. Candied onto the almonds? Imogen wasn't sure. But the salad was beautifully crafted and presented like a gallery showing. Probably tasted amazing, like that cold asparagus soup with Dungeness crab that white-gloved hands had just taken away.

The chefs were top-notch. Like Imogen wanted to be. But Elder Conway wasn't coming. He didn't even know who she was. Imogen Shah wasn't getting a show. And if her secret got out?

Well. That would be the end of the little Indian girl for good.

"Excuse me, sir," said the waiter now setting a salad in front of Mason. His name was Sam Davies. He had aspirations for film, and tonight was steeping in his role as a waiter. His lines sucked, limited to subservient pleasantries, but this was still his most significant opportunity so far. Even if the pay for this evening, and for keeping his mouth shut, hadn't been great (it was), that was *Harper Knox* at the end of the table. And to a lesser extent, that was *Donovan Bruce* at the door. If tonight's audition went well, maybe he'd end up in Harper's next blockbuster.

"Sorry," said Mason. The waiter had startled him. He couldn't stop thinking about Casey. The anchor that had steered him wrong for so many years.

He looked at Ella, then away. He didn't know that she was jonesing hard and that her thoughts had fallen from him into the darkness. He didn't know that if asked right now, she might even admit that yes, suicide had its appeal.

And that was without knowing that Noah had already uncovered her secret.

Mason knew none of this, and wouldn't have cared if he did. If he knew that his envelope blew the whistle on his plagiarism, he wouldn't even have been bothered about that.

His eyes went to Harper. She was watching him, then watching Summer, then John, then Heidi and Taylor and Ella. She wanted to know the truth about Casey or else.

Or else *what?*

Harper began eating her salad. Mason tried not to stare or wonder.

She wasn't thinking about accusations right now. Her mind was on the plan. On the steps. On Donovan, on Gavin Cash. But most of all on a girl and a small stuffed animal. A dog. On a feeling, which she kept right beside her heart.

Under the table, Teek reached for Taylor's hand. She took it. Their eyes met. There was comfort in that glance. Neither knew for sure just yet (and they hadn't the privacy to discuss it), but of all the pairings at the table, they were the only two who more or less knew each other's truths. Or at least, Teek knew Taylor's.

She didn't exactly know what was in her husband's envelope, but she knew a secret so much worse. It would be simple to connect the secret she knew to the lesser one that she didn't. They were cause and effect, after all.

She held his hand, thinking about how difficult things had seemed between them just a few hours earlier and how right now, none of that mattered. Anything could be worked out, and between them, there were no more secrets.

She thought of what he'd told her. About his guilt. How it

consumed him to hold it inside. She could forgive him ... couldn't she?

"Taylor," Simon said. "Teek told me you're some sort of networker now?"

Taylor considered pretending she hadn't heard. The last person she wanted to talk to — ever, really, but right now for sure — was Simon Wyatt.

"She's a collaborative coordinator for OutReached," Teek said after the silence yawned too long. "They put nonprofits together and help them pool their resources."

"So a networker," Simon said, chewing a mouthful of greens. "All those rich do-gooders looking to change the world. What kinds of ideas are they looking to fund? There must be finder's fees for that sort of thing, right?"

Nobody had spoken in a while, so Melissa stopped pressing the sharp tip of a nail file into her forearm. Noah stopped thinking about the twin boys who weren't his after all. John stopped wondering what, exactly, *had* happened to Casey Davis in the week between the infamous senior class party and her death. Heidi brushed hair behind her ear. Bindi went to do the same, but her tethered hand wouldn't permit it.

Taylor said, "Go fuck yourself, Simon." Then she mumbled, *"Maybe you can kill yourself, too."*

Simon half stood. Donovan eyed him, and he sat.

The last plate was Mason's. He picked at it with his fork. Then the waiter who'd delivered it stood erect at the empty head of the table opposite Harper and said, "If I could please have your attention, I'd like to introduce your second course for the evening. It's—"

Second Course

Locally Sourced Baby Greens
With Blood Orange Reduction Vinaigrette,
Grilled Pink Lady Apples,
Smoked Paprika Candied Almonds,
And Point Reyes Blue Cheese Crumbles

THIRTY

December 3, 2028

S wipe.
> *Swipe.*
> *Swipe.*

Today Ella felt particularly disaffected. The real world and the Ellaverse were skin to skin, but sometimes she felt the membrane between them. She saw her life from a distance, heard it as if through cotton. She had no sense of smell or taste. There was only the cold reality of touch — and forget about that touch being human.

Unless ...

But no. She swiped again, advancing images, trying to rush the thoughts from her mind.

Thoughts were like pills, candy in her hand.

There was an orange prescription bottle in her drawer, buried deep, in case of emergencies.

Is that what this was?

She needed an escape. Well, "escape" was the wrong word. Escape implied moving from a bad situation into a better one. Ella "went away." The benzos and the beautiful little opiates, when she could get them, were her parachutes.

Ella closed the stock photo website. Her first image was good enough after all. She went back to LiveLyfe, considered her post about the new clay teapots, and navigated to the ads manager instead. None of Unusual Artifacts' ads were performing especially well. Not a single one from the set her team had started on Monday. That's why Ella was building this new set. Her boss wouldn't care that her team had screwed up. She'd fire Ella if Unusual Artifacts failed on social.

She looked around the office. Jason and Diane were at the water cooler. Ella should get up and go over. Yell at them for their shitty work. Or maybe she could join their conversation. Talk about family, friends ... the latest episode of *Fat Vampire*, which everyone allegedly spent their cooler time discussing.

Diane laughed. A far-off twitter, but Ella heard it clearly. Jason smiled. Neither seemed to care that they'd done a terrible job on the ad set, leaving Ella to do it (again).

They sounded happy. She wondered what that was like.

"You need coffee."

Ella looked from the water cooler to Addison, her boss. "Sorry?"

"You don't seem awake yet."

"I'm okay."

"Kids keeping you up?"

"No."

"That's good." Addison took out her Doodad, tapped, and returned it.

Did she just send someone a text about me?

"Why?"

Addison laughed. "You just look tired."

Ella touched her hair, fussed with her collar.

"Is it ...?" Ella reached for a compact. She probably looked homeless.

"Never mind." She gestured at Ella's screen. "Is that the new ad set?"

"What? Oh, yeah."

"How are the LiveLyfe ads doing?"

"Better."

"Were they bad?"

"No."

Addison squinted, smiling awkwardly. "Okay. Well ... carry on."

She moved to leave. Probably because she'd already decided to check up on the ads, and start a paper trail.

"Addison?"

She turned.

"Do I really look tired?"

Addison shrugged. "I dunno. You're ... quiet."

"I'm just trying to focus."

"Good."

"Get these ads going."

"Always a plus."

"Make us some money," Ella added. "Get lots of new sales."

Awkward again. "Well ... we'll talk later."

Addison left and Ella wondered if that was a threat.

We'll talk about it when your father comes home.

The last set sucked because Jason and Diane had done it without her oversight, but the others were good. So why was she flailing?

You just look tired.

Maybe she *had* been overly quiet and in need of caffeine.

She pulled out her compact, opened it, then peered into the tiny mirror. She wiped it with a tissue but her image didn't improve. Noah had told her, just this morning, that she looked beautiful. But Addison was right; Ella looked like Swamp Thing. She was nothing but lines and shadows, and at only 29 fucking years old.

She stood, then caught Sara's attention in the cubicle next door.

"Oh, hey, Ella."

"Hey. Do you have any concealer?"

Sara laughed.

"Do you?"

"Why?"

"For this." Ella pointed at her worst spots.

"For *what?*"

"I look like an old man. And I have bags." Poking the area under her eyes.

"Yeah, right."

"Do you have anything or not?"

Sara turned toward her. "No, sorry. But seriously, Ella. It's like you're messing with me."

"What do you mean?"

"You have perfect skin. I *wish* I had your complexion."

Did Sara wish she had Ella's body, too? Despite her constant diet and exercise, she was still too fat and her clothes all looked terrible.

She went to sit. Sara called her back.

"Hey. Have lunch with me today?"

"Oh. Sorry. I can't."

"Meeting?"

"Yeah." It wasn't true, but Sara always had questions when Ella didn't eat lunch. Besides, she didn't feel like company. She was tired, fat, floating off in the Ellaverse, and probably about to be fired. She couldn't taste or smell or see right or hear right.

The only thing left was touch. And that was cold. Inhuman.

Unless ...

She was already on LiveLyfe. What would it hurt? She could poke around.

Ella blinked, and in the darkness saw horror. Then nothing at all.

She cradled her tablet so that no one would see that she'd moved from ads to personal research. She always felt drunk when she did this. Drun*ker*, anyway; these days she always felt at least a little drunk.

There were times when she lost herself entirely.

Who am I?

What do I do?

She had a husband, Noah, and two wonderful boys. What did it mean that she sometimes considered how they'd be without her? Or that she was sure the answer was *better*?

She could just go away.

But no, she had a job. She had a life. Never mind that her home was a sty despite the housekeepers, or Ella's attempts to play house. So what if she sometimes leaned on the vacuum to keep herself upright. So what if she occasionally found bruises she didn't remember getting and had once woken at 2 am in the downstairs bathroom, with no idea how she got there.

Her hands were sluggish. Torpor and agitation. She was slow but keyed up. A zombie with a monster's pounding heart.

And then she was looking at Chance Baskin's profile.

She loved all his beach photos. She'd taken some of the pictures, and it felt like a special kind of *fuck-you* that Chance had shared them with the world. Ella could see her shadow in a few of the photos, but she wasn't really there. Not in his photos, his world, or his life.

I want to be with you, Chance.
And he'd said, *You're married, Ella. You have a life.*
But with you, I feel—
And so do I.
His way of saying he didn't need her. Or *want* her. And why would he? Bags under her eyes, cheating, lying bitch that she was.

She last saw Chance eight years ago. Then for the last time a couple of years after that. And Ella saw him yet again for the very last time three years ago. Shouldn't she be seeing him for the very last time again right about now?

Her skin warmed with the thought of his touch. Her nerves crackled.

But her gut was already knotted. This was a terrible habit. A downward spiral.

If she messaged him now, he'd say yes.

They could meet. Today. Tomorrow. Every day for weeks, until he tired of her again.

Her finger hovered over the screen.
You're a wife.
You're a mother.
And yet, the burning abandon pulsed between her legs.
Think about the kids. Think about Noah. Think about ...
... about all those past disasters. About her history of acting first and never thinking later. About the scourged earth behind her. About her never ending betrayals. About the body in its grave.

She swiped Chance's profile away. Her palms were sweaty. Her eyes couldn't focus. Someone had dropped her from a very high place, and she was flailing down to her death.

She needed something from the emergency stash.

Valium. Xanax. Mother's little helpers.
Breathe, Ella. Just breathe.
As it had been at the funeral.

As she'd told herself in the church bathroom, after all those eyes said it was her fault.

A new profile. Taylor McKay.

She hadn't looked up her Girl Squad in years. Glancing through Taylor's profile now, she felt like an intruder. They'd all left on such uncertain terms, neither estranged nor friendly. What would Taylor think, if she knew Ella was here?

Taylor had married Teek, also from Bayshore. She hadn't taken his name. Was she independent, or was there something else?

Ella flicked through Taylor's photos. She'd aged so much better than Ella. She looked … *happy?* But Taylor had a shadow long before the bad things.

Her Friends list. All those old names making her shiver.

Ella's finger betrayed her and now she was looking at the profile of a girl much younger than herself, though they'd been the same age when it mattered. The girl had bright red hair and the radiant smile of someone with their entire future in front of them, and no idea that they were hours from death.

Casey Davis.

And the last post she ever made.

Going to the senior party tonight at Simon Wyatt's house. It's going
to be—

Ella stopped reading. She couldn't finish. It was too sad. Too tragic. Why was Casey's profile still up? Why had nobody taken it down? Eleven goddamn years it had stayed here to taunt her.

Ella's hand jammed into her drawer and emerged with a bottle:

Boyer, Ella
Alprazolam, 0.5mg
Take one tablet for—

But fuck the bottle's stupid suggestions. Ella needed it to go away and an overdose wouldn't be so terrible.

Two pills. She chewed them, to make them work faster, and the bitterness nearly made her retch. But within minutes her heart had stopped hammering and she'd gone past okay to kind of baked, false euphoria trekking an opiate's steps across her mind.

She swiped again.

Heidi.

How had Heidi been, these past years?

Because back then, even Ella had known that they'd done something wrong. But Heidi? Heidi had been—

THIRTY-ONE

May 19, 2018

—"Happy?"

Heidi hadn't been paying attention. She'd been gazing left, right, behind, forward, and yes, even up and down as they walked the concrete path through the grassy quad. The college was lovely now, during the daytime, but at night it was stunning. Heidi could practically smell the academia, the adventure, the possibilities of a well-lived future. A place where girls became women and boys became men. It was like walking through a dream. Someday soon, they'd be a part of it all.

"What?" Heidi asked.

Ella repeated herself. "I asked why you seem so happy?"

They walked a few more paces, hands in their pockets as they passed the black iron lampposts. The crisscrossing paths cut the quad into wedges, and most were full, despite the evening hour. A team playing pickup football, nerds preparing to launch a rocket, a few couples making out on blankets. The perfumed air smelled like a promise.

"Is that a trick question? I seem happy because I am."

"How can you be happy?"

"Because it went off without a hitch!" When Ella didn't react appropriately, Heidi sighed. "What, Ella."

Not a question. More like an accusation.

"Well ... don't you realize what we just did?"

"Yep: *Nailed it.*"

"She was crying. She was humiliated."

Heidi had seen that, yes. But sometimes friends messed with friends. Some girls cried for every emotion: sadness, happiness, fear, anger, frustration. It could have been anything.

Naturally, their prank had shocked Casey. But she'd eventually think it was funny. Probably pay all of them back. Heidi didn't know about Ella, but she planned to make out with the doors locked and the curtains drawn just in case.

"Oh, she was fine," Heidi said.

"She was *not* fine."

"Are you serious, Ella? It was just a joke!"

Ella shook her head, eyes down as they approached the Diamond Society house. "We should never have agreed to do it. We should have told Summer no."

Heidi shrugged. "Well. Too late now."

"It doesn't bother you at all? What we did to our *friend?* Not just setting her up, but *filming* it, too. Lacy was posting it to BayNet! That shit with Casey will be online forever and—"

"She'll get over it! It's a meme, Ella. Memes last like ten seconds! Do you remember that wedding dance thing from a few years ago?"

"No."

"Exactly. A week from now, nobody will remember this, either."

Ella didn't agree, but she wouldn't argue her point, or make eye contact.

Heidi wished that Ella would debate the issue so she could keep working the "it's no big deal" argument.

Ella stopped on the porch and looked up at the house. "I feel like shit, Heidi. That was wrong. I don't want to go in there."

Heidi rolled her eyes and sighed. "Okay, Ella. You wanna know why I'm happy? Because we did exactly what we were supposed to do. What you *agreed* we were going to—"

"I know I agreed. But—"

"And now here we are, after the unpleasant part, ready to get our reward. *Diamond Society*, girl!" Heidi took one of Ella's reluctant hands. "Do you know what this means? We've got a family here now. When we start at Coastline next year, we'll already have sisters."

"We *had* sisters. Taylor—"

"Screw Taylor! She didn't want to pre-rush and neither did Casey. We paid our dues by doing what Summer asked us to. Casey paid hers by ... well, you know. Taylor didn't have to do anything. What do you think she's gonna do when we tell her she's in at Diamond and that the sisters already said yes? Do you think Taylor's really going to turn it down?"

"Well ..."

Heidi tipped her head. "Ella. You can't be serious. Taylor's got that 'I'm so superior' thing going on, but there's *no way* she's going to turn it down. She wants to save the world and help poor people and whatever? Don't you think Diamond's philantropological ..."

"Philanthropic."

"Yeah. Don't you think those connections will help?"

Ella sighed.

Heidi took her by the sleeve and smiled. "Come on. We did the hard part. Let's at least enjoy the good part."

Ella sighed again, half-shrugging. They walked up the steps to the white double doors and rang the bell.

"This is so awesome," Heidi said.

An Indian girl answered the door. Someone they'd met before, but whose name Ella kept forgetting.

"Ohmygod. It's you." She turned and called into the house without pause. "It's the high school girls. Heidi and Ellie!"

"Ella," Ella corrected.

"Get the hell in here, you sluts." She reached out, took them both by the forearms, and dragged them inside.

There was a girl with strawberry blonde hair, a black girl with stunning green eyes, two girls who (in Heidi's opinion, anyway) were a bit pudgy for sorority life, and the black-haired girl they'd met before. She looked like someone had coerced her into coming and she eternally resented it.

The girls formed a circle. Some were tittering, others merely waiting.

"We're here to see Summer," Ella said when nobody spoke.

"Like we don't know why you're here," said the Indian girl.

"Holy shit. We have the internet. Did you know YouTube already pulled your video down? You're like, infamous."

"Of course *YouTube* pulled it down, Imogen," said one of the pudgy girls. "It's still up on—"

"—PornHub," the black-haired girl finished. "Imogen and I were just watching it."

That sounded like a joke, but there was no laughter. Heidi's stomach dropped. But that wasn't all that felt strange. There was a vibe in the air. The girls had circled them like returning heroes, but nobody had asked them into the parlor; no one had offered a beer; no one had asked them to sit. The six girls were in a halo around the newcomers, like a waiting tribunal.

"I can't believe you guys did that." The black girl shook her head.

"What Juliet said," the girl beside her concurred.

"Summer told us to." Ella's eyes flicked to Heidi, apparently trying to make peace by doing her part. They'd come this far, after all.

"Yeah, she did," said the other pudgy girl.

Silence.

"So, where *is* Summer?"

"Ohmygod, keep your panties on," Imogen said. "We called her."

Heidi hadn't heard anyone call anyone.

"I can't believe she got you to do that," said the blonde.

Now the praise seemed worded for Summer.

"So ..." Heidi said. "Did you guys all pre-rush?"

A few of them snickered. Then Imogen said, "Me and Melissa are rushing. The regular kind of rush, I mean."

"Summer, too," Melissa said.

Footsteps. Summer arrived from behind, parting the group like Moses.

It was strange that a pledge would be in charge of handling pre-rush, now that Heidi thought about it. Shouldn't Summer be subject to hazing and pranks, rather than dishing them out?

The mood changed again. Now it was Heidi's turn to wonder if they should have come.

Summer laughed. "So you really screwed her over, huh? Your best friend?"

Heidi swallowed. Her words now felt plastic, out of control. "We do what we're told."

Laughs. Summer looked at Juliet, then again at Ella and Heidi. "It's like you have no sense of loyalty at all."

The girls were still smiling.

Heidi tried to match them, but couldn't. Ella, beside her, looked horrified.

"Well ..." Heidi said.

"Do you really think we'd want someone in Diamond Society without any loyalty? Who would *do* something like that to a friend?"

"But—"

"Maybe you should go," Juliet said.

"Go where?"

"Back to mom and dad. Don't you have school tomorrow?"

"We can stay out as late as we want," Heidi said.

That got a laugh. *Thanks, ladies; we'll be here all week.*

The semicircle shrank. Juliet was in charge.

"So ..." Ella looked helplessly at Summer, who was hanging back with a satisfied smile. "So, Summer? Are we in?"

Juliet stood in her way. "Don't ask Summer. She's just a pledge. Well, she *was.* I guess this makes her official."

"*What* makes her official?"

But Heidi knew. So did Ella. They all did.

The girls laughed harder.

They were backing up. At the front door. Outside, onto the stoop. Heidi's backpedaling legs belonged to someone else.

Finally, Summer nudged the other girls aside and came to the front, centered in the open door.

"Summer ..." Heidi said.

"Thanks, you guys. I owe you one."

"For what?"

The room erupted in grotesque, unladylike laughter. Donkey brays and belching harpies. Summer gave them a smile and a wave, then the door closed. They could still hear laughing inside, telegraphed through the thick wood.

"What just happened?"

"Goddammit, Heidi."

"Are they ...? Are we ...?"

But Ella was down the steps, to the walkway, marching across the quad.

Heidi broke her paralysis and rushed to catch up. By the time she did, Ella already had her phone out and was tapping the glass.

"What are you doing?"

"What the hell do you think I'm doing?" Ella jammed the phone to her ear.

Distant and tinny, Heidi heard the phone make its connection, then ring.

THIRTY-TWO

May 19, 2018

The phone rang.

It was on a small, white-wicker end table. It looked nothing like a bedside nightstand but Casey was used to it. The phone was ancient. It had been bedside in her room since she'd been eleven — bright pink, handed down from her mom because she still believed in landlines. When Casey graduated and moved out, her sister Kimmy would inherit the thing. Have fun, kiddo ... it's the 1960s all over again.

"Don't answer it," Casey said.

Taylor was already reaching. "Hello?"

"Tell her to go fuck herself," she told Taylor from the bed.

Casey's voice — which her friend Jackie said had a sexy sandpaper quality — now struck her as particularly gritty. Thick with snot, probably. She'd certainly blown her way through enough tissues since yesterday.

"You don't even know who it is," Taylor said, covering the mouthpiece. Casey could hear a high-pitched voice, and then Taylor said into the phone, "Oh. Hey, Ella."

Casey gave her an irritated smirk.

Taylor continued, but even if Casey had wanted to pay attention (she didn't; Ella could rot inside a giant's foreskin, for all she cared), she was already finding it impossible. Her attention kept going to that shitty wicker nightstand and the dumb, old-fashioned pink telephone on its top. *A princess phone,* her mother had called it. *A princess phone for my little princess.*

It hadn't sounded ridiculous then. At eleven, she'd been excited to have any kind of phone. And now, it seemed so … so *wrong* that Ella and Taylor should be having this particular discussion through that childhood relic.

Seeing her innocent pink phone used for such base conversation was somehow indecent, like squeezing a stuffed animal between your legs to masturbate.

It made Casey feel — of all ridiculous things — *guilty.* She was the one who'd blocked Ella and Heidi on her cell, so they had to call her landline and hope that mom or dad didn't pick up.

Just like that, Casey felt like crying all over again.

As far as she knew, Mom and Dad hadn't heard the news or seen the videos yet, but it hadn't even been 24 hours. How long could it possibly take, and what would they think of their little princess then? What would *Kimmy* think? She was in middle school, where everything was a big deal and nobody knew what to do with their changing bodies and minds. Was there *any* chance Kimmy's friends wouldn't see it and show her? Any chance in Hell?

"Hang up," Casey said.

Taylor half-turned, still talking to Ella.

"I said, *hang up.*"

Taylor raised a finger, then turned the rest of the way. Casey rolled onto her back in surrender. Taylor was stubborn and bold. That had made her an excellent port in this particular storm. Same for keeping herself out of their stupid stunt in the first place.

Casey had heard by now why they'd done it, and if Taylor had gone to that stupid pre-rush thing, none of this would have happened. Taylor would have refused; she would have told Casey what Summer Nixon had tried to get them to do. Just went to show that Ella and Heidi couldn't be trusted to make their own decisions.

But the downside of Taylor's personality was that no matter what Casey wanted, Taylor was going to keep doing what she felt was best. She was loyal to Casey, but her larger loyalty was to the group. If Taylor thought there was a chance that the Girl Squad could survive this, she was going to try and save it.

"They *what?*" Taylor said.

"Tell her to eat shit," Casey said, half-sobbing. "Tell her to eat shit and die!"

"Hang on. What about pre-rush?"

"Fuck pre-rush!"

Taylor moved farther away from the bed, now stretching the pink phone cord in its long, undulating spiral. "Wow. That's terrible. What about Heidi?"

Casey felt like weighing in on Heidi too, but let the moment pass.

"Are you just leaving now? Where are you?"

Ella replied, but Casey couldn't make out her words.

"You're still at Coastline?"

Casey couldn't make out any of the chatter, but after a few attempts at interruption, Taylor cut in. "Of course. Look, I'm not going to lie. You screwed up. You screwed up really, really bad. You were a complete and total bitch. Truth, Ella? I want to kill you both. *Me.* Not just Casey. But—"

She stopped while Ella spoke.

"No, I won't. But I'm pissed at you, and I'm not going to pretend I'm not. You don't do shit like that to friends. You don't do shit like that to anyone! We both told you about the sort of hazing crap they do, and you walked right into it. I don't feel even a little bit sorry for you."

"Why would *you* feel sorry for *her?*" Casey demanded.

Taylor again held up that maddening finger.

"But ... Yes. Okay? Yes. Eventually." Chatter. Taylor laughed as she responded. "Oh, no. No no no no no. Trust me; you don't want to talk to her right now. She'll tell you all sorts of things that you won't want to hear, most of them true. You're not in a productive place right now, neither of you."

Casey sat up. Used, wadded tissues spilled from the bedspread to the floor. "Does she actually want to *apologize?*"

Moving the phone away from her mouth: "Yes, of course. But—"

"Fuck her!"

To the phone, Taylor said, "Did you hear that?"

"Fuck both of them! *Fuck them forever!*" Casey shouted.

"Yes. I'll tell her. But right now, I think you just need to stay away. What? Yes, I'm sure. With time. But you can't expect her to just forgive you the day after—"

"She thinks I'm just going to *forgive* her? Taylor, they *set me up!*"

"I know." Then to Ella: "I don't think you're a monster. I think you're stupid and gullible and that you got tricked. I'm glad you got what was coming to you. Heidi, too. I sure hope she feels half as sorry as you do."

"Fuck her sorry!" Casey opined.

"But you're not *monsters*. I'm sure she'll forgive you eventually. *Eventually*, Ella. In her own sweet time, taking as long as she needs to."

Ella said more. Taylor stopped her.

"I know you are. But really? That's just too damn bad."

And Taylor hung up.

Casey glared at her. "Why did you tell her that?"

"Tell her what?"

"That they're not monsters. That I'd forgive them eventually."

"Because they're not, Casey. They're idiots. You know how Heidi is. She'll do anything for approval."

"Fuck her."

Taylor sat on the bed beside Casey, then put a hand on her arm. "I know this is tough. But just ... you know Heidi's family. Her dad left them high and dry when she was only—"

"Good."

"—when she was only ten. After screwing his mistress and telling Heidi to help him cover it up. And her mom's such a piece of work. She *seems* together, but we both know she's not."

"Screw her."

To Taylor's credit, she didn't push it, but Casey knew she was right. Heidi had daddy and mommy issues. The Squad had more than once pried her away from bad boyfriends who would have beaten her up and broken her heart, and she always — *always* — sought approval from *anyone* she felt was above her. Summer Nixon had been no exception.

"I know you don't want to hear it, and I don't blame you," Taylor said, now stroking Casey's skin. "But Ella ... Well, she's really, *really* sorry. They just got caught up. She's heartbroken over this. You should have heard her. It got bigger than they thought it would. Took it too far. I guess some of the girls who busted in on you were Diamond Society, and they were kind of feeding the fire, goading everyone to upload before they could think about what they were doing. I really think Heidi and Ella thought it would be a prank, nothing public."

"That doesn't forgive anything."

"Of course it doesn't," Taylor said.

The room was quiet, save the distant sound of a lawnmower.

"Taylor?"

She looked up.

"I love you, Tay."

Taylor's mouth crumpled. She looked touched in a very specific way. It was with bittersweet nostalgia: the way a person looks when something they cherish is dying.

Normally, Casey's friends rolled their eyes when she gave her signature sign-off, but this time Taylor said, "I love you too, Casey." And somehow, that made it worse.

Within a minute, Casey found herself crying again. Taylor handed her a tissue, and before she knew it, her weeping head was in Taylor's lap.

Taylor brushed Casey's hair from her face.

It was a curse, being able to see. Front and center was that pink phone — her mother's, soon to be her little sister's.

A princess phone for my little princess.

Well, Mom? Look at your little princess now.

THIRTY-THREE

"Ohmygod. This vinaigrette is amazing." Imogen grabbed a waiter by the arm as he was setting down the final plate. "What is this vinaigrette?"

"It's a blood orange reduction, Miss. Grilled pink lady apples, smoked paprika candied almonds, and Point Reyes blue cheese crumbles."

"What's the next course?"

"Kona kampachi or lamb."

Imogen traded the waiter's arm for Melissa's. "Shit, Melissa. Have you ever had Kona kampachi belly? It's like a fish-themed orgasm."

"All orgasms are fish-themed. Except for guys jerking off alone."

"I don't get it." Then she got it, and laughed so hard the glassware rattled. "I'd get wet for a dish like that."

Imogen ate, making noises of pleasure. Taylor watched, not looking down at her greens.

"Speaking of getting wet," Imogen said, "do you remember Donnie from freshman year, Summer?"

Summer mumbled, taken by surprise at Imogen's sudden change of direction.

Imogen went on:

"Didn't you blow Donnie in that club, The Inferno, when you were shitfaced from those tequila bombs?"

Summer was at the opposite corner of the table from Taylor, but Taylor could still clearly see her skin redden. She and her husband tried deliberately not to make eye contact.

"Was it *Donnie* she blew?" Imogen frowned. "Or was it Marcus?" She tugged at Melissa's sleeve. "OMG; Marcus had the biggest cock. And it was all black, way blacker than him, like he'd gotten tired of his original little white one and ordered an upgrade. Did you ever see it?"

"Not like Mason's," Imogen said when Melissa didn't comment. Mason perked up, and the whole table looked at him. "No offense, Mason. You've got a nice dick, but it was nothing compared to Marcus."

"I'll bet his dick isn't as big as you think it was," Melissa said. "You just have little hands."

"I didn't jerk him off or anything, you freak! He just wagged it all over the place at parties!"

Summer tried to keep it in, but the stress was getting to her. She scoffed once, then covered her mouth with her eyes darting self-consciously around.

"Summer will tell you!" Imogen said, seeing her opening. She pointed.

"Girls ... let's ..." Teek's thought wasn't more well-formed than that. He must have been feeling Taylor's agitation, though, because he kept looking over, and now this lame attempt to stop the shop talk.

"Summer was always about the wieners in college," Imogen said. "Remember? She wanted to put a camera in the bathroom when guys were over. Right, Summer?"

Barely looking up, Summer said, "That was a joke."

"Oh, and it's just a coincidence that your big pledge test was a prank involving *wieners?*" Imogen pointed at Mason.

"Just one wiener," Melissa clarified.

John was looking at Summer, but Summer was still pretending not to notice, with diminishing success. Her face was red enough that Taylor swore it was reflecting off her blonde hair.

"Summer," Imogen said, stuffing salad into her mouth as if unaware she meant to keep speaking, "How did you even come up with that prank?"

"Hey, hey ..." John said.

"I mean, I'd never heard of anything like it. You got to see Mason's dick, got back at someone for stealing college guys, *and* got props from Juliet." Imogen held up her hand, seeming to assess it for size. "How big do you think Casey's hands were?"

"Okay, that's enough," Teek said.

Imogen took a butter knife from the table and wrapped her hands around it like a penis, seeming to measure the knife's length. She must have been satisfied because she set it down with a thoughtful little *mmmmmm*.

Fifteen seconds of silence passed before Imogen said to Summer, "The guy Casey was with. How big do you think *his* dick was?"

Taylor smacked her palms, face-down, onto the table. Her index finger hit her fork's tines and sent it into the air with a lazy cartwheel. It landed on her bread plate with a china-cracking clang.

"Will you SHUT THE FUCK UP?"

Leaning forward to see past Melissa and Teek, Imogen was hot to reply. "What's up your butt, Miss Thing?"

"How about you have some respect for the dead?"

"How about you eat my ass?"

"That's real mature," Taylor said. "Just what I'd expect from someone like you."

"What's that supposed to mean?"

They were standing. Not just Taylor and Imogen, but pretty much everyone.

Teek moved in front of Taylor, to intercept, and Melissa stepped away from Imogen to give her free rein.

"Maybe you should just keep your theories to yourself. You and your goddamn 'sisters.'" Taylor looked at Melissa, then stared hard — and long — at Summer. She was hard to read, trying not to engage because eleven years had made her the lovely Summer Merritt, but Taylor could still see the furious, cunt-of-the-year Summer Nixon bubbling under her skin.

With his hand across Summer's front, John said, "Let's all just sit back down. Take it easy."

Ella spoke up. "Why don't you let Summer speak for herself? Awfully quiet down there, Summer."

"I'm just trying to eat my food."

"Not barfing it up like in college?"

Summer wiped her lips with her napkin, then threw it down onto the table. "I never—"

"I said, *take it easy,*" John told Ella.

Summer said, "I guess you're going to try and blame this all on me."

"Well? Who's fault is it?"

"Yours! And hers!" Pointing at Heidi.

"Oh, that makes sense," Heidi said. "Go lick your masters' pussies some more, Summer."

"That's uncalled-for," John told Heidi.

"*Really?* What's she told you about her good ol' days at Coastline? Did she tell you that they just hung out all day planning parties?"

"I know plenty. I've known my wife since—"

"Since her slut-shaming days," Noah cut him off. "Embarrassing high schoolers to slit their wrists?"

"You stay out of this," John said.

"Why me? You're not even *in* this!"

"She's my wife."

Mason laughed.

"Got a problem down there, Mason?" John asked. "How's that resolution to be a decent father going for you?"

Mason stopped immediately, looking utterly confused.

Teek said, "She didn't slit her wrists."

Bindi: "What?"

Heidi: "What does that matter?"

"He said she slit her wrists."

Noah looked down, shook his head, and said, "Jesus fucking Christ, Teek."

"Hey, she's here to find out what happened, right?" Indicating Harper, who Taylor had momentarily forgotten. "*She didn't slit her wrists.*"

"I know she didn't," Harper said.

"And you know that Summer started it all," Heidi added.

"You sure jumped to do it, for something you were so against!" Summer said.

"I was tricked. You tricked us."

Summer gave one loud, hard bark of laughter. She looked at

Bindi. "She was tricked. You hear that, Miss Bridges? Me, your husband ..."

"Don't drag me into this," Bindi said. She was the only one still seated, zip-tied to her chair.

"The thing that matters," Melissa said, "is that she's dead."

Taylor lunged toward Melissa, but Teek was in the way.

As he held his wife back, Melissa smiled and said, "Slit wrists or popped pills, it just matters that she's fucking dead, and that nobody fucking killed her except herself."

"You bitch," Taylor said.

"You pretentious ass."

"You're amazing. Not an empathetic bone in your body, is there?"

"Hey, I didn't kill her." Melissa pointed at Ella and Heidi. "Those two did."

"Shut up, Melissa," said someone. Taylor was shocked to see that it was Summer.

"Them," Melissa clarified, now pointing at Summer, "and her."

"I don't remember you objecting. You and Imogen were all for it." Summer turned to Harper. "They thought it was hilarious."

"It was. So she's dead. That doesn't change the fact that Mason's O-face is ridiculous." Melissa kissed the air at Mason. "Do it for us now, pretty boy."

"Someone should shut your mouth," Mason said.

"Like someone shut Casey's?"

Noah said, "Will you *please* show some *motherfucking respect* for—"

"For who?" Melissa laughed. "You're all hypocrites. We all watched that video when it came out. I'll bet you guys beat off to it. Maybe some of the girls, too. Hell, I did once. Rubbed one right out. It was hot, until it got hilarious." She scanned the table. "I didn't know Casey. I guess in some abstract, cosmic way, it sucks that she died. But *I* didn't know her and *I* thought those videos were awesome and I'm not going to pretend, now that she's gone, that she was my best friend." Another bitter laugh. "Hell. We know what being a best friend of Casey Davis got her."

"Screw you," Taylor said.

"I'd say that *you* already screwed each other plenty. Some nerve you've got, talking about respect for the dead. Casey didn't kill herself until a week after that prank, so how bad could it have been for her? You." She looked past Imogen, at Bindi. "You're a shrink. If someone had an embarrassing incident like this, doesn't it seem like the worst time for them would be right after it happened?"

"Hard to say," Bindi said. "I didn't see her. She wasn't in school the week after."

"So nobody was fucking with her in the halls," Melissa said. "No post-prank hazing. I know she even went to that senior party because Melissa and I were there, too, as guests. Doesn't it seem strange, if the *prank* was the problem, that she'd wait all that time ... and go to a party?"

"Maybe it was her way of saying goodbye," Bindi said.

But Melissa was unconvinced. She sat back down and sipped her water.

"You ask me, something else happened. Something after the prank." Melissa nodded directly at Taylor. "Maybe something having to do with her 'three best friends.' It sounds like you were the only people around that week." Another sip. Then she looked at the sole remaining members of the Girl Squad and said, "Maybe *you* killed her."

Ella, Taylor, and Heidi looked at one another, then at Melissa. The entire table was waiting.

Finally, Taylor spoke. "You're a sick, twisted bitch."

Now tipping back in her chair, Melissa said, "At least I know what I am, Honey."

Taylor snapped forward, hard, and grabbed Melissa's envelope from her place setting. To her surprise, Melissa didn't flinch or intercept, just smiled up at Taylor as if she wanted her to take it.

"I'll bet there's some pretty dark stuff in here," Taylor said, holding up the envelope. "I'll bet what's in here would tear you apart."

And Melissa said, "Try me."

THIRTY-FOUR

October 20, 2023

Melissa was nervous.

And that was a blistering pain in someone's pimply red ass because Melissa Lynch *never* got nervous. She couldn't give a shit if she started a crappy delivery business that distributed its best wares for free.

And still, now, as she leaned with her ass against the table at the SouthTec banquet, Melissa was tense enough to press diamonds. She could feel it in her hands, with their black-painted fingernails gripping the tablecloth. In her rigid body and knotted back. Even in the way she kept catching herself smiling. Who smiled at a client function? Not this bitch.

You don't even need to go onstage. Nobody cares who you are.

But that didn't matter. Melissa spent her days spooling off shitty clickbait articles for her bosses at SHARED, and she was goddamn good at it. She could take any inane subject and make it addictive. Fat child actors? Botched plastic surgery? *For sure.*

But the best articles were about sex. Guys always clicked to find out what women secretly thought of their junk when they talked with their friends, and girls always wanted to know what the guys thought about the feel, look, and smell of their parts. Girls were easier to trigger. Less secure. More victim to media manipulation.

But for this last batch, the client had somehow tracked down SHARED's chief jaded writer and asked for something different. Something nonstandard, creative ... *personally inspired*. At first, the assignment's freedom had been delicious. Only once she was finished had Melissa realized she'd committed a horrible mistake: *She'd put herself into the work.* She *had* enjoyed working on SouthTec's campaign and *was* proud of the articles.

That was dangerously close to giving a shit.

What if the client wanted to talk to her? She was at their company banquet.

Who invited the PR firm's writers to the company banquet?

"Who are you?"

Melissa turned to see the guy she'd nicknamed Marty McFuckface, sampling cheeses from the appetizer spread. "I'm Melissa."

"And who *are* you?"

Stupid McFuckface. "I'm a writer with SHARED."

"What's SHARED?"

Fuck this guy. The moment she'd seen his mustache in that first meeting, she'd hated him. And, sure, Melissa hated most people ... but that stupid fucking mustache. He was like a hipster, but thirty years too old to pull it off. How could he not recognize her?

"We're your PR and social media firm."

"What?"

Oh, fuck you. Even "I don't know what you mean" would have been better. "What?" was just insulting. Like she'd spoken a foreign language. She hadn't worked with McFuckface directly, but she'd gotten ripples from his assholery throughout the entire campaign. Something would stall, and one of Melissa's people would say, "McCafferty doesn't like it" or "McCafferty wants a budget update." Him and his mustache. He even rode a scooter to work, then berated the people who drove trucks because they were murdering the environment. Vegetarian, she seemed to remember. One of the righteous, militant ones.

Melissa drew the sharpest arrow in her quiver. She had basically single-handedly gotten SouthTec the attention that had made this celebration possible, after all.

"I wrote the article series that got picked up by CNN."

"The Bengal series?"

"Yep."

Instead of being impressed, McFuckface scoffed. "Oh. Right." *Snort.* "Enjoy your free shrimp."

He left. Fucking McFuckface.

She needed a drink. Just water. Alcohol would make this worse. But on her way to the bar, she caught sight of someone leaving the kitchen in chef's whites who looked way too familiar.

"Imogen Shah?"

Imogen turned. For a second, Melissa thought she might not recognize her. It'd been ... what? Two, three years since graduation? But Imogen lit up, setting a tureen of something-or-other aside to rush over and take Melissa into a little Ewok hug.

"What the hell are you doing here?" Imogen asked.

"I work for this company's PR firm. Why are *you* here?"

Imogen spread her arms, displaying her coat and toque. "I'm a chef now!"

"You're catering this thing?"

"Oh, no ... I'm more a personal chef. But I know the girl who runs the catering company, and they tossed me a bone. She let me come in to help with sauces."

"Just sauces?"

"Hey, sauces are important!"

They stared at each other for a while, hands on hips. Imogen was beaming to see her old sorority sister, but even Melissa couldn't keep the pleasure off her face or out of her cold heart. Imogen sent the nerves away. It was downright Pavlovian, how her personality responded.

"So you actually became a chef, huh? Figured that was just more of your old bullshit."

"Here and there. You remember my goal from way-back?"

"'Screw your way through the football team'?"

Imogen slapped Melissa's arm. "To be on TV!"

Melissa laughed. "The era of the celebrity chef is dead, you know."

"That doesn't mean that—"

"And you're not a celebrity."

It devolved from there. Melissa was supposed to be mingling and accepting praise. Imogen, Melissa supposed, was needed in the kitchen. It changed nothing. They spent at least fifteen minutes catching up and falling into old patterns as other chefs came and went, looking at Imogen in a way that suggested maybe she should get back to work.

Melissa unloaded, without being remotely emotional. She told Imogen about the job, then finally about McFuckface.

"Wait." Imogen pointed, on the sly. "Are you talking about *that* guy?"

Melissa looked, surprised. "Yeah. How—?"

"Ohmygod, that guy sucks so many dicks. Like a big old *bag*. You could bring dicks in by train and dump them all over his face, and he *still* wouldn't have trouble getting through them all. He'd be like, 'More dicks!'"

Melissa, knowing how it blew her cover, laughed.

"He's been in the kitchen *three times*, Melissa. The first time, he had someone bring him back, and the other two times he just barged in. He said he could taste meat in the béarnaise. Who the hell puts *meat* in béarnaise?"

"What's béarnaise?"

"He was probably still getting aftertaste from all the goat dick. I told him there's no meat in my béarnaise. Then he demanded to see my workstation because maybe someone had cut meat on the same surface. And my knives. He stood there in front of the facility manager and insisted I re-sanitize my knives. As if I got to chopping chervil right after carving up some big-ass butt roast for the carnitas we're not serving, and that the *saucier* wouldn't have anything to do with. And he said he'd had better … Hey, are you okay?"

Melissa's attention had wandered. She'd gotten inside her own head again.

"Just edgy."

"*You?*"

"Shut up."

Imogen looked her up and down. "Wow, these guys really have you messed up." She seemed to remember something, then ran back into the kitchen. It took her a long time to return, but when she did, she was holding her purse.

"Sorry. Took me a long time to find it."

"Are you going to give me a loan or something?"

"No, idiot." Imogen reached into her bag and came out with an orange bottle.

"You're still taking those?"

"I have chronic anxiety!"

"I'm not taking that."

Imogen had already opened the vial, then slipped out one of the small white pills.

"Maybe you're not listening to me," Melissa said.

"Oh, don't be an idiot." She snagged a knife from the appetizer table, then snapped the pill into rough quarters. "Here. A half-milligram. It'll take the edge off."

"What is it?"

"Nyperal. I'm offended that you don't remember my medications."

"Isn't that what you gave Casey Davis?"

Imogen's face darkened. "That's not funny."

"I'm not trying to be funny. I'm talking about the senior party. Remember how she was freaking out and nobody knew why, and she wouldn't tell anyone? You gave her something to calm her down, didn't you?"

Imogen's darkness retreated. "Oh. Yeah."

Melissa looked around. Then got an idea. She raised the pill to her lips, then licked it.

"Gross!" Imogen said.

Melissa ate the pill.

"You're supposed to take pills with water."

"It doesn't taste like anything," Melissa said.

"So?"

"What would one of those full pills do to me?"

"For you? Knock your ass out for the night, probably."

"How fast does it work?"

"I dunno. Maybe an hour?"

Melissa felt her face go evil. "I've got an idea."

"What?"

"Grind one up and give it to McFuckface."

"What?"

"You heard me. He'll fall asleep with his face in the potatoes."

"We're not serving potatoes."

"Come on, Imogen," Melissa said, excited. "It'll be hilarious. Slip it into his Bernie's."

"Béarnaise."

"Whatever."

"Are you serious?"

"Of course I'm serious! He's insulting your food, insulting my work, and generally being a giant douche. Let him get what's coming to him. He'll never taste it in all that cream."

Imogen laughed, as though Melissa were kidding. "You really mean it," she finally said.

"Yes!"

"No way! I want to be a TV chef someday, bitch!"

Melissa sighed, then berated her friend into compliance. There was some protest, as usual. Friendly shoves from Melissa. Finally, Imogen went to the kitchen, then returned ten minutes later, dour.

"I can't believe I just did that."

"Enjoy it," Melissa said.

So Imogen forced herself to. She returned to work, and in the hour following McFuckface's unknowing consumption, she came in and out, reliving old Diamond Society days with Melissa. They theorized as to the whereabouts of some of their sisters, looking up who they could find on LiveLyfe to see who'd gotten plastic surgery or fat or poor or anything else worth mentioning.

Then there was a commotion from the dining room. Melissa laughed when she saw what it was: Tightass McCafferty had collapsed in his chair, dragging half of the tablecloth and its accouterments with him.

"Paul?" someone said. "Paul, are you okay? *Paul!*"

At first, Melissa wanted to guffaw as McCafferty tried and failed to stand, tried getting to his *knees*. He began to twist and squirm, the crowd yelling around him for air. The aging hipster was now on all fours like a dog, back heaving, his body half-convulsing.

His hand went to his throat. His face turned red.

"He's choking!"

Someone circled behind the man, trying to get him upright and into a Heimlich. But McCafferty was finding his strength; he pushed his rescuer away and heaved in a mighty, ugly suck of breath. He wasn't choking.

Someone shouted to call 911, but nobody moved.

He was upright, staggering between tables, looking for all the world like a drunk. There was a pain in her side, and Melissa realized that Imogen was gripping her with tiny iron fists.

"Oh my god!" Imogen said.

"He's just tired. He's just—"

McCafferty grabbed the edge of the nearest table, spasmed once, then unleashed a torrent of brown puke all over his neighbors' dinners.

The heave was a full-body maneuver, repeated three times before he went dry.

He collapsed halfway to the floor, grabbed just in time by a white-haired man in a tux. Several people eased him into a chair, bile in pools down the front of his shirt and tie and jacket. His breath was still rough but coming easier. His head swayed to stay upright.

Imogen couldn't help herself. She rushed forward, into a knot of onlookers. Melissa, keeping her distance, did roughly the same.

"What happened to him?" Imogen asked, even though she knew.

A middle-aged blonde in heels actually laughed. "Too much to drink."

Murmurs surrounded McCafferty, mostly asking the man if he was okay.

"It's better. I'm fine."

Someone said, *"Did anyone call 9 1 1?"*

But McCafferty raised an immediate (if sluggish) hand. "No. No, don't call anyone. I'm okay."

"Are you sure?"

"Too many whiskeys."

A man: "Jesus, Paul. You can't even sit upright."

"... and I haven't slept," McCafferty added.

A woman was beside him, gamely unflinching at the stench. Mrs. McFuckface, Melissa supposed. She said, half to her husband and half to the crowd, "I think maybe it's time we go home."

"You sure you don't want an ambulance?"

McCafferty laughed, but it was an exhausted laugh.

"I think we're okay," the woman said.

Melissa, feeling the crisis averted, turned to Imogen. That had been a near ballbuster, but the asshole would sleep it off and be fine. He'd got what he deserved. Mission accomplished.

Imogen, purse over her arm, was headed for the door. Not the door to the kitchen, either. The outer door.

"Hey," Melissa said. "Where are you going?"

But Imogen's eyes were wet. She refused to look over.

She hit the door.

Melissa followed, calling into the evening's dark. *"Hey!"*

Imogen turned. In a hard voice that Melissa never heard and could not have imagined, her former sister said, "Don't talk to me. *Ever.*"

THIRTY-FIVE

Simon watched the scene with interest.

Taylor stood with Melissa's ripped envelope in one hand and the creamy white card in the other, looking shocked. She hadn't expected Melissa to call her bluff, nor for her to elaborate and tell the story on her own.

"So it was her," Simon said, turning to Harper. "*She* killed Casey."

"I don't think that's what I said, asshole."

Melissa was sitting, contentedly sipping her wine. Simon felt an overpowering urge to do the same. He wanted to take his glass and belt it. Even with three drinks in him (not counting the ones before dinner), this felt too sober for so many memories. After a few second's indecision, he did as impulse commanded. It was an excellent wine.

"Didn't she die of a drug overdose?" Bindi asked.

"Yes," Harper said. "But it was a suicide."

Simon was flustered. It was becoming hard to think straight. Melissa's unabashed story had dredged up some garbage. His thoughts settled as Donovan came to Bindi, reminded by her speaking up, and finally cut the zip-tie binding her to the chair with a whispered apology.

Simon let him finish, then said, "Someone gave Casey the pills, though."

"You heard the story," said Noah. "*Imogen* gave her the pills."

241

"At the senior party! A week before she died! I just gave her part of *one pill!*"

"Why are you always carrying pills, Imogen?" Mason asked.

"I told you! I have anxiety!"

"Maybe you should take one now," Melissa said.

"Fuck you, Melissa!" Imogen blurted, turning.

Melissa shrugged. "Just a suggestion."

"How the hell could you tell that story?" Imogen reached for her envelope, tore it open, then held the white card up with something like bitter victory. "Word for word!" she yelled, showing the table a card identical to Melissa's. "Thanks a lot, bitch! Thanks for sharing *my* secret, too!"

"What did Casey take?" Noah asked Harper. "What killed her?"

"I don't know," Harper said, voice still mild and eyes assessing.

Watching her, Simon wasn't so sure of *that*, either. How could Harper know so much about her party guests, but have no idea what illicit substance had killed the absent guest of honor?

Simon searched for the place he'd made inside his mind, should anything like the Elmer incident ever happen again. It was good to have a place to go, where he could be calm and objective, calculate the best option in any given situation. That skill made him rich, before it turned him poor.

After a short silence, Noah extended an accusing hand toward Melissa. To Harper, he said, "If you're looking for someone to blame for Casey's suicide, I would start with the most soulless person here."

Melissa laughed.

"You think this is funny? You *poisoned* someone."

"Sure," said Melissa, rising to challenge Noah. "But it's just a coincidence that she picked that secret. It's not even the best one. You think you've got me figured out? You don't. I don't give a shit about secrets. I don't believe in them. It doesn't matter to me what people think — especially what any of *you* think. Yeah. I poisoned a guy."

She held up a hand, then ticked items off by folding down her fingers.

"I also stole three thousand dollars from a store I used to work at. Saw a guy get knifed, then ran away because it freaked me out, and never told anyone. A guy I liked was dating this rich bitch, so I had a techy friend plant some fake texts that made it look like she was cheating on him, then stole the guy away, and dumped him two weeks later. I've had three abortions. I use it as birth control because I sure don't use anything else. Speaking of sex, I've had at least two STDs. Never told my partners. I knew a guy who was gay and terrified of telling his parents because they were both strict, bible-beating evangelicals, but I told him to fess up to clear the air. I knew they'd disown him, but I wanted to record the whole thing for a sociology report. When I told my professor, he refused to accept my project on moral grounds. So I called his wife and told her that we were having an affair. I called with four fingers in my mouth and told her I was sucking him off *right now*."

Melissa turned to Harper. "So if you think I give a shit about whatever dirt you've got on me, think again. What are you going to do, ruin my life? I'm still here because I want to hear all of *their* secrets." She looked around the table. "Especially yours, Noah. Everyone knew you were in love with Casey, but I'll bet you secretly fucked a dog."

"You're sick," Noah said. "You goaded a girl into killing herself, and you don't even care."

Melissa didn't back down.

"That's right. I did." She looked at John. "You want to know what kind of person your wonderful wife really is? It was all her idea. She planned the whole thing. She set Mason and Casey up, got her girls to film it, then embarrassed Casey hard enough to never show her face again. And why? Because Casey didn't want to be part of her — *our* — stupid fucking Diamond Society. *And* because Casey seemed to like herself, something Summer couldn't stand to see in others. She seemed to have pride and self-respect. Summer kept seeing Casey around Coastline. A high school girl hanging around college; can you *believe* the audacity?"

Melissa shook her head, still meeting John's eyes. Then to Noah, and everyone she said, "We were all in on it. Everyone in Diamond Society, Mason in his way, her *best fucking friends,* and all of the hypocrites in here who let it happen, then didn't say dick when it did. At least I'm honest. Harper. *Girlfriend.* You want the truth? Yeah, we did some sick shit to Casey, but that's the world for you. Things don't always go your way, and even when you're flying high on the honor roll, sometimes you end up on the internet with a dick in your hand. But suicide? Bitch, it was *over a week* between the day we messed her up and the day she shuffled off this shitty mortal coil. And if she did kill herself because of some stupid prank? Well, then *good riddance.* That kind of weakness has no business in the gene pool."

A long moment passed. Melissa and Harper didn't break eye contact. The star was too calm. Simon looked on, waiting for her detonation. He had no idea why she cared so much about Casey Davis — why she'd gone to such great lengths to solve this mystery. But she did care. *Plenty.* And through the turmoil, she'd been entirely too cool. Something *had* to change.

But instead of blowing up, Harper said, "I agree with you."

Melissa, delightfully, looked slapped.

Harper stood. "Not about Casey deserving anything she got, of course, and not about 'good riddance.' But I agree that she didn't kill herself because of a prank. It's not just that time passed. It's the magnitude of the crime. I've seen the videos, and yes they are embarrassing. I sure wouldn't want *my* private moments exploited so hideously."

She gave Summer a meaningful look while John, speechless beside her, gaped.

"But it's like I said, Casey was stronger than some prank. What happened to her? Even the betrayal by those who meant the most to her?" Another meaningful look, this time at Heidi and Ella. "It was terrible. But it wouldn't have broken Casey. She was stronger than that — proof that what Ms. Lynch says is true. So the question remains: What's missing? What *else* happened to Casey that might have caused her to end it all?"

Down the table, Teek and Taylor were whispering. It had been going on for a while (Simon had noted it even during Melissa's tirade) but was ramping up, becoming almost heated. When all eyes turned to them, they stopped cold.

"*Taylor?*" Ella said, seemingly glad to see her compromised after all the abuse she'd taken herself. "*Teek?* Do you two have something you'd like to share with the class?"

THIRTY-SIX

May 12, 2029

This was the best/worst part, when the girl being held down by a half-dozen guys started to thrash and fight and kick and scream.

Teek had seen this particular video many times before, and it never failed to thrill. He had his pants around his ankles and an iron-hard meat pipe in his hand, countdown initiated. He wanted to synchronize with the part where the woman starts to cry. It couldn't be real, right? Teek even thought he recognized this girl from other videos — so yeah, she was probably a pro. But still, the way she cried? Oscar-worthy shit, if the Academy ever added that "Best Gang Rape" category.

10 … 9 … 8 … 7 …

And then a mechanical sound from the house's bowels. The garage door.

Fuck.

Teek was supposed to have all afternoon. He'd wrangled flexibility at the studio; musicians were night owls anyway. Taylor had never been able to swing anything similar — one reason his attempts to make nice on the whole Come-N-Eat fiasco had fallen apart. Sure he'd gotten them banned from their favorite trashy diner after that dumb dead spider joke, but the day shift didn't know, and if Tay had free time in the middle of the afternoon, they could have gone back.

Maybe that could have closed some of the distance, and spilled some levity into their darkening relationship. He could have made his old jokes ("Come-N-Eat: my two favorite things!") and earned her old smile.

But she was so closed off. Teek had no chance to heal the wound.

Well, for starters, maybe you could stop watching hardcore rape porn instead of having sex with your wife.

But Taylor never wanted to have sex. Or be close. Or even really talk to him. And it's not like Teek enjoyed his fetish. He hated himself for it.

She's probably not affectionate these days because you're into rape porn. She can sense it.

But Teek knew that wasn't the reason. Taylor was ... *sad.* That was the only word. It wasn't anger or irritation; it wasn't even depression. This felt environmental. Something Teek was sure he was somehow causing.

He grabbed the remote, killed the video, raised his pants, and managed to capture his tablet so he could pretend he was reading. But his jeans were tight over an obvious boner. If Taylor saw his face, she'd figure it out — not just the masturbation, but the means. So he rushed to the kitchen. There was an apron in the pantry. Maybe he could put it on, be quirky, pretend to be playful. And maybe, if he was very (very) lucky, he could talk Taylor into some fun times. His wife remained, in Teek's learned opinion, stupidly hot. When she wasn't sad, he loved her to pieces.

"Hey, sexy. How *you* doin'?" Teek asked as she entered. Big grin, turning corny into playful. Hopefully enticing.

"Hey," she said.

"I thought I'd do some cooking."

You? You can't cook tea. "Okay," she said instead.

Teek's grin stayed in place long after she left the room.

With his erection departing, Teek stowed the apron and peeked into the living room. Taylor was on the couch, sitting right where his balls had been a few minutes before when he'd been watching *Taken By Force 7* with 8k clarity.

He ducked back into the kitchen, his heart pounding. Too many close calls. He absolutely, positively, could not use the main TV for this, not ever again. He needed to go into his office or something. It didn't matter if he thought he had the house to himself.

Teek peeked out. "You're home early."

No reply. So he returned to the kitchen, unsure of what else to do. He heard Taylor leave the living room, then walk upstairs. Into the master bedroom, into the master bath. Two doors closed behind her. A familiar feeling descended, and Teek thought, *Shit.*

Taylor had been spending a lot of time in the master bathroom lately. Sometimes taking a bath (and not responding well when he came in to find her naked with frisky intentions), but often just *in there*, without a sound. It was her bathroom, not his. One of the sinks didn't work, so Teek had been using the bathroom down the hall. Just one more way that man and wife were more like roommates.

What did she do in there?

Probably just sitting in there, thinking about how her marriage was falling apart. The spark was gone; the champagne had lost its fizzle. They'd gone from loving to fighting to quiet ... and silence was deadly.

Given their beautiful start — and how dead things had become — only one thing could have soured her so completely.

She knew.

Yep. That was it. Taylor knew *everything*. She knew that while Teek liked all naked ladies, he enjoyed watching them when they were tied up and taken against their will the most. She had probably found his stash and watched every clip, somehow knowing that the parts where the victims protested loudest were always the hottest, and that when they cried it turned him on.

Shit.

Motherfucker shitbox cocksucking bastard.

It wasn't fair.

For one, Teek was 99 percent sure that even his nastiest videos were fake. And even if that still made him feel disgusting, wasn't it worth noting that he wasn't any less disgusted with himself than Taylor must be? Did she think he *liked* being into such filthy shit? No way. This was wiring. He'd tried to walk away, but it had been like a pastor preaching against pornography. You said *no* on the one hand, while the other went down your pants.

Teek felt like scum when he accessed his stash, and even worse afterward. A man who should never be a father or husband. One of those men who made things awful for everyone around them. But goddammit ... *he couldn't help the way he felt.* At least not from the waist down.

And now Taylor knew. Maybe she'd figured it out just now, seconds ago in the living room.

He should go upstairs. Confront her. *Confess* to her.

This frost had been there too long.

They'd always been a great couple, but things had waned and slowly died. No sign. No reason. Unless, of course, this had been the problem all along, and she'd been summoning the pluck to leave him.

Talk to her. Maybe she'd let you tie her up. Tell you to stop, and squirm when you don't.

But that made Teek feel like a thousand times worse. He loved Taylor, and the idea of her as the subject of his hated fetish — even in play — made him want to vomit. It made him sure (and up until now, he only suspected) that he didn't deserve her.

Then just talk to her. Ask her what's up. If she knows, she knows. At least you can get it out into the open.

But what if it's over? What if she leaves me?

Then at least you can move on. Think about it, buddy ... anything is better than this.

And that, at least, was true. Teek would take their old battles over this bullshit every time. Even now, he was thinking back to every look and cast-off glance. Every downcast word, her reluctant acceptance, the way she no longer seemed to participate in their relationship so much as acquiesce.

He walked up the stairs, ten billion pounds on his shoulders. What would happen, when they brought it out into the open? Would she shout? Or cry? Would she leave him? *Report* him? If any of that shit was real, it had to be illegal.

His bedroom door was ajar, so he stepped inside when his knock went unanswered. The bathroom was closed, so he waited. He moved into the hallway, paced, generally tried to make his presence known.

After three minutes, he knocked on the door. Taylor called back, "I'm in here," as if anyone else might be home.

Teek said he'd like to talk to her. Then he moved into the bedroom, sat on the bed, and waited.

She emerged a moment later with red eyes that Teek pretended not to notice. He patted the bed beside him.

"What?"

"Sit. Please."

Taylor sat but said nothing.

Teek sighed. He was no longer sure he wanted to confess. Was he *sure* she knew? And if she didn't, did he want to volunteer it? "Things between us have been ... you've been so quiet lately."

"Just been thinking about stuff."

"About what?"

Taylor thought, then looked away and shook her head.

She knows.

"We don't connect anymore," he said.

"You mean sex."

Something sharp entered his chest. "Not just sex. Let's start by talking about us. You and me."

"There's nothing to say."

"You don't mean that."

"I don't know what you want me to ... I ..." Again, she shook her head. This time it came with a sniff and a swipe at her eyes. She was still wearing mascara, now distressed.

"It's me," he said, swallowing. "That's it, isn't it? I—"

Teek didn't finish, because Taylor started crying.

And then she started to sob. First beside him, then against him, and finally into his lap. Teek wasn't sure why, but all that weeping made *him* want to cry. He was the problem; he'd done this to her. And yet she'd taken hold of him — the cause of her woes — for comfort.

"Hey," Teek said, rubbing her back, unsure of what else to do or say.

"Of course it's not *you*," she said, giving the last word intense, dramatic emphasis. She half-laughed, as if this was all tragically ironic. "I've been wanting to talk. I really, truly have."

With Taylor curled up against him, Teek couldn't see her face. So he looked out the window, baffled.

"I ... I've been seeing someone."

Fuck.

It was so much worse than he'd thought. Not only was Taylor going to leave him; she was cheating on him first. He wanted to feel anger, but it was too blunted by his sins — and given all their ups and downs, hiding his fetish was but one.

"*Seeing someone?*" he repeated.

"A therapist."

An inkling of relief. Teek exhaled. "Why are you seeing a therapist?"

"Because I can't do this alone. I tried. It was killing me."

Teek went silent, paralyzed by this new and baffling information.

She straightened, met his gaze. "She ... My therapist? She said I should talk to you. She's been telling me to for weeks." Taylor mimicked a knowledgeable voice, apparently quoting her therapist. "*He can help you, Taylor. That's what partners are for. He'll want to help, if he's as good a man as you say.*"

Teek's shame withered into guilt. He couldn't accept praise. Not now, not ever. "Tell me what?"

Taylor cried again, but after it was over, she told him a long, spooling story whose conclusion Teek couldn't guess until the end, when she finally offered the punchline. Apparently, his wonderful wife had repressed some childhood memories that were only now clawing their way to the surface. She told him the whole story of what she'd slowly come to realize, just as things between her and Teek began to slip: After every one of her Brownies meetings starting in second grade, someone had molested her. She didn't even know who it was because she'd blocked it all out. It could have been anyone — the scout leader, another parent, a brother ... maybe one of the older girls. Until a few months ago, she hadn't remembered any of it. But the thorn had been cutting her mind from the inside.

Teek held her, let her get it all out. Her manner was hesitant, as if ashamed. Teek kept telling her it was okay, giving her the reassurance she seemed desperate to get.

Why was she ashamed? It wasn't her fault; she'd been seven years old. She hadn't asked for it, or wanted it, or chosen it in any way.

It took a long time. Teek tried to be patient, but this was shredding his insides.

"The worst part is that I realized just a few days ago that there was someone else around. A second person, who let it all happen. Almost like they were standing guard, you know? Just ... just ..."

More tears. He couldn't believe she'd been holding onto all of this. Instead of leaning on him for support. A half-hour ago he'd ascended the stairs with a confession in his head. But at least today, Teek wasn't the problem.

Still, Taylor's revelation nipped at his soul.

Someone else stood by and let it happen.

Taylor gripped his arm, holding him like a life preserver.

Color had drained from the world. Thought was impossible.

"I need you, Teek. I hope you can forgive me."

"*Forgive* you? For what?" She didn't answer. "*Taylor.*"

She clung to him like flotsam, as if she might drown. Most people thought you could recognize a drowning person by the way they shouted and thrashed. In reality, drowning was silent. It came after the swimmer had tired out and given up. A hopeless bob, legs unable to kick, arms unable to rise. The dead simply slipped under.

"Taylor," he said again.

"I'm so glad you're here. You've always been here. I'm sorry I kept it from you. I'm sorry I've been picking fights. I just wanted to feel something. To get us back to normal. What I've put you through …"

Dagger in his chest. Dagger in his heart of hearts.

Guilt, like a tsunami. Not because of the porn.

He had to say something.

Someone else stood by and let it happen.

"You're such a good man." Trailing sobs. Undignified snorts, as her body spasmed, fighting through the last of it. "You don't deserve how I've treated you."

You're a good man.

But he wasn't. Not after what he'd done all those years ago.

He took her by the shoulders. "Taylor, there's something I need to tell you. About Casey."

THIRTY-SEVEN

Melissa was sitting beside Teek, close enough for him to see where her dark eyeliner had caked.

She'd be pretty if she wasn't such a horrible human being.

"It isn't nice to whisper," Melissa said.

"We were just talking," Taylor replied.

"Obviously. About what?"

"None of your business."

"Sure sounded like our business. I heard you say, 'Casey.' And you started up just as our lovely, psychotic hostess here was saying that one little prank wasn't enough to make Casey off herself. Seeing as Casey and her offing is the reason we're all here, maybe you should share."

Everyone was staring. Teek felt X-rayed. Suddenly he was sure they all knew what got him off when his pants were down. He'd slipped a peek inside his envelope while the others were shouting, and sure enough, his fetish was there — Harper probably had her private eye snooping into his internet provider's records. The table was judging him.

"It's between me and Taylor."

"Make it between the rest of us," Melissa said.

"No thanks."

Melissa snatched a hand toward his envelope. But Teek was faster.

The two of them traded stares.

"Oh, come on," Melissa said, leaning back into her seat. "We're all friends here."

Taylor snarled. "Leave him alone. He doesn't have to tell *you* anything."

Melissa leaned forward. "So it was something *he* told *you*. What, is he cheating? Like Heidi's boyfriend?"

"Let it go," Taylor said.

Melissa reached for Taylor's envelope. Despite the need to lean past Teek to get it, Melissa managed to pluck it away. Taylor reacted too late, nearly knocking Teek's water glass into his lap.

Melissa stood, backing off. Taylor stepped forward.

Melissa wagged a finger, smiling, then slipped it beneath the envelope's seal like a threat. "So he told you his secret. Did you tell him yours?"

"We tell each other everything."

Guilt punched Teek in the gut.

"Then tell us what you were talking about." Melissa's finger worked deeper beneath the string.

Taylor looked at Teek, her eyebrows raised.

Maybe I should *tell them.*

"*Taylor ...?*" Melissa's voice was high. Teasing.

"It's up to Teek."

"Teek?" Melissa said.

"No."

Taylor flinched forward as Melissa shrugged. She'd already ripped the envelope around the string enclosure, thin white fingers deftly drawing the cream-colored card from its home. She stopped, defeated. Melissa read the card silently, then rolled her eyes in Harper's direction.

"Oh, *what*, this was the best you could find on Miss Perfect?" She turned to the table and read, *"You were molested as a child."*

Teek put his hand on Taylor's arm, urging her to sit. Heidi put a hand over her mouth and Ella's bitch-face split into something like genuine sympathy.

Downstairs, through the exit behind Donovan, Teek could hear the clatter of servers massing, preparing to bring a new dish to replace their spent salads. Something smelled delicious — out of place in the middle of this psychological massacre.

"For fuck's sake," Simon said. "You couldn't find something that's at least her fault?"

Harper considered the standoff between Melissa, Teek, and Taylor, then let it pass.

Relief flooded Teek. They could handle the mystery without him. And as long as Harper decided not to push, it ultimately didn't matter. *Dead was dead, and the past was the past.* God knew he and Taylor had said that to each other, trying to believe it as they tried to salvage their marriage from this hideous twist.

"The party, then," Harper said. "Let's talk about Casey's night at the Bayshore senior party."

"Casey did *not* go to that party," Heidi said, half-laughing.

"Of course she did," Harper insisted.

"No offense," Heidi said, "but I know *you* weren't there. I was. It was the night after the prank. Why would she go to a big school party, where everyone knew?"

Noah shook his head. "She was there, Heidi."

Teek nodded. Taylor, Mason, and others did the same.

"I didn't see her," Heidi said.

Imogen spoke. "She was upstairs, hiding."

But Heidi still looked confused, not recalling Imogen at the party.

"Either way, who cares?" Bindi said, attention drawing blessedly farther from Teek. "The prank happened on Friday night, but she didn't kill herself until the *following* Saturday, eight full days later. The party was in the middle. Sounds to me like it was neither here nor there."

"Was it?" Harper asked Bindi, her shaped eyebrows high. "*You* were at the party, right? You were the chaperone. So tell us, was it well-behaved and social — just a gathering of friends?"

"Well—"

"It was a drunken fucking mess," Summer said.

"Why were *you* there?" John asked. "You were in college."

"Visiting old friends."

"How is this relevant?" Mason asked.

"She didn't come to school the week after," Ella said. "Maybe something happened at the party."

"Maybe someone saw her drinking alone at the party," Simon offered. "Maybe talked her into suicide. You know, as an easy way out?"

"That's stupid," Imogen said, staring at Simon.

"Hey. *Someone* gave her the gun."

"She didn't use a gun, Simon," Ella said.

"I'm using a metaphor, ever hear of it? How about you, Imogen?"

Imogen rolled her eyes.

"Who was at the party?" Harper asked.

"Everyone," Simon said.

"Every one of you?" Harper asked.

"*Everyone.* I'm *that* good of a host."

Mason said, "I didn't go."

Simon ignored him. "It was the party of the century. You want to talk with all the people who *might have* interacted with Casey? Anyone who might have teased her, made her feel like shit ... maybe got her upset or made things bad enough for her to end it? Okay, cool. Go get a yearbook, then start dialing. You're in for a long night."

Mason stood and threw his napkin onto the seat. "That's it. I'm done."

"We're not finished," Harper said.

"Yes. We are." Mason spread his hands wide, tossing his envelope to the table with a flourish. "Hey, everyone! I'm a successful graphic designer, but only because I took credit for someone else's work. *Boom!* Go ahead and tell the world. I don't care anymore." He mimed dropping a microphone, then turned toward the exit. "Y'all have a beautiful fucking dinner."

Donovan blocked the door.

Mason met him chest to chest. "You seem like a nice guy. I respect that you're just doing your job. But please don't fool yourself into thinking I can't get past you."

Donovan cleared his throat, barely holding his ground. Mason dwarfed him, like a kid facing an NFL lineman.

After a tense moment, Bindi stood. "Screw it. Mason's right. *My husband is cheating.*"

Simon smirked. "Is that what's in your envelope, or Heidi's?"

"Who cares?" She stood behind Mason, waiting for the door. "Put our secrets on a billboard for all I care. I'm tired of this game and want to go home."

Melissa took her cue and stood. "Drugged an asshole. Fuck it. Let's go, Imogen."

Imogen, who seemed to care more about their near-murder at the banquet than Melissa, didn't flinch.

Teek was resolute as well, with Taylor reluctantly abiding.

Heidi stood. So did Noah. Same for Summer, followed by John.

"Move," Mason said to Donovan. "*Please.*"

"Harper," Donovan said. "Maybe now's a good time to tell them?"

Heads turned.

"Tell us what?" John asked.

Harper seemed to consider, then finally sighed. "The main course will be out shortly, and you will want to eat it all, lest you throw everything off."

"Throw *what* off?" Mason asked.

"Your chemistry. The amount of food you eat matters a great deal, I'm told."

A waiter arrived to refill the room's glasses.

"What the hell are you talking about?" Mason asked the moment he left.

"You are free to go, as I said at the beginning. But I would *strongly* suggest that you stay for dessert. Crave's pastry chefs are second to none. We're serving *La Bete Noir* — 'The Black Beast.' A dense flourless cake with Valrhona, elderberry gelee, and toasted Marcona almonds."

She dabbed at the corners of her mouth, then set the napkin in her lap. "It also contains the antidote to the poison that was in your soup."

Taylor felt the bottom drop out of her stomach.

Mouths gaped. Eyes went wide.

"Sit, please. A fabulous pastry will *always* cure what ails you." Then her plastic smile vanished and Harper looked at each person in the room, slowly, deeply, and one at a time. On her face was a gauze of calm, covering the bubbling fury underneath. "Or at least it will cure those of you who I determine have nothing to hide."

THIRTY-EIGHT

Simon spent ten milliseconds digesting what Harper had just told them and another ten considering a nuclear option: leaping past John and Summer to take Harper by the throat. It only took a few more milliseconds to realize how stupid and pointless that would be, and so he stood down.

He had been watching Harper all evening, weighing her as an opponent. She was smarter and wilier than she let on; it took a con to know one. Harper wouldn't be holding the antidote in her handbag. And Donovan, if pressed, surely had a weapon.

Panic solved nothing. Cool heads always prevailed. So to anything but the most watchful eye, it would have seemed that Simon didn't react to Harper's news. Only Melissa, who'd been staring at him (Simon was kind of hot and she needed the distraction) saw his face change.

A flash of naked rage and then it was gone.

Bindi reacted plenty. Harper's words spun her in place by the door, putting her face-to-face with Heidi behind her. There was a flash of anger there as well, but the thing with Donald and his mistress suddenly seemed so far away.

Poison? Had she really said *poison?*

Mason, in front of Bindi, couldn't find his words. He was inexplicably thinking of Jessica. Specifically, he was thinking of how mad she'd be if he died tonight. *Punk-ass, went and kicked the bucket after knocking me up.*

Melissa, on the other hand, had been seeking death for years and considered it a friend. She knew more about the many ways to perish than most, cataloging and researching them like a prized collection. She'd even written a clickbait article: "The Ten Worst Ways to Die (Number Three Will Make You Vomit!)." She found herself wondering what Harper had used: arsenic, belladonna, strychnine, fucking Drain-O for all they knew. It would wrap its chemical hands around her throat at some point and squeeze her to death. Unless Harper decided she was innocent and among the privileged few whose dessert deserved antidote.

John was also thinking of antidotes. Many noxious substances had them; he'd learned that much in college. Epinephrine could reverse a barbital overdose. If someone ingested a heavy metal like mercury, it could be precipitated out by a liquified protein source, like egg white or milk. If you knew what you'd consumed, you were most likely fine.

But of course, only Harper had a clue.

John opened his mouth to speak, but something brushed by him. Noah, who'd decided he was through being a doormat. Ella had stepped on him for years. After learning the twins weren't his, he was through with laying down. Now was the perfect chance to put his money where his mouth was.

He rushed forward, toward Harper.

Donovan moved to intercept, but Noah got there first.

He took Harper by the shoulders and shook her.

"You poisoned us?"

Harper, unfazed despite the shaking: "Don't worry, Noah. If you're innocent, you have nothing to—"

"TAKE IT BACK! TAKE IT BACK RIGHT FUCKING N—!"

Donovan pressed the blue arc of a pocket-sized Black Jack stun gun into Noah's side, shoving 21 million volts through his body.

Everything clenched. Noah was sure that life was over and that his eyes were exploding.

He hit the deck two seconds later.

Ella, rising quite suddenly to her cuckolded husband's defense, stepped past his prone form, arms toward Harper, and got the same treatment.

Heidi, at the far end of the room, had half of her hand inside her mouth, trying to tickle her uvula. She heaved once, twice, and then John yelled to stop her.

"Don't vomit! It'll just—!"

John didn't get to finish *what* it was (*make it work faster, since the poison's already left your stomach*) because someone struck his shoulder from behind, knocking him into Summer's cleavage in a way that she would have found hilarious or perhaps even sexy in situations not involving mortal peril.

"I'm very sorry, sir," said a well-mannered voice. "Perhaps I can find you a moist towelette?"

A waiter, carrying a tray. He wasn't joking, either. John had racked the table on his way into his wife's breasts, and some fancy sauce was now staining his slacks.

"What?"

"My apologies. We will, of course, cover any damages."

"What the hell are you talking about?"

Six white-gloved waiters were circulating in the melee, distributing plates from platters. One server was making a loop, retrieving soiled silverware. He stepped over Noah and Ella with a refined, "Pardon my reach" as if diners at Crave frequently hit the deck while doing a little shake and maybe peeing themselves.

To Imogen, one of the waiters said, "You had the pan-seared kampachi belly?"

And Imogen, who still hadn't left her seat, was shocked into agreeing. A plate arrived before her — passionfruit and shallot soy yuzu and liliko'i. Imogen could barely manage a baffled *thank you*. The dish smelled heavenly.

As did the Gower salt marsh lamb breast with slow-baked onion, Sicilian pistachio puree, and nasturtium that someone had set at Heidi's place while she was working to return her salad from the depths. Just as she succeeded and threw up spectacularly into the corner (and all down her arms), Summer was receiving the same dish. She looked up at her waiter and whispered, *"Call 911. That crazy bitch poisoned us!"*

The waiter nodded politely and said, "Enjoy. The protein in your dish comes from a small farm in Scotland, and takes 28 hours to cook *sous vide*."

Heidi puked again. Taylor sat silently nearby, white as a sheet.

Teek panicked, now reconsidering his decision to stay silent. But he knew what would happen if he told the story now. Harper had poisoned them. If it turned out that she didn't already know what he did, what might she do next?

Not to everyone. You probably won't be walking out of here, but at least Taylor might.

And if you can somehow trade desserts with someone who's innocent, you'll walk out, too.

Simon was taking a different approach. In his mind, the whole party was one big social puzzle. A zero-sum game of the most extreme sort. He'd solved problems like this before, in life and business. When things went rotten, folks needed someone to blame. Right now, with no clear boogeyman, Harper might hold the whole room responsible. Wasn't it better to save someone than no one? Focusing the blame for Casey Davis was the sensible, logical thing to do. It was downright altruistic when you thought about it.

Summer? Yes, she makes an easy enough target. Everyone knows that Summer's a bitch. Everyone knows she'd ordered the prank that started it all. Miss Bridges was right; the senior party is a distraction. Nothing to see there. Instead, look only at Summer.

It felt right. One neck for the guillotine instead of twelve, and what excellent luck: the remaining neck wasn't even his. Summer was no big loss — and given what Simon knew about her, she wouldn't be able to fight back. She wouldn't dare.

And if Harper needed more people to punish, he could toss in Ella and Heidi. He had a little cache of secrets himself, thanks to a certain tech venture in his past. They had betrayed one of their best friends. Fuck them. They deserved whatever they got.

Meanwhile, Summer was wondering if she could deflect blame to Mason, who'd loved Casey and left her.

Ella considered blaming Heidi. Summer first, but Heidi too if push came to shove.

To her credit, Heidi was thinking in the inverse direction.

John stood and moved toward the man by the door.

Donovan saw his approach but was too absorbed in the melee to care.

This was all spiraling out of control. Donovan had prepared, but not for this. He kept a hand on his stun gun and his eyes on Harper.

But of course, her eyes were on the past.

Main Course

Your choice of:

Pan-Seared Kona Kampachi Belly
With Black Lava Sea Salt,
Passionfruit and Shallot Soy Yuzu, and Liliko'i

or

Gower Salt Marsh Lamb Breast
With Slow-Baked Onion,
Sicilian Pistachio Puree, and Nasturtium

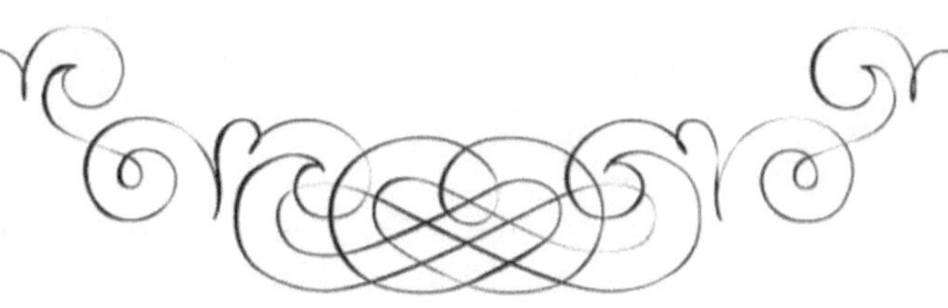

THIRTY-NINE

May 19, 2018

"Put him down, Kimmy," Casey warned.

Kimmy — technically fourteen but watching Casey with all the guile of a thirty-something — held the stuffed dog for a few more seconds before finally setting him aside. Casey knew her sister well enough to know what had happened in that pause: Kimmy had seriously considered doing the dog voice again, moving his little paws up and down to make it clear who was supposed to be speaking.

Casey's glare had stopped her. Despite their usual game of using her favorite stuffed animal as persuader-slash-ballbuster, Casey didn't want to hear more. There were lines to push and others to cross. Kid sisters walked that line carefully.

"I'm just saying," Kimmy said.

"You're always just saying."

"I'm just saying that—"

"See," Casey interrupted, "this is the problem. Announcing that you're 'just saying' something doesn't suddenly make me want to hear it. There is no freedom of speech in here. You want freedom of speech, go into your own room."

"I'm bored in there."

"Then go downstairs."

"I'm bored down there, too. Besides, even if Mom and Dad *were* home, they wouldn't let me talk about it."

"That makes three of us," Casey said.

Kimmy pouted, then rolled onto her back. Ranked lines of stuffed animals leaned between Casey's pillow and the wall, in rough order of size. Casey's and Kimmy's room were like two sides of a portal between parallel universes: similar in substance, but opposite in order. Every morning, Casey made her bed, lined up her animals, and organized her folders for the school day ahead. Kimmy tossed everything into one big pile and trusted the system to find her what she needed.

As Kimmy flopped back, one of the animals fell forward, somersaulting over the covered pillow. She picked it up: a blue narwhal named Spike. Kimmy liked holding Casey's animals. If her 18-year-old sister could have toys on her bed, then it must be okay for Kimmy to own them, too. Eighth graders were more serious than seventh graders. More into texting, Snapchat, and YouTube than the bracelet-making and dog posters Kimmy had been into a few years back.

She studied Spike, then returned him to his row. This was Casey's room, not hers.

She stared at the ceiling.

"Come on, Casey. If my big sister won't tell me how to handle dangerous stuff on the internet, how am I ever supposed to figure it out?"

Casey ticked her eyes toward her sister but said nothing.

Kimmy, seeing this, mumbled, "Probably end up with one of those kiddie porn guys. It's okay to send strangers pictures of yourself in the bathtub, right?"

Casey rolled her eyes, turning. "Fine."

Kimmy sat up.

"*Fine*, Kimmy, but don't think I don't know what you're doing."

Kimmy nodded, not wanting to jinx this spectacular moment of luck.

Casey met her eyes. She squinted semi-theatrically. "And don't go thinking you can manipulate everyone like you manipulate your family. You're going to drive Dad nuts when boys start calling. Don't make it worse for him by batting your eyes around school to get what you want. Boys only take it as encouragement."

"That's the idea."

"Promise me, Kimmy."

She rolled her eyes. "Fine. Promise."

"Luckily, you've got the family curse."

"What curse?"

"No boobs. Tall, and no boobs."

"I've got boobs." She didn't, though, compared to her friends.

Casey waved a showing hand around her unspectacular chest and intoned, *"Gaze into your future."*

They were close enough now that Kimmy could slap her hand away, so she did.

"At least you'll be able to play basketball," Casey said.

"Stop trying to change the subject."

Casey's smile vanished. She exhaled. "Okay. Fine. What do you want to know?" Then, a better question: "How much do you *already* know?"

Kimmy told her. And despite Casey's best attempts to keep the video of her and Mason from the world, Kimmy had already heard about it. She'd got the play-by-play from friends, heard both the mockery from enemies and the mumbles in Target (*That's that girl's sister!*), and had even seen some of the clip at Molly Weyland's house. She hadn't seen the most interesting part, with the guy's thing, but it was only a matter of time. She'd heard rumors that it'd gone off in Casey's hand and sprayed goo everywhere.

"Ew," Casey said when Kimmy reported this. "No."

"If it's gross, why would you do it?"

"It's not that it's gross." Casey paused. "For me ... at eighteen years old."

Sigh. *"I get it."*

"That didn't happen in the video." She looked away, then exhaled harder. "Dammit; I hate that this is how you're going to learn about this stuff."

"I *know* about handjobs, Casey." *Because duh.*

"You'd better not be—"

"Not *doing* them, dork. I just *know* about them."

"What do you know, besides the video itself?"

"Dunno. That you like Mason Pace?"

She wasn't sure about that. Right now, Casey neither liked nor disliked him. She needed time to understand what she felt — other than lethal levels of embarrassment. Her parents, during this first ...

what ... almost 24 hours? So far they'd pretended not to know, but they knew.

Everyone knew.

Right now, whatever feelings she may or may not have had for Mason were tangled up in all of it. She'd return his calls soon, and then she'd be able to face him. But not yet. Only over the past half-day had she finally begun to feel sort of okay again, when sufficiently distracted.

"I meant, what do you know about the prank?"

"What prank?"

"It wasn't just some random video of us ... well, *you know*. You got that, right?"

Kimmy shrugged.

Casey sighed, slid onto her side on the bed, and looked up at Kimmy with her serious face.

"Okay. That's kind of important." And then, as honestly as she could, Casey told her kid sister pretty much everything — except the genitalia-related bits that she would forever pretend Kimmy didn't already know. It wasn't just that someone had caught her and Mason in a compromising position. It was that she'd been set up and then broadcast.

"Are you serious?" Kimmy asked when Casey finished.

"Of course I'm serious. Didn't you see how *mad* I was when I came home last night?"

"I figured you were embarrassed. Molly's sister Brenna said you guys snuck off to get it on because you just couldn't wait. But I guess she also said you guys hooked up for the first time at the party, and I know you went out with him a few times before, and ..."

Casey held up a hand, eyes closed. She'd gotten whiffs of what Kimmy was saying already. As time passed, the rumors would only get worse.

"Brenna's an idiot. It's not true, Kimmy. They set us up, from start to finish. And we *had* been on a few dates before, like you said. It turns out we'd liked each other for years beforehand. Maybe we moved a little faster than we should have, but ... it's not like that. Don't believe what they're saying. Not for a second."

Kimmy bobbed her head. "Of course."

Seeing that simple nod, Casey envied her. She hadn't entered high school yet, or seen how bad it could get. Kimmy knew that kids could be jerks, but she was still naive enough to believe that her big sister always knew right, could see the direction of her life's ship and how to set the sails. A few years from now, Kimmy might look back and doubt Casey's protests. But for now, the fact that Casey said something was still reason enough to believe.

"Kids can be mean, Kimmy."

"I know that."

"You know it on a Crestmont Middle School level. You go to Crestmont because you live in this neighborhood. Bayshore is different. When you go there next year, it's because Mom and Dad had to apply to get you in, then paid buttloads of money."

"Because it's a boarding school. That's the cool part. You only have to stay at home when you want to."

"Because it's *exclusive*," Casey corrected.

"So what?"

"When not everyone can do something, the people who *can* do it get all snobby about it. You wouldn't believe the bitches at Bayshore."

"Oh my God, Casey. There's this girl in my science class, Carly Chester? She's such a bitch."

"I don't know Carly, but I'll bet it's Carly times a hundred at Bayshore." A small smile. "I'm talking maximum bitchitude."

"Carly put gum in this one girl's hair on the bus. On her *birthday*."

Casey scoffed. "*Gum. Amateurs.* At Bayshore, it's all psychological warfare."

"What do you mean?"

"The girls at my school know your innermost secrets. The stuff you don't tell anyone and the stuff you've always been afraid of or are self-conscious about. So, like, maybe you used to wet the bed, like all the time. They know it."

"How?"

"Dark magic. And what'll happen is, you'll keep coming home and your bed will be all wet. Someone sneaks in and pours water on it to mess with you, over and over again."

"Couldn't you set up cameras?"

"These girls are ninjas, Kimmy. Maybe you didn't hear me."

"You're making that up."

"If their family belongs to a better country club than yours, there'll suddenly be rumors everywhere that your parents can't pay tuition. People will offer to buy your lunch, and it seems nice of them, but you know they're doing it because they heard something, like you're dirt poor, or because they're just screwing with you. But only if you *already* feel inferior. See what I mean? They're inside your head."

"Bull," Kimmy said.

"Tell that to the girl who didn't get her first period until she was fifteen, then kept finding tampons in her bag for the next four years."

"Did that really happen?"

"You bet. And a ton more. *Man*, are you in for it next year. I hope nobody finds out I'm your sister."

But despite the truth of Bayshore's horrible girl culture (and, she was sure, an equally shitty boy culture, rife with adrenalized elitism), Casey was smiling. Kimmy always made her feel better, even when she wasn't trying.

Then Kimmy gave Casey one of her serious looks — the dramatic one she used in school plays or her numerous DIY film projects with friends.

"You can't let them get you down, Casey."

Casey barely refrained from ruffling Kimmy's wavy blonde hair. "Okay, kiddo. I won't."

"I mean it, Casey. Mom said you're staying here tonight."

"What, I'm not allowed to spend a night at home?"

"She said you might not even go back to school next week."

"Don't you want me around?"

"Be serious, Casey."

Casey's shoulders rose, then fell. "I just need some time. This kinda sucks, you know."

"If you don't go back, it'll get worse. Those bitches will talk about you and you won't be there to defend yourself."

"Well," Casey said, "it's true they smell fear."

"Promise me you'll go back on Monday."

Casey let her jaw hang slack and answered in a voice of overdone exasperation. "I'll *think* about it. But absolutely no promises, okay?"

"Okay."

Casey's face became normal again. "Either way, we still have tonight and tomorrow to watch movies."

"Isn't tonight the big senior party?"

Casey's answer was half-word, half bark. *"Yeah."*

"So ... no movie tonight."

Casey's head shook, red hair flying. "Oh, I'm not going to the party. No way, no how."

At this, Kimmy seemed deeply offended.

"No, Kimmy. Absolutely not."

"But it's the *senior party!* You've been talking about it forever! *Everyone's* gonna be there."

"Exactly. *Everyone's going to be there.*"

"Jackie would tell you to go and face them," Kimmy said, plucking at the sheets.

"Already did, earlier today. I should never have told you about each other. You're too much alike."

"So ...?"

"I said I'd go. But I changed my mind."

"You *lied?* You can't *lie! You have to go!"

"Kimmy, no! Screw them and their stupid party! This is my decision, and I say no. You can't know what this is like for me!"

"Casey!" Kimmy whined.

Casey put on her mocking face and replied, *"Kimmy!"*

They sat in silence for a few seconds — just long enough for Kimmy to marshal her argument. Then she carefully said, "You've been looking forward to this party. You really want to go. You said it was the send-off you all deserve."

"Yes ..."

"And now you're just going to give it up because of some dumb prank?"

"Not just 'some prank,' Kimmy. Everyone's talking about me right now — *everyone.* Not to be crude, but they've all seen me naked, kid. *Doing stuff.*"

"Stuff they all do too, right?"

"Not on YouTube."

"So? You got tricked!"

"And most people are hearing the version you heard, where I wasn't tricked — just *caught.* And besides, I told you, two of my 'friends' did this to me. The only Bayshore friend I have left is Taylor, and she might not even go. Who am I supposed to hang out with? *No,* Kimmy. Forget it."

Casey looked toward her dresser, already dreaming of soft

pajamas and popcorn at home. She was tired of this discussion. She'd be better tomorrow, but right now she wanted to forget it all existed. Kick back at home and pretend she was fourteen again.

When she looked back up, Kimmy was holding the stuffed dog, lips pursed as she prepared to do the voice.

"*Pweeese,*" Kimmy droned, speaking for the dog.

"Now, why the hell does *he* care if I go to some dumb party? He's just a dog."

Still in the voice, Kimmy said, "*Because if you don't go, those mean girls will think they got to you.*"

"They *did* get to me. But I'll get over it."

Kimmy moved the dog's stuffed arms up and down, animating the words. "*And I'm worried that if you don't go, Kimmy won't have a good example to follow when bad people try to get* her *down.*"

"That's kind of a low blow, don't you think?"

"*I'm only trying to give you tough love.*" And then Kimmy, because the dog couldn't, made an over-the-top frown.

"Put him down, Kimmy."

Kimmy didn't. "Pweeese, *Casey?*"

Casey sighed. "*Fine.*"

Kimmy's face lit up. "You'll go?"

"*Whatever,*" Casey said. Then she stared at the stuffed dog and told it, "Fuck you, Harper."

"He was only trying to convince you for your own good," Kimmy explained.

"Yeah, right." Casey stood and moved away from the bed and her pajamas, toward the vanity she'd grown too old for. Apparently, she was getting dressed in her party clothes. Apparently, she was donning makeup — both figuratively and literally putting on a brave face. "Nobody around school saw *his* boobs."

Kimmy picked up the dog. "He's naked all the time. If he was a girl, we'd *constantly* be seeing his boobs."

"Great."

Kimmy turned the animal over in her hands. He was brown, floppy, and even his collar was gender-neutral.

"What kind of a name is 'Harper' for a boy dog, anyway? It's better for a girl."

Casey was focusing on her reflection. "I can't believe I'm going to this stupid party."

"You're doing it because you're tough."

"I'm doing it because my sister is a pain." She reached for Harper, holding him in the traditional speak-for-the-dog pose. And in the same voice Kimmy had been using a moment ago, Casey said, *"Casey hates you for forcing her to go to the party."*

"Yes. Of course," Kimmy told the stuffed animal.

But at least Kimmy was happy. Happy *for* her sister's bravery, Casey supposed. But that didn't make going any more comfortable.

"And just so we're clear," the dog continued, *"Casey is only doing this for you."*

FORTY

May 19, 2018

Simon walked to the pair of jocks holding red cups of beer, touched each on the shoulder, and offered his most winning smile. He thanked them for coming. Asked how they were doing, wondered if the football team was going to beat Southern in the upcoming game. They were just a little drunk, but their inebriation wasn't the reason the exchange went well — that they didn't find Simon's check-in absurd or cheesy. Senior Fever took care of that.

Tonight, everyone was friends, from the most popular rich girl to the lowliest burnout — of which Bayshore had few, but which had still clustered tonight. The house was mingling. Comrades who had crossed time and space and high school together, about to disembark the crazy train and get on with their lives.

Simon's phone rang. Miss Bridges, the counselor and student council staff advisor who'd green-lit this party. After okay'ing it, and making sure all the invitations went out, Bindi found herself unable to attend for longer than the introductions. Simon knew that would happen. It wasn't easy to convince people that his ideas were theirs. Fortunately, he excelled at it. The skill would make him billions, now that high school was pretty much over.

"Miss Bridges! How's the symphony?"

"How did you know I was at the symphony?"

Dammit. Simon couldn't admit to deliberately steering the party based on her plans, but he recovered quickly, the smile still in his voice. "I can hear the lobby sounds in the background. You're at Silas Hall, near the stairs."

"That's ... how did you do that?"

"I've been there many times with my parents. Say hi to Jimmy for me. He's the usher with the gravelly voice who sits at the kiosk. Is this the night where they're spotlighting Vivaldi?"

"Why ... yes."

"I'm sure it's lovely."

"It is."

Pause. Simon kept smiling as two girls passed with admiring looks.

"So, um ... is the party going okay?"

"Everyone is having a great time."

"No alcohol, right?"

"What did I promise you?"

"Can I speak to your parents?"

Simon saw this coming, and he'd made a devil's bargain. Dad was seeing his secretary and Mom had been out of town for a week. Father and son pretended that neither knew the other's secret. Dad could go to whatever hotel he wanted while Simon told Mom he'd stayed home. If he contradicted Simon's story, that meant trouble with the missus. Another fortunate aligning of stars that Simon had arranged with a grin and a flourish.

"Of course." Simon moved into a bathroom for the echo effect, then spoke to no one. "Dad, it's Miss Bridges." He pushed the toilet brush around, creating sloshing sounds. With his face away from the phone, he said, "Hang on a sec" in a voice sort of like his father's.

He shouted as if something had gone wrong.

"Simon?"

"I'm sorry. Someone broke one of the toilets. He's fixing it right now." Then again to nobody: "Dad? She wants to talk to you."

"Wait, Simon — if he's in the middle of something ..."

"It's no problem. Please, just hang on a sec."

Simon made more splashing.

"Simon?"

"Yes?"

"Maybe you can just have him call me back in a few minutes."

"Aren't you at intermission?"

"Yes, but we just got out. If he can call in the next five or ten minutes, it'll be fine."

"Are you sure?"

"Of course." And she gave him a number.

Simon thanked her, called his father, and informed him that he'd just been cleaning a toilet. He gave him Miss Bridges's number. Then Simon hung up, knowing that she would enter the second half of Vivaldi assured that the party had its chaperones responsibly in place.

There was a pitcher of Long Island iced tea on the counter. Someone made it earlier because they didn't like beer. It smelled like 95% alcohol by volume and contained half of the liquor cabinet. Simon picked it up on impulse, then circulated. If a cup was empty of beer, he filled it with fire.

"Sadie! I'm so glad you could make it. And James ... are you two together?"

Simon moved on, through the kitchen into the dining room into the living room. His classmates were already making a mess. This gathering wouldn't get as sloppy as some low-rent frat party (that, Simon vowed), but cushions were off the couch, smashed chips were in the carpet, and motherfuckers weren't using coasters. But it was cool — Dad would cover for him, and the maid would have more work in the morning.

"Simon!"

He turned, said hello, asked if the group who'd shouted was having a good time. He reminded them that there was a pool outside, and a hot tub. No barfing in it, please.

There were nerds in his study. Of course; that's where the books were. Simon guessed they'd seen neither a party nor natural light in a while. They were pale and barely looked up from their phones or Switches or whatever. But they were his guests.

"You guys need anything in here?"

"We're good."

"Chips? Pretzels? Someone somewhere is ordering pizza."

"No, thanks."

"Come on. Brian. We went to elementary together. I *know* you like pizza."

"Okay, fine. Maybe some pizza?"

Another smile. "I'll send them down."

Then Simon dutifully found the group ordering pizza and sent them after the nerds.

Everyone would be happy tonight. This was the senior party alright, but it was *Simon's* party, too. And dammit if his guests would be less than cared-for inside these walls.

On the way down the big stairs, he collided with a blonde it took him a few seconds to recognize. "Is your name Summer?"

"Yes."

"Summer ... Nixon."

"Yeah."

"You graduated last year, am I right?"

"Yes, but Jason Granger said it'd be okay if—"

Simon smiled wide enough to show all his teeth. "You think I might not be okay with college girls at our party? Make yourself comfortable. Beer is in the kitchen; snacks are everywhere. Including on the floor." He laughed. "Who are your friends?"

Summer, seemingly overwhelmed by Simon's graciousness, looked to the two girls flanking her. "This is Melissa."

No response from Melissa, though Simon tried to shake her hand.

"And Imogen."

"Ohmygod, your house is like off the chain. What did this place cost?"

"At least ten bucks."

Imogen didn't seem to get it. So she said, "Do you have a movie room?"

"Just down the hall."

"A wine cellar?"

"Yes, though not in the cellar because we don't have one. Unfortunately, it's locked. Sorry. My parents wouldn't just kill me if someone got in there. They'd die themselves."

"Imogen," Melissa said, "stop embarrassing yourself."

Simon moved to go, but Imogen stopped him.

"Wait," she said. "Is Casey Davis here?"

"Casey?" Simon felt off guard. He had seen her, yes. He remembered because he'd been so shocked by her arrival. The last time he'd seen Casey, it'd been onscreen with her shirt off and her hand down Mason's pants. That had made things awkward, considering how friendly they usually were. But after he'd seen her — from across the room, while he'd been in the midst of other host duties — he'd lost her, and hadn't seen her since. Had she left?

"Casey Davis," Imogen repeated. "Red hair, skinny, looks kind of like—"

"I know who she is. Yeah, she was here. I'm not sure if she is anymore."

"Why?"

"Well, honestly, there was this 'incident' with Casey at Bayshore yesterday."

"I know about the video," Imogen said. "That's why I want to talk to her."

"Imogen," Summer said, taking her wrist.

"Get off! I told you I was going to talk to her, so just get over it." To Simon, about Summer: "I swear, she won't take no for an answer."

"About what?"

"Let's just find her first, at least," Summer said, now uncomfortable.

"I want to apologize, and she doesn't want me to."

"It's not that I don't want you to," Summer said.

"It's just that Summer look worse by comparison if she *doesn't* apologize," Melissa said.

"Shut up, Melissa."

Imogen turned to Simon. In a single breath, she said, "We're kind of the reason that all happened and it sounded really funny at the time and it got Summer into Diamond Society and us kind of too, but now it just seems shitty."

Simon blubbered. "You mean ... *You?*"

Imogen put her hands on her hips. "So where is she?"

Simon didn't know, but there were places he hadn't thought to check. Now acutely interested, he led them on an off-limits tour starting on the main floor and continuing through the rest, including in his parents' bedroom on the upper level.

They found Casey alone in the guest bedroom, her face red and her manner slow, a bottle of gin in her hand.

"There she is." Imogen left the group, rushed forward to sit beside Casey like an old friend, then said, "Look. That was super shitty of us. I feel bad. I'm really sorry. They are too." Pointing at

Melissa and Summer, who seemed more paralyzed than apologetic. "This one time, I was in the bathroom at a party, and I wasn't just sitting on the toilet; I actually had one leg up and was *changing my friggin' tampon* and this guy walked in and just stared right at me and I was like, 'Get out, you freak!' That was sooo embarrassing. So I totally know how you feel."

Imogen tried to put an arm around Casey, but she turned to look at Imogen like she had seventeen heads. "Get out of here."

"Look," Imogen went on. "It's not so bad. Stuff passes. And we didn't mean for it to be like that. It was Summer's idea and—"

Summer came alive. *"You went along with it just fine!"*

"Shut up, Summer! Do you know how this feels?" To Casey: "She doesn't know how it feels. She was born with a silver spoon in her vagina."

Impossibly, Casey laughed a little. Simon saw her eyes waver, realized how drunk she was. Had she circulated at all, or just come up here after pinching from the liquor cabinet? And if she was planning to do that, why come at all?

The bottle was half empty.

"Stop acting like you're a saint, Imogen," Summer snapped.

"Get out of here," Casey said — a little to Imogen, but mostly to Summer. "They *told* me you put them up to it."

"Who?"

"I SAID GET OUT OF HERE!" Casey blurted, anger like lava.

She seemed to consider throwing the bottle at Summer, then used her free hand to hurl a small, decorative box instead. It struck a bookcase nowhere near her head.

"Let's go," Melissa said. "Get some Cheetos or something."

"I don't like Cheetos."

"Fuck, you're stupid, Summer," Melissa said. Then they were gone, leaving Imogen and Casey on the bed with Simon still by the door.

The girls seemed to have forgotten him. Imogen, if she'd honestly been part of this, was making headway toward forgiveness with shocking velocity. Casey seemed to have spent her emotions on gin, moving through catharsis to whatever lay beyond. It was clear she wanted a friendly hand, even if it had so recently helped to stab her. Simon already knew Ella and Heidi were her enemies, and apparently Summer Nixon, too. Imogen must have been far enough away to be acceptable. It was the kind of comfort she might resent later, but for now Imogen had her hand on Casey's shoulder.

Someone passed behind Simon in the hallway, then backtracked. Teek Sheridan. He stood by Simon's side, took in the two girls in what had become a half-hug, and paused in reverence. His breath reeked of beer and in the corner of Simon's eye, Teek wobbled on his feet.

He had undoubtedly seen the video like everyone else. His thoughts, though immature, were obvious. Simon couldn't blame him. Wrong or not, that video had been hot. He'd never seen Casey that way before. Apparently, she was up for a good time after all.

"Are they making out?" Teek asked. Then quieter: "*Can I watch?*"

"Shut up, Teek."

"Who's that Indian girl?"

"Some college girl from Coastline."

"I'll bet they start making out."

"Get out of here, Teek."

But Teek didn't get out. Instead, he moved into the large room and sat on a big, puffy chair way back in the corner. Simon picked up a coat that'd been lying by the door and threw it at him, but Teek caught the garment and pretended to snuggle into it. There were other coats under him on the chair. Teek set down his beer and proceeded to make a nest out of the abundant outerwear, wrapping himself as if for a nap. If Simon hadn't seen Teek enter his cocoon, he might not even know he was there.

"I'm really sorry," Imogen was saying.

Casey started to cry.

"It's okay," Imogen said.

"I don't want you here."

But Imogen just patted her shoulder.

"Seriously," Casey said.

"Shh."

Teek eyed Simon. His eyebrows went up and down.

Simon gave him a look: *What are you, an idiot?*

"You guys can go," Imogen said to Simon.

"I want him to stay." She apparently hadn't noticed Teek.

"Why?"

"Because I don't like you."

"You just don't know me. I'm actually super cool. But I get caught up in shit. It's like a problem I'm trying to get past."

"Just ... just go."

But Casey was in a downward spiral, and it was clear. Not only was her body sloppy and her speech slurred and her eyes unfocused; her chest kept hitching at random intervals, her mood wavering and nowhere near controlled.

Then she just started bawling.

"Guys," Imogen said. *"Go."*

Simon backed up a step, but no more. "Is she going to be okay?"

"She'll be fine." Imogen eyed him, waiting for Simon to leave before she did whatever came next. But Casey was crying harder now, shoulders shaking, actually leaning into Imogen's chest. She was blabbering about *all she'd worked for* and *what her parents would think* and *how she was letting Kimmy down* — whoever Kimmy was.

Imogen fumbled one-handed in her purse, coming out with a pharmacy vial. "I have something that'll help you."

Casey was drunk, flagging.

"Casey? Casey."

She looked up, eyes red.

"Take one of these." Imogen handed the bottle to Casey.

"It hurts. This ... *hurts.*"

"I know. It will make the pain go away. Help you relax. You won't be able to see things clearly if you can't relax." She shook the vial. "They're just little ones. No big deal."

"I don't take drugs."

"It's not a drug." Her head tipped. "Okay, I guess it's technically a drug. But not that kind. I take these all the time for anxiety." Imogen put her purse on the floor and patted Casey's hand. "Seriously, honey. It'll help."

"Casey?" Simon said from the doorway.

"Give us some space, will you?" Imogen said.

So Simon backed away. He thought to ask whether it was a good idea to drink while taking pills, but Imogen sounded like a veteran. It'd be fine.

He was in the hallway again, then back down the stairs. Fifteen minutes later, his phone rang. Simon moved into the hall to take the call.

"Dad?"

"Hey, sorry to bother you," Simon's father said. "I wanted to let you know that I talked to that woman for you. Exchanged a few texts afterward, too, like she was still nervous but didn't want to call again."

"She's at the symphony. Probably texting from her seat."

"Oh. Well, anyway. Just so you know, I may have mentioned that you were watching *Die Hard* on the big screen, if that comes up."

"Okay. Thanks, Dad."

"Are you having fun?"

"Sure. Nothing like a hundred kids in the house to make for fun times."

"And everything's okay? I got the feeling from your advisor that I'm kind of on the hook if anything goes wrong."

"It's fine," Simon said, finding his temper suddenly short. He'd been trying to circulate, but he kept thinking of Casey.

"You're not doing anything you shouldn't be doing, are you?"

"I don't know, Dad. Are you doing anything *you* shouldn't be doing?"

Silence on the line.

"All right, son. Have a good night."

And he hung up.

Simon felt something (he wasn't sure what; the evening had birthed emotions from joy to lust to anger to fear, and it wasn't even ten), then turned his head to the staircase. Something was telling him (*compelling* him, really) to go back upstairs, to Casey.

But he wouldn't. He knew he shouldn't.

Simon turned to move into the kitchen and found himself up against Imogen's ass as she bent to look behind the couch. Confused, he waited for her to emerge, then raised his shoulders in lieu of a question.

"Oh, hey. Have you seen a purse lying around?"

"Is Casey okay?"

"What?"

"Casey." He pointed upstairs. "Is she okay?"

"Oh. Yeah."

"Those pills you gave her. Is that stuff okay to take when drinking?"

Imogen bent to look under the coffee table.

"I'm sure it'll be fine."

FORTY-ONE

"—Her fault! I'm telling you, it was—"

"Get off me, Noah. You know it was—"

"Bindi! Miss Bridges! *She'll* tell you that—"

And in that moment, amid all the shouting, a rough hand took Summer's arm.

She looked up; it was John. She'd glanced around moments ago and not seen him, then lost the thought in her panic. Where had he gone? Had she only been imagining his absence, scared out of her mind by the certainty of death?

John didn't seem like himself. Not even a tiny little bit.

"We need to go," he demanded.

"They won't *let* us go."

"We'll find a way. We need to get out of here, Summer." He looked toward what seemed to be a narrow utility door in the Buvette's corner, where Donovan was standing. He mumbled, agitated by something unknown. Something new, other than poison.

Summer stood in front of him, commanding attention.

"John. You have to keep a level head. Don't flip out on me."

"I'm not flipping out."

"You want to run, but you know it's stupid to try. Stay with me and keep your head on straight. I need your mind. I need you to be my rock."

"Goddammit, Summer, that's what I'm trying to do!"

Summer flinched. Then she yanked her arm away, moving from compliant to defiant in one swift kick.

"Didn't you hear her, John? *We're poisoned.* If we leave, we'll die!"

"Summer, I need you to trust me on this. We need to look for an opening, and then we need to run."

"That guy Donovan is blocking the door. He's got a taser!"

John grabbed and pulled.

Again, Summer snapped away. "What's wrong with you?"

"Now."

"Maybe you should explain."

"Later. Let's go!"

But Summer was resolute. She stood her ground. "Listen. That bitch did something to us, but she'll save the people she decides are innocent. Guess who doesn't look innocent at all right now?" She jabbed a finger into her chest. "We need to convince her that I'm not at fault. You need to help me, John."

"None of that matters. She's unstable, but there's a lot she doesn't know about what happened. If she discovers the wrong thing and it sets her off, who knows *what* she'll do?"

"What about what she's already done?"

"Summer, she ..." Exasperation. He looked again at Donovan. "Will you please just trust me?"

Summer stood even firmer. Alcohol was regressing her, making her more like the girl he'd met than the woman he'd married. Summer could feel the change, didn't care. She said, "Why?"

"Because I'm your husband!"

But for some reason, right now — maybe it was the mortal peril, the drinking, or the 2018 everywhere around her; maybe it was John's complacency where their mutual poisoning was concerned — Summer didn't feel like budging. Or being ordered around. Or being told "it's fine" when it so obviously wasn't. Or being harshly whispered at, like she couldn't see the writing on the wall.

Her hands went to her hips. "Where did you disappear to?"

"What?"

"I was looking for you a minute ago and didn't see you."

"I had to go to the bathroom."

"And Mr. Doorman just let you? Is that why you think he'll let us leave now, despite his weapon?"

"A waiter came with me! Jesus, Summer, who do you think I am? And it's not that I think he'll let us go. But he ... Well, he'll have to leave his post eventually, and when he does, we can—"

"What would he leave for?"

"He has to go to the bathroom too, sometime."

Summer shook her head, insulted by whatever John was trying to pull. One part of her mind knew she was irrational. The larger part didn't give a shit. "I'll stay put. *I* don't want to die." She jerked her head toward Donovan. "I *swear* he looks familiar. Where do I know him from?"

They both turned at the sound of retching in the corner: Imogen, following Heidi's example with a hand in her mouth. She heaved again. Imogen's technique was all wrong. Summer should step up, show her former sister how it was done.

"Please stop," Harper said.

Imogen saw Harper approaching and shoved her hand deeper. Around most of a fist, she said, *"Fuggyoh."*

Then the bile, all over the wall and window.

"It's left your stomach by now," Harper said, still with her acceptance speech voice. "It was in the *soup.* All you're doing by eliminating what you ate since is making it work faster."

Imogen answered by throwing up again.

"Donovan," Harper sighed. "If you would?"

Donovan whispered into his Doodad. Within two minutes, the waiters had returned with rags, a bucket, and mops. They cleaned up after Imogen, then Heidi. They helped Noah and Ella back to their proper seats, pulling them up from the floor in the aftermath of their tasing. One spritzed the air with something, and the acid odor disappeared. Then they were six-facing-six down the table again with their host at the head. Just a friendly little dinner party: twelve little Indians, all in a row.

And Harper said, "Try your main courses. The lamb and fish are both excellent choices."

Dead silence. Into it, Summer said, "You expect us to *eat?*"

"That's up to you," Harper replied. "But I'd suggest so if you want to live until dessert. We still don't have the answers we need, and time is quickly running out."

Exasperated and near tears, Imogen practically whined. "Why does it matter so much? What the fuck is the point of all of this? Who the hell was Casey Davis to you?"

Harper took a second before answering. The room waited. Then she said, "She was my sister."

Whispers. A ripple of fear. The mood changed, just like that.

"Casey had a sister," Ella said. "But her name was—"

"—Kimmy," Taylor finished. She looked at Harper. "Casey made fun of her because she hadn't inherited the red hair."

Harper sipped her wine with a humorless shrug.

Summer scanned the table. They all looked like animals in a snare, knowing the hunter was about to return. Soon, it would get ugly. The only way out of the snare was to put someone else in it.

"Tell us what you were whispering about earlier, Teek," Ella said. "Did something happen at the party?"

He sliced his meat, eyes averted.

"Oh, for fuck's sake." Simon set his fork loudly onto his plate. "We all know where this started. Without the prank, nothing else would have happened. If not for one stupid, cruel prank, Casey Davis would still be alive. Isn't that right, Summer?"

Summer blinked up. Simon's reputation had always preceded him, but she knew him better than most of the people here thought they did. Simon's look seemed to ask if she'd dare get dirty defending herself.

She glanced at John, then back at Simon.

Maybe she would. Maybe it was worth it. There was plenty that Simon had coming.

Blowhard. Salesman. Liar. Cheat. Deep down, a coward.

Oh yes. She and Simon shared secrets of their own.

Simon pointed past John, his arm close enough to get it bitten. "You want to know the reason your sister is dead? Talk to Queen Bitch right there."

Summer snapped. "Oh fuck your mother, Simon!"

But Simon didn't flinch. He swung his arm toward Imogen.

"And that one right there showed her how to do it," Simon told Harper. "The night of the party, Imogen gave Casey drugs."

"No I didn't." But Imogen was a terrible liar.

"Ask Teek! Probably what he was talking about earlier anyway."

Taylor opened her mouth, but Teek said, "That's right. I was there."

"You came in and got her to calm down," Simon said. "Then you took out a pill bottle and gave it to her."

"I gave her *one* pill!"

"You sure about that?"

"Of course I'm sure!" Imogen turned to Harper. "I just gave her one, I swear. I just wanted to help her relax!"

Simon was laughing.

"What's so funny?" Imogen demanded.

To Harper, Simon said, "She left her purse at my house." Then to Imogen: "You called the next day, asking if I'd found it. And I had — in the room I left you in with Casey. Are you sure the pills were still there when you picked it up?"

"She died a *week* later!"

"Of a Nyperal overdose. Same stuff you gave her." To Harper. "*Right?*"

"Even if she did take them, I ..." But Imogen was out of words.

Simon went on. "I asked Imogen about the pills after I saw her giving them to Casey. They made me nervous. I looked it up online afterward, and you're definitely not supposed to take them when you're drinking."

"I told her that!"

"After giving them to her?"

"It's fine if she just took the one ..."

Simon laughed again, ignoring Imogen, talking to Harper. "She gave Casey instructions, is what she did." He pointed at Summer. "*Reason to die.*" Then Imogen. "*HOW to die.*"

"That's ridiculous," Summer said.

Simon leaned forward, into John's space. John, keyed up well past his usual calm, shoved Simon back hard enough to rattle the plates. He flinched to retaliate, but John's expression stopped him. John's eyes flicked toward the door again, then to Summer.

Simon straightened his collar. "If you want to kill someone over Casey," he told Harper, eyes darting to John's, "kill *them.*"

Summer felt her mouth wanting to open, her fists desperate to clench. She could end this. Simon had plenty of dirt and Summer could prove it. The only problem was, that dirt sullied Summer, too — maybe enough to cost her a husband.

But under Summer Merritt's kind, adult skin was Summer Nixon, the white-hot bitch she used to be.

Summer stood. Looked at Simon's smug smile. Saw it falter. And said:

"Before you take Simon at his word, you should know ..."

FORTY-TWO

July 9, 2028

Summer knocked, noting for the hundredth time that the paint on Olivia's door was peeling. She should have John take care of that. There was a lot about the old woman's house that needed attention and wasn't their responsibility, but their neighbor should at least have the dignity of a pleasant first impression for visitors, if she ever got any other than Summer. She'd earned at least that much for her time on Earth.

"Who is it?" said a small, cracked voice on the door's other side.

"Good morning, Mrs. O'Connell. It's Summer."

"Who?"

"Your neighbor, Summer Merritt?"

"Are you with the tax office?"

Summer smiled, somewhere between sad and amused. She'd been coming over to check on Olivia nearly every day for almost eight months now — ever since her son moved to Florida for a job. It was scary how quickly her mind had declined. The tax office question was only a few days old, but she'd asked it every day. Summer wasn't even sure what a "tax office" was. Had Olivia gotten an IRS audit once, and that memory out of all of them was the one her loose wires had chosen to connect as her cortex fought to hold its integrity? Or was it something older than Summer, recalling a day when tax collectors came door to door like milkmen?

"No, Mrs. O'Connell."

"I don't like to open the door for strangers."

"You know me, I promise. Just look through the peephole."

The glass eye darkened. Then locks clicked, and the door opened. Summer was ready with a smile. Olivia, blessedly, smiled as well. If Summer had started this little pre-work routine a few months later than she had, the memory of Summer as a trusted friend (the visual half) might not have taken root. They had to go through the song and dance every day, but for now it worked.

For them both, as things turned out.

"I brought you some tea." Summer held out a cup.

"I can't have coffee," Olivia said, hesitating.

"That's why I make you tea. Do you remember?"

The lines on her face seemed to search for an answer. "No, I don't."

Summer had known that was coming: all part of the song and dance. Through trial and error she'd stumbled into the perfect response. She threw up her hands. "Oh well. That's one more for the Queen!"

Olivia cackled with delight. Summer smiled along. She had no idea what the expression even meant, if anything.

"Would you like to come in?"

"I would. How are you feeling?"

"Oh, I get along."

"Should we sit in the parlor?"

The spare room was an office if anything, but Olivia enjoyed thinking of it as a parlor. She sat in her chair without any trouble. Her body was doing fine. Her *mind* was on vacation.

Before sitting, Summer circulated, opening windows. It got musty in here. She always closed the windows before leaving, but as long as the weather held, airing-out was in their routine.

"It's nice to see you, Dear," Olivia said as Summer took her usual wing chair.

"It's nice to see you, too. Your TV is on. Were you watching the news?"

"Yes. Did you hear they elected that actor as president?"

"Which actor?"

"Ronald Reagan. You didn't hear?"

"Mrs. O'Connell, that was back in 1980. President Reagan died a long time ago." *And with Alzheimer's.*

"Did he now?"

"He did. Have you been playing your memory game with Alice?"

"Alice Kray?"

"That's right. Do you remember Alice?"

"Of course I do. I've known her since kindergarten. She and I were both ..." And Olivia went on, telling it again. Summer waited patiently through the story she'd heard a hundred times before.

"I made you that matching game so you could play it with her. They say that memory is like a muscle. If you practice, maybe you can hold on to more."

Olivia waved a hand to change the subject. "How is your family?"

"Good."

"What's your husband's name again?"

"John."

"Just got married, didn't you?"

"No, we've been married for eight years."

Surprise filled her face. "That long?"

"Yes. We have two wonderful children."

"You don't say! What are their names?"

The rest of the exchange played out. They went through this same thing almost word for word every time, then sat with hands in their laps. Olivia asked if Summer lived next door. Twice. Summer answered both times, kindly. It was amazing what the mind kept and dismissed. Olivia could recite all of her old phone numbers, but not her current address no matter how many times Summer reminded her.

Summer's hands worked in her lap. So much of this helped Olivia. But still, she felt almost guilty. Was it wrong to use Olivia like this? She enjoyed every second of Summer's presence, so probably not. Still, the newest part of their routine had gone on long enough that Summer knew it for the compulsion it was. For the addiction it was.

At first, she had hated that awful website that it seemed everyone was buzzing about. But the idea of "confessing" had wormed its way into her head, then burrowed like a parasite. She wasn't Catholic and wouldn't see a priest, and she'd be damned if she was about to log on and confess to her computer ... but on the other hand, admitting it all to Olivia? Her neighbor was the perfect vessel. She absorbed, unburdened Summer's soul, and then forgot. It was like plunging a filthy rag into a gleaming stream and watching the dirt all wash away.

Looking at Summer now, Olivia seemed to sense something wrong. Maybe that was conditioning. The confessions were almost daily now. As Summer's eyes watered, the old woman said, "Is something wrong, Dear?"

"Yes, actually," Summer said, looking at her hands. "I wonder if I could tell you something."

Olivia leaned forward and took Summer's hands in hers.

"Of course."

"I'm not a nice person, Mrs. O'Connell."

"Nonsense. You're a wonderful person."

"I lie. For fun. I don't even know why I do it. I find strangers and lie to them. I just make things up, spinning the most ludicrous tales. It started a year or two ago, and at first I'd lie about something small, like my age. One day it dawned on me that the person I'd told would never know. How could they? They didn't know me. They'd never see me again. The lie just ... vanished. It was infallible — something I'd always get away with."

Olivia smiled, still holding Summer's smooth hands in her wrinkled palms. "Every woman lies about her age."

"But it took hold of me after I realized that no one would ever know. The first time I told someone I had three kids instead of two, it gave me this strange thrill. I'd created a person, then made him disappear. Just like that."

She was getting upset. Olivia patted her hands.

"Now it's completely out of control. I told someone the other day that I was running for Congress. One time, just to see what would happen, I told someone that my brother murdered his family. I made the poor woman drop a carton of milk. It went everywhere."

Summer cried a little. It's not that her lies were harmful; it's that she couldn't stop. A few days without a whopper turned her into a junkie. Small lies no longer did the trick. She needed bigger thrills, worse infractions. And, Summer was increasingly sure, she needed a release from Olivia to prevent her utter destruction.

"You live next door, don't you?"

Summer sniffed. "Yes."

"And I think you have a husband. Have I met your husband?"

"Yes, you have."

"What's his name again?"

"John."

"You seem upset. Is everything okay?"

Her sin was washed away like filth in a stream.

So Summer went on. She told Olivia about the compulsive shoplifting that had just recently begun on the heels of her lying. The bulimia, under control after college but back after her second pregnancy, when the weight had stubbornly refused to come off. John knew none of it — and worse, she knew that keeping the secrets from John was just another part of her sick little game.

"I don't know what's wrong with me. It's getting worse, and I don't think it's going to stop."

Olivia waited, patient. With enough time, her face always cleared from concern to confusion.

Then Summer said what she'd recently realized but spoken aloud only twice. "I think I'm being punished, Mrs. O'Connell."

"Punished? Whyever would you be punished?"

"Because of something I did back in college."

"What did you do?"

"I made a girl kill herself."

Shock entered Olivia's eyes. Then, slowly, eventually, it softened.

"John doesn't know."

"Who is John?"

Her chest felt tight. Catharsis loomed like an orgasm ahead. Every visit now, she raced for a peak and then felt better. But also like an orgasm, catharsis was fleeting. She'd be back tomorrow for more: a strung-out deadbeat, desperate for a hit.

"John doesn't know the type of person I used to be. But he will. And do you know why? Because I swear one day, I'm just going to blurt it all out. I'll tell him about Casey and how I hated her and how, when she was so miserable after that dumb prank, I was so happy. I know why I hated her, but have no idea why it bothered me so much back then. She was with a college guy, supposedly. And it just bothered me, you know? This little uppity high school cunt with her red lips and stupid fucking red hair ... thinking she was good enough to be on *my* campus without *my* approval. Didn't even want to be in my sorority! She was *too good for it.*"

Really reveling now, in her petulant, mocking voice.

"And you know, one time I saw a psychiatrist. John didn't know, of course. She said I wasn't to blame. I didn't know what would happen. I wasn't happy she'd died, right? And I said no, I wasn't *actually* happy. But I was, I think. At the time — and maybe just for a little while — I *was* happy. I didn't know how miserable I was back then. I was always on top. Always in charge. Bayshore was *my school,* and after a few years, Coastline was *my college.* Even after Casey died. But I'm just sure, Mrs. O'Connell. I'm *positive* that John's going to find out about all of it. And then he'll leave me. He'll take the kids. And I'll let him. Because what kind of mother am I, keeping all of this up?"

Olivia kept enough of the story to make one assessment: "But Dear — you're not like that anymore. Now you're kind."

Summer was crying freely, taking tissues to mop her eyes.

"Still a liar. Still sick. Still fucked up in the head." She tapped her temple, realizing only after removing her finger that she'd made an imaginary gun as if planning to blow out her very real brains. Anger was in her now, red hot with nowhere to go. In the past, she would have taken that rage and punished someone.

But had it ever been about the other person, or had it always been about Summer?

Had Casey Davis died because of Summer's insecurity? She had never connected those dots.

"I swear, John will go, and my life will be over. He'll find out that I'm puking out half my meals, that I lie just for the hell of it. Including *to John,* of course, because that's the ultimate thrill. And worst of all is that we met because of Casey. The life I have? This great life that I'm pissing away? I owe it all to meeting John ... and I owe meeting John to what I did to Casey, because he was on the *Coastal,* and he came to interview me about the story. He met me when the guilt finally hit me. It made me soft, and John's the kind of guy who likes to help. He thought I *needed* help. But all this time, he's assumed Casey was a friend. I talk about it with him sometimes, but not once have I told him why she did what she did. He doesn't blame me because he has no idea. He feels *sorry* for me."

Understanding came and went from her eyes. Olivia was an empty vessel all over again. And that was great, but now Summer felt something missing and wondered if soon, her self-destructive adventures would need another level.

Olivia was great for confession, and confession was good for the soul. But what was even better for the soul? What did Summer crave?

Judgment, of course.

"When I told that therapist, do you know what she said? She said I was just a kid and that I made a mistake. 'Everyone makes mistakes. The important thing is that you learned, because learning made you better.'" Summer wiped her eyes, blew her nose. "But I didn't learn. Do you see? For years, I kept right on doing terrible things. There was this guy who came to Coastline a year behind me. Simon Wyatt. Even after the thing with Casey, he ... he and I ..."

"What is it, Dear?"

But not today. She couldn't talk about *that* today. So Summer went in a different direction.

"More and more, I wake up in the middle of the night and get this feeling that I'm rotten. Spoiled inside, like a bad apple. I put up a great front. I smile for my husband and my kids. I head the PTA, but I don't rule it like a bitch. John does well; we contribute a lot to charity. More than we can afford, maybe, but I insist. I volunteer for all of the food drives and even worked a season at a soup kitchen downtown. I help train therapy dogs. And coming to see you?" A bitter smile touched her lips. "I love coming to see you, Mrs. O'Connell. Not just to unload, but because I want to help you."

"I appreciate it. I really do."

"But no matter how much I do, I can't shake the feeling that it's all an act. I never stopped being the person I was. I'm one of the bad ones. That's what it feels like — like I'm rotten to the core, and that all I'm doing now to destroy myself is Hell casting its sentence."

"You musn't feel that way," Olivia said, her own eyes now rimmed with moisture, her hand still clasping Summer's. "You're so good to me. How can you be bad, if all you do is good?"

For the scantest moment, Summer saw blue sky behind all of the clouds. She almost believed it. Almost saw the logic.

Almost.

Summer watched the old woman's eyes. Wanted Olivia to hate

her. To cast her out. To call some unknown authority — hell, to call *John* — and turn her in.

But instead, Olivia's face softened. Too much time had passed. The filth was departing, washed from all but Summer's deep, dark soul.

"You look upset, Dear. Is something wrong?"

Summer smiled as best she could, knowing that today's confession was at its end, and told Olivia that everything was fine.

But it wasn't. This wasn't working. If confessing to her forgetful neighbor was enough to release the pressure, she wouldn't still feel this swelling inside.

This sense of countdown, of impending doom.

If Summer didn't find an outlet soon, one day soon she would—

FORTY-THREE

—**E**xplode. That's what the room felt like. Like it was about to explode.

"... that he blackmails people," Summer finished, looking at the other guests but still staring hard at Simon. "For kicks."

Simon tipped back in his chair, smiling wide enough to show all his teeth. The sound that came from his throat was technically laughter, but it sounded almost mechanical: *Heh-heh-heh*. Uncomfortable, not amused, and maybe a little bit dangerous. He glanced at Summer, as if in warning.

"*I* ordered the prank on Casey," Summer said, turning her eyes to Harper, putting her hand on her chest. "It was stupid. I've regretted it every day of my adult life. The Diamond girls told me to pull something nasty if I wanted to pledge, and that's what I thought of. Your sister got caught in the middle, and I'm sorry. But as much as I'm to blame for that, I'm not to blame for her suicide. What I did was terrible, but it's not what you're looking for."

Summer's eyes found John. She took a breath, but couldn't face him full-on, even for a silent apology. He hadn't known she'd pranked Casey before tonight, and who knew what he'd think of her after what was coming. The life she'd so carefully built on her buried past was crumbling, brick by terrible brick.

"Simon and I hooked up a few months after Casey died. He was a freshman at Coastline. I was a sophomore. He came to one of our parties, and we learned we had Bayshore in common. And he was ... well, you know how Simon is."

Meaning smooth. Charming. A snake in cashmere.

"Bullshit," Simon said.

"I could dig up the pictures." Summer remembered the photos and knew just where they were. John thought his wife was tame. She'd demurred when he'd felt adventurous, beaten into a different person by the time the two of them settled. But she'd been wild once, and had owned a treasure trove of porn to prove it. She'd been two people back then: her old self at the Diamond House (and for a few hot weeks with Simon), and the newer, better person she was trying to be whenever she was with John. She'd been so sweet and innocent around him, but surely her husband was doing the math, calculating the overlap, their courtship punctuated by torrid interludes with another man. She remembered being unable to stop her cheating, the guilt a parasite chewing its way to the surface.

Even then she'd been determined to break herself, to set herself to sabotage.

Simon shut his mouth.

"What attracted me to Simon was how reprehensible he was. I think I needed to be around someone worse than myself back then, just so I could compare. John was ..." She paused, unable to look his way. "John was too *nice* for the old me sometimes. He was on the staff of the Coastline newspaper, doing a story about the girl from Bayshore who'd killed herself. We met because he'd heard Casey and her friends had been pre-rushing Diamond Society. He knew about the prank, but not that I was behind it. I couldn't show him this other side of myself. But I had to show *someone.*"

She looked down at John. His stare was unreadable. Her fingers trailed toward his shoulder.

He stood, walked to the window, and looked into the night.

"Simon and I played this game. A grown-up version of Gross-Out, where we had to try and out-do the other with something awful we'd done. That's when I told him all about my part in the Casey Davis thing. And a lot more — things I'd never told anyone. Hazing. Hateful, hurtful things. But no matter how bad I got, Simon was always worse. The things I'd done were mean, but Simon's stuff was ... *deep,* I guess. Things I'd never even have thought to do because I kept my cruelty on the surface, like calling girls I didn't like fat or ugly. But Simon is a strategist."

"This is fun," Simon said, still smiling. "Listening to your delusions."

"I can prove we were together."

"So can I. But just because you secretly like it in the ass doesn't mean a goddamn thing right now."

Summer kept her face neutral, but his punch still buried itself in her gut. He'd said that one for John. A perfect example of what she'd been working to articulate. When it came to cruelty, Summer had been an amateur. For Simon, it was a beautiful instrument, and he was a prodigy.

"I never told anyone to share Casey's pictures and video," Summer said, trying to ignore Simon. "I just wanted Ella and Heidi to take pictures so they could show them to me to prove that they'd done it. I never understood *why* anyone shared them, either, until Simon told me about BayNet."

"BayNet ..." Ella said, searching her memory.

"I heard about that," Noah said.

Summer nodded. "It was an underground bounty program. Hot at Bayshore for like three months, until the school found out and blocked it from the network. You could snitch on something you overheard, or upload anything private, about anyone at all. It paid a bounty in Bitcoin. It was Simon's baby, paid for with his daddy's cash. He built it for leverage."

"What leverage?" Noah asked.

"Leverage on anyone, about anything. That's how Simon got ahead. Why things always worked out for him. Remember how Doug Nelson was going to be on student council until he suddenly dropped out so Simon could take his place? That happened because Doug was gay and terrified his parents might find out — and BayNet was all set to tell them. Being on student council was what got Simon into Coastline. His grades weren't good enough without it."

Simon laughed again, but she was getting to him. That look was back in his eyes — the one he'd gotten when he'd peeked inside Harper's envelope. A blazing fire of menace.

Summer focused on Harper, trying to forget the others. "It was just supposed to be Ella and Heidi taking pictures. That's the way I arranged it, but other people showed up. They were there because for the few months BayNet was running, spies were *everywhere.* Someone probably got a whiff of our 'pre-rush' scam and decided to follow them around. All I know is that the girls shared the videos and pics to BayNet and *BayNet* shared them with the web. Simon told me he got the notification when it happened, then made Casey's dalliance public right away."

Bindi said, "Why share the footage of Casey and Mason instead of keeping it as ... leverage?"

Summer sneered, then repeated what Simon had told her in their terrible bedroom game: *"Because he thought it was funny."*

"Such bullshit." Then to John's turned back, Simon said, "Do you know what your wife told me once? That she was a compulsive liar. She lies just to see what'll happen."

John turned his head, looking at Simon, not Summer.

"And hell," Simon continued. "That was a long time ago. If she used to lie about shoplifting back in college, I wonder what she'd lie about today. You wear condoms with this one, I hope?"

"That's enough," John said.

But Simon stood, spreading his arms to address the room.

"Hey, I just want everyone to know who it is that's telling stories right now. You two." He indicated Melissa and Imogen. "You've seen how Summer lies for fun, right? Caught her in a few, I imagine?"

Summer shook her head, resolute. She said to Harper, "It's true, about Simon and BayNet. Have your private investigator look into it. He's the one who—"

"—shamed Casey into killing herself?" Simon finished. "Oh. Yeah. It was all me. Convenient, isn't it? Summer's little fairy tale laying the blame on someone else."

"I don't lie," Summer said. But she did, of course. She'd told Simon all about her damages, including the compulsive lies. It'd been new back then, birthed not long after Casey's suicide. When she'd been with Simon, it felt more like a thrill than a sin. It was hard, facing him now. The guilt was back, deep and dark.

Simon chuckled. He gave a condescending shrug that seemed to say, *Whatever you want to believe, Summer.*

"Your middle name is Francis. How would I know that? I know all sorts of things about you, including BayNet."

"Just because you know some things—"

"You grew up in Festus, Kentucky," Summer went on. "Moved to

Cielo del Mar in 5th grade, after your dad sold his company. Then there was a scandal when the buyers learned that most of your dad's clients were defrauded. They sued, he went to jail, your family went shit-ass broke. Just another piece of trash."

"Right. *That* happened." But Simon's smile looked plastic.

"Your mom couldn't get a job. You almost got evicted, so she gave your landlord a 'job' instead."

Simon's eyes lit.

"When Daddy got out of prison, he made a whole bunch of money fast. Like, too fast to be legal. Taught you all you knew, right?"

"You have a mole on your back," Simon said, his voice hard. "I remember because I came on it so many times."

Summer was undaunted, avoiding John's eye. He looked ready to kill Simon or her; she had no idea which. She finally had Simon in the crosshairs, and under Harper's eyes.

"No morals at all. Puts up a great front. Simon Wyatt was everyone's pal, right? But inside, he's nothing like what you see on the surface. Tried to go to a psychiatrist once, didn't you, Simon? Hey, Miss Bridges — tell me what you think of his diagnosis ..."

"Shut your fucking mouth, Summer."

"Paranoia. Claustrophobia. Narcissism."

"I said, *shut it.*"

"And let's not forget about—"

Simon snapped and charged Summer.

A second later he had his hands around her throat, knocking Summer back in her chair.

She lost track of time in the panic. She saw the slow spinning of the Buvette's fan overhead, the nighttime twinkle of distant city lights through the big patio doors. Sounds stretched like taffy. She'd been using her right hand to spin her wedding ring. Now she could feel its points still pressing into her index finger.

Activity blurred overhead. Someone shouted.

Then Simon was being reeled back, away from Summer.

He spun toward the man who'd grabbed him. John, ready to fight.

But after a long look, Simon shook his shoulders to settle his coat. He turned his back for a few seconds, then met John's glare. Again it looked like they might fight. Again, they didn't.

Summer looked from the standoff toward the door, sure she'd see Donovan rushing to intervene with his stun gun.

But Donovan was gone, missing just like John had predicted. Gone to the bathroom, perhaps.

Maybe they could have sneaked away after all.

Simon raised his chin to stretch his neck, using one hand to right his collar and tie.

Summer went to John, but he moved toward the doors, putting distance between them.

With all eyes on him, Simon said, "Nobody here's a saint. Not me, not any of the rest of us."

The room waited for more, so he gave it to them.

"I saw Casey the night of the senior party. She was upset. Drinking in one of the upstairs bedrooms. But I talked to her and remember thinking that she was going to be okay. But after the party, things changed. Casey suddenly *wasn't* okay. That means that *someone* gave her a push."

"What are you talking about?" Taylor asked.

"Ask Imogen," Simon said. "She was the last one to see her that night."

FORTY-FOUR

Imogen had a mouthful of fish when Simon turned on her. She was distantly aware that she was in the middle of a life-and-death game, that she had poison in her stomach that she was attempting to quench by eating Kona kampachi belly (ha-ha, how ironic), and that the other people in the room were all preoccupied with a girl who'd killed herself more than a decade ago.

But Imogen didn't want to think about any of that. One level down in her mind, it was all so boring. A level below *that* (the level that understood Imogen Shah might be near the end of her short, portentous life), it was terrifying. So she stayed on the upper floor, thinking about the fish. All of the spices. About how she hadn't taken many selfies for her many social media accounts lately. About how in yoga tomorrow, Shaylene was going to be the instructor, and Shaylene was a masochistic *cunt*.

That fish-appreciating, selfie-meditating, yoga-ruminating part of her mind didn't even hear what Simon had said. It only noticed when suddenly, everyone was staring at her.

"Wait. What? You're on mushrooms if you think that."

Simon addressed Harper. "I went in to check on Casey. She was upset, but I got her calmed down. Then Imogen came in and whipped out a bottle of pills."

"I did not!'

"You did. Remember?"

Imogen remembered.

"Oh. Yeah. Okay, but it was only to calm her down because—"

"Just like she whipped them out earlier here," Simon said. "Are drugs your solution to *everything*? Do you always carry them, and hand them out like Tic-Tacs?"

Every eye in the room was on her. And not in the way she liked.

"Don't try to turn this around on *me*. Everyone knows that Summer and those two are the reason that Casey killed herself."

"Oh, *whatever*," Ella said. "Like you weren't laughing and pointing when she—"

"I never even saw her except for that night!"

"It was *you* we were laughing and pointing at," Melissa told Ella. "After you were stupid enough to fall for pre-rush. Remember?"

Ella looked ready for a harsh rebuttal but said nothing.

"She had a whole bottle of those pills, Harper," Simon went on. "I was talking to your sister, getting her to laugh because we kind of had that sort of relationship, and then Imogen busts out the Nyperal and was like, 'Here! Take these!'"

"Nyperal?" John said.

"That's what she died of! Imogen left her the whole vial and she just—"

"Oh, as if, Simon!" Imogen blurted. "She didn't even kill herself until like a week after she—"

"Using *your* pills! I looked those things up. I know how dangerous they can be, and Imogen didn't even care. Just wanted her to 'relax.'"

"That's what they're for! I told her to take *one*!"

Simon turned back to Harper. "She wanted me to leave the room. But I peeked back in, and they were popping those things like nobody's business. Both of them."

"Oh, whatever!"

"So you *didn't* give her any," Simon said. It wasn't a question. It was a statement full of *I-smell-bullshit*.

"No!"

"You didn't give her one right then and there, in the room. And then again later?"

"She didn't even open the bottle!"

Simon shook his head. To Harper: "She told me to leave them alone. Later, I found one of the pills on the floor. They were probably taking them together. Imogen must've told her not to take too many, then gave her the bottle. Told her to use them when the pain got to be too much and she needed an escape. Guess what happened a week later? She decided the pain was too much and took enough to 'escape.'"

Harper was looking at Imogen.

"He's lying, Miss Knox. I was going to give her just one of them, but I got distracted and I don't think she took any. She didn't even *want* any. But later I realized I'd left my purse and went back, but I ran into Simon first. He was all worried, too. Sweaty worried. So I told him to drive her home. Make sure she got away from the party because it wasn't doing her any good. Probably shouldn't have come. I felt horrible. It was funny at first, but what they did to her, that was pretty fucked up. So Simon's like yeah, I was just about to drive her home, and then he went back to do it. So *I* wasn't the last one to see Casey that night. *He* was."

Simon laughed, like it was all just a joke.

Imogen was on fire, all levels of her mind collapsing into a terrifying, infuriating stew. She looked at her plate and saw only a poison-absorber. She looked at Simon, seeing someone who was trying to hurl his responsibility her way.

"Are you *really* going to act like you didn't drive her home?" Imogen said.

"I *didn't* drive her home."

"Then why did you say you were going to?"

"I didn't."

Imogen replied gape-mouthed. "You ..." Then, turning to Harper: "*Bullshit*, Miss Knox. He's lying."

"*You're* the one who's lying!"

"Well, then what did we talk about that night, when I went back to check on her? When you ran into me."

"I *didn't* run into you." He laughed again, enough that it was getting obnoxious. Imogen had just had her nails done yesterday, but that wasn't going to stop her from clawing a bitch.

"In the upstairs hallway. Remember?"

Simon shook his head. "I talked to you downstairs, after you'd told me to leave you alone with Casey. I said I was worried about her drinking and taking drugs at the same time, and you said it'd be fine. I found your evidence when I was cleaning up the next day and came across one of your little pills on the floor."

"What makes you think it was mine? It might have been a birth control pill or a Tylenol."

"It had an N-shape cut out of the middle. I'd never seen a pill like it."

Imogen suddenly felt desperate. Accused. Caught, too. She had lost her purse that night, and her prescription. Casey had opened the vial after she'd left, then dropped one. But it wasn't her fault Casey had killed herself. She'd even gone back up to check on her, but now Simon denied it. What the hell was that about?

"Why are you lying?"

"I'm not lying. You were drunk."

"Yes, I was drunk. But I know it happened." *Inspiration!* She jabbed a finger at Teek. "Ask him! He was there!"

Teek shrank.

"Tell them! Tell them how Simon and I talked later that night!"

"I wasn't there. You're remembering wrong."

"Now you're *both* full of shit!" Panic was getting the best of her. A conspiracy was closing in. She throttled her frustrated tears. That night had been fuzzy, yes. She hadn't been used to drinking; her strict Indian upbringing usually defeated the daily life of a college girl. She'd been unprepared for the wallop of all that beer, but she still spoke to Simon in the upstairs hallway. And she was damn sure she'd seen Teek, too.

"Tell them!" Imogen shouted.

"I wasn't there," Teek said.

"Why are you doing this? I didn't tell her to kill herself! I didn't give her all those pills, at least not on purpose! Are you really this fucked up? Going to blame it on me when I was only trying to help?"

And goddammit, the tears were starting to come. Everyone was watching. Some of the people in this room were going to die tonight, and it felt sure that Imogen Shah would be among them.

"Fuck you, Teek! What, you're such a fucking ball-licker that you won't even admit you *saw us talking?*"

Teek had the eyes of a liar, and he cast them away. He looked like he was trying to make himself small, to avoid attention and do nothing. He would run if he could. Forget the other psychopaths in the room; Teek looked downright *nuts*.

"TEEK!"

Noah stood. "Teek wasn't in the hallway."

Imogen shut her mouth. Simon glared. Everyone waited.

He indicated Simon and Imogen. "But both of *them* were."

FORTY-FIVE

May 19, 2018

Noah walked up the steps, his heart pounding.

With each partial flight (there were three between Simon's main floor and the top of the stairs), the thunder in his ribcage gathered strength. He was lightheaded by the time he reached the top. Surreal for sure. And *terrified?* Well, that was a given.

At least you'll know. No matter what she says, good or bad, at least you'll have your answer.

Minutes from what felt like one of the most defining moments of his life, Noah argued for this venture to have a positive outcome. He and Casey were friends for sure, and they'd swapped a lot of personal stuff in small interludes over the years. She'd never really dated, not seriously, and other than that rather unfortunate thing with Mason, Noah would have said she was the kind of girl who shut guys down, made herself inaccessible. Getting a girl like Casey Davis required the goods, and the guts to try.

Noah had never had the guts. Not until today.

She likes you. Even if she never wants you as more than a friend, at least you know she likes you. She might be able to see how that could grow.

That was the optimist Noah. The louder voice thought the optimist was a hopeless idiot. Obviously, that voice opined, Noah was firmly in the Friend Zone. *If you don't go for the pussy, you're labeled a pussy,* Teek had told him. Not that Teek was any better. He'd liked Taylor McKay for a while, and done precisely dick about it.

But Friend Zone aside, Noah had chosen the worst possible moment to tell Casey his feelings. The loud voice inside him knew that; all of his friends would have told him that; anyone with a brain in their head knew it, too. Not only was she exactly one day past her last (sexual) relationship (and that's assuming she and Mason weren't still together, which they might be), she was pranked hard. Casey wouldn't want declarations of love; she'd want to hide under a rock.

But don't you see? That's why this timing is perfect, said the optimist. *If she'd wanted to be left alone, she wouldn't have come to the party. You saw the LiveLyfe post she made before coming here. She expects to have fun. She's brave, getting out there despite all the jackasses.*

And as to declarations of love? Well, Noah would play that one by ear. He'd missed his chance at the student council meeting after missing it five thousand other times with Casey. This — the last social event of their high school careers — felt like all he had left. But if the mood was wrong and he couldn't tell her how he felt, then he'd be a friend forever. She needed him now. She'd want his support. She'd want his arm around her shoulders and her hand in his. And if feelings got confused and they ended up leaning so close that kissing was their only option? Well, that would all work itself out, according to every teen movie Noah had ever seen.

He headed toward the bedroom where the now-infamous Casey Davis had apparently decided to show her face and then hole up sad. But there were two people ahead, talking. One he didn't recognize: a short Indian girl. The other was Simon.

The girl put a hand on Simon's chest as she spoke, smiling too broadly. She seemed not just drunk but *hammered*, slurring half her words.

"Seriously," she was saying. "That stuff is no joke. And d'ya know what? I get the feeling she's going to keep right on drinking."

Noah stepped closer. Simon's back was mostly to him and the girl was too soused to notice.

"It's like you said," Simon replied. "I'm sure she'll be fine."

"I should just go check."

The girl moved to head farther down the hall but Simon circled to stop her. This brought his face more straight-on to Noah, and his eyes flicked up to see him. Noah gave a miniature wave, but Simon seemed distracted. His usually smooth manner was fractured, his voice all-business.

"Imogen?" Simon said.

"That's my name," she slurred.

"No offense, but you're really drunk."

"What can I say? I'm having fun. I should go to high school parties more often."

"You know the expression, right?" He put a hand on Imogen's arm when she tried to push past him again, toward the end-of-hall bedroom that Noah assumed must contain whoever they were talking about. "Two drunks don't make a right."

Imogen took a minute. Then, suddenly, she started laughing. Simon smiled along, but his smile still looked out of sorts, his hair mussed. She finally nodded, accepting her state.

"You're right. Fine. I'm fucked up. But seriously, she needs a ride home."

"I'll see that she gets one."

"I can't do it. Because I've been drinking." A laugh. A moment of abstract sobriety.

They awkwardly parted. The girl glanced at Noah as if she didn't see him, and then he was alone in the hallway with Simon.

Noah approached as Simon ran a hand through his hair, making it pretty again.

"What was that about?" Noah asked.

Simon ticked his head toward the room behind him. "Casey is here. She's kind of messed up."

"Messed up how?"

"Wanted to come to the party, then decided she didn't want to be here after all. She's got a bottle from my dad's liquor cabinet."

Noah jerked a thumb toward the girl that Simon had called Imogen. "Who was she?"

"Goes to Coastline. Said she wanted to help. To cheer Casey up."

"Okay."

"But I don't want her to help. She was involved."

"'Involved'?"

"With that prank. On Casey."

Noah's spirit left him. His shoulders deflated, understanding. "Oh." Then he moved to walk around Simon. "I'll go and check on Casey."

"She's *out*, dude. Can't handle her liquor. There's nothing to check."

"Still," Noah said.

Simon's eyes ticked back and forth. He exhaled. His mouth set, he exhaled one more time, and then he put a hand on Noah's shoulder and leaned close. Had he really thought Simon seemed uneasy when he'd been talking to Imogen? The kid could run for Senate.

Quietly, Simon said, "Look, dude. I know you like her."

"No I don't."

"Everyone knows. Everyone but her."

Noah felt naked. He wasn't sure what to say.

"Believe me, you don't want her seeing you right now. She's barely holding her head up. And she's mean. Pissed about what happened yesterday and blaming everyone. You go in there, she'll decide you were in on it. Forget about making a good impression. Forget about wooing her while she's puking on your lap."

"Did she take some pills? That girl said she took—"

"Casey said she didn't take any and I believe her. I seriously doubt she could open a childproof cap right now. She's shitfaced. I need to drive her home."

"I can do it, Simon. I can drive her home."

Simon gave a good-natured laugh, then used the hand on Noah's shoulder to turn him around. They began to walk back toward the stairs.

"My party, my mess. I appreciate the offer, but I got it. Just gotta grab my coat."

Big grin. Simon slapped his shoulder and disappeared.

Noah stood alone in the hallway listening to the party. The air smelled like yeast; he wondered how Simon would erase the olfactory evidence before his parents came home.

Wasn't Miss Bridges supposed to be here? *And* Simon's parents? He had an impulse to find the counselor and ask her for guidance. Casey wouldn't blame him, would she? She couldn't possibly be as whacked out as Simon said. Even if she was, he could carry her down the stairs, to her chariot. He could give her a warm shoulder to lean on. He could show her that he was there, that he was on Team Casey. He didn't care about the prank. Yes, it had hurt to hear she was with Mason — and then, shamefully, to look the video up and see it. But Noah could rise above. He could be the bigger man.

He turned. Headed back toward the room where Casey lay in her stupor.

But before he was halfway down the bedroom hallway, he heard stirring from the room at the end. She was up! Hope rose, stupid as it might be. He could talk to her now. Be there for whatever she needed, including that ride home that he'd be happy to take off Simon's hands.

He went to the door. Listened. Someone was rustling about, bashing into things. Hell — maybe *breaking* things, for all the chaos.

Noah knocked. No one answered, so he knocked again.

"Casey?"

The reply was immediate, dipped in acid: *"Fuck off!"*

"Casey? It's—"

"I said fuck off! Get the fuck out of here!"

Noah flinched back. For a few seconds, he could only stand with his knuckles a half-inch from the wood. Simon had been telling the truth. Her voice was sloppy and furious, choked with tears. She'd worked herself into a frenzy up here, boozing out about how those girls had wronged her. It sounded like she'd snapped at Simon, and now it was his turn. But he hadn't said who he was.

No. That's the coward's way out.

His inner voice was like ice. It would tolerate no arguments. Noah had bitched out at the council meeting like he'd bitched out every single day for years. This was his last chance to be a good guy, to be brave and show her what kind of man he was, how he'd always do the right thing no matter the cost. Maybe the booze and the anger really would make her hate him tonight. But wasn't that better than nothing?

"Casey? It's Noah. I'm coming i—"

The door wrenched open. The brushed chrome doorknob slipped through his fingers. Then Casey was right there, inches away.

He could smell the light, strawberry shampoo mingling with the piss-sour reek of alcohol on the outbound train of her breath. Her usually sparkling green eyes were accusatory, as if she meant to reach for a weapon and gut him. Her hair was a mess. Her mascara made black fingers on her cheeks, reaching for her throat.

"Can you hear? I told you to go away!"

But she wasn't just defending her sanctuary. She was leaving — drunk for sure, but ambulatory after all.

"But ..."

"Get out of my way, Noah!"

Noah watched her as she moved by him, noting the way everything was just a little off. She was wearing a skirt and sweater combo that matched her emerald eyes, but the skirt was askew on her hips. The sweater looked stretched, nearly torn. Peeking back into the room, he saw why: the place was in tumult. That's what he'd heard before knocking: Casey trashing the room in a red-headed temper.

"Where are you going?" he demanded.

"Home!"

"Casey!"

But she kept on marching, the purse on her shoulder banging into the wall. Something rattled in one of the pockets.

Get her, Noah. You know she can't drive. Don't let her get away.

Be a man for once in your life.

He moved up beside her. She created more distance, walked faster.

"How do you plan on getting home?"

"How do you think?"

"You can't drive, Casey."

"Don't tell me what I can do!"

"Listen to me!" He reached for her, almost got her purse strap. "Goddammit, will you slow down for a second?"

She didn't. He reached again, this time grabbing the purse.

Casey didn't let go and a tug-of-war ensued. It had to look like kids fighting over a toy. But when the purse opened between them, he reached in and grabbed Casey's keys.

Then he let go and raised his other hand, pacifying.

"Give me my keys, Noah."

"Not until you talk to me."

"I don't want to talk to you! Why the hell would I want to talk to anybody?"

"Fine. You don't have to talk to me. But you're not driving home."

"You going to tie me up? Pin me down so I can't escape?"

"Calm down." Hand still up, begging for mercy. "You want to go home? Fine. Just let me drive you. I don't like beer. It tastes like piss."

She snatched for the keys. She briefly had them, but Noah's hold was better, and when Casey's grip slipped, the recoil sent her back into the wall.

She bent at the waist and started bawling.

Noah reached for her. "Casey? Are you all right?"

She tried to swat him away, but she was sobbing too hard.

"Casey?" He touched her shoulder, then took her by the wrist. "Come with me. Let's talk."

"No!" She wrenched from his grip. "Go away! *Leave me alone!*"

Her voice became unintelligible, choked with sobs.

"*Casey!*" Noah got hold of her wrist again, meaning to help her upright so they could go somewhere private. Nobody was witnessing this, and he wanted to keep it that way, for Casey's sake. "Come with me."

"*NO!*"

"Casey, *come with me, will you?*"

As he was dragging her upright by the left hand, her right hand swept around in a big, dramatic arc and slapped him impossibly hard across the cheek. He let go, blinking.

"What?" she said, her wet eyes full of fire. "Now everyone takes a turn?"

"What are you talking about?"

She was furious and distraught, unable to marry both emotions. Sobs alternated with angry little jabs as she struggled to her feet.

"I'm not your toy. I'm through taking shit from all of you."

"Casey, I ... I'm trying to *help* you!"

"*AND I DON'T WANT YOUR HELP!*"

She was up and past him in a second. Then she sniffed hard, wiped at her ruined eyes, and stormed toward the stairs.

FORTY-SIX

"Oh," Simon said. "That's right."

Melissa barked sarcastic laughter.

"It was a busy night." Simon looked reasonably at Imogen. "I'd had a few beers. I forgot you came back up."

"Or you were lying," Imogen said. "Why were you lying, Simon?"

"Why were *you* lying, Imogen?"

"How am I lying?" She turned to face Harper, who seemed perfectly civil, wine glass in hand, looking for all the world like a woman who hadn't threatened a dozen people with death. "I'm not lying. He's the one who's lying."

"You said Teek was there," Simon said.

"I made a mistake!"

"Well, so did I."

Imogen made a face, frustrated but unable to argue with Simon's suddenly cool tone.

"So who took Casey home?" Harper asked.

"Nobody, as far as I know," Noah said. "Maybe she walked. Or called for a FASTr. Simon came back with his coat looking for her a few minutes later."

"Did *anyone* here take Casey home?" Harper asked.

Many people around the table mumbled, eager to score points. But nobody had done it or knew who had.

"Why was she so mad, Noah?"

"It was like she blamed all of us. The whole school. Even her friends."

"I can't imagine why," Summer said. "It's not like her friends all turned on her or anything."

"Oh, *fuck off,* Summer. If it weren't for you, none of it would have even happened."

She turned to Heidi. "If you hadn't agreed, it wouldn't've happened, either."

"Great comeback. Did your overlords at Diamond House write that for you?"

Summer looked at Heidi like she was mentally deranged. "What are you, six years old?"

John spoke up, looking at Harper. "You're her sister. Did she say anything strange when she got home?"

"I was already asleep. The next morning, she didn't come out of her room. Didn't want to talk to me at all. It was like she'd gone backward, after how well it seemed like she'd felt the night before, all things considered."

"What's more likely is that the night before was a false high," Bindi said. "Like she was in shock. Being around everyone again probably triggered her. Made all her defenses crumble. That next day, you were probably just seeing how she'd been feeling all along, deep down. Casey going to the party probably wasn't the best idea. I get that she was trying to face her demons, but it seemed to remind her that she *couldn't* face them instead. Not yet."

Harper fixed on Bindi a second too long.

"Are you sure, though?" John's temper was back to neutral after his dust-up with Simon. He turned to Harper. "I mean ... how was she over the next week? Before ..."

Summer looked at John. "Why? You didn't even know her."

"I wrote that article, remember? For the Coastline paper?"

Harper looked at John. "You were on the *Gazette?*"

"Yes. It's how I met Summer. I looked into your sister's case, as part of a project."

Harper seemed to consider this. Then she said, "She was really bad for a while, but I don't trust my memories. I was a child. I brushed it off because I thought mostly about myself, like all kids. I was gone all day at school and Casey stayed home. She finally let me back in a little later in the week, and I got the impression that she was feeling better. She wasn't on LiveLyfe or anything — just kind of avoided all social media because ... well, you can imagine why. But she did say she'd been talking to a few friends. I just took it as a good sign that she was on the phone, but I don't know who she talked to."

"I talked to her," Taylor said.

Heidi and Ella both stared down at their poisoned plates.

"What did she say?" Summer asked.

Taylor gave Summer a hard look but then responded.

"Nothing, really. That she was okay. I asked her about the party because Noah told me about how she was that night, but she said she'd 'just gotten fed up.' Like everything hit her at once."

"Like she hit Noah," Melissa said.

"She told me to tell Noah she was sorry about that. She was drunk; she wasn't thinking straight. She knew he was only trying to help. And she must have forgiven him since I know he visited her later in the week."

The room looked at Noah. Based on what Taylor had said, he'd probably just earned himself a dessert full of antidote. Taylor, too. John struck Bindi as 50/50. He was innocent in that he hadn't known Casey, but guilty by association for marrying the Queen Bitch of the West.

"But didn't she seem ... *off*?" John asked.

Mason turned to John. "Off how?"

"Just ... *off*. Not her usual self."

"She'd just been slut-shamed on the internet," Simon said. "So yes. *Off*."

"More than that, though," John said. "I ... heard she was acting weird that week. Like maybe something happened at the party."

"Who did you hear that from?" Harper asked.

"Summer, I think. Or someone else I talked to. I doubt I still have my college notes from that long ago, but I feel like someone said the party was ... *weird*."

"It *was* weird," Ella said.

"Maybe that's because you'd just gotten your friend to kill herself," Melissa said.

There was a long silence. Harper surveyed the room, casting her judgment across it. The main course was almost over. Dessert was coming, as were their endings.

Bindi yawned. It wasn't late, but she already felt tired. Looking around the table, she wasn't the only one. The poison was already working.

"She wasn't getting better."

Heads turned toward Simon.

"I went to see her in the middle of that week, too," Simon continued, softer than usual. "I cut fourth-period math on Wednesday or Thursday and drove to her house because I was worried about the stuff that Imogen gave her. I noticed that the pill bottle wasn't in Imogen's purse when I found it, so I figured Casey took them. When I got to her house—" He shrugged at Harper. "—*your* house, I guess — I think I caught her off guard. She didn't have time to compose herself and make like everything was okay."

Simon looked at Harper with something like apology, then went on.

"She was drinking. *Heavily.* She didn't want to invite me in. I insisted. I saw the liquor she probably hid when her family was home, and when I peeked into her room, I saw those little white pills lined up on her nightstand."

"'Little white pills'?" John repeated.

Simon nodded. "The Nyperal. Her taking it made me nervous. I told her I was worried about her. We all were. The whole school. But she just laughed me out of the house. She said that nobody cared. Or gave a shit at all."

Something in Donovan's pocket must have buzzed because he slipped out his Doodad and spoke into it. Then he whispered to Harper and she stood.

"The kitchen says dessert prep is underway," Harper announced. "The elderberry glaze is tricky to get just right. And, of course, there is the matter of adding the secret ingredient." A tiny smile. "Well, at least for some of you."

Murmuring. Fear punctuated the room's fabric, rich with the scent of adrenaline.

"If I could sum up our findings thus far," Harper said, "it appears that almost everyone in this room is at least somewhat responsible for what happened to Casey, or culpable in the years of cover-up that followed."

She looked at Summer, Mason, Ella, and Heidi. "Some of us *did* things."

She looked at Taylor, Teek, Bindi, and John. "Some of us *hid* things."

She looked at Melissa, Imogen, Simon, and Noah. "And some of us *knew* things, yet failed to act."

She cast a long, slow gaze around the room and said, "If I were a betting woman right now, I'd put nobody in the clear. And if it were *my* neck on the line? Why, I'd spend the fifteen minutes or so we still have before the Black Beast arrives on our plates to find the answer to one simple question: *Who among us was most responsible for Casey's death, and who was merely an accessory?*"

Harper picked up her napkin and prepared to sit.

"You won't get away with this," Ella said. "Money might buy you secrets and accomplices, but when a bunch of people suddenly die one night at your restaurant, you can bet the cops will come knocking."

Harper took this in, then finished sitting. She composed her napkin on her lap just as the waiters returned to clear their places in preparation for the final course.

And she said, "You're absolutely right, Ella. The police will surely come knocking. In fact, my people have explicit instructions to call officers to Crave before we all leave for the evening."

Nobody spoke.

"But as to whether I will get away with it?" She laughed. "Contrary opinions aside, I'm quite sure that something happened at the senior party. And I'm quite sure that if she hadn't gone to that party, Casey would still be alive today."

Waiters circulated, snatching forks, trading them for clean ones.

"Friends," Harper said. "You were the ones who killed my sister, but I was the one who made her go that night. Without me, she would have stayed at home. Without my insistence, she would have stayed safe."

She sipped her water, then went dead cold.

"Burn the building, burn my reputation, then burn in Hell for all I care. I don't *want* to 'get away with it.' I ate the same soup as all of you ... and I know what will not be in my dessert."

FORTY-SEVEN

Thirteen little soldiers, sitting in a circle.

Thirteen little murderers, desperate to flee evil.

Summer Merritt, formerly Summer Nixon, who'd cleaned out her closet almost every day in front of her senile neighbor to clear her conscience (and with no idea that if she did the same using the Contract Confessions website she found so repugnant, that she'd be confessing to her husband), was feeling decidedly drowsy. It was the foreign substance in her system slowing her down — beginning the process that, if left unchecked, would cease her heart and breath.

Still, she couldn't stop watching the elegant profile of the Hollywood star beside her. She'd seen the *Life, Liberty,* and *The Pursuit of Happiness* trilogy like most of the Western world, and in an attempt to prove herself cultured, she'd even sought out *The God Particle* online and found it more bold than amateur or pretentious.

Before tonight, Summer would have called herself a Harper Knox fan. And why not? She was talented, elegant, and one of those rare people who took your breath away. Twenty-four years old and already a Hollywood heavyweight; slim features unshaped by cosmetic surgery because she frankly hadn't needed it yet. Harper was younger than Summer and more beautiful than she'd been five years ago at 24, though their looks were similar: wavy blonde hair, fair skin, blue eyes, noses sharp and upturned enough to cut cheese.

She was like a mirror for Summer — a supernormal version of reality showing Summer what she might have been, had things not gone so wrong. And yet, it seemed like they'd both been holding blackness inside. Within a few hours, they'd probably both be dead as doornails.

John Merritt sat beside her, a husband with more secrets than just the obvious one. He'd promised himself that he'd come clean to Summer within two weeks or end his secret site for good. He'd even considered making a confession himself, were he a customer willing to set an example by sampling his own goods.

John had a good thing going these days, and for it, he'd trapped himself in a classic non-moralistic moralist's dilemma: knowing he should change but frankly not really wanting to. The submissions he parsed daily — stuff like Mason's confession that he'd unwittingly led a girl to suicide, sure, but also mind-crushing disclosures like those from the wife-beaters, self-mutilators, kiddie-fiddlers, and the like — were eating his soul.

Yet the money was good ... and if John was honest with himself (and we're talking dark-closet, under-the-basement-stairs levels of honesty), he was addicted to those bits of people's lives. Sure, it was corroding his faith in ... well ... *everything*. But it was delicious. Compelling. Like a gory accident or a shameful diary.

He'd learned the lust of secrets early on. If there was a seed within him that birthed Contract Confessions, it was as old as the cancer that broke Summer. As old as what had broken Simon, who sat beside John, quieter than the others, making lists in his mind.

On Simon's lists: pros and cons. Rights and wrongs.

To Simon, life had become an equation that he needed only to balance. He could picture an enormous scale inside his mind: not a triple-beam like they used in science class, but one like on the statue of Justice. That scale had two trays. In order for one to go up, the other must go down. In order for one side to weigh less, something else, by nature, must weigh more.

Simon's insides weighed plenty. Not as much as the guilt plaguing Summer, Ella, Heidi, and even Mason, though in a logical world it sure seemed like Mason's guilt should weigh ounces to the tons carried by the women. Or milligrams, perhaps, compared to the guilt heaping Teek. His tray would slip too low if left unbalanced. If what Harper said was true, then Simon might be in deep shit. As far as he could tell, Noah, Taylor, and Bindi seemed the safest — but then again, maybe nobody was.

He could wait for the dessert course and steal Noah's dish, but that felt like slim hope. Noah would probably fight back, and Donovan might intervene to make sure Noah got what was coming to him and that Simon did not. He could try to run to a poison control center, but again: Donovan at the door with his stun gun, and likely guards in the lobby.

That left sabotage as his only viable option.

Simon knew he had to come up with something bad enough to thrust on someone else — something that would make them look worse while making himself seem better. He'd tried it with Imogen, but more might be required. He should reinforce her story, for one. Tell them all again how he'd gone to Casey's house mid-week to check on her (he hadn't), how he'd seen Casey popping Imogen's pills (he also hadn't), and how sure he was that Casey had been planning to kill herself from Go (he definitely hadn't, and still wasn't sure today).

Harper seemed to feel that something had happened at the party to make things worse for Casey. That meant opportunity. So now he looked from person to person, motionless in his chair versus the drooling, panicked chatter he heard from so many of the others, spooling stories in his mind. He'd learned so much about Bayshore's people from BayNet, about *these* people. There had to be something he could use. *Someone* he could throw to the wolves.

Melissa? Imogen again?

Ella and Heidi and Summer were already implicated. Their target was too obvious.

But what about Mason? Or Noah?

In the grand scheme of things, Noah, the fourth guilty little soldier sitting clockwise from Harper's left, was sinking in machinations, thinking of ways to spear Simon without any way of knowing that the man was thinking of doing the same to him. In Noah's estimation, Simon would make a damn fine sacrificial lamb. Chances were, three or four obvious candidates in the room were dead already, but the puzzle was missing a piece.

He agreed with Harper. Casey *was* strong; she *was* too resilient for a single embarrassing prank to end her life. Casey *had* been "off," as Summer's husband called it, both at the party and after. Something *had* upset her, and she hadn't copped to it when Noah visited the morning of her death.

As far as he could tell, she'd been alone in that room upstairs for an hour or more, drinking and popping pills. Maybe that was Imogen's fault. Maybe it was Bindi's for failing to chaperone, or maybe it was Mason's fault for disappearing on Casey rather than showing solidarity as the other victim of the prank.

But of the people in the room, beyond the obvious scapegoats, Noah would have chosen Simon. He didn't want to admit why, and maybe even couldn't have said if pressed. Perhaps it was because Casey had always liked him more than Noah. Perhaps it was because Simon had lived what appeared to be a perfect life without a cheating wife who'd given birth to boys who seemed to be his sons, yet belonged instead to a man his wife couldn't stop stalking. Maybe it was because Simon, unlike Noah, had gone after what he wanted in life, rather than shrinking from it. Or because Noah had never said what he wanted to Casey, and never could.

Who had kept him from going in to speak with her that night? *Simon*, who he'd stopped to talk to in the hall. If only he'd gotten into the room sooner. Whatever had been tormenting Casey in there might not have happened.

He might have saved her.

He might have loved her.

None of that was true, of course. But just as Noah had spent his adult life burying regret and obsession, so had Ella. Even now, she was nowhere near self-aware enough to notice the cosmic coincidence that linked her to the former friend she'd helped torment to death: Casey dead by pills, Ella trying hard on a subconscious level to take enough to join her.

But beneath the level of consciousness, Ella had always known. She had always been her own worst torturer — the fly in her own ointment. She, like Heidi two seats down in our clockwise roll-call, had lied to be happy, had fucked to be happy, had shopped to be happy, and had self-medicated to be happy. And like Heidi, each of Ella's well-intentioned vices had served her as a double-edged sword.

Both had slit their own throats. Both had dug their own graves. Both had self-flagellated for eleven long years. Not in words and not in a way they'd ever been aware of, but the abuse had been there all the same.

Ella, beaten. Herself holding the whip.

Heidi, broken. Herself wielding both hammer and ax.

Between them, Mason was remembering the week between the prank and Casey's suicide. Earlier Miss Bridges said that he'd called the office over and over, wanting to discuss the problems with young Miss Davis. He wondered if it was too late to tell her that she'd been right.

The problem — and if Mason was lucky, this would be a temporary issue — was that he *knew* he hadn't placed those calls. But memory was plastic; a person could come to believe just about anything he wanted to. Trauma victims misremembered their pasts all the time. Their brains changed reality to cope. Teek had even told that story earlier, about Taylor, about how she'd been molested for years and forgotten all about it.

So he tried to believe. Tried to "know" that he'd called to check on Casey. Because that would have been the noble thing to do.

Mason thought on the week in question, about those calls to the guidance office. He almost remembered making them now, even though most of his mind insisted he hadn't. Because why *wouldn't* Mason have called? Why *would* Mason have more or less ignored the whole thing, trying in only the most half-assed ways to reach Casey and let her know that he had her back? It's not like he'd spent that week thinking only of how the whole thing affected him. It wasn't like he'd been a selfish jock. It wasn't like his friends had laughed about the video, shared it on their cell phones in the locker room, and ended the friendly hazing by offering Mason a slap on his back.

Mason was a good guy. He'd done his best to help Casey. He'd called the guidance office. He'd chastised people for laughing. He hadn't noticed that while the prank sunk Casey like a brick, it increased his status at school.

He *wasn't* a bastard.

The eighth and ninth guilty soldiers, past Heidi and the slowly disintegrating perception of herself as a woman with her shit together (though honestly, that wall had always been spun sugar solid and in her darkest hours she damn well knew it), were Taylor and Teek.

They stood alone at the table as a couple with most of their secrets mutually divulged — and that included the worst of them. The fact that Teek's nasty rape porn fetish remained under wraps held little comfort. The fetish was bad, but nothing compared to the reason he'd already given Taylor to disrespect and despise him. The fact that she hadn't simply walked out that night was a miracle, and a large part of Teek kept waiting for the other shoe to drop.

Had Taylor misunderstood him when he'd told her? Had she gotten the wrong impression? Ever since that night, he'd kept wanting to bring it back up just to be sure — while simultaneously never wanting to discuss it again.

He'd been sure he would repulse her. That she'd stop sleeping, slap him, announce his atrocity to the world. Instead, she'd gone silent. She'd stopped spending all that time in the bath. In a quiet, horrifying kind of way, she'd almost returned to normal.

It was wrong. This wasn't how things were supposed to be.

Where was she crying? Who was she telling? She'd never brought it up, other than in wordless glances that broadcast her hate. Or love?

It made no sense. Even now, she was holding his hand.

She gave it a squeeze.

Save us, that squeeze seemed to say. *If we're to survive tonight, someone else needs to die.*

The secret dangled between them by one thin string: a sword of Damocles, swinging above the table.

There was no talking. Few made eye contact. Nobody stood, or stirred. There was no panic. Only the ticking time. And inevitability.

Melissa. Imogen. Both thinking about Harper in their own way. For Melissa, it was a feeling of justice. Would she die? Probably. That was okay. When the time came, Melissa was sure that she'd fight out of instinct. But did it really matter if she'd been dead forever?

Imogen felt the opposite. She wanted very badly to keep on living. Imogen didn't realize it, but if the room filled with water, she'd stand on her friends to keep herself afloat. It wouldn't have made her proud, but it also wouldn't have shamed her. It would have made her human. She didn't want for grand choices, never had. Her goals were simple. She wanted connection; she wanted admiration; she wanted to indulge her loves and avoid things unwanted.

Back in college, Imogen had gone along with something she shouldn't have because it was easy. She'd tried to atone, and now it looked like her attempts to help Casey had gotten the girl killed. Imogen didn't want to think about that, just like she never wanted to think about the time she'd almost accidentally murdered McFuckface.

If she lived through tonight, would there be Nyperal to soothe her nerves?

Maybe she *was* addicted. And maybe if she quit all at once, she'd find herself unable to cope.

Imogen didn't care.

Tonight had taught her that she wasn't any good at facing the past, and that the best way to get over something was to block it all out. It wasn't self-deceptive. It was honest. And in the end, the results were the same. If Imogen survived this dinner, she'd never harm anyone again, even by accident. She'd cook; she'd stick to the most frivolous corners of social media for the dopamine it promised her brain; she'd live her tiny and probably insignificant life. Most importantly, she'd stay away from Melissa Lynch. Imogen loved her and always would. But Melissa was trouble. She liked to shake things up. Imogen did not.

Nor did Bindi Bridges, who sat at Harper's right. She'd always done her best. Never broke the rules, cheated, partied too hard, or purposefully abdicated her duties. She was even vanilla in bed — something that even as she hated Donald, part of her was now lamenting. Could she have kept him interested? Probably not. Donald was a hunter-gatherer. Men were wired to fertilize whatever willing females they could find, and the hunt was part of the thrill. Bindi knew that from her work with patients, of course, so could she blame her husband? No. That meant blaming herself. It was so much more comfortable to blame Heidi.

Let's be honest: Heidi had it coming. Even when it had seemed Heidi had been fucking some other woman's husband, Bindi had judged her. She wasn't supposed to, professionally speaking, but she had. Heidi had no self-control. It was bullshit that she'd stolen a man from someone with plenty.

Heidi probably would die tonight. Officially, that was tragic. Unofficially, it was fine.

Bindi's subconscious let itself feel that way, and her conscious would never know. It could bury this. Down the road, Bindi would convince herself that she'd tried to help Heidi, just like Mason would convince himself that he'd tried to help Casey. Just like Noah would believe he'd been in love and not a coward, just like Imogen would believe she'd made Casey's final days easier rather than handing her the means to die.

At the table's head, lastly, sat our lovely host for the evening: Harper Knox, formerly Kimberly Davis. The internet at large knew her old name, of course, but only her most devoted fans (those that scared her a little), would have known without a reason to look.

Joan Crawford was born Lucille LeSueur; Cary Grant had grown up as Archibald Leach. Almost nobody could recite those names without looking them up. That suited Donovan fine. He'd accepted Harper's fame in the way he acknowledged her darkness. The fact that nobody recognized him as the man on the arm of one of the world's biggest stars meant he could run errands in peace.

Harper had anticipated this night for many years. She took a moment to savor it, just as she'd soon savor her dessert. She looked around the table: Bindi Bridges, Imogen Shah, Melissa Lynch, Teek Sheridan and Taylor McKay, Heidi Blanchard, Mason Pace, Ella and Noah Boyer, Simon Wyatt, John and Summer Merritt.

She'd heard all their stories. She'd learned all their excuses. Something was still missing, and with luck — with the pressure applied and time running out — she felt certain that she'd learn it before the bodies hit the floor, including hers.

All had played their part. All had something to hide. Even John Merritt's arrival had been an unexpected bonus. She hadn't realized his part in this. But of course, was it any surprise what a site like Contract Confessions had to hide?

Satisfaction percolated through her, along with growing fatigue. She was feeling the drug's torpor, same as her guests. Right now it seemed she could sleep for days, and soon enough she would. The time was finally here. After years of waiting and plotting, this was all about to be over.

She turned to Donovan. At first, he wouldn't look at her. *Couldn't* look at her, in spite of all he'd already done. But then he felt her gaze and softened. Turned to face her. And they exchanged a bittersweet smile.

Harper and Donovan knew that no matter what happened next, none of the desserts would have an antidote, and not a single one could save them.

Donovan was still watching the woman he loved. Eyes quiet. Expression downcast. Mouth tight.

This is right, Harper silently told him.

In return, Donovan seemed to sigh. His look said, *I know.*

Then Harper's eyes circled the table. There were six guests on each long side, plus herself at the head. Each with their secret. Each having played their part. Each guilty, in their own way.

And she thought:

Thirteen little soldiers, waiting for their deaths.

Thirteen lifeless bodies, breathing their last breaths.

Dessert

La Bete Noir
("The Black Beast")
Made with Valrhona Chocolate
And Elderberry Gelee
And Served with Toasted Marcona Almonds

FORTY-EIGHT

March 23, 2027

arkness. Fuck you, darkness.

The thought circled Donovan's mind like detritus in a drain. He could almost see his worries like specters through Harper's dark mansion. In the kitchen shadows, dark things played like ghostly children. Only light could banish them, but this time even when Donovan flicked the switch for the overheads, he barely felt better. The shadows remained, clinging to the dark beyond the windows at 3am. They were getting stronger. Harper's demons — no longer precisely *Harper's*.

He boiled water in the electric kettle, then poured it over a teabag of Spicy and Sweet. A grocery store brand, same as Donovan could have bought before he'd moved in with a multi-millionaire. Strange, to see wealth and fame from the inside. Harper was mobbed whenever she left the house. Going to the gym, walking the dogs, getting a mocha — ordinary things the paparazzi seemed not to believe stars stooped to do. But they were just people. Didn't they laugh when happy, cry when sad, and bleed when wounded like anyone else?

Donovan, preparing Harper's herbal tea for the fourth night in a row, knew that better than most.

He left on the overheads, blaming forgetfulness but knowing

deep down that Harper had infected him, that he was beginning to feel the nighttime too. Now he coveted the light like a thief.

On his way back to the bedroom, he turned them all on.

Be gone, things of the darkness.

He sat on the enormous bed. Harper shifted beside him but kept her back turned.

"Give it up," he said.

"I'm sleeping."

"You haven't been sleeping for an hour now."

"Yes I have."

"Get up or I'll pour this on you."

She rolled over. Their eyes met. He didn't see the star, larger than life before him. He saw Harper, who he'd found in Home Depot. Harper Knox, who had loved him the moment she realized that he knew who she was and didn't give the thinnest of shits. Her eyes were red with fatigue. Her hair was tousled. This was the beauty he loved most, different from what the world got to see. Vulnerable, honest with the absence of glamour.

"If you keep getting me tea at this time, it'll become a habit. You'll teach our bodies that this is when we're supposed to wake up."

"You're awake anyway."

"But you'll reinforce it. We'll keep waking up in the middle of the night forever."

Donovan handed her the cup with a shrug. "Then we'll play games. It can be our thing."

She sipped, grateful for the company. Even if this was becoming a habit, that was better than the dreams that seemed to beat Harper in her sleep.

They sat in the silence under four switches worth of lights.

"What is it, Harper?"

"Nothing. Just restless."

But that was a lie. They had been together for months, and this had hit her weeks ago, whatever it was. And now the effects no longer stuck to nighttime. Donovan could see it in her daytime fatigue, little changes in the brightness of her smile, in the way she carried herself. It wasn't going to leave until she looked it in the eye. Whatever had been bothering Harper was here to stay.

"Tell me the truth," Donovan said. "I'm not above tickling you until you pee yourself."

That got a smile. Then after a second, "How old are you?"

"Too old to sleep in a bed with pee in it," he said, raising his hands in claws. "So you'd better talk fast."

She waited for him to let it go. When he didn't, she sighed.

"Something from a long time ago. It's in my head all the time now, like a puzzle I can't solve."

"A puzzle? But you've seemed so sad."

She sighed again, then set the tea aside.

"All right. It's about my sister."

"I didn't know you have a sister."

But he knew from looking at her face that that was exactly the problem. She didn't *have* a sister; she'd *had* a sister. The fact that she'd never told him went hand in hand with whatever was keeping her awake. Secrets, like anything, obeyed the turn of the soil. They never stayed buried for long.

"Her name was Casey," Harper said.

THEY LEFT the therapist's office. It wasn't helping. At all.

"Fuck this, Donovan. I told you. I already did the therapy thing."

"When?"

"When I was thirteen. My parents made me go."

"The same parents who wouldn't go themselves?"

"I shouldn't have told you that," Harper said.

"Your estranged parents who—"

"They got weird. They hate that I changed my name."

"To the name of their late daughter's favorite stuffed animal."

"Donovan ..."

"Kimmy ..." he mocked.

Her face became serious. "I told you not to call me that."

"I see. Is that the tone you use when your parents call you 'Kimmy'?"

"I'm 22 years old, Donovan. Would you like me to call you 'Donny'?"

"Ah. My mistake. *Kimberly*. Or do you prefer Kim?"

"Knock it off."

They were in the car. His car. The five-year-old Camry, not the Mercedes. He took her hand. "Look at me."

Harper kept looking out the window.

"Look at me," Donovan said. "I'm very handsome. It should be easy."

Harper turned but held her frown.

"You freak out when called by your given name and chose a juvenile touchstone that couldn't possibly be more reminiscent of the memory you refuse to deal with as your professional name. Tell me. What did Casey call her room?"

"'Casey's room,'"

"What else?"

"Fine. 'Fort Knox.'"

"*Knox.*"

"Were you reading my diary?"

"You've said it in your sleep."

"So?"

"You're having trouble sleeping. It's affecting your work. Your mood is different. I'm worried about you, kid."

"I'm fine."

"You need to keep going to therapy."

"No."

"If you don't face it, it'll get worse."

"I'll think about it," she said.

～

SIX MONTHS LATER. Harper hadn't returned to therapy. Donovan found her in her office, typing. When he came through the door, she snapped around and immediately tried to close the window. But she wasn't fast enough.

"Who is Summer Nixon?"

"Nobody."

He sat sideways on the arm of her easy chair. "Do you know when someone says 'nobody' and it's believable? When they close windows like they've been looking at porn and get all sweaty."

"I'm not sweaty."

"You've been saying that name in your sleep. Was she an old friend? A friend of Casey's?"

Harper's eyes clouded. Her hair was mostly blonde, but in the sun, it shone slightly red.

"So ... *not* a friend."

She started to cry. Alarmed, he wrapped his arm around her. "Hey. Hey. It's okay."

"She's gone, Donovan. My sister is gone and I'll never see her again!"

Donovan said nothing. He just waited until it was all out. Casey was gone and had been for nearly a decade now, but Harper had never let herself grieve. Kids weren't supposed to take losses well. They were supposed to lose their shit, then act out until it was over.

Harper never let that happen, and her parents' embargo on talking about Casey hadn't helped. The issue must have gnawed at them from the inside. Harper's parents were separated, and she spoke to neither of them. It didn't take a genius to understand why. Each of them reminded the others of the girl they buried at age 18, then erased from their shared history.

Harper finished sobbing and looked into Donovan's eyes. He was startled to see the face of Kimmy Davis, thirteen years old and lost all over again.

She met his gaze, her eyes like cool blue sapphires. "She didn't just commit suicide. She was driven to it."

Donovan let that settle. And then he said, "Tell me more."

～

"YOU SEEM UNEASY ABOUT THIS, FELLA," said the handsome man with the long blond hair and permanent stubble.

Donovan denied it.

"I wouldn't be worth what she's paying if I couldn't see that. Maybe it's something you and me should talk about."

Donovan looked past Gavin Cash, down the long hallway leading to his inner office. Harper was still in there, sitting behind Gavin's big steel desk like a damsel in noir. The two of them were standing man to man.

"What these kids did to her sister? It's pretty dark. You gotta see that."

"Of course I do. But this ..." Donovan was at a loss for words. He stopped talking, smelling the flypaper overhead, peppered with corpses.

"This what?"

"It's like ... *revenge.*"

"It *is* revenge. Thought you were smart enough to have figured that out by now."

"If you tell anyone about this," Donovan finally said, "her lawyers will—"

"Tell me something, cowboy. Do you love her?"

Donovan, startled, stammered out an "Of course."

"Then there are two options for you, way I see it. Either you can help, or you can get out of the way. I suppose you could make an argument that tattling on her yourself is love, too, but that's pussy talking."

Donovan assumed this meant that *he* was a pussy, not that Harper's vagina was calling the shots. Although with a guy like Gavin, he supposed it could be either. "I wouldn't do that," he said, offended.

"So you either stay with her and you stand by her, or you get out and let her do what's needed."

"How about the option where we work through it without resorting to spying on kids from her sister's high school? You know ... *within* the law?"

"Ain't nothin' I do that's outside the law, friend. You say otherwise and we got a problem. Now, if she's got designs to blackmail these kids with what I dig up? That's on your girl, not on me."

"She'd never do that."

"Maybe," Cash said, digging for gold between his teeth. "But if she did, I know I'd wave the flag for her. Some of these kids? *Shit.* One of them is fucking the counselor's husband. One's got two kids with another, but they're cuckoo eggs."

"What?"

"Not his," Cash explained. "She fucked some other guy, and her hubby doesn't have a clue. That guy Simon, he's committed six kinds of fraud. Felonies, good in total for a life behind bars if they got him on all of them. And two of the sorority girls? Hell, man, they *poisoned* a guy. Nothing official, but it ain't hard to see what happened if you dig, you dig? And all of that's *on top of* what they did to her sister. They got it comin' — no question."

"Didn't your mother ever tell you that two wrongs don't make a right?"

Cash laughed. If he'd been wearing a cowboy hat, he'd have tipped it.

"That's cute. You got a beef? You'd better talk to her." He pointed toward the office. "I just do what I'm hired to do. You slumping around and pouting ain't gonna change nothin'. Like I said, you got two options. You either hop aboard or you let it go and leave her. I've been in this business a long time, and I've seen people like her and I've seen people like you. You can try and talk her out of it, but you ain't gonna be able. I see it in her eyes. So, friend, if you're not into this, maybe you should cut out now. Save yourself some heartache."

Donovan met his eyes for a long moment then said, "Fine. I'm leaving."

But he didn't.

FIVE WEEKS LATER, Donovan decided to break it off for good.

He walked in to find Harper sitting beside the bed with a vial of pills and a bottle of whiskey. And she didn't drink whiskey.

"What's this?" he asked, already unnerved. "Got a headache?"

"You were right. I should let it go."

"Let what go?"

"All of it. Casey. There's just no point."

Her lifeless tone chilled his blood. They'd been together a year and a half, and he'd seen her ups and downs. She wasn't well, and the degree to which this was true had only smacked him in the face over the last few weeks, as he'd seriously considered his exit. Now the signs were everywhere.

The old cuts on her upper arms? And the stories she told, about how she used to drink in college? She said she'd partied like the rest of them, but so many of Harper's stories ended in blackouts.

He'd pieced the rest together, hiding his eyes from the truth that was becoming ever more apparent. The boyfriends who'd abused her but whom she never left, the daredevil behavior, the eating disorder that came and went, the dour, hopeless way she talked about herself when the spotlight was gone. Even her fame was manic. Harper didn't act because she enjoyed it; she did it because she needed to be someone else. She needed attention like a vampire needs blood. She sought out negative reviews, bemoaning and reveling in them in tandem.

An ugly truth was suddenly obvious to Donovan: Harper hated herself and always had. She'd probably suffered from undiagnosed depression since the day she refused to attend Casey's funeral. Her self-confidence was overcompensation, plain as the nose on her magnificent face.

She sipped a tumbler of amber whiskey. No rocks, surely no water.

"Harper. You need help."

"You've helped me."

"Not enough."

She picked up the vial and shook it.

"What's in there?" Donovan asked.

"Nyperal."

The temperature fell fifty degrees.

"Isn't that what your sister—"

"One pill makes you larger, and one pill makes you small."

"Harper, look at me."

"And the ones that mother gives you … don't do anything at all."

When he moved toward her, she snatched the vial like Gollum with Precious.

"Harper!"

She smiled, said nothing.

"How much have you had to drink?" The bottle was half empty. He'd never seen it before. She was a wine drinker, with an extensive cellar.

"Go ask Alice," she said.

"Give me the pills. They're dangerous. Especially with alcohol."

"So I've heard. So a little birdie told me."

"Who told you? Gavin?"

"And Casey, of course. She told me by taking a ton while drinking like a sailor, then never waking up. Though I never connected the dots until Gavin said something. Isn't that strange?"

"Give them to me, Harper."

"Why? You were right. I never dealt. It's like you said: I need to face the pain. Well, I faced it. And I've made a decision. It's so much easier than what I had planned."

"You're not supposed to face it alone."

"I'm through with therapists. I'm just … *through.*"

And she started crying again.

Donovan held her. Took the bottle, which now she released easily — able, at least, to still feel something other than oblivion. Holding her, Donovan felt love, pity ... and the longer he sat with it, eventually frustration. Irritation.

Anger.

Then outright *fury*.

Over the past month, Harper had planned and planned, building around what Gavin had fed her. She told Donovan she'd *been* planning for a long time — ever since Casey. The angst of it all hadn't hit her until some quiet part of her brain finally decided it was time to turn her old plans into a new reality. She hadn't grieved in the usual way, but Harper hadn't turned her head as he'd thought. Instead of weeping, she focused on her demons and gave them all names.

Summer.

Ella.

Heidi.

And what she'd built inside her mind, over the last ten years? From the corners Harper had shown him a Machiavellian masterpiece.

Holding her, Donovan wondered at himself. He'd waffled, refusing to choose a lane. He'd done nothing. Occupied space. A pussy like Gavin had said.

Either you can help, or you can get out of the way.

What had been holding him back? What was preventing him from being there for her?

Why wasn't he waving her flag?

They'd done this to Casey.

They'd done this to *Harper.*

His Harper.

"There's no point," she said, her voice still wet with tears.

"Tell me again. Tell me what you'd do to them if you could."

Donovan looked out across the hills. It was dark again, and this was when the shadows came, reaching out with nighttime tendrils to wrap themselves around his beloved's neck.

The temperature dropped. His anger settled into something new, less helpless. And in a voice he barely recognized, Donovan said, "Tell me again what you'd do to make everything right."

FORTY-NINE

Dessert had yet to arrive. Nighttime had come to Cielo del Mar, and the haze from the seaside boardwalk was — from the perspective of fourteen people holding court fourteen floors above the street — dominant over the glare from below. It seemed stiller than a coming storm should. Darker, as if the world itself didn't care.

From Crave's top floor, the French doors of the Buvette looked west, toward where the sun had set just hours before. Standing nearest to them, Donovan was the only one among the party who heard the waves. A curious breeze from the sea brought their sound through the windows, but only barely. As with all glass in the Buvette, the French doors were shatterproof. Harper had thought of that just as she'd thought of everything.

When my guests panic, they might throw chairs, or their Doodads, or even hack at the glass with a knife. If they break free — even if they fall to their deaths to do so — it will ruin all the fun.

Donovan made sure to swap the glass. Same as he had the invitations printed and helped Harper procure the poison. It broke his heart, seeing the final act play out, seeing his true love yawn as it took effect. She hadn't needed to join them; that was the one thing in this whole out-of-control affair that bothered him most. She could have her revenge without going gently into that good night. But try as he might, he'd been unable to stop her. Unable to stop any of it.

This is how it must be. I've always known that I'd go the way Casey went. It's not spontaneous. It's calculated. I won't be talked out of it, Donovan. I will do this with or without you ... but I will do *it.*

And with her declaration made, what was he supposed to do? Commit Harper for her own protection? Call the police? A logical man might have done either, but Harper had handled her plot like she took care of everything else. She boiled the water slowly around Donovan, getting him agreeing to those steps that seemed harmless. He'd said yes to the mildest parts, then more and more. *I only want to scare them.* But then it got worse. And worse. Now here they were, dead on their feet. And there wasn't a damned thing that Donovan could do.

He'd told himself, *I will go along with it until I find a way to stop it.* Or even better: *I will go along so I can stop it.*

But there'd been no way to stop it, and he shouldn't have been surprised. Harper had outsmarted him, just as she'd outwitted her sister's tormentors. She hadn't told him about her plans to lace the soup. He'd watched her pour powdered white pills into the wine as it decanted, and when she'd been away, he'd swapped it for an untainted vintage. But Donovan's missing spine had turned out to be one more thing she'd anticipated.

When Harper announced that she'd poisoned the soup instead, he'd been surprised as anyone. And now here he was, supposedly protected by Harper's wealth, but a bringer of death nonetheless.

He looked at his watch. Now time was the enemy.

"I'll make you a deal," Simon told Harper. "My network has billions in assets. I can make things happen if you'll just make sure I get one of the good desserts."

"You have nothing I want. Nor does your network."

"I heard you want to do arthouse, but are locked into a six-picture deal. I can make that deal go away."

"Bullshit," Melissa said. "I have better Hollywood connections than you do."

"Like she needs Hollywood connections," Summer said. "From either of you."

"You know who was responsible," Simon went on. "Let the rest of us go. As a show of good faith."

Harper leaned forward. "What if my faith isn't good?"

"You said you'd give an antidote to the innocent."

"So tell me, Simon. Which among you are innocent?"

"Me, for one. I took care of her. Tried to take away the pills when Imogen was practically feeding them to her."

Imogen picked up her water goblet and threw it at Simon. It missed by a foot, sailing between Simon and Noah, past the rug where it detonated on the tile. A waiter scurried in with a mop and a dustbin as if he'd been waiting.

Mason went to help. Donovan saw him slip out his wallet and hand it to the waiter. But his pennies were nothing compared to the encrypted offshore transfers already arranged for tonight's staff.

"No thank you, sir," the waiter said, declining the wallet.

"Just call someone." Ignored, Mason spoke louder. "Goddammit, just make a call!"

"Have a lovely evening, sir."

"*Fuck!*"

"Please sit down, Mr. Pace," Harper said. "Getting excited will only pump it through your bloodstream faster."

"*AAAAAAAAAAA ...!*" Mason rushed around the table and straight at Harper.

Donovan caught Mason in the side with the Black Jack and dropped him to the floor.

The others were starting to rise. He whispered into his Doodad. Within thirty seconds four of the waiters arrived with the kinds of guns that used bullets.

"Please," Harper said. "I need to know what happened."

"They *told* you what happened!" Bindi screeched.

"They told me what I already knew. 'Casey was pranked; Casey got sad; Casey took her life to ease the pain.' But you didn't know my sister like I did. You didn't know her strength."

Donovan took a step without thinking. All night long, Harper had held her veneer. All night, she'd been the queen of frost. But now, as she fought her sluggish muscles to stay awake, he could see the other Harper Knox between the cracks. *His* Harper. The soft, quiet, beautiful woman life had never allowed her to be. She'd been soured long ago, blighted before she bloomed. Because of these people. And she wouldn't want them to see her sweat.

"Harper ..." But she shook her head, waving him away.

Harper continued. "My sister would have never killed herself over a prank. I saw her all week. She was hurt, but getting better."

"Drinking," Simon said. "Taking Imogen's drugs."

Harper met Simon's eye but spoke to everyone. "Something happened to her. I just need to know, and it'll all be over."

Movement. Taylor had almost spoken, then said nothing. She looked caught as all heads turned, brown eyes darting to and fro.

"Taylor?" Ella said.

"I knew it. She was in on it, too. Wasn't she, Ella? Heidi? Taylor's not Miss Goody Two-Shoes in the end, is she?" Melissa's face wore its usual biting sarcasm, but then she yawned and it changed. She put her hand to her chest and breathed — slowly, like an experiment. And finally, Donovan saw the fear. She didn't want to die.

"Shut up, Melissa," Heidi said. And shockingly, Melissa did.

"Ms. McKay?" Harper said.

But Taylor looked lost. Helpless.

"Dessert will be here soon. I need to know who gets what."

"Nothing." But Taylor's hand, from Donovan's perspective, was visible on Teek's knee. It wasn't laying flat, like a sleeping dog. It was upright, in a claw, like a searching spider.

"It was Summer's fault," Noah said when Taylor said nothing.

Summer whirled around to Noah. "Fuck you. It's your wife's fault if it's anyone's. Hers and Heidi's."

"Sit down, Noah," Ella said.

But there were beads of sweat on Noah's brow. His eyes were wild animals trapped in tiny cages. His breath was barely there, his arm hairs standing on end. "I loved her! I'd have done anything for Casey! I tried to help her! I tried to save her!"

"Noah ..." Ella said.

Noah turned as if he might snap at her, but instead he defended his wife in the most unflattering way. "Ella is stupid! She does first and thinks later, but she never means it — and *believe* me, she's spent eleven years being sorry. She's paid her dues, Miss Knox! She's addicted to everything. Probably tried to kill herself. She sits at home and—"

"Noah!"

"Shut the fuck up, Ella! Just shut your fucking mouth!" He turned to Harper. "I know what's in her envelope. My kids aren't mine. I'm not stupid. I know. And go ahead, tell the rest of the world. She cheats and she insults me, but I still love her. Not like I loved Casey, not in the same way, but I do love her. She never meant to hurt

Casey. She loved Casey, and what they did has eaten her insides. Let us go. Please, just let us go."

"Mr. Boyer, I—"

"And me," Heidi said. "Do you have any idea how much therapy I've taken just so I can—?"

"*She* meant it," Bindi said, surprising the room. "Heidi means what she does. She's so rotten, she'll never learn."

Heidi looked like a bullet had found her.

Melissa said, "Kill us all; who fucking cares?"

Harper stood. Not because she wanted the room's attention, though she did. Donovan could see the real reason — to make sure she still could. He almost went to her, eager to put his arm around her. But he felt the slim objects in his jacket pocket and told himself, *Not yet*. There was a time for everything, and his ace was for later.

He watched her waver, taking the table's edge for support.

"Donovan. Call for dessert. Tell them that—"

But a stern voice — one the room hadn't heard in so long, it had nearly been forgotten — said, "Wait."

Teek was standing. Beside him, Taylor had his hand, trying to pull him back to sitting. She whispered his name, but it was like he couldn't hear.

"Yes, Mr. Sheridan?" Harper said.

"I know what happened that night. I know what turned things around for Casey — what messed her up so bad, she couldn't recover. Not at home. Not with the support of her friends. Not until she was gone. I know who's responsible. If you have to blame someone, I know who. And why."

A moment.

"Who?"

"Me. And someone else."

Again, the room waited. Mason was halfway to standing. Summer looked eager. Beside her, John's attention seemed almost rabid. He looked at Donovan, but the sentry flinched quickly away. At Noah, who seemed lost after his outburst. At Simon, who looked prepared to kill. At Melissa, whose bravado had deserted her. At Imogen, who for once had nothing to say.

"Teek." Taylor's voice was near tears. "Teek, you don't have to do this."

"I'll tell you what I know," Teek said, ignoring Taylor. "What *nobody* knows except for my wife, who I only recently told. And Casey, of course, who never deserved to die."

"Teek," Taylor said. *"Please."*

"I'll tell you on one condition." He looked down. "Taylor protected your sister. She was there when Casey needed her, when nobody else was. She did her best. She's suffered for no reason. I want your word that she'll go free. Do what you want with me and everyone else, but let my wife live. Promise me that and I'll tell you everything."

Harper considered then nodded to Donovan. He spoke into his Doodad so no one could hear.

"You have my word. I swear on Casey's memory, Taylor is safe."

Teek swallowed. Looked down at Taylor, who sniffed, eyes still fixed on her husband. Donovan had witnessed their earlier tension, had seen this unspoken thing eating them up and forcing them apart. Now, it didn't seem to matter. The past was where it belonged, and this was Teek's confession. Something not in the envelope. The missing piece that Harper hadn't known, but that she'd sought through life and death and pain and misery.

And Donovan could see: Whatever it was, *Taylor had forgiven him.* Teek wasn't who he used to be — whoever that was. Just as Kimmy Davis was corrupted into Harper Knox, and the wreck of Summer Nixon had tried so hard to birth Summer Merritt.

It was enough to bring tears to Donovan's eyes.

"Well?" John said, leaning over the table. "What happened? Who was it?"

Teek swallowed.

And said:

"It was—"

FIFTY

May 19, 2018

Teek blinked. His eyes weren't working. Probably because he was shitfaced to an extent that he suspected nobody had ever been before.

He wasn't sure whether he'd thrown up, but based on his questionable whereabouts and the fact that he still couldn't see, he'd either gone to sleep or blacked out.

"I take these all the time for anxiety," said someone in the blackness. Or semi-blackness. More like brownness, now that Teek's wits were returning. Then, in that brownness with light around the edges, the same high-pitched voice said, "Seriously, honey. It'll help."

Something shifted on his face. Fabric. He was covered with ... a coat? He seemed to remember a coat. But he still felt too drunk to figure out what it was, in part because he didn't care. It was warm in here, and trying to face the outside world with all its bright lights felt like something a fool would do.

"Casey?"

Someone else. A voice farther away than the first. A male voice, Simon.

He was asking about Casey. Teek's mind was still full of fog, but at least he'd figured it out. He'd come upon Simon in the upstairs hallway. He had been looking into a bedroom, where Casey and some college girl were sitting on the bed. He had thought they might be drunk too, about to make out. That would be hot. Teek had talked to all who'd listen about Casey being so much wilder than everyone had imagined, whaling on Mason's throbber while he tickled her honeypot. And everyone with an internet connection could sneak a peek at her milky whites. He'd thought they might do it again, so when Simon told Teek to leave, he'd made himself at home in the big chair.

Teek remembered this all in a haze. He was superbly fucked up, catastrophically uninterested in focusing. His brain went in and back out of the semi-sleep, refusing to surrender the song.

"Give us some space, will you?" said the college girl.

Shuffling. Maybe Simon leaving?

The room was dim; only one good-sized lamp on an end table beside the bed. It was shaped like an irregular trapezoid, and Teek's chair was back in the shadows. He'd plunked himself in plain sight, but he'd been forgotten.

Whatever was over him shifted with his breathing. Just a little, so that one eye could see.

The college girl took Casey's hand. They spoke low: a bummer because Teek couldn't hear what they were saying, but potentially beautiful because it might have been the whispers of drunken lovers. After a few minutes, the college girl got up and went to the door. She was obviously going to close it so they could start making out, but she left instead. Teek waited for her to return but with nothing to occupy his mind, he blacked out again.

An unknowable amount of time passed. Maybe minutes, probably closer to an hour.

Teek woke to the sound of voices, his head slightly clearer. Like he'd shaken off some of the alcohol in his system, graduating from shitfaced to plastered. The coat was still on him but as before, his eye was still free to scope his surroundings. He didn't even have to pee. This was the life.

The new voices were Casey and Simon's.

"I can imagine how you feel," Simon said.

"No, you can't."

"Okay. I *can't* imagine how you feel. You win."

Casey smiled. It was weak, but there.

"I'm really sorry that happened to you, Casey."

"Thanks."

"Is there any chance you can see it as a success? You know, on a performance basis, with Mason?"

"That's not funny, Simon."

"Okay. How about on a presentation basis. If it helps, the reviews are flattering. People are saying that you must work out."

"Knock it off."

But Teek could see a reluctant, eye-rolling half-smile. People loved to hate Simon, but even his friends (and Teek was foremost among them) mostly liked him because he had no pretense.

"I'm just trying to find a way to reframe it that you can get behind."

"I just want to forget it ever happened," Casey said.

"Obviously that's not going to happen. You're stupid if you think people will just forget."

"Right." Casey held her face for a while, then quietly cried. Simon stood and closed the door, then sat back beside her on the bed. He took her hand. That was unexpectedly tender, for Simon.

"Shit passes. You know the internet."

"Except that even if people stop paying attention, it stays online forever."

"Hey," Simon said, "if you don't want me to try and make you feel better, I'll leave."

Casey took Simon's hand and patted it. "No. Stay." She slurred a little, still drunk herself.

After a moment, Simon said, "So. You and Mason."

She laughed. "We'll see."

"I thought I heard you had a boyfriend. Before Mason, I mean."

"That's just something my friends tease me about." Her face darkened.

"Fuck them," Simon said. "I got your back."

"Thanks ... Simon?"

"Yeah."

"Did you see the pictures? Or the video?"

He paused, but then said, "Yeah."

"Shit."

"Don't let them shame you for it, Casey. Be proud."

"*Proud?*"

"So you got caught. Everyone's fucking around. People said you were an ice queen before that shit happened."

"Great."

"Now, they see that you're just a normal girl. With her ... needs."

"Dammit, Simon."

"Hey. You opened my eyes."

"That wasn't my intention."

"It's okay."

She sniffed. Simon wrapped an arm around her and said, "I got you."

"Thanks, Simon."

"I always liked you, Casey."

"You're not terrible yourself."

He put his hand on her thigh, near the knee. Teek suddenly realized that he should have announced his presence a while ago, and was now officially a peeping tom. It wasn't his fault. He wasn't camping out in a closet. He'd been here the whole time — had even claimed his seat in front of them. If he'd blacked out for longer, he'd only be waking right now.

Maybe he should say something. Shift positions, pretend to be sleeping.

Instead, he kept watching.

Simon leaned toward Casey's face.

She pushed him back and moved her legs, escaping his hand. "What are you doing?"

"*Shhh.*" He leaned in again, eyes closed.

This time she put a hand on his chest. "Simon. Seriously."

"Come on, Casey. High school is almost over. It's now or never."

Her blouse was askew, undone a button too far. His hand slipped inside to cup her breast. Even from here, Teek could see the flash of a bra. She pushed again, but he held fast and began to knead. Finally, she gave him a big shove and in one swift movement, smacked Simon hard across his face.

"What the fuck, Casey?" The velvet was gone from his voice, his tone now indignant.

"What's wrong with you?"

"What's wrong with *me*? *Nothing's* wrong with me. You don't want me to make a move, don't give me signs."

Standing now, while Simon sat. "*What* signs?"

"The way you're talking. The way you're looking at me. You just said you liked me."

"As a *friend!*"

He took her hand. "Come on, Casey. Sit down. You're hysterical."

She snatched her hand back. "Are you *kidding* me? I'm *hysterical?* I'm at a party, alone, drinking, just wanting to get the hell out of here because I'm humiliated. Yesterday was the worst day of my life and today isn't much better. And even if none of that was happening, I'm with Mason. As of *yesterday!*"

"Sure doesn't sound like you and Mason are anything."

"Who cares? You think I'm open for business now or something?" She snatched a cover-up from the bed and marched toward the door.

Simon caught her by the wrist. "Sit down, I said."

"Let go of me."

"I want to talk about this. You go off half-cocked, you're going to say some stupid shit because you're not thinking."

"Like how you just grabbed my tit? Yeah, that's crazy of me to have a problem with."

"You were asking for it. You want me, and it scares you."

Teek watched, his pulse slamming like a bass drum.

Casey's face filled with over-the-top amusement. She'd never been more shocked or delighted by anything in her life.

"I *want you so much it scares me?*"

"Goddammit, Casey. I'm lined up to go to Coastline next year, but it's probationary. It's easy for you. You just waltz in with Daddy's money and—"

"And my excellent record? My good grades? My four years of *really hard work?*"

Simon's face firmed: all business. "It's not so easy for me. You say one stupid thing and—"

"Don't flatter yourself. I don't want anyone to know you put your fucking hands on me."

She went for the door.

He yanked her back. "You aren't listening to me."

"Let go of me, Simon."

He pulled her close. Rotated so her back was to the wall. Teek was sure he'd threaten her or something. Instead, he looked at her for a really long time. Then he kissed her again, hard.

Casey pushed back, but his hand went to her inner thigh, climbing higher.

"What the fuck is wrong with you?"

But in the rooms below, the music was loud. People were shouting. Upstairs was officially off-limits. He was the only one seeing this. The only one able to intervene.

But what would he do?

Anything. Do anything, *you fucking coward, before it's too late.*

But Teek was frozen. Paralyzed with a sick blend of fear, a perverse thrill, and plain old drunken stupor. His mind kept craving a blackout. His eyes kept wanting to close.

Simon pushed Casey toward the bed. Locked the door. Advanced on her, then caught her when she tried to run, seeing as Teek saw that Simon meant business.

Do something. Just stand up, open your fucking mouth!

But Teek's muscles betrayed him. So did his mind.

He sagged, still rooted in fear and reluctant arousal.

And watched it happen.

FIFTY-ONE

Donovan watched Harper as Teek finished his story.

Nobody other than Teek had spoken for a while. They were all aghast — except for Simon, who Donovan had to pull aside under threat of his stun gun until Teek finished talking.

Harper was no longer composed. Her face no longer pristine. She'd had Cash on this case for years, and a patchwork of other PI's for longer than that. None of them had uncovered anything like this. Harper had always maintained that the official story couldn't be the whole story — that Casey would never have killed herself over what some assholes thought of her.

But a violent rape? A downward spiral, from which she'd let nobody help because it seemed everyone had shamed and then turned on her? That would do it.

Simon tried to laugh. Donovan had never known Casey, but he knew her through Harper's memories, and what she had meant to the woman he loved. He had to restrain himself to keep from hitting Simon with his elbow, taking him down, kicking him until every last breath was out of his body. He had to remind himself: *Stick to the plan.* If Simon was suddenly dead from bludgeoning — or if his body showed any signs of physical trauma — the whole mess would fall apart.

"He's so full of shit," Simon said.

Taylor shook her head. "He's not full of shit."

"Really. So he just sat there covered in coats, pulling his pud."

"I was drunk," Teek said.

"Too drunk to *speak?*" Simon turned to Harper. "He's lying."

But Harper didn't think so. She rose from her seat and lunged across the table at him. Her hair was a frenzy; her cover girl lips pulled back from pristine white teeth.

Across the long table's center, water glasses canted and broke, silverware clattered and the tablecloth bunched. Harper's legs, now off the ground, kicked wildly, one shoe on and one lying on the rug. She was almost six feet tall; the lunge easily covered the table's span. She had Simon by the lapels, and looked about to bite him by the time Donovan shifted his attention to her.

One of the armed waiters nabbed Simon before he could do any damage. Before he could go after Teek, at whom he was staring daggers.

"*He's lying!*" Simon bellowed, arms now clasped behind his back. "*I never touched her!*"

But while Donovan helped Harper off the table and the waiter held Simon, nobody paid attention to Noah. He swiftly crossed the short distance between them and hit Simon impossibly hard in the gut, folding the asshole in half.

Simon tried to fight back, gasping for breath, but Noah wasn't too proud to fight at an advantage. He hit Simon again, this time in the jaw. So much for leaving no marks. Simon tried to kick while the waiter held him, but he overbalanced and almost fell.

Simon came up with his hair in insane tangles, eyes livid.

"*I didn't do anything!*"

"Fuck you, Simon! That's why you wouldn't let me see her! Why you said you'd take her home instead of me! What were you afraid I'd see — Casey on the bed with her clothes ripped off?"

Harper dragged Donovan away. She whispered in his ear, "Kill them. Kill them all."

"Harper."

"Fuck them." Then, realizing she should broadcast to the room instead of just Donovan: "*FUCK ALL OF YOU! It's over! You're all dead!*"

Teek came forward. "Wait. You promised. Taylor—"

"She's no better than you are!" Harper glared at Simon. "Rapist!" Then she stabbed a finger at Teek. "Accomplice!"

Taylor rose. "He didn't 'accomplice' anything! He was—!"

But Harper's accusing finger practically jabbed Taylor in the throat. "Conspirator! Enabler!"

"He just told me a week ago!"

"And now you're holding hands! Like newlyweds! Do you lay still for him in bed? Shout protests while he fucks you?"

"You promised she'd be safe!" Teek yelled.

But Harper's face belonged in an asylum. She was having trouble breathing. Between blue-eyed, wild-haired stares, her palm kept going to her chest. "Nobody's safe. Casey wasn't safe. She thought she could trust friends, but one by one they all betrayed her."

One by one she pointed at Heidi, Ella, Taylor.

"Her man didn't stand by her," she pointed at Mason, "and her loverboy didn't even help when he found out that something was obviously wrong." Centering on Noah.

"It would have been too late!" Noah said.

"Not too late to stop her suicide. Just like the people in charge failed to see." She pointed at Bindi. Then she made the rest of the rounds, starting with Melissa and Imogen. "You helped hurt her." Then Summer. "You started it all." Finally, John. "And *you*, Mr. Merritt? How many horrible things have *you* kept secret? How many criminals are still free because of you?"

Summer looked at John, apparently clueless as to how he spent his time.

"You're all feeling tired now, aren't you?" Harper put a hand to her chest. "Soon you won't be able to breathe. Soon you'll all be dead. Have you learned your lessons?"

"We've learned!" Mason shouted. "We were just kids! You want to kill Simon? Go for it! But *please*, give the innocents in this room our antidote!"

Donovan was pulling Harper toward the exit. This was bad, but there was still the potential to make it worse. Neither of them had anticipated a rape, and the revelation had unhinged her. He knew Harper better than anyone, but right now he had no idea what she might do.

Donovan's back bumped one of the remaining waiters, bearing dessert. They delivered plates topped with dense black cakes as the muttering and pleading continued, as Donovan ushered Harper toward the exit.

A sinister smile touched her lips. "There *is* no antidote. But please. Enjoy your desserts anyway."

Out of the room. Through the door, which Donovan locked and bolted.

The waiters were gone; only Harper's dozen guests remained inside. She'd specifically requested a shatterproof glass door to the Buvette, instead of a solid one. This was the part she'd been looking forward to most.

She pressed her face to the glass, kneeling now as the drug did its work.

Inside, pandemonium reigned. They either hadn't heard Harper about the antidote or didn't believe her. They were climbing over each other to eat the cakes — *all* except for Simon's — throwing kicks and punches, determined to rip each other limb from limb in the hopes that at least one of the desserts around the table was laced with salvation.

But Harper wasn't lying; there was no antidote. It wouldn't be long. The room was thick with labored breath. Hands went to chests as they exerted themselves. She'd timed it perfectly. With her dose delayed, Harper would be awake to watch it all happen.

Within minutes, the first of them — Heidi — had collapsed.

Then Bindi, then Noah.

And one by one, the rest of the guilty.

Donovan and Harper watched as the rodostazem did its work, benzos stirring within them like wildfire, binding to the GABA receptors in the brain.

Donovan had read the Physician's Desk Reference entry on it, just to make sure. Side effects included:

Drowsiness. Dizziness. Problems with thinking and memory.

Slurred speech. Sore gums. Nausea, diarrhea, constipation.

Blurred vision.

Headache.

And *death.*

FIFTY-TWO

May 1, 2029

This time, Donovan didn't wake to find Harper already restless. He wouldn't need to sneak through the dark mansion or fear their mutual shadows; he wouldn't need to boil water and make her tea. Unlike so many other nights, Harper was in the small office off the bedroom, light on. Working.

He went in. She must have heard him, but her back was to the door and she didn't react. He put his arms around her, hands sliding along her silk robe.

He kissed her neck, then her cheek. "Do you know what time it is?"

"It's 3:12 am." She tapped a small clock on the desk as if there wasn't one right there on her screen.

"Maybe I didn't mean that question literally."

"Then maybe you shouldn't have asked it literally."

"Aren't men supposed to be direct, and women obtuse?"

"I don't know. Do you mean that question literally?"

He slid his arms away, pulled up a second chair, and sat beside her. "What are you working on?"

"Take a guess."

"Dinner?"

"Of course."

He looked at the screen. "Do you really need to have Kona kampachi flown in?"

"Of course. We're not animals."

Donovan watched her work for thirty quiet seconds. She was as beautiful in her obsession as she was in her precision. She'd been composing her grand act of revenge since long before he'd met her, and now that the time was near, she'd been working almost ceaselessly. She still had the busy schedule of an A-list actor, so her real work happened at night.

"I'll sleep plenty soon," she said whenever he asked. It was a joke — and something Donovan very much planned to either talk her out of or sabotage if he could — but even so, it cut him deep. Harper planned to end her life. It wasn't sad for her, or happy, or relieving, or troubling. It was as matter-of-fact as the redundant clock on her desk.

"You still want me to greet the guests as they arrive?"

"Yes. You're the only one I can trust."

"We've got a problem if I'm the *only* one you can trust. I can't cook and I drop plates when I serve."

"I should clarify. You're the only one I can trust quite this much. The others will do their jobs and then keep their mouths shut. You will get away clean — and if we're lucky, even Crave will carry on."

"That's what you're worried about? *The restaurant* carrying on?"

Harper stopped her relentless typing and turned to him with sympathy. "My mind is made up, Donovan. I know you don't agree with my decision, but this is how it has to be. You will escape scrutiny simply because you are you. I am me."

"You don't have to end your life to get away with this, Harper. Especially since you don't even plan to—"

She put a finger to his lips.

"No. My darling."

She resumed typing. The plan's outline was more detailed than the to-do list for a week-long festival.

"If I greet them," Donovan said, "won't they recognize me? We've been photographed together on the red carpet. Everywhere."

"No offense, sweetheart, but celebrity chasers only care about the celebrities. If you were famous, we'd be an item worth talking about, but you're not. It's hard to imagine any of these specific people thinking you look more than vaguely familiar."

"And you're just going to get them to talk? You think someone will shout a confession?"

Harper laughed softly. "I doubt there's anything to confess. We *know* what happened for the most part. I just want to remind them. The senior party feels like a mystery box, but she came home half-drunk and all the way pissed. They must have gotten under her skin. I want to know what was said, but it can't be worse than what Ella and Heidi did. Or what Summer *made* them do."

Donovan yawned into a long breath. Harper's tablet was beside the computer, with Gavin's full profiles on each of the guests pulled up for reference. He took it in his hand, swiping through. He stopped on a pair of photos: Summer in high school, and Summer now.

"Don't you want to kill her?" Donovan asked.

Harper smiled, of all things.

"Or Ella? Or Heidi? Aren't you worried your first reaction will be to just get in there and ... I don't know ... smack them to death?"

"There are worse things than death, darling."

He didn't want to ask, but he was in this deep already and had to know. "Like what?"

"Remorse. Guilt. Regret."

"I see."

"Secrets," she added.

"There's nothing wrong with secrets. Right now, I'm keeping one from you." He meant their anniversary gift, but he might also have meant his plan to swap the tainted wine for clean wine so she would end the night breathing. He smiled at her, enjoying the duality despite the hour and topic.

"There are secrets we keep only from others, and secrets we keep from ourselves," she said. "The first brings joy because they don't truly deceive."

"What if someone is cheating?"

"Then it's a secret she's keeping from herself, as well as her significant other."

"What if she's *not* keeping it from herself — just from him?"

Harper smiled at Donovan as if he were naive. "Everyone needs to be able to face themselves. If you've done something you know is wrong, you don't admit it and go on. You tell yourself a story instead. That way you can believe what you want, that you are who you want to be. Nobody hates themselves. Those who believe they do have simply told themselves another lie — one about who they want to be, versus who they *actually* want to be."

"I don't know if that's true."

Harper turned toward him. She took the tablet and studied Summer's photos.

"Look into the eyes of the older photo, Donovan."

"Okay."

"Now look into the eyes of the woman Summer has become. What do you see?"

"She looks bitchier in the older photo."

"But ironically, freer. That was before she was held in bondage."

"Held by who?"

"By herself. I don't need to torture Summer, Donovan. She's doing it to herself. It's eaten her up, that secret she's holding. It's devouring her from the inside out, like cancer."

"So ... what. You forgive her?"

"I will. After this is over."

"And Ella? And all the others?"

"Rebirth can come to anyone, so long as you can look inside, acknowledge, and let it go."

"Including you?"

Harper put her hand on Donovan's.

"I sent my sister to the party. I didn't try hard enough to help her when I might have made a difference. It doesn't even matter if something else happened; either I sent her into it or I failed to acknowledge it. There's no blame I'd put on them that I couldn't also lay onto myself."

"So you should do as you want them to. Look inside yourself, acknowledge your guilt, and let it go."

"I can't. There's one difference between them and me."

"What?"

"Who I am?" She sighed helplessly. "*All* I am today. None of it would have existed without the thing inside me. All of them—" She indicated the tablet. "—have become twisted versions of who they were supposed to be. Some changed for the better, like Mason and Summer, and others for the worse: Ella and Heidi. But at their core, they are all still themselves. But not me. I wouldn't be who I am without what Casey's suicide forced me to become."

Donovan felt a chill. "And what is that?"

"Cold. Calculating. Driven. Obsessed. *Twisted.* You've only seen inches of me, Donovan. I was thirteen when it happened. I never grieved, never told anyone about how I forced Casey to go out until I told you."

"You didn't know. You can't blame yourself for—"

Again, she laid a finger across his lips.

"I changed my name. I became someone else. I don't know who Kimberly Davis was, or who she might have been. Our secrets define us, but in my case it's literal. I don't know who I'd be once this was over. It's not like I can just open up, forgive myself, and let it all go. How would I go on?"

He put his hand over hers, on the arm of the chair. "With me. You'd go on *with me.*"

She let the moment pass, no reason to swim in the same old debate.

He said, "It's just not fair."

"What's not fair?"

"That they should go on, and you won't."

"You act like you *want* me to kill them."

"No. I like your plan. Let them think they're poisoned; let them freak the hell out. They think they're dying when the mild dose hits them and they start to fall asleep. They look God in the eye. When they wake up, it's almost a literal rebirth. It's downright Christian of you, Harper. Far kinder than I'd have been in your shoes."

"They will still suffer. They will still pay for what they've done."

"But ..." He sighed again. "... well, *you* will suffer the most."

"I won't suffer at all."

"You know what I mean."

"Living on is its own breed of Hell. And if something rears its head? If we find out something we don't already know — that Gavin hasn't uncovered? That's when you call the police. Have them ready after you're gone but before our shaken guests emerge. They will arrest whoever we tell them to. My money goes a long way, dear. Lawyers might get them out of the jails you send them to, but they'll be on warning. It's good enough."

"Good enough for who?"

"For me." She put her palm against his cheek. "For you. For *Casey.* And that's all that matters."

"I'll do you one better. Same plan — but instead of just one person dying, *nobody* dies."

She gave him a look. Then he stood, giving up for now, and wrapped his arms around her.

They exchanged a kiss. "Don't stay up too late."

Then Donovan returned to the bedroom alone, closing the office door and killing the light.

In the darkness, he whispered, *"I'm not giving up on you."*

FIFTY-THREE

As Ella felt her life ending, her second-to-last thought was of Casey Davis. Not in the way Casey had been the subject of *everyone's* thoughts this evening, but of Casey before things went bad, before Ella had sold her soul for nothing.

Ella's specific memory, if anyone had been able to see it from the outside, would have looked almost insignificant. The Girl Squad, sitting around Casey's dorm at Bayshore, taking an online quiz to find out whether they were sex addicts. The quiz had clearly been written for men.

Does your penis ever get raw from abrasion? Ella had asked Casey.

And Casey had said, *No. Only my balls.*

Heidi had been taking a sip of soda when Casey said that, and it squirted up the back of her throat and out her nose, dribbling down the front of her shirt. Taylor found that unendingly hilarious. They'd stayed up half the night afterward looking for new quizzes for men. Heidi learned that she'd been dating women just like her mother. Casey had all the symptoms of low testosterone.

Inside Ella's mind, Casey kept laughing. They all did. It felt like a thousand years ago. Like it had all happened to a different person.

Ella's final thought before dying was of Noah. Not her children; Noah.

It spilled from her deeper well like a montage:

Noah running into her during her first year at Coastline, when she'd been independent and alone, alienated from Taylor and unable to face Heidi just as Heidi had been unable to face her. When Ella had been trying to make her way solo after so long in a group, skirting the Diamond Society house, as if the place were radioactive. Noah laughing with her in the dining commons as they reconnected about Bayshore, avoiding the most painful moments among them.

Noah on their third date, wanting to take her hand but unable. Ella finally taking the initiative — and again when they parted, when she was the one to advance for a kiss.

Back then, his reluctance had seemed shy and sweet rather than spineless. Even at age 19, he was vulnerable and naive. Ella was guarded. *Jaded.*

Noah on their honeymoon.

Noah when the children were born, after she'd cheated one too many times and gotten caught in the most demonstrable of ways. Genetics offered evidence but Noah, who was still his brand of sweet, hadn't seen it. Ella remembered how unfair it had seemed: the guilt she felt watching her husband hold one twin and then the other, knowing that in a healthy life, this should be the happiest of times.

Ella's dark days, and the tiny ways — even when she'd been at her most twisted, her most addicted, her most raw and hateful, her most loathing and unlovable — that Noah's presence had made it all right. There hadn't been many good days at the end, she thought with her final breaths. They'd fought a lot and weren't going to last. But she supposed that even if she couldn't be loving, Ella had probably loved him just the same.

Even as her consciousness faded, she could feel her slowing heart as her center. Wrapped around it was the darkness she'd invited inside, then nurtured like a parasite. Noah said that she was stupid and didn't think before doing. He'd also said that she'd paid her dues (that was impossible) and that she'd probably tried to kill herself (she hadn't, though she had seriously considered it). Then he'd said the worst thing of all. The dagger in her heart.

She cheats and she insults me, but I still love her.

With that, Ella slipped into the abyss. Into the sweet release of death.

And then ...

FIFTY-FOUR

A sound. There was sound in Hell.

Ella listened for a while, hearing the *Plink-plink-plink* of the Devil playing the banjo. That, in its way, *did* make sense. Nobody considered Hell's aural landscape, but it had to have one, right? And surely it had banjos and bagpipes.

Despite being dead, her eyes fluttered open.

It happened slowly at first, her vision returning to the red interior of her eyelids, then only reluctantly yielding to the brightness of a room it took a while to recognize.

It came slowly; the room was unusual, and Ella was sprawled on the floor.

Neither made sense.

But then she remembered the start of the evening and its dreadful unfolding. Finally, the *coup de grace* in which the famous Harper Knox had locked them all in the dining room to die. She hadn't looked magazine-cover beautiful then. She'd looked insane, ready to rip out every throat in sight.

And why not? Now that Ella's eyes were open, she remembered Teek's story and how she'd felt hearing it.

If not for the coming desserts, she would have taken a fork to Simon's throat.

Harper's voice, raging without the silk she used for her interviews:

FUCK ALL OF YOU! It's over! You're all dead!
And so they had been.
So why was she alive?
Ella sat up, looking around. The plinking she'd taken for Satan's bluegrass was water dripping from an overturned goblet onto a purse.

There must have been an antidote-laced dessert after all. Maybe just one, and she'd gotten lucky. She had scratches on one forearm: scars over a Black Beast cake she'd battled Bindi Bridges for. Her arm was still sore from where Imogen and Melissa had both gripped it in a scrabble for another cake. They'd been working together, Ella remembered, but had turned on each other with the prize in sight.

"E— *Ella?*"

She looked back. Noah, also with his eyes open. "What happened?"

In a movie, she would have reached for him, wrapped him in an embrace and told him that she was so glad to see him again, that she'd thought it was over, that she'd loved him all along and that she'd make it right no matter what. Instead, she took his hand and helped him to sit up beside her. He put his palm on her shoulder. She didn't shake it away. Something inside her broke and she fought a sudden, excruciating urge to cry. She didn't hate the urge. It meant she could feel. That she might still be human after all.

Ella shook her head. Not far away, Heidi and John were stirring. There was an odd noise in the score: a Doodad, chirping as if with an incoming message. As if whoever was on the other end didn't know the recipient was supposed to be dead. John's, maybe? Or Summer's — a woman who apparently hadn't been murdered either.

John moaned and rubbed his forehead. He looked at his watch.

"What time is it?" Noah asked.

"4:15."

It was dark outside. So obviously A.M.

"We ... did we all just *fall asleep?*"

John answered Noah, sounding authoritative and not nearly as surprised as Ella felt. She caught his tone but not his words because as she'd started to stand, Ella spied Taylor from under the table, propped up on one arm, her other one rubbing Teek's shoulder to stir him. Her eyes were on Ella. Fixed, staring, moist at the lower lids.

She hates me.

Taylor was glad that she and Teek were alive ... but bothered that Ella was, too.

But then she said the strangest thing. The most inexplicable, least sensible, least logical thing that she could have told Ella ... or Heidi.

"I've missed you."

Ella's dam began to fracture. A hot tear rolled down her cheek — one, then another. She met Taylor's stare and said nothing, but Taylor must have gotten the message anyway because she did another strange thing: she smiled.

Imogen was on her knees. She wobbled onto a chair. From down low, Ella couldn't see what Imogen saw, but it must have been something on the table's surface. Ella heard the shuffling of paper. Then Imogen said, "What are these?"

Another bleat.

The Doodad was near John, as if it had spilled from his pocket when he'd collapsed. Its screen went bright, then dark after several seconds.

"She must have messed up," Noah said. "She tried to poison us, but she fucked it up."

Ella looked past the other waking guests, to the glass doors. Everything behind them was dark. No sound from below. They'd have to check to be sure, but Ella was willing to bet the twelve of them were alone. Alive or dead, Harper Knox and her helpers were gone.

Then there was a sound. Beyond the glass. Faintly, Ella thought she could hear traffic. A big truck, maybe, starting up at an intersection. Sirens, too, off to fight a fire.

The Doodad chirped again, lighting with its second reminder.

Ella glanced around, then dared a look at its face. Before it dimmed again, she could see the message from a blocked number:

Worked perfectly. She's fine but furious. Make the most of your second chances.

The screen dimmed as a hand closed around the Doodad. Ella followed its arm and found herself looking John Merritt right in his eyes.

Ella opened her mouth to ask an obvious question, but John gave an almost imperceptible shake of his head.

She looked at Noah, then back at John. Again, he shook his head: *Quiet. Trust me.*

So Ella — who'd never been good at trust but who found herself willing to give it a go — subtly nodded back.

Mason was up, kneeling between Melissa and Simon, both of whom were still lying down.

Melissa said, "Fuck this hangover."

And Mason, who'd been shaking them both, said, "Simon? Wake up and face the music, asshole."

John extended a hand and helped Ella to her feet. As she rose, her arm brushed the brick of the Doodad now in his pocket.

Worked perfectly. She's fine but furious. Make the most of your second chances.

The shake of John's head; her decision to trust.

No big deal. It wasn't the first time Ella had kept a secret.

FIFTY-FIVE

Two hours earlier

"Mr. Merritt."

John turned and saw Donovan just inches away. He'd somehow missed his approach. He'd been entirely too focused on what Harper had said and was, honestly, still freaking the fuck out even as Donovan took him by the arm and began to reel him away from the table.

Fear seized him. John and Summer were young and they had children. Neither was interested in dying.

A fabulous pastry will always cure what ails you, Harper had said moments ago. *Or at least it will cure those of you who I determine have nothing to hide.*

The past minutes flashed through his mind's eye like the final thoughts of a dying man:

Noah shouting for Harper to take it back, to undo what she'd done.

Heidi vomiting, even though the soup would have already left her stomach.

The waiter accidentally bumping John into Summer's tits, then apologizing as if spilled sauce, not murder, were the offense.

I'm very sorry, sir. Perhaps I can find you a moist towelette? We will, of course, cover any damages.

Then the waiters circulating as everyone panicked to serve the main course: Fish or lamb, as in: *to the slaughter.*

John, caught between terrified, baffled, and furious, stared at Donovan. But he let the man drag him off by the arm while Summer was distracted, while everyone in the room continued to shout and face mortality.

They went through a nondescript door in the Buvette's far corner without anyone the wiser. John noticed it earlier and figured it was a supply closet, but it turned out to be a service hallway. With the door closed and the chaos muted, Donovan's careful, servile nature disappeared. They were now two men: equals, not captor and tormentor.

"What the hell is going on here?" John demanded. "If Harper thinks—"

"With all due respect, I'll do the talking. We don't have much time, or someone will notice you're gone."

"So what?"

"I need to tell you something, but until all of this is over, nobody can know. Not even your wife. I need you to promise that it stays between us."

"Why?" John didn't venture into Donovan's ridiculous request for a promise. Even if he swore, why should Donovan trust that he'd keep his word? Only one of them had poisoned the other, and John couldn't help but feel a burning need to even the score.

"Because few people can truly keep a secret, but I know you can. We know about Contract Confessions. We even know that Mason submitted a confession a few days ago."

"How can you—?"

"It's not important. Swear it to me, John. If I wanted to harm you, there are much easier ways. You have to believe I'm here to help. But the only way to get through this is to let it play out. Harper has a plan for tonight, and believe me, she's thought of everything. If she has any inkling that it'll fail, she'll find another way. Right now you and your wife are alive, but you could easily end up dead."

"No shit. She already told us that—"

"There's no poison. Right now, you're safe. Keep your mouth shut, and we can keep it that way."

"There's no ... *What?*"

Donovan twirled a finger in the air, impatient. "You've all been given Nyperal. It's—"

"I know what Nyperal is."

"Of course you would. Sorry. That's why we're here. I need your help."

"Maybe you should explain," John said.

"She mentioned her man Gavin Cash. What she didn't mention was that he's been looking into all of you for *years* now. *Many* years, if you count the research she did on her own. She knows everything, down to the kind of porn you like. Well, not *you*. As far as her guy could tell, you don't even watch it."

"It changes brain chemistry," John said, unsure of why he felt the need to explain.

"Exactly why we're talking. Not porn, I mean, but ..." He started again, clearly feeling the press of time. "You weren't supposed to be here, John. She invited Summer. When I tried to send you away at the door, it was to spare you all of this. Harper overrode me. Even though she didn't expect you, she was happy to have you. She'd learned about you because of your ties to Summer. The idea of Contract Confessions? It's delicious to her."

"So what?"

"I know what you studied in college. When you started Pete's Place, I know it began as a pharmacy."

John nodded, confused by this deluge of information, trying to keep up.

"Casey Davis died of a Nyperal overdose. We think Imogen gave it to her."

John shook his head.

"Harper's given you all a milligram, in your soup like she said."

"That much will ... what ... knock us out for a few hours?"

Donovan nodded. "All but Imogen, who has a tolerance. She was given more so it'd be enough to put her out, but not enough to kill her. The idea *isn't* to kill any of you, John. It never was. Harper's not a murderer. Considering what she's been through — what your wife and others *put* her through — she's more forgiving than I'd be. I'm protective of Harper. Frankly? I think your wife and her friends can go to Hell."

"Now wait just a—"

Donovan held up a hand. "She just wants to scare you straight. Harper believes in second chances. You've all already swallowed enough of the drug to make you sleep and nothing in the desserts will change that. But if you let on *in any way* that you know you won't die tonight, this will all fall apart. Money can cover a lot of sins, John, and Harper has a ton. I can't guarantee that her Plan B and C will be as harmless. So you can't tell Summer. Or anyone. *Ever*. She's put so much in place. If she knows we talked ..." He practically shivered. "Let's just say that there are people outside of this building — not just me and Harper and the chefs and waiters she's paid off — who won't react well."

"All right." John supposed it was an easy enough thing to agree to since it changed nothing. And that, come to think of it, was what made this whole thing so strange. "If I can't tell anyone and we're all going to survive anyway, why are you telling me at all?"

Donovan's pupils were darting back and forth, and his fingers were shaking. "Because there is someone who *isn't* supposed to survive."

"Who?"

"Harper."

John took a moment to process. "She's going to kill *herself* instead of killing us?"

Donovan nodded. "I can't stop her. Or talk her out of it. She was supposed to dose the wine. I swapped her wineglass, but she changed it to the soup. I guess she didn't want to leave the room to swallow pills."

"How much has she taken?"

"Six milligrams."

John nodded. Harper couldn't weigh more than 130 pounds even at her height, and she'd put away a lot of wine. Six milligrams, taken with alcohol, was enough to kill even Mason, the biggest among them.

"I need your help, John. I'm doing what I can to walk the line — letting this play out so Harper will finally let it go and you can all get on with your lives — but my plan was always to save her. Once this has passed, I think she can move on, too. There's a reason she wanted to use Nyperal for tonight. There is theater to all that she does — even this. I *know* her. Killing herself later on, after she can't make a statement? There's so much less appeal. You have to help me. Help me get Harper through today. Help me let her see tomorrow."

"How?"

"I looked it up. There's an antidote, isn't there?"

"Yes. Flumazenil. You have to call 911 and ..."

Donovan shook his head. "She has to believe you never knew. She doesn't want to kill you, but she needs you to learn her lesson. Everyone has to see tonight through Harper's lens, not mine. If she thinks the evening didn't go off for you as she planned? Right back to Plan B. Plan C. She has an alphabet of them, believe me."

"It's not simple. Flumazenil isn't something you can just slip into her soup."

"What, then?"

"It's an injection. You have to deliver it intravenously."

"Like through an IV line?"

"Like heroin, with a syringe. Do you have any idea how to do that?"

"No. I need you to do it."

John shook his head. "It works too fast. Thirty, maybe sixty seconds at most. She'd see me, and she'd know."

"Can you teach me, then?"

John extended his arm, rolling up a sleeve. "Inside of the elbow, just like when you give blood. Hold the vein down, so it doesn't roll, then insert the needle at an angle. Think of it like spearing a straw with a pin. You'll be able to do it if she's unconscious, but no guarantees that you won't make a mess."

"She can be unconscious?"

"Obviously, earlier treatment is better, but if you need her to believe that the rest of us ..."

Donovan saw the point. "Right. Okay." He inhaled and exhaled as if steeling himself.

John lowered his arm, rolling the sleeve back down. "Once the needle is in, pull the plunger back. You want to see blood enter the syringe to make sure you're in the vein. Then squeeze it into her, slowly but not too slow or you'll still be in there as it takes effect. You'll need maybe 15 or 20 seconds to empty the syringe. When she starts to breathe normally again, she'll squirm and you'll lose the vein."

"Okay. I can do that."

"You haven't asked the obvious question," John said.

"How do I get it."

John nodded. "Flumazenil isn't a controlled substance, but you do need a prescription. Unless you already have a supply, it's not the kind of thing you can just walk in and buy."

"That's where I was hoping you come in. You used to own a pharmacy."

"That's right. And I could get in trouble for arranging something for you, but it's not like being busted for missing Oxycodone or Fentanyl. And that brings us to the *other* obvious question. Why should I help you?"

He met John's stare. The tables had turned and both of them knew it.

Donovan had blown the secret that neither he nor Harper were killers. Although they'd perpetrated one hell of a vigilante show, it was ultimately harmless — and it's not like anyone in the room had done anything to merit execution. Their crime against Casey had been a cruel, stupid prank. Right now, John held all the power. He could call Jeremy at Pete's and get what Donovan needed in a blink, but why *should* he?

Harper and Donovan wanted everyone in the Buvette to psychically gut themselves, to turn on each other, to expose their darkest lies, to face their deaths, and then to spend the rest of their lives shitting in fear that it might happen again.

Now, Donovan wanted John to let it unfold unimpeded. Maybe Donovan was right that Harper's Plan B or Plan C would be worse, but that was true whether she died or not. Maybe Harper Knox was just one more person about to get what was coming. Maybe under that logic, John should wash his hands and allow it to happen.

But even thinking it softened him. John was furious, but he'd studied pharmacology to save lives. He'd worked in a pharmacy for a while and did a stint as a volunteer EMT. Donovan and Harper would never make it to an emergency room, or they would be too stubborn to try. John was probably her only chance.

"You heard what those people out there did," Donovan said. "Harper has suffered her entire life because of it. Please. Try to understand."

"'Those people' include my wife. And she's not who you think she is. Not anymore."

"Then don't do it for Harper. Do it for Casey."

John considered.

Do it for Casey.

Why the hell should he care about Casey? Why the hell would Donovan think he *might* care, even a little?

John looked at the ceiling, sighed, then extended a hand. Donovan looked at it, not understanding.

"What?"

"Give me your Doodad. Mine isn't worth shit in here."

Donovan fumbled the thing to John so fast that it almost dropped. "Don't call the cops."

A neutered threat. John wouldn't call the cops because he believed Donovan that letting Harper and her hidden cronies think this hadn't gone off well might be worse than going to sleep and riding it out, not because he was ordered.

He called Jeremy's cell, then told him he had a private situation that needed help. Jeremy didn't ask; people with means O/D'd on benzos all the time, and few wanted it public.

"Anything," John said into the Doodad. "Do you have Lanexat? Oh, sure, Romazicon is fine. Yes. Yes." He gave Crave's address and asked him to hurry. "Thanks, Jeremy. Really appreciate this."

John hung up, handed the Doodad back, and looked at Donovan.

"He's going to bring you five syringes, all loaded and ready to go, within a half-hour if he can. I gave him your number so he can text when he's close, so be ready to go down to meet him. Give him cash. A *lot* of cash, because Jeremy deserves this even less than the rest of us. You got it?"

"Five syringes?"

John nodded. "It's all he can afford to have unaccounted. He said he'll number them for you with a sharpie, one through five. Give her the first one just like I told you, drawing back to be sure you see blood, then delivering it over 15-20 seconds. Wait thirty seconds after you're finished. If she hasn't responded at all by then, moving around or breathing better, wait another minute and give her the second syringe. If she *still* doesn't respond, wait a minute and give her number three, then the same pattern for four and five. Don't fuck up the order; they're different dosages. And don't give her any more after she starts to wake up. You don't want her to have more than she needs."

Donovan nodded. "In the vein, pull back and see blood, push it in slowly. Wait thirty seconds and if she doesn't start waking up, wait a minute and give her the second one, and on through all five."

"All five *if needed,*" John clarified.

"What if she's still unresponsive after all five?"

"Then get to a hospital and tell them exactly what you did, and expect one motherfucker of a scandal if they save her, or an even bigger scandal if they can't."

Donovan nodded again, grimly this time.

"So are we done here?" This was the angriest John could imagine feeling after potentially saving a life.

"Yes. Thank you, John. Really."

"Go fuck yourself."

John led the way back toward the Buvette. Donovan stopped him at the closed door.

He looked back. With an almost sheepish face, Donovan said, "Remember. Don't say anything to anyone. You have to pretend you think it's real."

John just stared.

"It's for the best. Not just for me and Harper. For everyone."

John went for the knob, but again Donovan put a hand on his shoulder.

He turned, now inches from punching Donovan flat. "What."

"I have your number. We'll remove the jammer when we go, after everyone is asleep. I can text, if you want. To let you know. If you care. The number is scrambled. It can't be traced."

"Let me know what?"

The next was hard for Donovan to say — and as determined as he was to loathe them both, John couldn't help but be affected by its raw emotion.

"If she lives."

And on its heels, Donovan's ridiculous plea played again in his head.

Do it for Casey.

For the poor dead girl, about whom more than half the room seemed to care so much.

"Fine," John muttered. "Text me."

"Oh. And John?"

"Jesus Christ. You don't know when to stop, do you?"

"After you wake up, when you leave, be sure to take your envelopes with you."

"Fuck you. Clean up your own mess. I don't ever want to see them again."

John looked back at Donovan, waiting for his refusal to land.

But Donovan looked like he hadn't understood. Or like he wanted to make a correction because *John* was the one who didn't understand.

"I'm not talking about *those* envelopes," Donovan said.

FIFTY-SIX

" Simon? Wake up and face the music, asshole."

John ignored Mason, keeping his eyes on Ella, knowing she'd read his Doodad's screen. Unless she was an idiot, she would see right through Donovan's text. It wasn't fair. He'd done what he thought was best; he'd made the hard choice and now they'd all survive until morning — including Harper, who might or might not try to end her life again.

Donovan requested a no-win scenario with a semi-happy ending, and it came down to a minor betrayal in exchange for a life. He'd made his choice — and especially following Teek's story, it had felt like the right one. Even as Harper ranted and raged and lost control, it had seemed to John that she'd been in the right — not relative to Noah or Taylor or even to Summer, Ella, or Heidi, but certainly to at least a sixth of the night's roster.

Casey had been raped, and that changed the game. He was glad he'd helped Donovan save her, despite it all. And judging by the approaching sirens, it seemed Donovan had placed at least one final call of his own, and even the wrongdoers would get what they had coming.

But if Ella spoke up? If she thought he'd helped plan this, rather than trying to mitigate it? Hell, she didn't even need to accuse him.

She only had to ask the question.

He watched her, sensing Imogen shuffling behind him at the

table, seeing the others rouse on the floor below him, hearing the sirens.

Shockingly, Ella nodded. And then her eyes told John something he never thought he'd see her say, given what he'd learned tonight:

We all deserve the benefit of the doubt.

Maybe she knew. She had an addict's manner, and if Ella was hooked on the right stuff, she'd needed a stronger dose to knock her out. Maybe she had never descended into the sleep of the benzo naive. Perhaps Ella had seen Donovan do his life-saving work. Maybe, she'd heard his phone call to summon police for Simon, or his mutterings about a helper in their midst.

In the end, it didn't matter.

"What the hell is this?" Imogen asked from behind him.

John turned away from Ella, toward the table. Imogen had a large gold envelope. It was just like the ones that had started their evening, except that these were new, and the originals were gone. Unlike the first round, the new envelopes were unmarked. There were twelve on the table — one for each — but at a glance they were all exactly the same.

Mason looked over, seeing the others migrate toward the table. He straightened, delivered a hard kick to Simon, then walked to join them. "More secrets?"

Bindi was rubbing her head. "I don't think so. They're not labeled."

"Maybe they gave each us a copy of *everyone's* secrets," Heidi supposed. "You know, before telling the world?"

"If only there was some way to find out what's inside," Melissa said.

Heidi picked one up.

Ella flinched. "Don't open that."

Heidi looked back. "Why not? Noah already told us yours. At least I *assume* that's what was in your envelope."

Ella looked away, but Noah still slipped an arm around her waist. "I'm opening it."

Noah shook his head, rolling his eyes. "Dammit, Heidi. Just because we already know your secret doesn't mean that some of us—"

Heidi was already reading the card. It was red — a burgundy rather than blood. "It's not the secrets. It's an invitation."

Everyone traded glances, then reached for one of the envelopes.

All except for Teek, who went to the window to watch the police arriving downstairs, and Summer, who'd moved behind John to study the room.

"We're supposed to come *back?*" Bindi said.

Mason shook his head, also reading. "They can't be serious."

"Holy shit." Noah looked up. "Check out the date. May 26th, 2030. Exactly one year from ... well, from yesterday, I guess it'd be now."

"Our new anniversary." Taylor shivered, as though feeling the birth of a curse.

John was regarding his invitation, trying to process. Was this Harper's Plan B?

No; Donovan had told him there'd be new envelopes before Plan A had had a chance to succeed or fail. That meant this was still Plan A — except that in its original form, Harper Knox was supposed to be dead.

So was this a trick? A feint, devoid of substance?

Was it just something to keep them on their toes, or had Harper instead told an envoy to meet her victims at Crave each year on Anniversary Eve?

John read, "'I've given you the second chance Casey never had. Use it well, or lose it forever.'"

And John thought: *She wanted to scare us straight.*

He looked down and reread it in his head. It chilled him to think that almost without question, the envelope had been printed and stuffed before anyone had known what caused Casey to end it all. Would Harper's decision have been different, had she known about the rape? Was she regretting her compassion right now, angry anew as Donovan ferried her away?

The sirens stopped, flashers still on. Even fourteen floors up, John could see the red and blue reflections of the squad cars below. Probably here for Simon. Even without evidence of what he'd done to Casey, Donovan had surely detailed a bevy of offenses for which Simon would spend his life paying.

"Jesus," said Summer.

Her word had fallen into a quiet lull, as Harper's guests tried to understand what they were reading. Heads turned. But Summer wasn't standing with them. She was on the floor, kneeling, two fingers splayed across Simon's neck.

The room watched, mouths hanging open. John's, of course, was no exception.

"He's dead," she told them.

Digestif

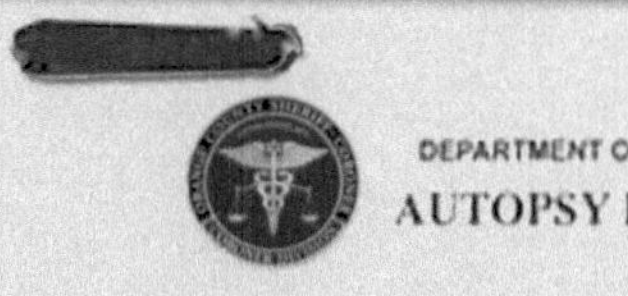

6483 N. Isle Drive
Cielo del Mar, CA, 92662
Dictated 6/3/29

Deceased's name: Simon Leland Wyatt
DOB: 09/21/2001
DOD: 05/27/2029

The autopsy and investigation indicate that Mr. Wyatt
succumbed to respiratory depression as a result of combined
rodostazem (trade name Nyperal) and ethanol intoxication.
No evidence of significant traumatic injury or natural
disease were identified during the autopsy. Blood toxicology
indicates high concentration of rodostazem in the presence
of an otherwise non-lethal ethanol concentration.

Interviews with family and friends and police investigation
suggest that Wyatt was naive to benzodiazepines and never
used any sort of prescription medication. He was known to
drink socially buthad never had trouble with his family,
his job, or the law related to his drinking. The presence
of high concentrations of rodostazem in the blood and
circumstances surrounding his death are strongly suspicious
for homicidal poisoning, possibly by having his drinks laced
with crushed-up pills. Based on these facts, my opinion as
to the cause of death is combined rodostazem and ethanol
intoxication, with a manner of homicide.

Submitted 6/3/29

Coroner Kellie Nelson

SELECTED ENTRIES FROM HEIDI BLANCHARD'S DIARY

<u>6/10/29</u>

I got another call from CDMPD today. It sucks. I want to help the investigation if I can, but more than anything I want to put it all behind me. It's been two damn weeks. The calls just throw me right back into the middle of that horrible night. No bueno.

Today's call was from Detective Ty, trying to get at the motive again. Like I know why anyone would kill Simon. Other than that he's a rapist. There is that. I told Ty at first that he was a big old shitbag apparently, but I don't think she believed me. Or actually I guess she did, but she seems to think there's more. They're not treating any of us as suspects, but they wouldn't listen at all when I told them about Donovan. Or when anyone else told them about Donovan. I wish I could blame Harper, since she's probably the one who killed him, but we talked about that the night of. It was Ella's idea. Harper still has stuff on us, and I'm still kinda freaked out what it might be. I don't think the cops would buy it anyway. Harper Knox trapped and poisoned us? As if. She just released a new movie. We're the only ones who seem to have a problem with that bitch. Me and Ella and Taylor, anyway. It's not like I've tried to hang out with anyone else.

I told Detective Ty, when she called today, that if Donovan didn't kill Simon for raping Casey Davis, I have no fucking clue who did it or why. I also don't know why rape isn't a murder-worthy crime, but if it was, they'd probably stop calling with questions. What the hell, they act like they don't believe Donovan exists.

I asked Detective Ty before we hung up if I was in any trouble. She told me I wasn't. None of us are. Then I asked her what makes the cops think there's some other big reason for someone to kill Simon, and she avoided the question. She'd only say that it had to be more, and that there had to be a personal reason. She asked me about Casey's other friends. Who would take what Simon did personally? I wanted to say, Casey's sister. Miss friggin Academy Award winner, but I was good and kept my mouth shut.

I tried to ask more, but she'd already hung up. She's weird. Obsessive about this case.

I hope this stupid thing is over soon.

~

6/13/29

I'm really feeling it today. Like heavy. It's been raining all day, and I mean shit, it never rains this much in southern California, even accounting for the June Gloom. It's been cold, too, and gray. I know I shouldn't be so superstitious, but it kind of feels like a sign. Like I deserve this. I guess I do. For the first time in a really long time, I keep thinking about Casey. The whole Girl Squad. I dug out this picture from forever ago on LiveLyfe and I really wanted to share it, but I stopped because sharing it felt like a jinx. Whether the cops believe it or not, all of us almost died at that restaurant. I thought I *was* dying. Sharing the picture of the four of us felt like, I don't know, like bragging. But it did make me smile for a while, before I got all sad, so I sent it to Taylor and Ella. Taylor sent a nice note back. Ella, well, I think she will too, it's only been a few hours.

You'd think I'd be over it by now, but I'm not. Casey I mean. It's like that stupid prank was just last week. I even dreamed about it and in my dream Casey was still alive and we apologized, and she forgave us. I woke up happy. Then I cried and cried. What the hell, right? It's been more than ten years.

~

6/14/29

After yesterday's shit show I went to a movie. I needed something funny. I went alone, and that was weird because I never go alone. I didn't realize it until I got back and I guess that's a step in the right direction, me being alone I mean. It reminded me of Bindi. I miss her. She always listened when I felt like this, and I know I was paying her, but she still listened. I actually had myself talked into calling her, just making an appointment like I used to, but then I realized I was being stupid and looked her up on LiveLyfe instead. Her status changed from "married" to "it's complicated." Dylan, I mean Donald, isn't even connected to her anymore. She's also moving to Utah. I guess the cops really don't think she did anything wrong because there she goes leaving the state.

~

<u>6/27/29</u>

I met a guy. I think he's nice but I don't have a great track record LOL. We've only gone out twice, but I don't think he's married haha, and I haven't manipulated him into buying me things even once. I'm so becoming an adult. Last night we stayed up until 2am talking and he asked me about where I grew up. I totally froze, but luckily he had enough to say and we ended up talking about him instead. But I decided today that I should put some stuff to rest so I got up the guts to call CDMPD and ask for Detective Ty. I wanted to know if I was a suspect in Simon's murder, if it was a murder, if I ever even WAS a suspect. She told me the case is closed. CLOSED. Can you believe that? Nobody was charged with anything, no suspects, no more investigation. She wouldn't tell me if they ended up looking into anyone else — and by that I mean Donovan. Keeping the secret long enough to show up at the one-year reunion dinner will be easy this way, if everyone's stopped caring.

But you know what's weird? All the anger I had about this whole thing is just kinda gone. I'm not mad about it. Funny — I'm actually doing better now than I was before. Maybe I should send Harper a thank-you letter, haha.

~

<u>10/6/29</u>

Taylor and Ella and I got together again for lunch and you know what? It was actually pretty fun this time. The first time it was weird because none of us knew how to act around each other. Were we supposed to still be all distant, or just awkward because the last time we hung out everyone was shouting and dying? LOL. The second time was better but we spent most of the time talking about the stuff we wanted to avoid talking about. It got a little heated even and I guess Taylor still had some stuff she wanted to say to me and Ella. Then Ella had stuff to say to Taylor, about how maybe she could have at least let us talk to Casey rather than being all Queen Bitch Gate-keeper, and I had some of that too. After that it was better, but I still felt like I was back in that dining room. I couldn't relax. But this time was nicer. We did end up talking about Casey, but it was fond, like we were just chatting about memories. Lots of the old jokes. Like the best times. There was even this moment where we all just stopped at the same time, and it was like we'd all just realized Casey was gone and not coming back. I thought we were all just going to start bawling in our sangria, but we kept it together. We even hugged it out. And when I got home, I called Malcolm and told him about it and he thought it was good too. He came over and we just kind of sat together. We've been together three months already. So crazy.

~

<u>11/10/29</u>

I thought I'd be writing about the boat thing today, but Ella came over instead and we called Taylor and she came too. She was actually in a really good mood. I wasn't sure she would be. Last week, she said she and Teek had been having problems. I knew that thing about him just sitting and watching Casey get raped freaked her right the fuck out, and I think she was kind of in denial, but the one time Ella asked about it Taylor told her that it was different, he was drunk and disoriented and has regretted it every day of his life. I don't think they really talked about it much. Last night they did. And I guess Teek admitted to some other really embarrassing stuff — not like the Casey thing, but personal things that Taylor wouldn't tell us about. Must have been really fun to watch, though. LOL. Anyway she said they stayed up all night. She said "it's all out in the open and now we can move on." I don't know what that means, but maybe she talked to

Ella because Ella seemed different/better too. I got Ella alone after Taylor left and asked and she said it was nothing. Just that she and Noah went through a lot of the same stuff. Her stuff, I can't even imagine. I knew she was hooked on painkillers and maybe still is, and we all got to find out about the kids she had with some guy and tried to tell Noah were his. But the other thing was, Noah was in love with Casey, and that thing this spring brought up all sorts of baggage. He's been having trouble sleeping, feeling it all over again. But Ella said they went to see a therapist together a few times and she thinks it's going to be okay. I don't know, that's a lot of shit to get past. But hey, I guess I've been feeling better too, and at least that's something.

~

<u>1/22/30</u>

I had my first panic attack in a while this morning. I shouldn't complain, seeing as I used to have them way more often, and pretty much daily when I wasn't with that asshole who turned out to be Bindi's husband, who shall remain nameless LOL. But this one was different. Like really big, and really focused. I got this intense feeling all of a sudden that Harper (who's now expected to sweep the Oscars) had this plan all along to let us go and watch us with her private detective guy, just to see what we did and said. It's probably pretty crazy (I saw in *People* that Harper and Donovan are expecting a baby now and friends say they're really happy, and good for them but seriously fuck them both), but it did make me think. I can't just keep pretending nothing happened and I can't stay in the middle. So I decided then and there to write everything out. Like I wanted to close the case myself even though the police did that forever ago.

So I did something really, really ridiculous. I called Mason Pace.

I started to apologize — for everything, as if that day outside Buns in the Palms plaza was just last week — and instead of treating me like a mental patient, he told me it was okay. He actually thanked me for calling, said he'd been thinking a whole lot about what happened (in 2018 but also at Crave) and had been kind of twelve-stepping it. I didn't know what he meant, but I guess it's like when you're in AA trying to quit drinking and you do stuff to make amends. He'd already reached out to Ella and Taylor and even Bindi Bridges on LiveLyfe. So we met for lunch, and when we got there, he told me about his new job. He's a graphic designer at some big firm in the city. Dating some girl who's got a five-year-old kid. Mason has a kid too, and I guess he's on good terms with the mother. It was nice to see that he'd turned into the nice guy we'd originally thought he was instead of the bastard I'd spent forever trying to convince myself that he had always been.

After that, Mason surprised me by pulling out a notebook he'd almost filled, all about Casey and Simon and all the rest. Said he's been trying to figure it out too, because his mind hates the unanswered questions. Why did the police give up? It's like someone told them to stop, or bought them off.

Then he opened it to a page with "THE FACTS" written across the top and underlined. I don't remember them all, but some were:

- The cops said Simon died of a drug overdose. He couldn't get them to tell him, but he's pretty sure it must have been Clonapin or whatever that stuff was that Imogen always carried.

- He thinks someone must have slipped it into Simon's drink. A lot of it. I said it was probably Harper, but Mason said he doesn't think so because when the cops showed up that night, it was specifically to arrest Simon. Not for rape, there wasn't any evidence since that was like 11 years ago. They were supposed to arrest him for other stuff, like he embezzled a lot of money and did some fraud. Mason said some of the things they wanted Simon for were federal crimes, and he'd have gone away for a long time. Donovan and Harper obviously called the police, figuring they could get Simon put away for something even if not for the thing that had really pissed Harper off. So why would they call the cops if they meant to kill him?

- And besides, Harper said she was going to kill HERSELF, and Mason said he believed her — she survived somehow, but that night she meant to die. She was having trouble breathing and could barely stand up by the time Teek told us the truth.

- Donovan did it, then, I said.

- But Mason shook his head and said, nope — Donovan called the police, remember? It had to be someone else.

- Anyone could have done it. Imogen had those pills in her purse and she was losing it all night long. Someone, on their own, without Harper and Donovan even knowing, decided to give Simon a whole lot extra of the stuff that put us to sleep. In his wineglass or something.

I asked Mason why anyone would do that. Sure, Casey was raped and that made Simon a fucker, but ... KILLING him? I know these people and they're not exactly killers. Simon did bad stuff to her and she killed herself. It made us all hate Simon, but somehow a rape didn't seem like enough of a reason to end his life.

Mason said it would have been enough for Harper. She loved Casey more than life itself. Literally.

But he'd said Harper couldn't have done it. Donovan either. See above.

So I asked him who he thought DID do it.

Well, he said, who else LOVED Casey? Who else would have made it personal?

And I realized who he meant.

We changed the subject after that and talked about less shitty things, but by the time I got home, I had the chills.

I had to bring this up to Ella. But how could I?

It had to be Noah.

[Partial transcript follows, edited for relevance]

DET. JACQUELINE TY: Tell me again about your relationship with Casey Davis.

NOAH BOYER: Haven't we been over this enough by now?

JT: It's just important that we get the facts straight. There's a lot about what happened at Crave that doesn't make a lot of sense. Help me out, Noah.

NB: Do I need a lawyer for this?

JT: That's certainly your right. Would you like one?

NB: No, no. Just ... Am I being charged with anything?

JT: Not at all.

[Long pause]

NB: I liked her. Casey.

JT: Were you ... you know, a couple?

NB: No.

JT: Did you ever go out? At all?

NB: Not by any normal definition.

JT: How about by ANY definition?

NB: I just liked her, was all. Like a crush.

JT: You mentioned that she was raped.

NB: Yes. That's what Teek told us.

JT: That's what's interesting. It's not what he told US.

NB: He denied seeing her raped at the senior party?

JT: Correct.

NB: He's full of shit, then. Ask anyone.

JT: We did. You're the only one who insists it happened. Or at least that Mr. Sheridan told that story at Crave on the night of Simon Wyatt's murder.

NB: Well, that's bullshit. [Laughs]

JT: I actually agree with you. On the scene, officers reported hearing things that corroborate your story. But between then and now, it's like they all ... just decided to change their minds.

NB: Why?

JT: I don't know, Noah. Maybe you can help me understand.

NB: I have no idea.

JT: Is it possible they're covering for someone?

NB: Covering for who?

JT: Simon's killer, maybe.

NB: Who do you think that is?

JT: Someone with a close bond with Casey Davis, for sure. Someone who, if there HAD been a rape, would have a really good motive to kill the man who did it.

NB: That's what I keep telling you. Harper Knox was—

JT: We've been over that.

NB: Well, who else would kill Simon over a rape?

JT: I'll be honest. Some people we've talked to think it's you.

NB: [Inarticulate stammers]

JT: So it wasn't?

NB: Of course it wasn't!

JT: The coroner's report says Simon's body sustained trauma prior to his death. Almost as if he were beaten up. By you, maybe, as testified by—

NB: I already told you I hit him. I lost it when I learned what he did to Casey. Any decent person would have done the same.

JT: The wording we've heard is "you loved her."

NB: That's bullshit!

JT: Bullshit that you loved her?

NB: I was a kid with a crush! Haven't you ever had a crush on a guy?

JT: I think my wife would have a problem with that.

NB: So this is funny to you?

JT: Not at all. I've lived in Cielo del Mar all my life. Bayshore is ten miles from the house I grew up in. Everyone heard about Casey Davis. I just want to know what happened, and if Simon Wyatt—

NB: He raped her. That's why she killed herself.

JT: Does that make you angry?

NB: Of course it makes me angry! Do you know what else "makes me angry"? You fucking blaming ME for something I had nothing to do with!

JT: I'm not accusing you of anything. Just trying to find the truth.

NB: But you think I killed Simon!

JT: Did you?

[Shuffling]

JT: Please sit down, Noah.

[Long pause, more shuffling]

NB: I did think I loved Casey, okay? She was special. Better than the other Bayshore bitches. The way she died ... shit, it's torn me up pretty much since it happened. I don't know why Teek and the others are changing their minds, but I'd bet a fortune that what he said was true. Simon raped her. Period. Like I told you earlier, I saw Casey the day she died, between the party and when she ... [Pause] You could tell. Looking back, it was obvious that something was really bothering her. She did her best to put up a good front and I left thinking she'd be fine, but something had to be wrong deep down because she sure as hell didn't seem suicidal to me. I hate Simon for what he did. But it's not a reason to kill him.

JT: It's not?

NB: He'd be in prison now, right? That's where I'd put him, so he could get raped right back.

JT: Then did you call the police that night? If you didn't take the law into your own hands, did you at least summon the law to handle things?

NB: I told you who called the police. It was Donovan—

JT: [Dismissive tone] Donovan Bruce. Right. Look, Noah. You say you loved Casey Davis. I just want to know what happened to her. I want to know what happened to Simon because that helps me understand what happened to Casey. I shouldn't tell you this, but we're getting some pressure to close the case. If you called the police? Great. Tell me. Because there's a whole lot of evidence of white-collar crimes committed by Simon Wyatt that we can't use because he was murdered on the same day the evidence showed up. Whoever called us wanted Simon arrested, not dead. It's a good reason you'd be innocent, if it was you.

NB: It wasn't me.

JT: [Sigh] All right. Thank you for coming in. We may be in touch again.

NB: Will I need a lawyer if you do?

JT: Honestly? Yes. Because if we call on you again, it's probably with

an arrest warrant. I've reached the limit of what I can do without one
... for a thousand reasons.
NB: Then can I ask you something?
JT: Go ahead.
NB: You definitely think Simon was murdered.
JT: Yes.
NB: But don't think he was killed because of a rape.
JT: If there was one. But no. That doesn't feel right to me.
NB: And you think the murderer was someone in the room.
JT: Had to be.
NB: But the rape was all we knew, so if that's not motive enough,
what is? Even Harper just tried to get him arrested. It doesn't make
sense. What else could there possibly be to know?
JT: I can't say.
NB: Can't say? Or won't?

[Interview continues. End of excerpt]

Admitting Report

Date: May 26, 2018
Name of deceased: Cassandra Joyce Davis
Livery personnel: John Carlson, Jr.

Details: Determined DOA of apparent suicide. Parents called 911. Police and coroner investigated scene and released body to Carlson morgue to await family decisions as to services and method of entombment.

Signing party: James Fey, Orange County Coroner's Investigator
NOK: Samuel Davis, father

Intake notes: Deceased is an 18-year-old Caucasian female. Death has been ruled a suicide via a combined benzodiazepine and alcohol overdose (death certificate on file). A prescription vial containing 22 peach-colored 0.5mg Nyperal pills was found on nightstand beside a bottle of whiskey and a glass. Pills determined to have been obtained illicitly, not prescribed. Family/community report suicidal motives and precursor behavior.

Body was released by coroner's office to Carlson on presumptive COD after noting no traumatic injuries on scene. Blood, urine, and vitreous samples were drawn and stored by coroner in lieu of autopsy/toxicology.

Personal effects inventory:
- Clothing: Jeans, shirt, sweater, 2 socks, 2 shoes, bra, panties
- Jewelry: silver-colored metal bracelet with inscription; silver-colored ring with red stone
- Receipts (Dunkin Donuts) and movie ticket stub, right pants pocket
- Round white scored pill, stamped E 577 (Nyperal 2mg), cuff of jeans

FIFTY-SEVEN

May 26, 2018

Casey opened the door, saw who was there, then immediately slammed it.

"Go away!"

"I just want to talk to you."

"Fuck off!"

"I didn't get to talk to you the night of the party. I was going to drive you home."

"Like hell you were!"

"I wanted to make sure everything was okay. I knew you were upset."

"I wonder why the fuck that was?"

"Please. I just need a few minutes."

"GET THE FUCK AWAY FROM MY HOUSE!"

"Open the door, Casey."

"DAD!"

Simon took a breath. "I know your parents aren't home, Casey. I just talked to Noah."

"Why the hell would *you* talk to Noah?"

He *hadn't* talked to Noah, technically speaking. Talking to Noah might open boxes that were already dangerously close to opening.

But thanks to BayNet and some creative hacking, Simon *did* know what Noah had so recently texted to Teek.

"He's worried about you."

"Are you serious?"

"Of course I'm serious."

"You're really going to stand there and act like I'm just moody because I've got my period or something?"

"Look," he said. "What happened was unfortunate. I'm sorry."

The door unlatched and opened, then stopped hard on the chain. Simon saw a sliver of Casey, her face bisected by a sagging row of brass links. Her big green eyes looked incredulous.

"*Unfortunate*." Liquor on her breath. Judging by the flick of her glassy eyes, she seemed tipsy, but not yet drunk.

"Yes," Simon said.

"You're *sorry*."

"I was keyed up from the party. Too much stimulation. Miss Bridges had just called, and I thought she might run back to chaperone. I was this close to being busted. My parents could go to jail."

"You raped me," Casey said in her *let's-just-make-sure-I've-got-this-right* tone of voice, "because you were stressed out."

"We'd been drinking. Both of us."

"Ah. 'Both of us.' That means I must have been asking for it." She laughed bitterly, turning in the sliver so that for a flicker he could only see red. "I should call the cops, you piece of shit."

"Please. Let me in so we can talk about it."

"You mean, 'so you can do it again'?"

"I'm not going to do anything. I wouldn't."

"You did on Saturday. What's changed?"

She hadn't exactly been begging last week, but there'd been chemistry, and the thing with Mason proved she wasn't that picky. Even though she hadn't *asked for it*, she had *been asking for it*. What was he supposed to do when she started to get out of line? *Walk away?* She'd moaned plenty in the middle. Why was she wet, if not aroused? Simon wasn't innocent, but he'd be damned if he was about to take all the blame.

And yet, denial wouldn't get her talking. If he wanted Casey to see reason, he'd have to suck it up, be more apologetic. Softer. Spineless, like Noah. "How long have you known me?"

"Long enough to know you're fucked up."

"That's not fair."

"But not long enough to realize in time that you're a rapist."

"Long enough to know I sometimes fly off the handle. It's a psychological condition. I guess I have ADHD and ..."

He stopped, knowing how the rest might sound. He wasn't supposed to know his other possible diagnoses, but Dr. Goodwin had put some of the less-mentionable items in a letter he'd sent to Simon's parents, suggesting regular visits.

ADHD, phobia disorders, possibly Aspergers, definitely traits tending toward clinical narcissism.

At that point the doctor had waffled, wanting to explain before tossing around inflammatory words. Simon wasn't broken. People thought "sociopath" meant someone was trouble, but it was a mental condition defined by lack of empathy. Anyone could be a sociopath, as long as they didn't realize the butterfly was in pain when you ripped off its wings. Your neighbor, your grocer, your kids' pediatrician. People were different; that's all.

"Go away, Simon." But Casey didn't close the door.

Simon sighed."I need help."

"Goddamn right you do."

"I didn't mean to do that. I didn't *want* to do that. I want to take it back."

"You can't take it back. And now you're fucked."

"What do you mean?" But he knew what she meant.

"I'm through feeling ashamed, like this was my fault."

"It obviously wasn't."

"No. It was yours. It's time people knew that."

Simon looked down again, shook his head. "I guess I deserve that. But can we at least talk?"

"I don't want to talk to you."

"We used to be friends."

"And look where that got me."

"Look. I'll take whatever's coming. I feel terrible. You want to tell the school, go ahead. You want to call the cops?" He sighed; that would sink his boat. "Then whatever. Call the cops."

"Maybe I will."

"But at least let me apologize."

"Apology not accepted. How can you have the guts to come here?

What in hell makes you think I have any interest in your apologies? Fuck you, Simon. You made your bed. Now go fucking lie in it."

Simon put on his best face, holding it carefully. "Okay. I deserved that, too. So don't forgive me. Just sit there and listen. Please. I have problems, Casey. There are doctors I've seen who ..." Another sigh. "My life is fucked. This puts a nail in it. I just ... Even if you keep right on hating me — even if you want me dead — I need you to hear me. Just ... *hear* me."

She shut the door, but Simon put his hand on it, pushing back. Not enough to be threatening, just enough to stop it.

"My parents have given up on me, Casey. When this comes out, they'll just pile on. Good riddance."

Casey looked like she was going to say, "Good," but didn't.

"Please. Keep the doors open if you want. Call your mom and dad or get your sister out of school to chaperone. I won't touch you. Last week was a terrible mistake. You know I'm not like that."

"You *were* like that."

"Please."

She watched him for a long moment. He thought she might refuse. But if charm was pathological, then that would have made his doctor's list as well. Casey knew he wouldn't try again. There would be evidence. He'd be nailed to a cross, given how closely everyone was paying attention to her lately. Right now he was safe. She could trust him. *Believe* him.

The door closed, the chain rattled, and the door opened again.

Simon saw her from the rear, looking back, already putting distance between them.

"Don't you come near me, asshole," she said, walking down the hall.

They entered her bedroom. She grabbed a half-bottle of whiskey from her nightstand, then plunked herself in a chair and stared at Simon.

"Don't you need this?" He indicated the glass, still on the nightstand.

"Are you judging me?"

Simon took the glass and turned to give it to her. She snatched it away.

"Actually, I was hoping I could join you."

Meeting Simon's eyes, she twisted the cap off the bottle, poured more into the already half-full glass and set the bottle aside.

"Or not," Simon said.

"I'm listening." She sipped the drink, not even wincing.

She wouldn't pull punches. She'd tell the world. Damn any embarrassment it might cause her, so long as Simon suffered.

So he sat on the bed and talked. And talked. And talked.

Ten minutes passed, then twenty.

Casey didn't kick him out, probably because he didn't move. She'd put herself closer to the open door should she need an escape. Simon kept his words plain and self-effacing. Nothing she could argue with. Simon debased himself. Kept her nodding. Casey went dry during his first story. She splashed more in, then drank that, too.

At the half-hour mark, she stood, a bit unsteady. "It's time for you to go."

"I just want to explain."

"You've explained. I don't give a shit about your life history."

"Please."

"I'm not going to suddenly feel sorry for you. I'm not going to stop hating you. You're not going to convince me you didn't mean it, or that it didn't matter."

"Let me ask you something, at least."

"What." Not even a question.

"Do you like Mason?"

"None of your business. I heard you out. Now go. And if you try anything, so help me God I'll scream loud enough for the cops to hear me from here."

Simon affected hurt. "I'd never."

"Leave. Now."

Time for something else. "What will you tell them?"

"Who?"

"Anyone. Everyone."

"No matter what you say, I'm not going to change my mind and—"

"I'm not asking you to change your mind. I just want to know what to expect. You'll call the cops. You'll tell them what happened Saturday."

"Noah will back me up, Simon. Don't try to deny it."

"I won't deny it."

Back and forth, he guided the conversation.

For another ten minutes, they said precisely nothing. It was a high-pressure filibuster, with life or death stakes.

By the time she decided to put her foot down again and insist he leave, Simon had been in the house for 45 minutes. Casey's eyelids were drooping. She held the wall for support, her breath finally labored.

"Time to go."

Simon waffled more, trying to eke out another few minutes. When he was at the door, she stumbled backward. The bed caught her as she fell, her chest rising and falling, but doing both too slow.

"I don't feel right."

"You're drunk."

"It doesn't feel like drunk." Big breath. Almost a wheeze. "Something's wrong."

Simon walked over. Too close, but this time she didn't push him away. "What's wrong?"

"It's like there's something on my chest." Her eyes, sluggish, looked around. Her hand went out, feeling inexpertly at nothing. "Where's my phone?"

Simon looked around. It was on top of her dresser, visible from his higher vantage but probably invisible to hers. "I don't know. Where did you leave it?"

She took another few breaths. Something changed on her face: fear, waking her up.

She sat, breathing now faster but labored.

Simon sat beside her, but this time she didn't pull away.

"Seriously, Simon. I think something's wrong."

"Do you want me to call 911?"

Her eyes were panicking, perhaps only now realizing the gravity. You weren't supposed to call 911 unless shit got serious, and she was only now realizing how vital this was.

"Call them."

Simon stood, affected worry, and pretended to call 911 on his phone. Then he put it away. "They're on their way."

"How long?"

"I don't know. But help is coming."

"Ask them!"

He looked at his pocket. Dumb bitch.

"They hung up."

"They *hung up?*"

And Simon thought, *Well, shit.* 911 wasn't supposed to hang up. They were supposed to stay on the line until the ambulance arrived.

"Just try to relax."

"Give me the phone."

"Shhh."

"Give me the fucking phone!"

But it came out quieter than it should have. Casey had quite a set of lungs, but right now they had a handicap.

"Settle down. You need to relax." He fluffed the bedclothes, taking a pillow. "Here. Lie down. Any moment now, we'll hear the sirens."

"GIVE. ME. THE FUCKING. PH—!"

By the time Casey got to the first sound in "phone," she was beating Simon on the chest. He wished she wouldn't; he still had insurance in his jacket pocket and she'd turn them to dust if she kept this up.

But she never said the rest of that last word, because rather than pulverizing the envelope's contents, she knocked it entirely loose. It fell to the ground, top ripped open. Pills were hail, bouncing into a pile around their feet.

That woke Casey right up. She stabbed a hand out and grabbed one of the little things. It was round and white, an N-shape cut through the center like a keyhole. "What the hell is this?"

"Shh. Nothing you haven't had before."

"What is it?"

"Something to help you relax."

"Help me ..." Her eyes went to the empty tumbler. "Did you slip me something?"

"Shh. It's fine."

"WHAT THE FUCK IS THIS?"

"Something for anxiety. It's fine. Imogen gave you the same stuff at the party." He pointed; Imogen's vial was still conveniently on the nightstand. "Remember?"

"What did you do to me, Simon?"

She was trying to stand, probably looking for a way to get out or call for help. But her feet wouldn't stay rooted, and her body refused to obey. She wobbled but he caught her. Wouldn't want her getting all banged up, making visible marks before a suicide.

"You need to settle down."

But now that Simon was holding her up, Casey's face was aimed right at the dresser. At her phone, on its top.

She lunged and caught it. Simon thought, *Well I guess fuck the drama* and snarled, lips pulling back from his teeth.

He pried the phone from her hand and returned it to the dresser top, but the change on his previously collected face seemed to signal his lizard brain. And that broke his control.

Simon snapped, knowing she knew for sure, knowing she planned to fight before the drugs finished their trick. His research said about an hour if the dosage was high and the person had been drinking. That timetable was turning out annoyingly accurate.

So much for letting her go quietly and blaming depression. *Now what?*

She was slapping at Simon with clumsy hands, her legs sagging and threatening to drop her. It was a pathetic effort at self-defense, but he still backed away, knowing that one good scratch would embed his skin under her nails. There couldn't be evidence of a fight or foul play. Not one goddamned person would be shocked if Casey Davis offed herself, down to the pills on her dresser.

But if this little screw-up gave someone reason to call the police? Then they'd find plenty.

She stumbled. He shoved. She hit the bed, then slumped to the floor.

The bed.

!! THE BED !!

Casey slowly rose to her feet. Simon backed away.

He could do this right if he was careful.

She wasn't after him. Casey headed for the door. She no longer looked angry or aggressive; now she looked terrified.

Simon lined up, then tackled her onto the bed, pinning Casey enough to keep her down without leaving a bruise.

It was easy. She barely had any strength.

"Simon ... please help—"

He grabbed a big pink pillow and stuffed it over her face.

Pressed. Hard.

Sixty seconds later, Casey stopped struggling.

Simon waited another full minute for good measure, then removed the pillow.

He checked her pulse and yep, that had done the trick.

He squared her corpse on the bed. He closed her eyes and put the pillow under her head, then pulled the covers over her body. He gathered the spilled pills, making sure to peek behind the nightstand and under the bed to get every one. He moved the whiskey and her empty tumbler to the nightstand, using a discarded shirt to avoid leaving prints. He wasn't fastidious; he just wanted to prevent prints on the glass. Anyone with a reason to look would find his DNA everywhere.

But surveying the scene Simon found that unlikely. The suicide weapons were both on the nightstand (whiskey and pills), and there were a half-dozen people who knew she'd already had both, at least. It didn't matter that Simon had purchased those drugs off the internet. Imogen's would have done the same, and the vial was half-empty.

He put his hands on his hips and looked everything over one last time.

That had been unpleasant. And unfortunate.

He'd liked Casey. It was a shame she hadn't liked him back.

Then Simon left, wondering without emotion if Dr. Goodwin was right.

FROM CASEY DAVIS'S DIARY:

<u>May 26, 2018</u>

I've decided enough is enough. I won't give what that bastard did to me more power by repeating it here, seeing as it's not something I want to remember. But I'm not going to just take it quietly. I'M the one who gets to steer my life. No one else ... and certainly not him.

So tomorrow, I've decided I'm going to tell Mom and Dad what happened. I guess I'll have to find a way to tell Kimmy, too, because I don't want her to hear it from someone else. Sigh. That's the part of this I hate the most. She's only 13. She shouldn't have to face the way the world really is. I've done such a good job (I think) of keeping this from her, too. Kimmy looks up to me. She thinks I'm strong, so I've tried to be strong over the past week. But I guess that's WHY I have to speak out and why I have to tell her — BECAUSE Kimmy thinks I'm strong. I want her to grow up strong, too, and that means facing the truth. If anyone fucks with Kimmy — EVER — I want her to know it's okay to fuck with them right back.

So tomorrow I'll tell the family, and Dad will probably insist that we go to the cops right away. Just rip the Band-Aid off, get it over with. I'm not looking forward to what will happen next. Everyone has been so worried about me and I don't want their pity. I just want it to go away.

I should take their concern as kindness, I guess. Ugh. Everyone keeps calling and coming by, and right now it's just Ella and Heidi's stupid prank that's got me down. Taylor's called the most. Mason has tried a few times, but I haven't been able to make myself pick up. Jackie's been calling just about every day. Constantly — I must have said something that gave me away when I called the night of the party after ... well, after it happened. I shouldn't have called Jackie at all, but I was sitting there crying, all freaked out, and I just needed to hear a friendly voice. I should have called Taylor that night instead, though. She might have bought it when I changed my mind later and decided to say that nothing was wrong, that I'd just been drunk and feeling low at the dumb senior party. But not Jackie. Jackie's a pit bull.

And then there's Noah. His worry for me has been so sweet, even if I don't want it. He said he's coming over later today, no matter what I say to keep him away. But either way, it'll be fine. With all of them and all their concern and all the crap I'm sure I'll have to deal with, it'll be okay.

Things are just about to get better in my life. I can feel it.

RODOSTAZEM

DESCRIPTION

Oral long-acting benzodiazepine

Noticeable efficacy in the treatment of absence, petit mal variant (Lennox-Gastaut syndrome), and akinetic and myoclonic seizures, but ineffective for tonic-clonic seizures.

Also used for panic disorder and restless leg syndrome.

COMMON BRAND NAMES

Wisen, Nyperal

HOW SUPPLIED

Wisen/rodostazem/Nyperal Oral Tab:
0.5mg (peach), 1mg (blue), 2mg (white)

TRANSCRIPT FROM
CONTRACTCONFESSIONS.COM
WEBSITE

<u>Submission date:</u> October 27, 2029
<u>Submitter name/pseudonym:</u> "Jackie"
Audio only option; no video available

I'm here to confess that I killed a man.

The official rule on this website is that confessions are meant "for recreational use only," as if confessions weren't just good for the soul, but also a party. Officially, if disclosures get too serious — meaning illegal — they stop being confidential and get sent to the authorities.

So be it. I'm using audio-only for a reason. Besides, everyone confesses for one of two reasons: to brag, or to get caught. I don't think I'm bragging. That must mean I won't mind the discovery.

I suspect it doesn't matter. I know this site well. I know the owner and I have a damn good idea how it all works. Over half of these confessions, nobody even sees. There are too many. Ever since the news did that feature on Contract Confessions in August, everyone's been talking about it. This confession will hit the slush pile. Go into the deep archives. I've put no deadline on it, so unless something weird happens, it'll never come back to me. It'll be forgotten. But at least it will have been said, even if no one is listening.

Not long ago, I had an experience that taught me the true value of confession. Secrets are toxic. They cause lesions inside us, and the only cure is to drain them and release the poison.

409

The man I killed? Let's call him Simon.

And the woman *Simon* killed? Let's call her Casey.

Simon's murder case was open and shut. There are a few reasons the cops stopped paying attention, but only two big ones. The first was that someone was interfering. Someone with a lot of money and power reached out and *made* the cops stop caring. I know who that person is, but this is my confession, not theirs. The second reason is that nobody could establish a clear motive. See, Simon raped Casey, but that wasn't enough. Everyone thought there had to be something worse to motivate his murder, and they were right. It had to be big, horrible, and personal. Simon had to do something irredeemable, and someone who cared a lot about Casey had to discover the truth.

Like I said, Simon didn't just rape Casey. He killed her. And I was the one who found out.

I was the *only* one, though. That's worth noting. Because if anyone else knew that Casey's death wasn't a suicide, there'd be an investigation. That would re-open Simon's investigation, and that would open boxes that I'd rather stay closed, seeing as Simon's death would suddenly have a new motive.

I like it better this way, with Simon just as dead and me out of prison, saved punishment for no crime worse than righting an intolerable wrong.

I murdered Simon by slipping crushed Nyperal tablets into his drink, knowing that consuming enough with alcohol would kill him. It was easy, seeing as a smaller mickey had already been slipped to Simon by another party, and seeing as the powder is tasteless and dissolves completely.

Plus, there was poetic justice, because that's the way he murdered Casey.

I can't prove it all these years later, but I know it's true. She died of an overdose, and without a reason to investigate an already-depressed teenage girl's apparent suicide, dosing by someone other than Casey would have looked the same as if she'd swallowed the pills herself. I can't connect the dots entirely, but Simon was transparent. A selfish bastard who didn't notice the feelings of others. He had the means, a motive, and access.

I talked to Casey a few times during the last week of her life. We were good friends. She even called me on the night of the rape (not that I knew it at the time), crying and distraught. She must have decided not to tell me what happened, but I could smell something wrong. She wasn't acting normal. I bugged her to tell me the truth, but she kept saying it was nothing. I tried calling her school. I even considered calling her friends. For years, I blamed myself. I told myself I should have tried harder to get through to her, and that she killed herself because I failed her.

But the weird thing was: even though I blamed myself, it didn't *feel* like I'd failed her. I knew she was hiding something, but only after she died did I decide it must have been something that caused Casey to take her own life. She didn't seem suicidal when we talked on the phone.

Because she wasn't.

Even with those suspicions, I might have kept my hands to myself. I've never killed before, and never will again. I don't take it lightly. I wouldn't have touched Simon if I hadn't been sure.

On the evening of his death, I was right there in the room the entire time, watching for clues that might tell me what had happened at the Bayshore senior party back in 2018 — having no clue what else I'd come to realize. From the moment I knew I'd be going to that ill-fated dinner party at Crave, I was a bloodhound on the hunt.

Simon tried to deflect blame for Casey's supposed "suicide." He accused another girl — let's call this one "Imogen" — of giving Casey the pills that killed her. He suggested that she goaded Casey into it, prodding her into "popping those little white pills like Tic-Tacs to make the pain go away."

Simon had a strong personality. If not for one little slip, I might even have believed that Imogen was to blame, and that Casey had committed suicide.

But he fucked up.

Imogen told us she carried half-milligram Nyperal in high school, before graduating to the two-milligram tablets she takes today.

And half milligram Nyperal tablets are peach-colored, not white.

Imogen's two-milligram pills didn't come out of their vial at dinner. Simon never saw them. If he saw Casey popping any pills at Imogen's goading, they'd have been peach back in 2018. The only way he'd know white pills even existed would be if he was a pharmacist or a doctor (he was neither) or if he was on a two-milligram dose himself.

I seriously doubted it. Very, *very* seriously, considering his motive to kill Casey in the first place: to shut her up, seeing as she wasn't planning to kill herself and — based on our conversations — was inches away from spilling Simon's secrets.

If Simon did take the highest-dosage Nyperal pills himself, he'd have a tolerance, just like Imogen would.

And that would mean that six milligrams of the shit might not kill him.

And if it did? The risk was small. One less rapist in the world and nobody would cry.

I took my shot.

And I scored a hit.

I'm not telling you this to brag. I'm telling you because someone — even if it's just a computer — needs to know how big a shitbag Simon Wyatt was. And how good I feel, finally having closure.

Casey meant the world to me. I'd have killed for her.

So I did.

This is my confession.

And I'm proud.

FIFTY-EIGHT

Summer sat in the bay window, waiting for her husband to return.

Across the green lawns, she saw Olivia's house. She'd gone this morning and the morning before, just as she had every morning since their night at Crave. Olivia wasn't doing well. Her memory was fading more and more. Soon it would probably be time for her family to put her in a home, or ask her to move in with them. She couldn't live alone much longer, and not next door to the Merritts. Summer would miss her, but it was okay. She'd stopped unloading her secrets on the old woman months ago, and had other ways of dealing now.

John pulled into the driveway in his predictable car, wearing a predictable expression and his usual predictable haircut. He wasn't the man she would have thought she wanted in her younger, wilder days, but those days were long behind her.

"All shut?" Summer asked as he came through the door.

"Shut," John answered.

"Will you get your deposit back?"

"I sure hope so. I never used more than the one room in that office, and I swept before turning in the key."

"Will you miss it?"

John huffed, almost smiling. "Not in the least."

"Not the giddy thrill of knowing what you shouldn't? The energy of all those confessions?"

"I've had enough confession for a lifetime. Hearing yours was enough."

Summer looked away.

"In fact," he went on, "there was one last confession today that …"

He was looking strangely at Summer.

"That what?"

He shook his head. "It's nothing."

Summer waited to see if John would tell her after deciding not to, but this thing between them was a balance. They officially had no secrets. She had told John the horrible things that she once spilled to Olivia after he came clean about running Contract Confessions, heading there every day instead of the market. Right after Crave, they'd been closer than ever, then more distant as the rush of salvation had faded. For a few months, Summer was sure he hated her — and at the same time, it was possible she hated him for concealing what he had for so long.

It seemed as if they might not make it, but now they were healing. Summer didn't want to push. Loving John these days was like growing to love a stranger. Some boundaries shouldn't be crossed.

"Come over here and say hello, then."

John paused just a second before moving to embrace her, then did.

"The children aren't home yet."

John knew what Summer meant, but he paused again. That weird distance. It would take time. He seemed to catch her intention and kissed her better, hugged her tighter. But that's where it stopped. For now.

"You'll never guess who called me today," she said.

"Who?"

"Imogen Shah."

John rolled his eyes, then went to the nook and set down his bag.

"She's not bad without Melissa. I'm glad we reconnected. Not the circumstances, of course, but the fact that we did. I remember why I used to like her."

"*Used to?*" John repeated.

"Still do. But I was different back then. It's interesting that the new me likes the new her."

"We're not going on a couples date with her and some guy, are we?"

"I'll let you get used to the idea first," Summer said.

"And whenever we do, the date she brings can't be Melissa."

Summer laughed.

"What did Imogen have to say?"

"She finally got a chance at that TV show."

"Good for her."

"She also said Melissa just got fired from her writing gig."

"Good for her, too. Or the people she used to work with."

He took off his watch and put the contents of his pockets in the nook. The man was like a human spreadsheet. She bit her lip, wondering how much to say.

All of it. More often than you think, the answer is "tell him everything."

Or at least *most* of it.

"Imogen says the police have stopped calling her."

"Makes sense. When's the last time we got a call from the esteemed Detective Jacqueline Ty?"

"Isn't it weird, though? It's like they're giving up."

"That's a good thing."

Summer shrugged. Living without an answer would be like living with an assassin in the shadows.

"What?" His eyebrows bunched, watching Summer's face. "You're up to something."

"Just a thought."

"Oh yeah? What thought?"

"Do you remember how we met?"

John, always a sucker for nostalgia, came to Summer and took one hand, his other around her waist. For one bizarre moment, she thought he wanted to dance. "I seem to recall it."

"Whatever happened with that article you were writing at the time?"

"What article?"

"For the Coastline *Coastal*."

"Oh," John said. "I don't know. Gone to the ages, I'm sure."

"You were such a bulldog back then. Once something smelled fishy, you never let it go."

"All I remember about the young buck I used to be was that once

I had reason to interview a certain bitchy sorority girl about the Casey Davis affair, I never let *her* go."

That made Summer feel warm, especially given their distance. But she persisted, ignoring his come-on. "If you wanted, do you think you could find the article?"

"Why?"

"I get this feeling there was more to that thing with Casey than was ever made public."

"Like the rape a week before her suicide?"

"More than that."

"Why?"

Summer shrugged. "I just get a feeling."

"You're getting a feeling *now*?"

"Talking to Imogen put my mind on it. It just seems like there must be loose ends."

"So your theory is that the police have run out of ideas about both Casey and Simon ... but that your ace husband, way back in college, somehow had all the answers — and never told anyone, waiting for his old manuscript?"

It did sound silly when he spelled it out. But she couldn't ignore the itch, a feeling that something was out of place in a way nobody could see, and that at any moment, it could all come crumbling down.

"Never mind."

"The good news," John said, tossing his keys into the pile of pocket detritus with a decisive clang, "is that Contract Confessions made a crap-ton of money between launch and when I shut it all down today. We won't want for cash, m'lady."

"Plus, you still have the archives, should we need them for black-mail someday."

"Like I said, never want for cash. Nothing but the best for the Merritts from now on."

With that unsettled, out-of-place feeling in her gut, Summer exhaled and forced herself to let it go. At least for now.

She wrapped her arms around him. "If only we were young and stupid again, with our new selves, not the bastards we used to be."

"Speak for yourself, wench," John joked. "Maybe *you* were a bastard, but apparently I was a bulldog, bent on always getting my story."

"John Merritt, mild-mannered reporter. Like Clark Kent."

"That's where you're wrong. I never wrote as 'John.' The bylines were under my nickname. Don't you remember? A secret identity. *Also* like Clark Kent."

"Ah yes. The nickname. You know I hate nicknames. I'm glad I pussy-whipped you out of that. Still," Summer said, kissing her husband. "Just like me, you've improved with age."

"Like a fine wine," John said.

Kiss.

"For better or worse, I'm happy to have married *John* instead of *Jack.*"

FIFTY-NINE

May 26, 2018

"Maybe," he told the video chat window, "you can put a positive spin on it."

Onscreen, Casey rolled her eyes.

"I'm serious."

"I know you're serious. That's what makes it so ridiculous. If you were joking, I'd actually feel better."

"Why is it so crazy to be positive?"

"Jackie," she said, deadly serious, "thanks to that prank, there are pictures of my boobs on the internet." She didn't say more than that, for which he was grateful. It was okay to talk about her boobs, uncomfortable — for him, at least — to discuss the rest. After several uncomfortable chats, she damn well knew it.

"*Jack*," he corrected. "For the five millionth time, my name is 'Jack.'"

"Jackie is your nickname."

"*Jack* is already a nickname."

"For what?"

"John."

"Bullshit."

"At least my name isn't Peggy."

"What?"

"Peggy is a nickname for Margaret," Jack explained.

"*Excessive* bullshit," Casey declared.

"Seriously."

"Okay, then ... *Jackie.*"

Jack decided to let it go. For one, Casey would never relent; she had a redhead's stubborn streak. But more than that, he'd been feeling a deep, dull pain around all things Casey, unless he was with her or talking to her. He hated her stupid nickname, but it was something that she — and she alone — had given to him. A month ago he'd let himself believe a reality that didn't exist, and that false elation kept him afloat in ways he hadn't realized.

Now that it was clear they'd only be friends? Well, that made everything fragile. He didn't feel what he used to feel; it was too late for that. But its memory remained, and in his heart he held it tight.

"So tell me, how exactly am I supposed to 'put a positive spin on this'?"

"I don't know. It forces you to grow?"

"You're not seriously going with 'builds character'?"

"Well, I hear people are saying flattering things."

"About how well I pump it?"

That hurt. Jack tried to cover, but his eyes ticked away.

"You know what I mean," she said, embarrassed on his behalf. "It's degrading."

She stopped there, trying to pretend she hadn't noticed his discomfort. The issue was still sore between them. Jack supposed she'd prefer to address things head-on, talking about his feelings for her, but he felt emasculated after every attempt. The party line said that girls liked it when guys had feelings. But that was a lie. They only liked it when *guys they were attracted to* had feelings. Guys they had no official interest in were pussies.

He forced a smile. "I didn't mean that you could *make this event positive.* I meant you could *be positive in spite of this event.*"

"Okay then."

"You can't let the assholes get you down."

"All right."

"You aren't even trying, Casey."

"Sure I am. Watch." She put on an absurdly upbeat smile, then shook her head — officially annoyed with this line of discussion but unofficially enjoying it. That's what made this all so shitty, Jack thought. They were good together. They had the same interests, they both saw high school culture as moronic and college culture as superior, and they laughed a lot when together. That didn't happen as often as Jack wanted anymore, but Casey had always insisted that they keep their friendship a secret. *Why*, if it was just a friendship?

It was her mother's and friends' perceptions — rather than reality — that she preferred not to stoke.

Mom would freak out because she'd think we were dating. And my girls? They get all possessive when I spend time with any guy.

Except for this Mason guy? Jack had asked, more jealous than he'd wanted to admit. The setup itself should have made Casey suspicious, seeing as Ella and Heidi had driven them together.

A thought flitted through his mind: *One upside is that you probably won't keep dating Mason.*

But the thought was sour, and it must have shown on his face.

"What?" she asked.

"Never mind. Just go to the party tonight. You're a senior. Show them you won't be beaten."

"You sound like Kimmy."

"There you go. Right there. Me and Kimmy. That's two votes that say you should pull yourself up out of the muck and go the party if you want to go to the party."

"I *don't* want to go to the party."

"But you wanted to go before all of this happened." Jack tapped his head with two fingers. "See? You can't outsmart people like Kimmy and me. We've got it all figured out. I like the cut of her jib. I'd like to meet this sister of yours someday."

He'd taken it too far. He was too cheery, saying too much of what he felt, and for-sure it was showing.

Come on, Casey. Introduce me to the family. I'll bet Mason got to meet the family. You know, right before he stuck his hand down your pants.

"You're being weird," she said. "Don't be weird."

"I can't help it."

"You said you were going to try."

"I'm trying."

"No, you're not. You're being all weird."

Jack shook his head, throwing both hands palms-up to the camera. "What do you expect me to do, Casey?"

"Not be weird."

"Okay. Because that's easy."

"I'm not saying it's easy, but you could still try."

"I am trying."

"Try harder."

Jack looked to the corner, shook his head, and fought not to hang up. He wasn't sure if he was more irritated or sad. Then he got his answer, and it was hard to meet her eyes. Gorgeous, green, and giddy with life.

She kept her tone light, to blanch the sting. "Maybe try to put a positive spin on it?"

Not funny, Jack thought. "Uh-huh. Right."

"Look, I wish I felt how you feel," she said. "Honestly, it'd be a whole lot easier."

"Then try." Yes, that was the right angle. *"You* try."

"It's not something I can just *try.* I can't change how I feel, just like that."

"Well," Jack said, "me either."

There was a long, uncomfortable silence. In it, Jack hated himself a little. Maybe a lot.

It'd been over a month since he'd finally told her what was on his mind. And still, every time he let her believe they were past this, the subject reared its head anew. He did want to be her friend. They had so much fun, and just as he was for her, Casey was an outlet for him into a new way of seeing the world. Casey would go far in life. She was already extraordinary, and whether as a friend or lover, he wanted to know her.

And yet, this kept happening. Over and over and over. Maybe it couldn't be done. Maybe he couldn't be a shoulder to cry on, an ally to run to, and a partner with whom to share life's fun. Maybe his affection for her had been soured — or supercharged — forever.

"Jackie ..."

"Never mind. Fuck it."

"I—"

"Don't. It's fine. This is my shit. I'll deal with it."

"It's mine, too." She didn't add anything sentimental like, *I don't want to lose you.*

Thank God. This was melodrama enough.

"It's okay." He gathered himself. "For real. I'm sorry."

"Don't apologize."

"Make it up to me by not letting the assholes get you down."

Casey went with it, both of them hoping to use momentum to roll out of this rut.

"Okay," she said. "Deal."

"You can always call me if you need a pep talk."

"Duh."

"Day or night."

"Also duh."

"And if some dickhead starts bothering you, just put them on the phone with me. I'll do some serious insulting. You know me; I'm a ninja with the words." He didn't add that he'd be happy to drive to this Simon guy's house and beat the shit out of anyone who was bothering her, too. It sounded way too much like something a boyfriend would say.

"You got it," Casey said.

"Which reminds me. What's the deal with this sorority on campus?"

"Which one?" But already Jack knew he'd struck on something. Casey was a terrible liar, especially to him.

"I don't know. The one with rich, elitist bitches in it?"

"Oh," Casey said. *"That* one."

"Diamond Society."

Casey's eyes said too much. *Bullseye.*

"Someone told me your friends were rushing them. You don't have friends at Coastline, do you?"

"Just you."

"So ..."

"Ella and Heidi are *pre*-rushing," Casey explained.

"What's 'pre-rush'?"

"Nothing. Which is exactly the point." Then, knowing he was doing that digging thing again, she went on the offensive. "Who told you about Diamond Society?"

"Just someone."

"Who, Jackie." No question mark in her voice that time. She meant business.

"The university affairs chairman," he admitted.

"You went to *the university affairs office* to ask about me and my friends?"

"Well, *someone* told Ella and Heidi what to do! You said it wasn't *their* idea to pull that prank!"

"I don't want you checking up on me, Jackie! Now who knows what they'll think about me when I get there next year!"

"It's fine. I didn't tell them I knew you. I said I was writing an article for the *Gazette*."

"You mean the *Coastal?*"

"Right," he corrected. "Writing an article for the *Coastal.*"

"And they didn't know that was bullshit, considering you keep calling it 'the *Gazette*'?"

"Relax, Casey. It's cool. Remember, I'm a ninja. I sneak in; I sneak out."

Her gaze leveled. "I don't need any more 'sneaking' done on my behalf. Okay?"

"I was just curious if Diamond Society was involved."

"Who cares?"

"Because if they're hazing, it's against the terms of their—"

"Seriously, let it go."

"I just figured I'd go over there. Casually, you know?" He shuffled papers, found one yellow Post-It note. "The guy said I should talk to a girl named ... 'Summer Nixon.'"

"STOP."

He stopped.

"No more. Okay? I can take care of myself."

"What about this Summer girl? Did she mess with you?"

"Jesus, Jackie. You really *should* join the newspaper. You're like a dog with a bone."

"My meager upbringing makes me scrappy." *One more try.* "But just ... Close the loop for me. One more thing and then I'll let it go."

"What."

"Was she? Messing with you?"

"Jackie ..."

"Just a yes or no."

Silence.

"No. Okay? Summer Fucking Nixon is perfectly lovely. She rides unicorns. She farts perfume. I love her so much."

"Are you being sarcastic?"

"Jackie. I answered your question. Can you please just drop it?"

Slowly, Jack nodded.

"Now. Listen. I need to get ready."

"Okay," Jack said. "I'll let you go."

"We can talk tomorrow."

"Okay."

"And maybe do the museum soon. *If* you're good and stay the hell out of my business. You're not my big brother."

Big Brother. Ouch.

"Got it?" she said.

"Got it."

"I'll talk to you later."

"Stay positive."

"I'll try."

"Don't try," Jack said. *"Do.* Like Yoda."

"Okay. Gotta go. Love you, Jackie."

There was a long pause. She hadn't meant that literally; it was how she signed off with friends.

"I mean—"

Jack couldn't resist. He cut her off.

"I love you too, Casey."

Then he killed the window, suddenly alone with his hammering heart. If he kept that kind of thing up, it would only cause problems. But it sure had felt beautiful to say it.

Jack sat in quiet for a few moments, feeling the oddest emotion. It wasn't happy; it wasn't sad; it was neither nostalgic nor hopeful. It was all four at once, nearly too much to handle.

He opened a new window and went to LiveLyfe. To Casey's profile, naturally, just to make sure she was planning to do as she'd promised. She lived on social media. Whether Casey went to the party or stayed home, she'd let LiveLyfe know her intentions.

There were already shaking dots at the top of her feed, telling him that she was typing. Seconds later her update appeared, arriving all at once like a magician's trick. And true to her promise, her words were positive. Upbeat. Seeing the bright side of what was coming.

Going to the senior party tonight at Simon Wyatt's house.

Casey entered a blank line. Then, below it:

It's going to be pretty killer.

ENTER THE TRUANTVERSE

When it comes to stories and the worlds they live in, books are only the beginning.

Visit JohnnyBTruant.com/join to get my best books sooner and cheaper than the other stores.

My list doesn't suck like so many author email lists. Seriously. It has unicorns.

AUTHOR'S NOTE

WARNING: Enormous spoilers ahead!

We've written some complex books in the past. *Axis of Aaron* flipped between true and false memory and required regular check-ins between me and Sean as to "what's real?" *The Beam* was complicated enough as a single series, but became a delightful boondoggle the moment we authored several more series in the world, all with lore and characters that twisted through history like a braid. *Devil May Care* actually had two timelines and three endings. I had to draw myself a color-coded map, complete with indexed milestones, to write my way through that one.

Despite all of that, I'd give *Pretty Killer* the title of "most difficult" of all our tales. "Complicated" isn't quite right because although there are lots of twists in the book you just finished, I don't think it comes across as *complicated*. "Difficult" is closer, from our perspectives. But even that doesn't tell the right tale, because "difficult" usually implies unpleasantness. This book wasn't unpleasant to plan or write at all. It was a rich, twisting, many-layered delight. One that took approximately five billion story meetings to figure out, and was hard as hell to hammer into what we knew it could be.

But all for the joy. *Only* for the joy.

More than anything, *Pretty Killer* is about secrets. Specifically, it's about what our secrets do to us if we pen them up inside, unable to confess. Ella and Heidi's secrets about what they did to Casey turned them both neurotic and addictive, neither of whom could stop self-medicating in one way or another. Teek's gave him a compulsion he loathed and gut-eating guilt. Summer's turned her kind, but always with that old edge just below the surface, threatening to erupt. John's secret gave him a quest for revenge, but also a voyeuristic interest in the secrets of others: Contract Confessions, which made him a fortune yet ate him alive.

Writing about secrets, ladies and gentlemen, is not easy. When things are out in the open in a book, characters are able to discuss them so the reader can learn them. What's more: they can discuss those things so *the other characters* can learn them. In a story like this one, though, where everyone keeps their secrets inside until forced to reveal them, we had to find sly ways to let you (the reader) know that something was amiss and interesting ... but not tell *too* much so that you, too, could still surprised at the appropriate time.

Done right, hinting at unrevealed secretes combined with the timely exposing of *parts* of those secrets (sometimes to the reader, sometimes to other characters while *excluding* the reader, and sometimes to both) creates a layered reading experience that you'll hopefully want to revisit. Our goal was for you, once you finish *Pretty Killer,* to feel as if you'd like to read it again.

Example:

When Simon first runs into Taylor and Teek outside Crave, Simon is all smiles while Taylor is cold. Throughout that scene and the first two-thirds of the book, she's rude to Simon for a reason that nobody (other than Taylor and her husband Teek) can understand. She takes constant pot shots at him and snipes even when he's at his most charming. Toward the end, we learn why: It's because Teek very recently confessed to Taylor that he witnessed Simon raping Casey Davis. Taylor is angry and still deciding what to do, but Simon doesn't know that and Taylor's not going to say it aloud. In addition, we as authors didn't want to let *you* know Simon's secret just yet. So we hinted, made you wonder ... and then revealed it when the time seemed right.

There's a lot of that in *Pretty Killer:* a ton of seemingly baseless comments, little slips, and little *almost*-slips. Remember, near the beginning, when John was able to identify Imogen's pills by sight? That should seem a little odd for a grocer, but makes sense once we learn that John has enough pharmacology to know how to kill a man without being detected. Or remember when Melissa and Imogen think they used to see John with Summer on the college quad, yet they bicker over whether it was when Summer's hair was blonde or dyed red? That's because they'd been seeing him with Casey and only *thought* he was with Summer, yet couldn't trust their own fallible memories.

Again and again as I wrote this draft, I tried to walk the razor's edge of hinting at something unseen, then pulling away from it. I tried to *almost* reveal something through a character's actions ... and then have that character interrupted, or decide remembering wasn't worth the effort. Sean gave me the start of it in the outline's start-stop rhythm. Then, as the story diverged from the outline (which it did entirely by the end), I had to make the whole thing sing.

Writing is tricky when one character has a secret, but *all* of ours did. And in all cases, different permutations of folks knew each secret: Imogen and Melissa knew each other's; John knew Mason's but Mason didn't know John knew; Summer knew Ella and Heidi's; *you* thought *you* knew John's at the start but found out at the end that his true secret was much deeper. Harper knew most of the secrets at the beginning except for the most vital among them (Teek's about Simon, which they all learned — but also John's about himself and Casey and the way she really died, which nobody else *ever* learned except for you as the reader). Even Donovan was keeping secrets: from Harper, about his plan to sabotage her plan to kill herself, adding his own twist to her plans to scare all of the others straight.

Hopefully, by the end, you understood all of the secrets that mattered to the story's unfolding. And hopefully, seeing the whole of the tapestry, you're curious to go back and read it again — this time, knowing the truth. And if you do so, you might notice on re-reading that Summer can't find her husband during the time Donovan swipes him aside to ask about antidotes. You might notice that Donovan, in turn, is missing when he runs down to receive those antidotes from John's pharmacist friend. You'll see new nuance in comments that seemed random the first time through. You'll notice glances that, at first, appeared to be meaningless — but that now say something like, *I know what you did, you bastard.*

Creating this story with its many reveals and layers was a fantastic sort of literary workout for us as authors. It strained muscles we didn't know we had. It forced us to stretch in ways we didn't know we could bend. It put us in your shoes, as the reader, because we had to ask: *How should we denote a change in timeline? Does every chapter need a time index? Whose point of view should we write each chapter from, so that if we were readers, we would understand just enough but not more?*

There was a lot of interesting research required for this book (see the acknowledgements section, to follow, for those stories), but more than anything we were challenged to put it together like a grand jigsaw puzzle ... while never overplaying our hand. *That* was interesting. We tried very hard to give you enough red herrings and false finger-pointing to confuse the outcome, but I have no idea if we succeeded.

One question I had was, *Is it obvious that Simon will end up being the bad guy?* And the answer was, *Yes, I think it's obvious.* But in a weird möbius of logic, making our "bad guy" the most obvious *bad guy* felt safe because it's rare that the culprit in books and movies *is* the person you think. "He's too obvious," we hoped you'd tell yourself — or at least consider, totally confused. "That means he *can't* be the villain!"

Other questions I had:

How can we convict Simon of one crime (rape, which everyone assumed drove Casey to suicide) on a conventional level while also leaving a deeper crime (murder) unrevealed to all but two people: Jon, who'd exact silent revenge, and you as the reader?

How could John be in love with Casey and nobody else know ... and yet, somehow end up at the Crave dinner party anyway? (He met Summer when he went to investigate Casey, yet never told Summer about his true past.)

How, in the end, could we show the reader that John killed Simon without having John just come out and say, "Yo! I'm John, and I killed Simon!" AND, for bonus points: *How can we leave clues all along that, in retrospect, clearly pointed to John's involvement ... but do so without anyone knowing it was John those clues implicated?*

See, there are rules to good fiction — especially good fiction that teeters on mystery, as this book does — and whether or not readers feel we succeeded in the "good" part is irrelevant to us trying our best to follow the rules.

One rule is that we, as the authors, aren't allowed to silently collect clues and hold them back until the last minute — at which point we drop them and say, "Boom! Here's what happened and that you had no way of knowing if the author hadn't stepped in!" No, the true version of events as revealed in *Pretty Killer*'s final chapters had to have left traces — and you, watching the scenes throughout the book, had to have been able to notice them. That means that Taylor, who knew about the rape, had to act toward Simon the way a woman would react to her friend's rapist. The other guests had to have seen and heard about John in the past, if they all went to Coastline. Donovan and John had to come and go as they made their plans and sometimes be absent from the dining room without drawing too much attention. And if John truly was in Casey's life, there needed to be hints of him in the others' stories. Our task, then, was to obscure what you saw: to keep Casey far from the story's camera when she was with John in the others' memories, and to have her call him by a nickname: "Jackie" (so much more embarrassing than "Jack") rather than "John." And so on and so on, through layers of obfuscation.

Books like this are a labor of love for us — a love letter to the written word. *Pretty Killer* won't sell nearly as many copies as something highly commercial like *Invasion*. It won't reach as many people or earn us as much in royalties. And yet, writing *Pretty Killer* took three or four times as long as those more conventionally successful books. We wouldn't do it if it weren't for the pure joy of telling the story.

So if you enjoyed this book — and especially if you see some of the little nuances and easter eggs and quiet mentions that you think most people will miss, or if you feel compelled to re-read the book and experience it again — I hope you'll drop us a line at help@sterlingandstone.net and let us know that by the most important metrics of success as writers, we succeeded.

We're grateful for you.

— Johnny B. Truant
    September 7, 2018

ACKNOWLEDGEMENTS

I usually fly pretty fast and loose with that persnickety thing others call "reality." Also troublesome and not usually worth our attention are "veracity," "plausibility," and "research." We even have a saying around here related to this that pays homage to our first book together (*Unicorn Western*) while also summing up the various tricks writers use to hide the fact we're talking out our asses: *Put a unicorn in it.* Because if you put a unicorn in your novel — even if she's just standing off to the side in one scene and does nothing — you as the author can point to her when readers complain that you got something wrong. "There's a *unicorn* in this story," you can explain. "Clearly this story takes place in an alternative world where the usual rules don't apply!"

Unfortunately, *Pretty Killer* offered very little opportunity for unicorns. We were forced to try and sound sensible, and get our facts straight. (And by the way, I'm being a little sarcastic. We don't rely on unicorns in every book. Just most of them.)

I'm sure we still screwed some stuff up in the book you've just finished, but with this being one of our more special stories, it felt important that the twists and turns be plausible. We wanted to sit our reader down for an exclusive dinner, delve into murder of a pharmacological nature, and reveal the final clues through the eyes of folks who included police and coroners. Doing so required a lot of experience we ourselves didn't have — detailed holes that we found ourselves unable to plug with unicorns.

As such, we're deeply thankful to a few friends for the help they provided us before, during, and after we wrote this story.

The course-by-course structure of *Pretty Killer* was something Sean invented and I found to be thematically important during the draft. It was important that Crave be an exclusive place to make that work, though, and neither of us (fancy though we are) knew enough about *haute cuisine* to bullshit our way through our guests' dinner menu. To help, Sean reached out to his old friend Roberto Martin, a professional chef who's cooked for many very famous celebrities whose names he's not allowed to divulge. (He could tell you, but then he'd have to kill you. Probably with Nyperal.) Roberto scoured the culinary landscape to make a fitting potential last meal for Crave's party. He also told us a few tidbits about the food Crave would be serving, and I couldn't resist working some of them into the draft in a way I hope wasn't obtrusive. Maybe we all even learned something. Did *you* know Kona kampachi belly was flown from Hawaii's big island on ice, to be served sashimi rare? I sure didn't.

After I had the book's outline in hand, I turned to figuring out some of the very important details that vanish into the story's fabric, but without which the story wouldn't work at all. The drug used throughout the story — Nyperal, a brand name of the generic rodostazem, both of which we totally made up and don't actually exist — was the most vital of them. At first, I thought I could wing it. X person would illicitly overdose Y person on Z drug, and all would work out. But of course things got much more complex than that, and I realized I needed a drug that could jump through hoops: useful but commonly abused at lower doses, deadly at higher doses, unde- tectable by the methods our story would employ, and (most impor- tantly) subject to the misidentification that nearly lets Simon get away with his deed ... while allowing "Jackie" to catch him when nobody else can.

I was rubbing my temples on all of this when our friend and fellow author Juliet Fisher (who also happens to be an ex-pharma- rep) volunteered her help on "any drug stuff." At first I thanked her and moved on, but very soon I went back to her and started asking questions. This discussion quickly became pivotal to the plot. We had to mix and match some real drugs with some made-up qualities (and of course a made-up name for our weapon of choice), but Juliet's help was invaluable in steering it all. The best twists in *Pretty Killer* never would have come about without her, and I'm absolutely not just saying that.

Toward the draft's end, I realized that including a few pieces of "found paperwork," presented without narrative interpretation, would be the best way to let the reader see what had really happened without our true killer needing to stand up and give a *Scooby-Doo*-type villain's monologue about how he did it. That had me creating a whole bunch of crap I had no business creating, like coroner's reports, police interviews, and funeral home intake forms. I thought I could bullshit my way through them, but quickly realized I'd be an idiot to try.

Fortunately, I've got some knowledgeable friends. I called on Adam Richardson (an ex-cop who runs the very helpful WritersDetective.com and has been cool to me, Sean, and our third partner Dave ever since he found our Self Publishing Podcast) and my college buddy Robert Shott, who just so happens to be a forensic pathologist working for a county coroner's office. I see Bob once a year or so at a reunion poker weekend and he always has many gross stories about untimely death. Things I've learned from Bob whether I wanted to or not include: some death scene bodies are collected in a bucket, decapitations aren't as rare as you might think, and you eventually get used to the smell of rotting flesh. (Fun side note: also present at those poker weekends is Eric Alexander, a geneticist who I thanked in the acknowledgements for our book *Dead City*. Now if I can just write a book that relies on interventional radiology (Tim) and corporate accounting (Mike), I'll have tagged everyone.)

Between Adam and Bob — both of whom were very patient with my many rounds of "what if" questions, and both of whom took blocks of text from this book and rewrote better, less egregiously incorrect versions thereof — we were able to craft some postmortem acrobatics that should, for the most part, be plausible. If mistakes remain, rest assured they're mine.

So to Bob, Adam, Juliet, and Roberto: *Thank you!* We quite literally couldn't have written this book without you.

Johnny B. Truant
    Fall, 2018

ALSO BY JOHNNY B. TRUANT

Winter Break

Pattern Black

Pretty Killer

Cursed

The Bialy Pimps

Namaste

The Target

La Fleur de Blanc

Axis of Aaron

Devil May Care

Screenplay

The Island

Burnout

Sick and Wired

UNICORN WESTERN:

Unicorn Western

The Wanderers

A Fistful of Magic

Shimmer to Yuma

The Man Who Shot Alan Whitney

The Spectacular Seven

Open Meadows

The Unforgotten

The Magic Bunch

Unicorn Genesis

~

FAT VAMPIRE:

Fat Vampire

Fat Vampire 2: Tastes Like Chicken

Fat Vampire 3: All You Can Eat

Fat Vampire 4: Harder Better Fatter Stronger

Fat Vampire 5: Fatpocalypse

Fat Vampire 6: Survival of the Fattest

The Vampire Maurice

Anarchy and Blood

Vampires in the White City

Fangs and Fame

Game of Fangs

~

INVASION:

Invasion

Contact

Colonization

Annihilation

Judgment

Extinction

Resurrection

Save the City

Save the Girl

Save the World

Longshot

~

THE INEVITABLE:

Robot Proletariat

The Infinite Loop

The Hard Reset

Cascade Failure

Reboot

En3my

~

DEAD CITY:

Dead City

Dead Nation

Dead Planet

Dead Zero

Empty Nest

~

THE DREAM ENGINE:

The Dream Engine

The Nightmare Factory

The Ruby Room

The Pandora Core

The Engine Convergence

The Tinkerer's Mainspring

~

GORE POINT:

Gore Point 1

Gore Point 2

Gore Point 3

~

THE BEAM:

The Beam: Season One

The Beam: Season Two

The Beam: Season Three

The Beam Season Four

The Beam Season Five

Future Proof

Plugged

The Future of Sex

~

THE TOMORROW GENE:

The Tomorrow Gene

The Eden Experiment

The Tomorrow Clone

Null Identity

~

COMEDIES:

Everyone Gets Divorced

Greens

Fiends

Decoy Wallet

~

NONFICTION:

The Fiction Formula

Fiction Unboxed

Iterate & Optimize

The Story Solution

Write. Publish. Repeat.

The One With All the Writing Advice

www.ingramcontent.com/pod-product-compliance
Lightning Source LLC
Chambersburg PA
CBHW030337010826
48973CB00004B/1041